Sherlock Holmes Never Dies

Collection One

Studying Scarlet
The Sign of the Tooth
The Sandal from East Anglia
The Bald-Headed Trust
A Case of Identity Theft
The Hudson Valley Mystery

Craig Stephen Copland

Copyright © 2019 by Craig Stephen Copland

All rights reserved. No part of this book may be reproduced or transmitted in any form or by any means, electronic or mechanical, including photocopying, recording, or by an information storage and retrieval system – except by a reviewer who may quote brief passages in a review to be printed in a magazine, newspaper, or on the web – without permission in writing from Craig Stephen Copland.

The characters of Sherlock Holmes and Dr. Watson are in the public domain, as are all of the original stories that served as the inspiration for the stories in this book.

Published by:
Conservative Growth
3104 30th Ave., Suite 427
Vernon, British Columbia, Canada, V1T 9M9

ISBN: 9781711336893

Dedication

To my parents, Jim and Dorothy Copland, who instilled in me a passion for reading and provided a loving home in which books of all sorts could be enjoyed.

Contents

Studying Scarlet 1
The Sign of the Tooth 89
A Sandal from East Anglia 159
The Bald-Headed Trust 223
A Case of Identity Theft 293
The Hudson Valley Mystery 379
About the Author 501
More Historical Mysteries by Craig Stephen Copland 502

Dear Sherlockians:

These six novellas are *pastiche* stories of Sherlock Holmes. The characters of Sherlock Holmes and Dr. Watson are modeled on the characters that we have come to love in the original sixty Sherlock Holmes stories by Sir Arthur Conan Doyle.

The settings in the late Victorian and Edwardian eras are also maintained. Each new mystery is inspired by one of the stories in the original sacred canon. The characters and some of the introductions are respectfully borrowed, and then a new mystery develops.

If you have never read the original story that served as the inspiration of the new one—or if you have but it was a long time ago—then you are encouraged to do so before reading the new story in this book. Your enjoyment of the new mystery will be enhanced.

Some new characters are introduced and the female characters have a significantly stronger role than they did in the original stories. I hope that I have not offended any of my fellow Sherlockians by doing so but, after all, a hundred years have passed and some things have changed.

The historical events that are connected to these new stories are, for the most part, accurately described and dated. Your comments, suggestions, and corrections are welcomed on all aspects of the stories.

I am deeply indebted to The Bootmakers of Toronto (the Sherlock Holmes Society of Canada) not only for their dedication to the adventures of Sherlock Holmes but also to their holding of a contest for the writing of a new Sherlock Holmes mystery. My winning entry into that contest led to the joy of continuing to write more Sherlock Holmes mysteries.

Over the next few years, it is my intention to write a new mystery as a tribute to each one of the sixty original stories. They will appear in the same chronological order as the original canon appeared in the pages of *The Strand*. Should you wish to subscribe to these new stories and receive them in digital form as they are released, please visit www.SherlockHolmesMystery.com and sign up.

Wishing joyful reading and re-reading to all faithful Sherlockians.

Respecfully,
CSC

Acknowledgments

I discovered both *Gone with the Wind,* and *The Adventures of Sherlock Holmes* while a student at Scarlett Heights Collegiate Institute in Toronto. My English teachers – Bill Stratton, Norm Oliver, and Margaret Tough – inspired me to read and write. I shall be forever grateful to them.

My colleagues in the Oakville Writers Group endured the drafts of the various chapters of the story and made valuable suggestions. My dearest and best friend, Mary Engelking, read several drafts, helped with whatever historical and geographical accuracy may be present, and made insightful recommendations for changes to the narrative structure, characters, and dialogue.

For the very idea of writing a new Sherlock Holmes mystery I thank the Sherlockian Society of Toronto, known to members as the Bootmakers. They posted a story contest for a new Sherlock Holmes Mystery. I entered and was fortunate enough to be one of the winners. So, I kept writing more Sherlock Holmes mysteries

Studying Scarlet

A New Sherlock Holmes Mystery

(An Unauthorized Parody)

Chapter One

Your Momma

Our beloved Queen Victoria passed away a year ago. All of England, indeed the entire Empire was saddened, but there was a universal feeling that *the old girl had done it well.*

Throughout the Empire a pall, a lethargy, had descended. The old order had changed, but the new one to which it would yield its place had not yet begun.

From the poor level of our Baker Street Irregulars all the way to the earls and lords of the land, we simply waited, wondering what the new era would be like. The Prince of Wales, the heir apparent, was no longer a dashing *bon vivant*. He had become a portly, bearded sixty-year-old grandfather and all of his subjects agreed that he had finally grown up and was ready to take his rightful role as the head of the greatest empire the world had ever known. In June of 1902, the crowned heads of the world gathered in London for the coronation. Half a million citizens were given free dinners and tins of chocolates as part of the celebration only to have the event itself postponed because Albert Edward was ill with a severe pain in his gut. Now, in early August, he was feeling better and on Saturday would be crowned king at Westminster Abbey.

My health, so damaged in Afghanistan, had fully recovered. My medical practice had expanded following my purchase of the files of the aging surgeon in Marylebone whose affliction with St. Vitus Dance had led his patients to seek alternative care. This connection, added to my military pension, was providing me with a solid income of well over three hundred pounds a year. I was rising early, greeting each day with resolute happiness. I was engaged to be married this fall for the third time and was quite certain that together with my lovely wife we would enjoy life until our days together on the earth were done. I could not have been more content.

Sherlock Holmes could not have been more miserable. Without a truly creative criminal with whom to match wits, without any unusual nefarious puzzles to be solved, Sherlock Holmes was indulging overly often in his dangerous seven percent solution and complaining about the petty and utterly predictable cases that had been presented to him for the past year.

From time to time I would hum a few lines from our dear friends Bill Gilbert and Art Sullivan that I knew would rouse him from his sullenness:

When the enterprising burglar's not a'burgling
When the cut throat isn't occupied in crime
He loves to hear the little brook a-gurgling
And listen to the merry village chimes

Holmes would be sure to respond with "Blast it, Watson, if you must be humming tunes from the stage could you not, at least, remember something from that infernal nonsense *Pinafore?*"

"Yes, of course, my dear Holmes," I would reply, "but you must admit that our times are splendid. Truly the best of times, are they not?"

Mind you, there was still much crime in London. On the hour it seemed someone's house would be broken into. Somebody would rob a shop or flog a cabbie for his fares. Almost every day some poor soul would be murdered. In the past week alone, three men had been done away with, each in a different part of London, and all by garroting. The newspapers were trying to create a panic, warning citizens about *the mad garrotters*. Years earlier they had done the same and caused a panic that swept the city. Such morbid fears about evil doers had a wonderful effect on the sale of newspapers, as the barons of Fleet Street had proven a few years back with the titillating stories of the infamous Jack the Ripper. But these were all just normal, everyday crimes; nothing truly, ingeniously, diabolically evil, and sufficient to warrant the intense energy of London's most famous detective.

"No, my dear Watson, we do not live in splendid times. We live in very dangerous times, the worst of times," remonstrated Holmes. "The Empire is crumbling. The Americans are eating into our trade and the Germans into our naval superiority. Britain is forming all sorts of unholy alliances with unpredictable countries. The Boers gave our army a thorough run for it, and the world cheered them on. Some youth tried to murder the Prince, and the Belgian authorities let him walk away. Anarchists are on the move everywhere. They are not murderers of the usual garden variety that kill for money or jealousy. They are fanatical in their beliefs and intent on mayhem and destruction of the established order.

"Yet none of these cases have come to me, Watson. Those sorry chaps at Scotland Yard treat every death as if it were just one more unsolvable murder, and I receive nothing but the most trivial of clients wanting help with the most commonplace of problems.

"Look at this, Watson," he snapped as we, or at least I, enjoyed Mrs. Hudson's breakfast of perfectly poached salmon. "Another pathetic, jilted American woman seeks my help in tracking down her philandering husband, who has no doubt run off with the governess and the family trust account, and was last seen swilling gin in Southwark!"

He as much as tossed the letter onto my plate, sat back, crossed his arms and scowled.

"A junior constable or even a brainless newspaper reporter could find her husband for her. Who in the deuce gave her my name? And she condescends to have her employee write the letter for her."

The letter was typed and bore the letterhead of the Dorchester Hotel on Park Lane. The lady may have been estranged but was clearly not without means.

> # The Dorchester
> *Park Lane, Mayfair, London*
>
> August 2, 1902.
>
> Dear Mr. Holmes:
>
> I am informed that you are currently in London and are normally to be found in your rooms during the morning hours. Therefore, I will call on you at 8:00 am tomorrow.
>
> My employer and I require your assistance in locating her estranged husband who is believed to be living in London. Your services have been highly recommended.
>
> Yours very truly,
>
> *Hataniah O'Donnell* (Miss)

"The impertinence, do you not agree, Watson? How utterly presumptuous. Some Irish spinster who has come back to Britain thinks she can just walk in at any uncivilized morning hour and demand my services."

"Well now, Holmes, she is an American after all. You cannot expect the same manners and deference that our English spinsters would exhibit. But we still have a good twenty minutes before she arrives, so enjoy some nourishment and brace yourself. I am sure that you will be able to summon your usual gracious composure and send her on her way."

We concluded our breakfast, and Mrs. Hudson cleared away the dishes. Holmes removed himself from the table to his armchair and lit up his beloved pipe. At 7:50 am the bell rang.

"Confound it!" Holmes shouted, "She has even come early! Mrs. Hudson, you can just leave her standing out there in the rain until the hour strikes."

"I shall do nothing of the kind, Mr. Holmes. She may wait in the hallway if you insist but it is miserable weather outside and I shall bid her enter."

For a moment, I thought he would fly into a rage, but he took another draw on his pipe, cocked his head to the side and said, "Very well then. If I must be so treated, let us redeem the time by making sport with her. A game of wits, Watson. Are you up for it? Mrs. Hudson shall bring her card and tell us three pertinent facts describing her. You and I, Watson, shall deduce three additional facts each about her, and we shall see who reasons more of them correctly. If the morning is to start by being wasted, then we may as well put our wits to work. What say, Watson, are you ready?" He had stopped slouching into his armchair, was sitting up straight and rubbing his hands together.

"Oh, very well, Holmes, if you must. But not one hint of disrespect to the lady."

"Of course not. When have I ever shown disrespect to a visiting American?"

I thought it better not to answer that. "Please, Mrs. Hudson", I said, "let the poor soul in before she catches her death of cold, and then bring us her card."

Mrs. Hudson gave us a sideways glance, sighed, and proceeded out the door and down the stairs. A few moments later she re-appeared with a sly smile on her face and presented a white calling card to Holmes. I came and stood behind his chair and together we perused it.

Hataniah Mary O'Donnell

Head Foreman – Domestic Affairs
Beulah Plantations
Fayette County, Georgia

"Very well then, Mrs. Hudson," said Holmes. "Three facts about her."

"She is American."

"Oh, come, come, Mrs. Hudson, we already knew that."

"That is true Mr. Holmes. But it is also true that she is, you might say, very American."

"Yes, go on."

"She is well-dressed in a fine black satiny dress with a full skirt, a black quilted jacket held together by a platinum clasp chain, and has a hat such as an American woman of a certain age might wear to church."

"Indeed. And one last piece of data."

"She is not young, and she is most certainly not starving. There's two for you sir. Now get on with your game. I will not be rude to any guest on my property just so you two layabouts can amuse yourselves."

"You go first, Watson," said Holmes, ignoring our landlady's rebuke. His look spoke volumes as if to say that he had already discerned the poor lady's entire life story.

"By her name, she is Irish," I said.

"Watson," Holmes said with a strong tone of impatience, "I had already observed that from her letter. Surely you can do better."

"Fine, if you must," I muttered. I was not at all comfortable with the rudeness we were showing to a guest, even if she was American, by making sport about her while she stood waiting. "She is from County Cork." I was not sure of this but had treated some Irish folks by the same name who claimed to have come from there. But of course, with the Irish, you can never be sure. "She left Ireland as a young lass during the great famine some forty years ago, and if it were not for the current situation regarding her employer's husband, she would have never returned, having found a much better life on the other side of the pond. There. Is that good enough? Now please, Holmes, get on with your deductions, get this silliness over, and display better manners to your client, even if you are going to decline your services."

Holmes took a deliberately slow inhalation from his pipe and then blew it out even more slowly. He could, at times, be exceptionally exasperating. I looked over at Mrs. Hudson expecting her to be glaring at Holmes, but she was standing serenely in front of the door frame not looking at all vexed. Indeed, she looked somewhat smug.

"Not bad at all Watson, although at least half the population of America who have Irish surnames fled the sodden island during the famine. And yes, I do believe that the O'Donnells were from the south of the country. So solidly not bad. Let me add just a few more details. This woman, Miss Hataniah, was the daughter of a professor at Trinity College, Dublin. She entered a convent as a teenager, displayed a spirit too contrary for the nuns, was expelled – most likely there was a young man involved – took the women's business diploma at the Alexandra Girls School, had a fight with her family, got on the boat to America, attached herself to a bank in Atlanta, where she met her employer's husband and entered his business as a typist, eventually working her way up through the ranks to the high responsibility she now enjoys."

"And how, dear Holmes, did you come to those conclusions?"

"Elementary. I shall explain them over lunch but first let us see just how right I have been, and then graciously dispose of our impertinent American. Mrs. Hudson, will you please," he said, gesturing that she show our guest in.

Mrs. Hudson departed and we heard her ask our guest to ascend the stairs. The sound of the footfalls on the stairs was telling. They were slow. The first ten stairs were climbed, and then the sounds stopped.

"Ah yes," said Holmes, "She is truly old and heavy."

Then the next four stairs. Then another rest. Then the final three.

Mrs. Hudson turned to Holmes and me, and with a face straining to be straight, announced, "Mr. Holmes, Dr. Watson, Miss Hataniah O'Donnell."

The woman who entered the room was not tall, perhaps no more than five feet, but she was indeed large. I estimated close to thirteen stone. Her bosom could only be described as excessively ample. Her dress, jacket, and clasps were exactly as Mrs. Hudson had described. She was elderly and her hair was gray and woven into braids that were neatly coiled around the top of her head and nearly covered by the black felt hat that would have been stylish in London a decade ago.

Holmes stood staring at her, uncharacteristically speechless and exuded an air of being completely discomfited. The woman standing before him was anything but what he had deduced. She was a very dark-skinned woman of African descent. Her face was deeply lined and of the consistent color of a fine Belgian chocolate.

Mrs. Hudson gave me a quick look and a smile. I returned her look with a small nod. As unspoken co-conspirators, we both took a secret delight in seeing our truly genius but occasionally pompous friend nonplussed, and we knew that we would be remembering this morning for many months to come as we chortled behind the back of the great detective.

Sherlock Holmes recovered his composure quickly, gave a very slight bow towards Miss O'Donnell, and began his well-practiced *Thank you for your interest in us, but our specialty is not appropriate to the problems with which you are dealing, but please let me recommend one of my esteemed fellow detectives...* but he never even got the first words out of his mouth before Miss O'Donnell had marched fully into the room, passed under Holmes's nose, and dropped her body with a resounding thud into Holmes's armchair.

"Yessums, dem sevteen stairs is mo lac seven hunred when you is seventa seven years ole." Her accent and dialect identified her as a citizen of the Deep South. "Don't just be standing looking hangdog boys. Set yourselves down. I ain't going nowheres for a few minutes. And pardon me, ma'am, could you be so kind as to bring an old lady a cup of hot tea? And I don't suppose you got anything so civilized as bourbon in this here place, but a teensy bit of Irish whiskey to cools it down would be appreciated. Thank you much, ma'am."

Mrs. Hudson was positively beaming at her and replied, "Of course Miss O'Donnell. You just stay where you are. There's a pot on the stove waiting for you. And I do believe we have some excellent Irish holy water in the cabinet." With that, she departed.

Again Holmes started to say something, but the formidable presence in the room cut him off and firmly stated, "I told you boys to set yourselves down. May as well. Once a lady sets herself down, it be alright for the gentlemen to do so. Didn't your mommas never teaches you that? So set down, I said. We got some talking to do before I gets. But there's no business before I finishes my tea. Why thank you, ma'am. That do look like a perfect cup of tea. Much obliged."

With that, she took a long, slow sip from the tea cup, closed her eyes and smiled. "Now you knows it ain't quite as good as bourbon, but a fine cup of tea with something to fortify it is all the proofs I needs that there be a good God up there in heaven and He truly done loves His children."

"We do welcome you," I began, "not only to our home but to our fair town of London. It must be quite a strange place to you. Many visitors coming here for the first time do find it rather overwhelming." That was as far as I made it into my well-practiced welcome speech.

"Y'all call this a fair city!? *Fair.* London's a horrible place. Why t'ain't done nothing but rain cats and dogs since we arrived, and when it don't be raining it be fogging and smelling like something half-way between a gator swamp and a cow fart. Y'all got some pretty shops, but you got yourselves some powerful nasty weather, and we already learned some powerful nasty folks here. So sooner we done our business and get back to Atlanta the happier we'll be."

A wounding of my civic pride moved me to respond, but Miss O'Donnell held up her hand and said "Shush. You boys just pipe down till I finishes my tea; then we'll talk." She said this with an air of someone who was used to giving orders and so I and, to my surprise, Holmes both meekly obeyed. For the next two minutes, nothing was said, and we watched her serenely sipping her tea, looking around the room, and giving Holmes and me a good visual inspection.

"Very well boys. Yous is hired."

With this, Holmes jerked his head up and coughed on his pipe smoke. "I beg your pardon, madam; I have no idea as to how you go about conducting yourselves in Atlanta, but that is just not the way we do business here in England. You know nothing at all about my colleague, Dr. Watson, nor me, and we know nothing about you or your employer. Both of those pieces of information must be discerned before we will engage our services."

Miss O'Donnell just smiled back at Holmes. It was not only a friendly smile, it was positively condescending. "My employer is out in her carriage and I'll go and fetch her now, and y'all can meet her and listen to her story. And y'all will want then to be of use to her. Mark my words on that one. As to what I needs to know about you boys, I already knows enough. So yous is hired."

"I regret to inform you, madam," Holmes responded with controlled indignation, "I cannot see how you could possibly know sufficient about us. I may have some modest reputation here in London, but I doubt that anyone in Atlanta has ever heard of me. And pray tell why your employer would send her foreman instead of presenting herself to us if she wishes to be our client?"

"Oh, my dear boy," she said, "she is a very busy lady, and she has to send off telegrams and letters and do correspondence, and she knows, because she knows me all her life, that I will know who to trust and who not to. And I trust you boys, so yous is hired."

"Then pray tell me just what it is that you think you know about us madam since you have not asked us a single question and we have revealed nothing about ourselves to you."

She rolled her head back and laughed heartily. "Don't you know, you don't have to be asking questions all the time. You can learn all you needs to know just by looking round at little things. Them little things, they tell you all you need to know about someone."

The irony of the situation was delightful, or I should say that it was to Mrs. Hudson and me. It was all we could do not to join in her laughter. Holmes's face slowly softened and his intense innate curiosity took control.

"You are, madam, absolutely correct. But please tell me just what it was that you observed that led you to such a friendly conclusion about we two gentlemen on whom you had never set eyes until a few minutes ago. I assume that someone recommended us to you? The bobbies? Scotland Yard? Who?"

Again she laughed. "No, my boy. I didn't ask no police. I just took myself down to the kitchen of the hotel, and I asked the cooks and the help. And they say that famous detective Mister Sherlock Holmes be the best in the business. So we came here. And I see right away that what them folks says is correct, so I hires you."

"And how did you see that they were correct?" pressed Holmes.

Miss O'Donnell furrowed her brow and stared briefly at Holmes. "If you must know, sir, it goes like this. When I was waiting outside your door, I sees two pair of men's boots. Right nice they were. Expensive. But nicely shined and well cared for. So that tell me that the proprietors of this detective agency not be poor boys, because if you could not afford decent boots, then yous not much of a detective. But then I sees that the boots is two different sizes, and that says there be two boys here, not just one. That gets me wondering if you boys is a couple of them sodomite boys, like your wild Mister Oscar that we hear all about, if you knows what I mean."

"I beg your pardon, madam," I interjected, "but Sherlock Holmes and John Watson have never had anything but the most honorable of friendships and I . . ."

"Oh now don't you go getting all het up, Doc. Mrs. Cutler, that's my employer, and I don't care where some boy wants to warm his sausage, if you know what I mean. It don't make no never mind to us long as he be doing what we're paying him for. But I know that the minute I walks through your door that y'all ain't that way inclined."

"Indeed, madam," said Holmes, becoming quite intrigued with our guest of a decidedly different hue, "and just how did you discern that?"

"Well sir," she continued, "It could not have been more obvious. As soon as I was in your parlor, Doc here give me a quick once over an I knows he is one of those men who knows what a woman looks like without no clothes on."

"Madam! I object. How dare you!"

"No offense, sir, none in the least. You can say what you want, but what a gentleman says and what he thinks is two different things. It be just that any man who's been married he knows things that no bachelor or sodomite boy can, because they don't know. But any man who is or has been married he do know. And a woman know when a man know. That's just something all women know. And besides that, I sees that you got a teensy white mark on your fourth finger on your left hand where you used to have a wedding ring, so that tell me all I needs to know about you. And as for you, Mister Sherlock, I just has to see the way you were looking at me, and I sees nothing at all, meaning that you be no more than a steer who forgot what it's like to be a bull. So no disrespect, gentlemen, this is just what any woman knows.

"And then I looked around your room here and it tells me everything else I need to know."

"Quite remarkable, madam, and just what did you learn about us from examining our abode?" asked Holmes.

"Well sir, if you must know, this room be all neat and clean and all, and that is a good sign, but it's for darn sure that there ain't no woman living here, and that you ain't no sodomite boys neither, because neither a woman nor a nice sodomite boy would have so much expensive quality furnishings and have it look so ugly. You got more stuff and colors going on in here than I can shake a stick at. Looks like the dog ate the artist's whole box of paints and then come in here and done his vomit.

"No offense, ma'am," she said, turning to Mrs. Hudson, "I know you must try powerful hard to keep two bachelors from going ugly, but it can't be helped."

"Yes, my dear," said Mrs. Hudson, "I do try, but as you know . . ."

"I know. Oh, I know. And I see that Doc here got his copy of the *Lancet* and he's been reading it so he must be a diligent doctor. And you, Mister Sherlock, you got shelves full of books on chemicals, and criminals, and you already finished today's newspaper and set it down all mess up like you read it right through. So you must be smart, at least for an English man. And then I looked at all these little knick-knacks and whatchamacallems all over the place, and they've all been given to you by women because no man would buy them for himself. And no man gives presents like these to other men.

"Just look you. There is a photo right here beside where I'm sitting and it says 'I shall think of you always' and signed *I.A.*, and on your mantel there's a snuff box in carved ivory, and over there on the wall is a painting of somebody's cottage with flowers all over it. Everything in this room says you boys have been given gifts by happy women, but no names is attached. So that says that you not only done your job real good, otherwise nobody would give you nothing, but that you done lots of good jobs for women who were grateful because they needed you to be real discrete and all.

"And then I looked at the wall," she said, pointing to the open expanse of plastered wall on the far side of our parlor, "and there is a whole bunch of patches that've been painted over, and those patches is in the shape of the letters *V* and *R*. And that says to me that some damn fool's been doing his revolver shooting practice here in the parlor. So, you boys may be powerful strange, but one of you, and I'm expecting it be you, Sherlock, is one very good shot. And that be a good thing if we be needing protection. So what else do I need? Now if y'all will excuse me, I will go back down your stairs and fetch my employer."

"Truly remarkable. Absolutely remarkable!" gushed Holmes looking as if he had just met his doppelganger. "But please, madam, permit me one more question before we move on to the concerns of your employer. Why did she not just come into our rooms directly herself? It would have saved her considerable time and you could still have imparted all of your remarkable discernments to her?"

"Oh, she's a very smart woman, sir. And she hates to waste time. So, she sent me up here for to check out you boys and then go and tell her if you be like all those other English boys we met, you know, all those who're arrogant, obnoxious, and stupid to boot, or if you be otherwise. So now I knows and I goes and gets my employer."

With this, she placed her two hands firmly on the arms of Holmes's chair, leaned her large body forward, and with an effort raised herself and found her balance on her feet. She started walking slowly towards the door.

I rose to my feet. "May I assume, Miss O'Donnell, that you have concluded that we are not like the rest of the English boys. We thank you for the compliment," I said as she shuffled towards Mrs. Hudson, who was offering her arm to assist her down the stairs.

"I can only say for sure that y'all ain't stupid. The rest will have to wait. And you may as well stop calling me Miss O'Donnell. We be Americans and we don't stand on silly, pompous formality. I'll be calling you Doc, and you Sherlock, so y'all may as well be calling me Momma, because that's all anybody has been calling me for going on sixty years." And with that, she slowly descended the stairs.

Chapter Two

Starlet

"It is sad that I must stand on my principles and decline to take a case that is about nothing more than chasing American husbands," said Holmes with a sigh, "as it would be a thoroughly enjoyable diversion to work alongside such a remarkable woman. Yes. Delightful.

"Hmm. And what have we here?" he continued, as we peered down into the street from our bay window. "Our Momma is leaning into a very well-polished carriage with as fine a uniformed driver and brace of horses as we ever see on Baker Street. I believe that is the coat of arms of Knightsbridge Livery on the door, is it not Watson?"

"Yes, indeed it is," I said. "Oh. Look, Holmes, there is a third member of the entourage." We observed first Momma, followed by a tall gentleman in a morning suit, and then by a lady covered in a forest green cloak, completed by an ermine-fringed hood covering her head. They entered our door and we heard the group of them ascending our stairs.

Mrs. Hudson opened the door and the first to enter it was a young man. He could not have been much beyond seventeen years old. The most striking thing about him was his height. Sherlock Holmes himself is tall and lean, somewhat over six feet, but this young gentleman had half a foot on Holmes, which, thanks to years of being so lectured by Holmes, I immediately discerned were partly due to the heels of his boots. They were a military issue and of high quality, with noticeable wear on the instep section and up the side of the foot, clearly indicating some hard use in a stirrup. He had jet black hair and strong aquiline features, although his ears seemed a little overly large for such a handsome face. His shoulders were already broad, and even with a morning jacket and waistcoat, it was obvious that there was not an excess ounce of fat on his powerful, young body.

He was carrying a rather large portmanteau, which he immediately dropped just inside the door, and in a couple of long strides crossed the floor. With a gleaming guileless smile, he held out his hand to Holmes, who instinctively accepted it.

"Good morning Mister Holmes," he said as he pumped Holmes's hand firmly, "It is an honor to meet you. You have many fans and followers in Atlanta. I am Reginald Cutler, but everyone calls me Reggie, so please do. And you," he said, turning to me, "must be Doctor Watson. All of my fellow cadets read every one of your stories in *The Strand*. They will be most envious to know that I have been in your presence." He shook my hand as well and moved back towards the door and stood at ease beside it.

His friendly and humble confidence, without a hint of affectation, was highly pleasing. He was very young to have acquired such ease and social grace and it spoke of a very admirable job by both his family and his schoolmasters. I could see that Holmes had drawn the same conclusions as I, and wondered what else he had seen in this impressive young gentleman.

As expected, Momma climbed the steps much more slowly than our young Adonis. She entered the room huffing and puffing, with a fine bead of sweat now on her furrowed brow. Without a word, she walked decidedly across the room and again deposited her heavy frame in Holmes's armchair. Had it been anyone else to have twice so violated his *sanctum sanctorum* Holmes would have had a fit of apoplexy, but he acquiesced with a smile and went so far as to briefly place a warm hand on her shoulder.

Now our attention was turned to the figure standing in our doorway. Had I been given to the vice of profanity I am sure I would have gasped, "Oh . . . my . . . God!" for standing in our presence was the most magnificent embodiment of mature female pulchritude that I had ever gazed upon. She had a striking and queenly appearance, holding herself not just confidently but regally. The four-inch heels on her over-the-calf laced-up boots added to her natural stature, making her as tall as Holmes. Her rich black hair, streaked with strands of silver, fell from the crown of her head to her shoulders. The faint lines across her high forehead and the small crow's feet at the edges of her bright emerald eyes added depth to her utterly arresting visage. The upper part of her face bore an unmistakable resemblance to the young man who now stood beside her. Her lower face narrowed into a perfectly rounded V and her mouth, irresistibly accented by perfectly applied lipstick, was a weapon that could disarm any man as it closed into a girlish pout or broadened into a smile.

After removing her cloak and handing it to an attentive Mrs. Hudson, in a manner almost identical to that of the young man's, she strode across the floor towards Holmes. Her dress was a rich burgundy velvet. The yoke was just low enough to expose the upper circles of a god-given bosom. Her puffed sleeves covered her arms only to a place just below her shoulders, exposing firmly defined upper arms. What caused me again to come close to gasping out loud was the cut in the side of her dress that extended well above the knee, permitting a flash of her leg and lower thigh with each confident step she took. She offered her hand to Sherlock Holmes, who, carefully maintaining his impassive face and composure, accepted it.

"Good morning Mr. Holmes. You really must forgive our intruding on you at this ungodly early-morning hour, but I am a lady in rather urgent need of your services, and time is of the essence."

"Please, madam," he gestured towards the settee, "do make yourself comfortable, and I am sure our good Mrs. Hudson can organize a cup of her finest tea. And would you take some toast? It is still very early, and I fear you might not have had the time to enjoy breakfast."

"Thank you, sir," she said as she lowered her perfectly contoured body onto the cushions. "We did indeed depart from the hotel at a very early hour and had time to take our breakfast by Marble Arch before coming to see you. Why, good morning, Dr. Watson," she said, looking directly at me, "my son is such a devotee of your intriguing stories about our favorite detective. Is that not so, Reggie?"

"Yes, mother," replied the tall young gentleman, "I am planning to return to Georgia with as many autographed copies of the latest *Strand* as I can fit into my baggage."

"Now, Mr. Holmes," she said, turning to face my esteemed companion, "I do expect that you are about to tell me that my situation is precluded from your services, but I assure you that it truly is not, and if you will permit me to present my situation, I am sure that you will agree and respond to our request for your assistance."

She did not wait for Holmes to respond as it was quite obvious that he was being given no choice in the matter, but that acceding to her demands was not at all against his wilting will.

"My husband, who I must now locate without delay, and I met during those glorious days, now lost to all but memory, immediately before the War for the Independence of the South. We became enamored of each other during that tragic war, and eventually married after it ended, during that time falsely termed by Yankees as our "Reconstruction." Our marriage was passionate, but you might say tumultuous. We were blessed with the gift of a beautiful daughter, who was killed in a dreadful accident while she was still a child. I conceived a second time, but, unfortunately, I miscarried, so our having more children was not to be. My husband chose to live apart from me for some time after that. But I returned to my family's land and restored it, hoping that by doing so he would be drawn back to me, and indeed, he was.

"He stayed briefly, but then he left again, only to return. This pattern repeated itself several times. It was in part a result of both he and I being very strong-willed people and entering into what we both came to regret as furious clashes. But it was also the result of who, in his heart, my husband is as a man. The sedate life of managing a plantation was not his cup of tea." Here she turned to Mrs. Hudson. "And speaking of which, I do thank you. This is excellent.

"My husband, Captain Brett Cutler, in his heart and soul is a soldier of fortune. He has an overpowering weakness for believing in lost causes once they're really lost. So, for the past thirty years he has been a very highly regarded mercenary consultant to generals, rebels, politicians . . . anyone who was fighting a battle for a cause that Brett would support, but that had almost no hope of ever triumphing. He bore no allegiance to any nation except to the now vanquished Confederate States of America, which, Lord willing, will someday rise again, but that is another story. Seventeen years ago, during one of his returns to Beulah – the name of our plantation – I, perhaps in desperation, suggested that we take a honeymoon to make up for the one we had never had when we were first married. The place I selected had become recently famous as the honeymoon capital of America. I am speaking of Niagara Falls, the great cataract beside the Canadian border."

"Yes. Yes. We have all heard about this romantic location," said Holmes. "I believe that our Mr. Oscar Wilde, with whom Momma seems familiar, described it as the second great disappointment of American married life. But pray, please continue."

"To my surprise, Brett agreed, and we spent two very, shall I say, intense weeks. We went on delightful tours, stood arm in arm beside the raging waterfall, bought each other some very fine and personal gifts on the Canadian side of the border where all of the British merchants from Toronto have their shops. In the lovely hotel overlooking The Falls, we engaged in what I believe you would term conjugal interludes that were passionate and pleasurable beyond description. I was kissed, and kissed often by someone who knows how. My husband, even if by then being a man in his early fifties, was still heavily muscled, very athletic, a gifted and generous lover, and wonderfully endowed. I assume you understand what I am saying, gentlemen."

"Of course, madam," I snapped. I was aghast at hearing this far-too-frank allusion to what for decent English people are strictly private matters. I was particularly appalled that a mother would be making such statements in front of her young son, who, though manly, was still a callow lad many years from marriage. I glanced first at Momma, who was all but ignoring her employer and lost in the enjoyment of her second cup of tea, which I gathered the generous Mrs. Hudson had thoughtfully adulterated to her taste. I then looked toward Reginald on whose behalf I was deeply concerned, knowing that he would be terribly embarrassed if not humiliated by his mother's indiscreet description of his father. To my shock, he was still standing comfortably at-ease, but fixing his gaze on his mother in a manner that could only be described as adoring. Inwardly I groaned and despaired that America would ever become a civilized country. Then on she went . . .

"Sad to say, we ended our time together with an enormous quarrel. It was over my demand that he return to Fayette County and to our land. Land, I believed in my heart, was the only thing worth fighting for. I wanted Brett to love our land the way my father did and return and assume his duty as one of the leading landowners in North Georgia. He steadfastly refused to do so, insisting that the only way he would ever return would be in a coffin, at which time they could elect him a member of our city council.

"Brett departed directly from Niagara Falls to parts unknown. I returned to Atlanta, seething with a mixture of anger and passion all wound up together but obligated to do my duty as the owner of one of the largest plantations in Georgia. The following months and years were very profitable as we expanded our acreage and cotton production, and our lumber business, and continued to rebuild our fine city. But they were personally painful as I had no idea where my husband was. I heard nothing from him after that honeymoon, and to this day have had no personal communication from him.

"To my surprise, I realized that at some point during that passionate time beside The Falls I had conceived. I had believed that, given my age and having been told that after my miscarriage I would not be able to have any more children, the chances of my being fertile were non-existent. But here I was in the family way and no idea where on earth my husband could be found."

"My dear lady," I said in my most doctorly consoling voice, "I am sure that must have been a very trying time. But be assured that we have dealt with many sensitive family situations that had the potential for scandal, and are more than prepared to use the utmost discretion in all of our services to you."

The woman looked at me as if I had just emerged into civilization from the jungles of Borneo. Then she broke out into a pleasant peal of laughter.

"Oh my, oh my, doctor. You have obviously never been to Atlanta. Why, after our dreadful war in which so many of our men were lost, for a woman of my age to have a living, breathing husband at all and not be widowed was a blessing. To have one who was not all crippled up with war wounds or gone all Tom o' Bedlam in the head was rare. And to have one who was known to be handsome and wealthy and generous, even if not physically present, was to be considered most fortunate indeed.

"And there was no doubt that Reginald was his father's son. All they had to do was look at him and he had Brett written all over him; the spittin' image, as we say in Georgia.

"And as for scandal. Fiddle-dee-dee! We are Americans. As Brett once told me, 'With enough courage, you can do without a reputation.' It also helps if you are one of the wealthiest women in the city and provide reliable employment to over three thousand people irrespective of their color, and give fair wages and help build the hospital for our veterans. Why then you can ride stark naked down Peachtree Street like your Lady Godiva and receive nothing but smiles and reports in the papers about your charming eccentricities."

Holmes said nothing and continued to fix his gaze on this quite unusual woman. Momma continued to sip her tea, and the boy continued to gaze on his mother with unabashed admiration. I could do no more than sputter, "Yes, of course, madam. Such things would be highly irregular here in England. But I am sure that your husband was thrilled with the prospect of another child, especially a son who has grown up to be such a handsome young man. His father must be very proud of him."

Her face fell. I observed a tremble in her lower lip. "No, Doctor Watson, his father is not proud of his son. Neither is he un-proud of his son. My son's father does not know that his son even exists."

She paused here. This was an issue of some pain to her, and even such a supremely confident woman had to take a moment to recover her emotional equanimity.

"Brett has never returned to Atlanta. I have sent him many letters informing him about Reggie. Whenever I received news of where he might be found, I posted yet another letter. I sent them to India, to Russia, to Japan, to Greece, to Serbia, and most recently to South Africa . . . to anywhere and everywhere on earth where there was turmoil and in which a soldier of fortune might be serving a worthy cause.

"Every one of my letters has been returned to me unopened and marked 'Whereabouts Unknown.' To this day, Brett does not know that his son is the pride of the new Georgia Military Academy and the idol of every debutante in the city."

Here I glanced up again at the young man. He was looking down at his boots and blushing. How unusual that a young lad could be so proud of his mother even as she boasted about his father's endowment but then so embarrassed when she bragged about him.

"Permit me to ask the obvious question," Holmes finally said, breaking his silence. "Why now? Why after all these attempts to locate your husband have you taken it upon yourself to come to London to try to track him down in person?"

"In May Reggie graduated from the Georgia Military Academy with exceptionally high honors. He has received acceptance with full scholarship to our most prestigious school in the South, the Military College of South Carolina. We know it by its more familiar name of The Citadel. His father also attended The Citadel, after being expelled from West Point, and had outstanding accomplishments. He still holds the school's record for many of its military, sporting, and academic contests. Now Brett, being Brett, failed to graduate due to some charges laid against him for some minor misdeeds connected to bringing girls into the dormitories, alcohol consumption, and feeding some sort of nutrients to the faculty members' horses, causing them to have diarrhea during a parade day.

"His writing essays in the school newsletter criticizing in the most severe terms our politicians and the military leadership of our Southern regiments, and noting how much more prepared were the regiments in the North, made him very unpopular with some of those in power. Although, looking back, he was absolutely correct in his assertions and sadly all too prescient. He now is esteemed by the school, and they claim him as one of their own even though they also expelled him so many years ago. His providing funds for their new armory has not hurt.

"But they do have one inviolable rule concerning admissions. The Citadel must act *in loco parentis* and requires all parents of cadets to sign permission forms giving them this unrestricted right. These must be signed by both parents unless one of them is known to be deceased. Since Brett is believed by all to be alive, it is required that he sign the documents. Forgery is out of the question, not because I would not hesitate to do it but because I am sure it would be found out, bring dishonor to my son, and destroy his opportunity for a brilliant military career.

"The school term begins on the second Monday of September. It is now the third of August. There is little time available to us, and so I have left my affairs in the capable hands of my Head Foreman for Agricultural Operations, Sam Magnus, and have come to London to find Brett. I placed advertisements in your newspapers announcing my presence and asking and indeed offering to pay for any pertinent information. I have recently met with three of his closest business associates, who confirmed that they had recent communication from him, believed him to be either in London or nearby, but had not personally spoken to him nor could they confirm his whereabouts. Since I told you at the outset of this conversation that time was of the essence, I am now here requesting your services, Mr. Holmes."

Sherlock Holmes raised his head, and his face took on a puzzled and somewhat pained expression. "Mrs. Cutler, I cannot but admire all you have accomplished in your life and in that of your son, and I am honored to be solicited by someone so esteemed as yourself, but my special province is in matters that are not only criminal but require an exercise of logical synthesis. While your concerns have been distressing and your ability to rise above them most inspiring, there is nothing you have told me that in any way involves the breaking of the law. Doing dastardly things to the digestive tracts of horses is the closest you have come, and I'm afraid that even that does not constitute a crime."

She responded with a feigned smile. "Now don't you go jerking your chin at me Mr. Holmes. I said a moment ago that I had made contact with three men in London who had carried out some recent transactions with my husband although sight unseen."

"Yes, ma'am," I confirmed, "You did indeed tell us that."

"The names of those three men are: Donald McQuarrie, a banker in Mayfair; Boas De Groot, an importer with an office in the City and a warehouse in the Docklands; and Brendan Fitzsimmons, a solicitor on Bedford Row. Now . . . do you see why I am here?"

Mrs. Hudson uttered a fearful gasp. I could not speak. For a quick second, Holmes clasped his hands together.

The three men she named were the three who in the past few days had been murdered by the mad garrotters.

"Your police, your Scotland Yard, and your newspapers are all reporting that these men had no connection to each other, and that they just, unfortunately, were in the wrong place at the wrong time when a murderous gang of thugs came along, garroted them and robbed them. That silliness is what they are saying, is it not, Mr. Holmes?"

"Indeed, it is, and, as usual, they are quite wrong," replied Holmes.

"Yes. There is a connection, and it is my husband, Captain Brett Cutler. They were all in contact with him during the past year, and now they are all dead. So that is why I am here, Mr. Holmes. My husband's life is quite likely in danger, and I need your help to protect him."

I asked her, "Have you spoken to the police or Scotland Yard, Mrs. Cutler?"

"I spoke to them yesterday afternoon as soon as I learned about the third murder. They were very officious and sympathetic and all but made it quite clear that they could not help me look for a husband who would not be found. I do believe that they thought I was just one more American woman searching for some wayward husband, who had emptied the family's accounts, run off with the governess, and was now hiding out in London. I must confess that I was more than a little disappointed that they could be such obnoxious fools."

I could not resist a glance in the direction of Sherlock Holmes. He had been called many names in his career but never to my memory obliquely referred to as an obnoxious fool. I stole a glance at Mrs. Hudson as well and noticed that she was biting her lower lip. Then we noticed Holmes glaring angrily at both of us, so we had to look at the floor and pretend to be inspecting the carpet.

Holmes turned to the woman who had most assuredly become our latest client.

"Mrs. Cutler . . ."

"Sir, if we are to be working together to protect my family, I would prefer that you address me as Starlet, which is how I am known to all in Atlanta. Indeed, it is how all the men of my age, what few there are in Atlanta, address me. Those men and I shared four years of war, and it gave us the right to be familiar with each other. I expect that you and I are about to enter some dangerous times, and a more informal form of speaking to each other would be quite acceptable."

"Thank you, Miss Starlet," said Holmes. Using a client's Christian name took a concentrated exercise of the will on his part. "Leave these matters in our hands. We shall do everything in our power not only to protect your husband but to bring these murderous thugs to justice. I must, however, correct one of your misconceptions."

"Yes, and just what might that be?"

"You said that the obvious connecting link between the murders of these three men was some form of communication they had with your husband sometime during the past year or two."

"Yes. Why, what else could it have been? The police know of no other business, family or social connection they had to each other."

"My dear lady. The connection to your husband was only secondary. They all shared a much closer tie in their business dealings. They all had a direct meeting with the same person during the final days before their deaths." Holmes paused, waiting for Miss Starlet to comprehend the gravity of what he had said to her.

She stared at him blankly for a few seconds, and then her eyes widened with a look of fear and shock. "Yes. Of course. Their immediate link with each other was not with Brett. It was with . . . me. Those murderers have been following me. And Momma. And Reggie. And now three men are dead. Most horribly murdered. I led those villains to those three innocent men."

"Yes, I fear that what you say, Miss Starlet, is indeed what has happened, but there is no way you could have known that," said Holmes. "We do not know why they were following you, but we must acknowledge that not only is your husband in danger but most probably you, your son, and Momma are as well."

Miss Starlet retained her regal posture and demeanor, but I noticed that she was squeezing her right hand and pressing her thumbnail into that section of her index finger that is just behind the first knuckle. "Gentlemen," she said in a deliberate tone, "I have been through many difficult times in my life. I do not fear for myself, nor to lie, steal, cheat, or kill if I were forced to. However, three men have already died for no other reason than their contact with me. The two people who are nearest and dearest to me on this earth are sitting in the room. Their lives may be in grave danger, and it would be because of my actions. I do not blush to admit that I am quite frightened, and I place myself in your hands, seeking your guidance for our safety."

Holmes had been drawn into one of the roles that had made him such a great detective. He would assume his destined place as the protector of the fairer sex and would leave no stone unturned, no enemy unvanquished until his charges were restored to safety. "Miss Starlet," he said, "you may trust in our devotion to your needs and those of your family. But now I must ask that you reveal to me all that you have learned about your husband's activities since your arrival here in London. As you said, 'Time is of the essence.'"

She nodded. "We arrived in London ten days ago. Last year I received some pieces of correspondence from London regarding transfers of funds and properties from Brett's accounts but have heard nothing at all now for several months. Since these were my only sources of information, I began with them."

"Entirely sensible," I said with an affirming nod.

"All three of them acknowledged that they had had some contact with Brett in the past and that, following his explicit instructions, they had forwarded various transactions over to me. But they also were quite certain that they had never been informed of his address here in London, and that they had heard not a peep from him in person in over two years. I suspected that all three of them were withholding some information from me, but they would say no more than what I have just told you.

"I requested that they turn over to me whatever papers or other records they possessed, which they did."

"Indeed?" queried Holmes, "with no objection?"

"The objections were dealt with. Before his departure from America, Brett had left fully signed and sealed documents giving me power-of-attorney over his affairs in the event he could not be located. I merely had to produce these, and such records as they held were given to me. They are all in the valise that my son has brought with us. You may look over everything," she said.

"We shall examine all of the contents very carefully, you may be sure," said Holmes. "Our first priority, though, is your safety. You may assume that you will be followed unless we take evasive precautions."

"We are grateful for you concern. We departed the hotel at such an early hour this morning that I am sure that no one has followed us here."

"I am certain as well," said Holmes, "We have seen no one looking up from Baker Street, and had they sought to conceal themselves, we would have had a report from our splendid company of Irregulars."

"Who they?" said Momma, who had long since lost interest in her fortified tea and had been following every word of the conversation since the issue of danger to her family had been voiced.

"*They,*" said Sherlock Holmes, with a warm smile towards Momma, "are the best troop of spies in the city, and I am sure that when you meet them, they will endear themselves to you as much as they have to me. You may also be sure," he said, turning back to Miss Starlet, "that our adversaries will be watching your hotel and on seeing you return will immediately realize that they missed you this morning on account of your early departure. They will not make that mistake again tomorrow.

"So please follow these instructions to the letter," said Holmes. "I shall send a note to Master Toby St. John, the head doorman of the Dorchester. He is a stalwart yeoman and regards the safety of his guests as a divine trust. I will ask him to furnish young Reginald with a cab driver's uniform. I'm sure that he can come up with one large enough. Some of our drivers are as tall as your son, and you will just have to cinch in the belt and trousers. With a good top-hat, that should be enough to get past our enemy's lookouts. As for you, my dear lady . . ." he paused here, touching his fingertips together, "the most reliable disguise would be to have you dressed as a man."

"Whoa there, Sherlock!" said Momma. "That just ain't fittin'."

"And just what do you mean, my dear Momma, by 'ain't fittin'?"

Momma lowered her head and glowered back at him. "If something ain't fittin', it just ain't fittin'. And what you're suggesting just ain't fittin'. That's all."

Holmes looked over at Miss Starlet who gave a nod of acquiescence towards Momma and then looked back at Holmes with an expression that said, "and just what might be your next best suggestion?"

Holmes looked intently at Miss Starlet. I could tell that he was redrawing her striking figure in his mind and seeking to imagine what possible disguise could conceal her identity. His smile indicated that he had decided on an alternative. He raised himself from his chair and retired briefly to his rooms. He returned, bearing in his hand a mane of flowing red hair. "Then Madam, you will have to wear this wig and I am sure you have an evening gown with you, one that could be described, shall we say, as daring. As you depart the hotel just before the breakfast hour, please have your red hair in a somewhat disorderly fashion. You may attend to your rouge and lipstick in the cab."

"Mister Holmes!" Momma burst out, "I never but once seen hair that color in my whole life. Everybody that sees that and her flaunting her bosom before three 'clock in the afternoon'll think she's no more than white trash, a high-priced woman of ill repute!"

"Thank you, Momma. That is exactly what they need to think. Could you play such a role convincingly, Miss Starlet?"

"I could have danced with Abe Lincoln if I'd had to, so I am quite sure I could do what you ask," she responded with a sly smile. "I have just the dress in mind; the one Brett made me wear years ago when he was demanding the same theatrical effect. I brought it with me. With my young and handsome driver, the most observant of spies shall be thoroughly fooled."

Dear me, can this woman honestly be pleased to dress up like a prostitute and have her son drive her through London? My question was being answered in the affirmative. Merciful heavens. These Americans.

Holmes now turned towards Momma. "And you, my dear lady; I shall have to ask to remain at the hotel, but please make yourself visible from time to time in the lobby and the dining room so that their spies will believe your entire party is still in the building."

"I can do that," she answered, still frowning at Holmes and Miss Starlet. "I could even have the dining room send up lunches for four just to fool them some more."

"Splendid," exclaimed Holmes, "I am quite sure that you missed your divine calling as a detective."

"No, sir. The good Lord called me to be an honest Christian woman."

Holmes was struggling for a rejoinder but admitted defeat and simply rose from his chair, offered his hand to Momma and said, "Then allow me to assist an honest Christian woman to her carriage. I shall see you two tomorrow morning at the same time by our front door. And please, young soldier, leave the valise where it is. By tomorrow morning, we will have gleaned all there is to learn from it."

Mrs. Hudson interposed herself and took Momma's arm and helped her down the stairs. Miss Starlet and Reggie followed. From the window, we watched them drive off towards Hyde Park.

Chapter Three

Briany

Sherlock Holmes's complexion had visibly altered as it always did when his spirit was enlivened and he was engaged in hot pursuit of the latest evil doers. He moved with deliberate energy as he made notes and plotted out his route to the undoing of his adversaries.

Holmes reached for the valise and laid it on our table. He opened the latches and looked inside without saying anything. It contained three distinct bundles, each tied up with a ribbon to which a note was attached identifying its origins.

He turned to me. "We have entered a very dangerous game, my dear friend. It is not only afoot, it is running very quickly and we shall have to make haste to get in front of it. Otherwise our lovely client's husband's life will most certainly be shortened, as may be hers. We are dealing with very dangerous killers and there is no time to waste. I shall first organize the Baker Street Irregulars to bring us every shred of information available about a small band of garrotters and then make visits to the offices of the recently deceased.

"I shall need your assistance. I do not have adequate time left in the day to investigate all the data pertaining to the murders of these three unfortunate men and at the same time thoroughly examine the contents of this valise. So, my dear man, may I prevail upon your good graces and ask if you would be so kind as to review these papers while I haste myself about London. I ask only that you would seek in them the data that I would were I perusing them.

Of all people you are the most familiar with my methods. May I beseech you accordingly, my good doctor?"

"Of course you may," I assented, "but I fear I shall disappoint you yet again as no matter how many times I have observed you at work I have never fathomed the methods you employ to see details that are so obvious to you and missing to my dull eye. But I shall do my best and have a report for you upon your return."

"I could ask no more, my dear friend," and with this he departed the rooms and descended the stairs. I heard his bird whistle sound and from the window could see the ragamuffins he so endearingly termed his Company of Irregulars assemble around him for a minute. Then he leapt into a cab which forthwith began to move at breakneck speed south on Baker Street and toward the City.

My day's task, long and exacting, was laid out in front of me. I trust that my dear readers will bear with me as I plod my way through the details of my discoveries.

I started by sorting and sub-dividing. The first group of documents concerned shipments from various parts of the globe which arrived at the Port of London and were handled by the agent, the late Mr. de Groot. The bills of lading and way bills all noted the ports of origin—Singapore, Colombo, Rangoon, Tokyo Bay, Calcutta (several times), Vancouver, San Francisco, Rio De Janeiro, St. Petersburg . . . almost every major port on earth. The names of the ships were duly listed and all documents were appropriately signed and sealed. What was unusual was that in the entry for the size of the shipment many were marked a "Grade 1", the smallest, no more than a cigar box. Yet every one of them was also accompanied by a certificate of insurance from Lloyds and the rating of every certificate stated "Maximum £10,000." The "Protection" entry was invariably marked "Grade 10"—the ship's safe in the captain's quarters. Scribbled on the waybills were some markings in pencil with letters like "D" or "R" or "E" or occasionally "Au" or "Ag."

I did not have to be Sherlock Holmes to deduce that our wayward husband, Captain Cutler, had been sending back packets of gold, silver, diamonds and precious gems from the various corners of the earth in which he sought his fortune, and a considerable fortune it was indeed.

Within two hours I had completely sorted the shipping documents and arranged them chronologically. Over the past fifteen years our man had roamed the earth. It appeared that each of his temporary sojourns corresponded with some type of conflict. He had been in Burma when the Burmese were giving the BEF a bad case of the Irrawaddy Chills; in Shanghai while the Chinese and the Japs were having a go at each other; in western Canada while thousands of men "crazed for the muck called gold" were trekking their way to the frozen hills of the Yukon; in the Dominican when Teddy Roosevelt and his silly Roughriders were storming San Juan Hill . . . and so it went. It began in Paris with the uprising of the Commune and had ended just over two years ago in Pretoria. After that, nothing.

Interspersed with the highly valued and insured shipments were some rather curious ones. Every year without fail in early August and again in early December there were copies of shipping documents for articles sent to Calcutta. These were handled by a different agent who I gathered was a correspondent office for Mr. De Groot, and were all marked "D.G.H." They were not large items in size and had no insurance certificates. They took place like clockwork during the early years but then, for no apparent reason, came to an end eight years ago.

Holmes had often observed that you could tell as much about a man from his bank book as you could from his diary, and so I duly studied the details of Captain Cutler's financial transactions. Since 1864 he had maintained an account at a bank in Liverpool. Beginning in the 1870s there were large deposits exceeding a thousand pounds on an irregular basis that I cross-referenced with the shipments of gold and gems. Every quarter during the early years he sent £3000 to the account of the Beulah Plantation in Atlanta. Later this increased to £4000 and then £5000. Irregular payments were recorded to several firms that included Beretta, Colt, Remington and Rolls-Royce. There were miscellaneous payments to accounts at Harrods, Fortnum and Mason's and several of London's better haberdashers, and some smaller sums were sent to a Barings branch in Calcutta, but these had also been curtailed eight years ago. Then, starting a little less than eight years ago, transfers to an *O'Brien Trust* appeared and continued quarterly up until the latest recorded statement of the immediate past month. The cash balance was consistently maintained at just over £20,000 and when it exceeded that amount there were transfers to Hitchens, Harrison and Co. who I knew to be one of the major brokerages on the London Exchange. I assumed that our man was purchasing securities and wisely not leaving his funds in unproductive cash. Our Captain Cutler was a very wealthy man and an astute manager of his financial affairs.

Throughout the records various transactions had been initialed. Prior to 1898 they were clearly signed as "B.C." which I concluded were those of Brett Cutler, our wayward husband. Thereafter a different set of initials appeared. In what was clearly a female hand were the initials "B.O." Given the impressive size of the transactions this Miss or Mrs. BO must be a woman of competence in whom our man placed great trust. Suspicions concerning our man's fidelity crept into my mind and I feared that the heart of our lovely client might again be broken. But *honi soit qui mal y pense* and so these thoughts I had to banish from my mind as I turned to the thick file of documents that had come from his solicitor.

Most of what I found in the now deceased solicitor's file was received correspondence related to various business transactions. Many of these letters could be referenced back to shipping and financial entries and none seemed unusual given Captain Cutler's dealings in arms and shipments throughout the globe. There were two sets of personal correspondence that I set aside. The first were of incoming notes bearing the letterhead of St. Andrew's Mission. Prior to 1890 the location of the mission was given as Calcutta. Thereafter it read Kalimpong, Bengal. The notes were addressed consistently to "My dear Brett" and signed various as "John" or "Rev. John" or "Dr. J" and during the later years of 1892 to 1894 as "Daddy G". The contents were very brief. Some contained a note of thanks for a contribution received related to the construction of a library or dormitory. Others referred to the progress of "B". "B still reserved after loss but bearing up well" read one of the early messages. "B took first in maths" read another dated early on. Most of the later ones likewise referred to the remarkable accomplishments of this young student who was only identified as "B". The last note, dated in 1895 was a little longer and informed Brett that B had graduated and on Prize Day walked away with several academic first prizes as well as ribbons for swimming, athletics and riding. Whoever this young B might be, he was most assuredly an outstanding student. No more notes were received following the graduation notice, except for the odd one again thanking Brett for his monetary contribution to the Scholars' Fund.

The second set of notes bore the handwriting of two different men and were an exchange of quickly dashed off correspondence between them. They had used the same sheet of writing paper both to send the original note and upon which to scribble the hasty reply. Those originating from 'B' bore no letterhead at all prior to 1893 but were on the finest quality linen paper. From 1893 until 1898 they changed and were on paper supplied by Brown's Hotel in Mayfair. After that date they were once again on the same blank pages. Those initiated by the other man, signing as "AE" were embossed with a coat of arms that I recognised but to which I could not immediately attach a name, my memory of English heraldry having faded since my school days. The cryptic messages all appeared to concern the activities and movements of someone referred to as "The BH." In response to a note from B stating "BH present in the Khyber" AE had replied "Yes and arming the Boxers." From a location identified only as "Sand" was a request from AE, "Is BH in BEG" the reply came back from B "Many as well as on the Venz. Side.", and to which a third note was added "They are leading us to war with the Yanks." Others were in a similar vein except for one from Paris where B had written "Tiger confirms MB was behind Commune."

These and all other papers I laid out neatly in separate piles according to the subject matters and chronologically ordered for Holmes to peruse upon his return. I postponed asking Mrs. Hudson to send in supper and waited for Holmes to return, which he did shortly after six o'clock. He looked tired and hungry but bearing that look of determined satisfaction I had come to know when he was hot on the trail of a worthy adversary. He sat down at our table and poured himself a glass of brandy. Mrs. Hudson appeared soon bearing one of her unfailingly appetizing platters; this one of roast duck.

"Thanks awfully, Mrs. Watson," I said to the good woman.

As soon as we had finished eating I proudly displayed my work and offered some of my insights. Holmes listened politely and said little except the odd murmur of "Yes indeed." Or "Yes. Well done Watson." As his praise was always highly economical I felt quite pleased with my accomplishments. He took my notes and the files in hand.

"Please do not disturb me for the next fifty minutes, Watson. A three pipe review of the data is necessary."

Following supper and into the early evening, Holmes said not another word but merely smoked his pipe and looked over my various piles of documents, examining some quite closely with his glass.

Precisely fifty minutes later he put down the last letter, stood up, proceeded to the corner of the room and retrieved his violin. He tuned it briefly and began to play one of his familiar favorites by Brahms. This was unbearable.

"Really Holmes," I remonstrated, "you must say something. What have you deduced from your day and from my hours of work."

"Oh, yes, of course, my dear Watson. How thoughtless of me. First thing tomorrow morning we shall reunite our client with her husband and take steps to protect them for they are in great danger from the most ruthless of villains." With that said he placed his bow once more upon the instrument and returned to Brahms. I knew better than to expect anything more from him until morning.

I rose early but Holmes was already up and out of 221B Baker Street. From the window I watched him as he stood at the corner of Park Road chatting with a troop of his Irregulars. With a wave from the detective his spies scampered off and he returned and came up the stairs.

He sat down to breakfast, tucked in heartily to the kippers and toast that Mrs. Hudson had laid out, and engrossed himself in *The Times*.

At 7:55 I heard a carriage on the street below our window and looked down upon a very finely appointed hansom cab, with a tall driver strikingly attired in a navy blue uniform with flashing gold braids, buttons, epaulettes, and top hat. He descended from his perch at the back of the vehicle, opened an umbrella to offer protection from the rain, unlatched the door, and gave his free hand to his passenger. She stepped out onto the pavement and I inwardly groaned at what our neighbours would think about our latest client. For there emerged from the cab a tall woman with shoulders and arms uncovered in the early morning, a dress with cleavage cut so low as to give a clergyman heart failure, and a mane of red hair such as would be unknown outside of County Cork.

Our clients ascended the stairs and we could hear them laughing and giggling about their disguises. "Oh my, would not Belle have been proud of me? Do you think she would have hired me Reggie?"

"Only if she wanted to take the best clients away from all the other girls. Mother, you look utterly irresistible!"

They continued on in their rather vulgar repartee as they entered the room and proceeded to inform Holmes and me of their triumph in leaving the hotel, not only undetected but with glaring stares from the breakfasting patrons and a wink from Toby the doorman.

"Mr. Holmes, Mr. Holmes" began Miss Starlet, "How can I thank you? Knowing that you agreed to protect us so lightened my heart that we did not spend the afternoon in our hotel. I know that it was a little bit risky, but I told our driver to go directly to Harrods.

"I just had to see what the latest fashions are for the Fall in London so we stopped by the ladies' department and, well, my goodness, they had so many beautiful things to look at."

"Oh my. I introduced myself to the head shoplady and said I was sorry that I had so little cash with me otherwise I would love to buy my entire fall and winter wardrobes from her. And didn't she just give me and odd look and say, 'Madam, we do not need cash. You could just put everything on your husband's account.'

"My darling husband it seems has had an account with them for going on thirty years and has bought some beautiful fashions for women during that time. Well, Mr. Holmes, even if you would not be proud of me, I am sure that your dear Mrs. Hudson would," she said with a beaming smile directed toward the good lady, "because by the end of the afternoon I made sure that more damage had been done to that account than had been done in the past thirty years. If we all do make it out of this crazy time alive then Reggie, and Momma, and I will all be the best dressed folks on Peach Tree Street."

Holmes smiled warmly, having enjoyed their tale of retail adventure. "As much as it pains me to make the request, I will have to ask you to change from your current costumes into something more appropriate for a morning drive through London."

"Oh, must we really?" replied Miss Starlet, her face drawn into a well-practiced pout. "Very well then, you are such a spoil sport sir. But I have the most beautiful new white summer dress so I shall not complain." With an impish smile she made her way to one of our back rooms. Her tall handsome son followed bearing a carpet bag in which I assumed he carried more acceptable attire.

They returned forthwith looking splendid in fine quality outfits. Miss Starlet looked at Holmes and with feigned seriousness asked, "Kind sir, do tell this now respectable lady what news of her wandering husband?"

"We are off to Mayfair," announced Holmes, "to pay a surprise visit to your husband and," he added, looking at Reggie, "your father."

The gay smiles slowly vanished from the faces of Miss Starlet and Reggie, struck from their mouths by some invisible hand. They exchanged a glance of apprehension between them and then rose and without a word walked toward the door and descended the stairs. Holmes and I followed and once at the curb of Baker Street I hailed a four-seater, lucky to find one so readily on such a close and rainy day.

As we drove south on Baker Street toward Oxford I made a few remarks about the weather and tried to add some levity to the moment by repeating Momma's appraisal of London but to no avail. Our clients remained stone-faced, which puzzled me as we were about to accomplish the mission that brought them across the pond in the first place.

Holmes, who I have long admitted was a far better judge of the feelings that people are having in the hearts behind their brave masks than he let on, reached across the cab and warmly covered Miss Starlet's hand with both of his. "My dear, there is not a doubt in my mind that your husband will find you every bit as attractive as he did in the past. You have only become all the more lovely with the passing of time."

She glanced at him and gave a forced smile. "Four decades have passed since he looked upon me as a pretty and head-strong young girl and told me that I was no lady. That girl doesn't exist anymore. Nothing turned out the way I expected. Nothing. I fear that now that I have become a lady he will no longer see in me that pretty girl that he once desired so passionately."

"No," said Holmes, "he will not, but he will see an exceptional woman who will be his loving partner and helpmeet until death do you part."

"And you, young sir," he continued, turning to Reggie, "are about to meet a father who will be exceedingly proud of his son."

"Thank you, Mr. Holmes," Reggie said, "I confess to an inward fear that I would find it very trying if a father who had abandoned me not knowing of my existence were to do the same thing again after becoming aware of it. My lessons in courage failed to cover events like this one."

"I have no son," said Holmes, looking at Reggie directly, "but if I were to suddenly discover that I had one I would give thanks to Providence if he were to be half-way close to who you are. You will be just fine, mark my words."

"Thank you, sir," the boy replied, "you are being thoughtful."

"May I again ask you" said Miss Starlet, having somewhat recovered her composure, "where it is that we are going?"

"To Mayfair," said Holmes, "your husband has rooms at Claridges. As we enter I must ask you please to follow my lead and play the game with me."

We had driven down Park Lane, turned left into Brook Street, and arrived at the door of the recently restored and re-opened Claridges Hotel, which had once again returned to its status as the most respected and exclusive in all of London. Holmes led the way up the steps, breezed confidently past the attentive doorman, and approached the desk of the porter.

"I bid you good morning sir, my name is Sherlock Holmes." The porter raised his eyebrow while Holmes continued. "Our visit to your most reputable establishment is only for good reasons, I assure you. I am certainly not here to investigate anything untoward. This American lady, Mrs. Smith, is my client. Her son, Theodore, has completed his schooling and is about to engage on his grand tour of our fair land and the Continent. While doing so he will need a continuing place to return to and I have recommended that he take rooms at Claridges."

"Why thank you sir. Our reputation is very dear to us and knowing that our most famous detective attests to our quality is a very kind compliment," the porter replied with an authentic smile.

"You must understand, however," Holmes said, "that people in the colonies hear only those things about London that the most miserable of our reporters on Fleet Street tell the world, and so they fear that our streets are filled with cutthroats and villains, and our hotels with touts and swindlers. I have brought Mrs. Smith here today to prove to her that her son will be completely safe and secure."

"Of course, sir. The blackguards of Fleet Street do the nation no favors by such inflammatory stories."

"I heartily agree. So, may I impose upon your fine hospitality with two requests. Would you be so kind as to show young Theodore here a set of rooms? We have noted that you have several vacancies posted. And may I also, in strictest confidence of course, be permitted to see the list of your continuing residents so that I may assure his mother that they are all of the highest moral character and will be a welcome presence in the forming of his character?"

"We do not normally offer the names of our residents to inquiry, sir, protecting as we do their privacy," the porter said, "but as you have assured me of your treating it in confidence, and as I rather suspect that were I to withhold it then Sherlock Holmes would find another way to obtain the information all the same, I will let you observe our list."

From beneath his porter's desk he withdrew a small register and opened it to a marked page and spread it in front of Holmes who gestured to "Mrs. Smith" to join him in looking it over. Holmes smiled at the porter, closed the register and handed it back. "Thank you, my good man," he said, "although I am not personally acquainted with all of these august persons I can confirm that not one of them is known in any way other than the most positive to Scotland Yard. And now, sir, if you will give young Theodore a tour of the available rooms I will, with your permission, show this good lady what an excellent job Mr. Doily Carte has done not only in making Claridges a pearl of fine design but the safest in London from fire or thievery. After I do so I will return to your desk and fetch Theodore."

"By all means. We are very proud of our grand hotel. And please, Master Theodore, let me show you to what I am sure will become your most enjoyable home away from home," said the porter and with that he departed with Theodore in tow. As soon as he was out of earshot Holmes beckoned me and Miss Starlet to his side.

"He's not here," said Miss Starlet, "You said he was living here but his name was clearly not on that list. We might as well leave."

"I must ask you, my dear Miss Starlet," said Holmes, ever the teacher, "what did you observe about those names?"

Miss Starlet shrugged her shoulders and responded somewhat quizzically, "Nothing unusual. There were about thirty names, all Lord such-and-such or Earl of so-and so. Almost all striking me as oh-so-English, but certainly no Brett Cutler was inscribed."

"He most certainly was on the register and is living in room 435," said Holmes. "Let us proceed."

She looked at him with a glance of disbelief but said nothing and followed him up the staircase.

"Are we just going to walk in?" asked Miss Starlet.

"No, my dear, we are not just going to walk in. We are going to knock and if no one answers we are going to break in," answered Holmes.

At the door marked 435 we knocked and indeed there was no answer. Holmes procured from his pocket a small case that I had last seen when we burgled the residence of the vile Charles Milverton. It contained his collection of exquisitely designed locksmith's tools and, taking one of them in hand, he quickly picked the lock of what I am sure Claridges had advertised as being the latest in safety and security. We entered a room with high ceilings, floor to ceiling windows opening to a small balcony, very fine quality flooring, and lush velvet draperies. There were several paintings on the walls that seemed to be of the most recent avant-garde style from France. Rather blurred and smudged to my mind but then I was no connoisseur of art.

"Your husband continues to have very fine taste," I observed trying to disguise an inkling that the fine taste we were observing betrayed the hand of a lady of considerable breeding and hardly that of a soldier of fortune.

Miss Starlet said nothing. She walked slowly and aimlessly about. "Either he has found a classy mistress or this is not Brett's place at all," she concluded. It was apparent that she thought the former alternative the most likely and was not in a good humor.

"He does live here, stayed here last night, and will most likely be returning presently," said Holmes.

"How can you possibly know that?" asked Miss Starlet.

"The tobacco ashes in the ashtray are from the Golden Virginia brand. The maids clean the rooms every day in the late morning and again in the evening and no maid of Claridges would be working here long if she were to leave an ashtray unemptied and unpolished. These ashes were dropped by your husband this morning before he left the premises.

"Before he returns," said Holmes, "would you and Dr. Watson please look into all of the armoires, drawers, and closets and see what you can find. I will fetch our young Master Theodore from the front desk."

With that, Holmes departed the room.

Miss Starlet and I entered one of the bedrooms and began to investigate the closets. She opened a large armoire and examined some of the clothing that was hanging in it. She lifted out a fine cotton shirt and held it up in front of her. "These are his size but I do not recognize any of them. Nor these suits, nor the coats," she said.

"I do not think it likely that a man of your husband's wealth and activities would still be wearing the same clothes as he did seventeen years ago," I offered.

"I suppose you are right," she said while still looking from top to bottom of the armoire. Then I heard a gasp and watched her fall to her knees. She reached into the floor of the armoire and brought out a set of men's boots. "These are his. These are Brett's. I gave them to him." Her voice trembled slightly with barely disguised intense feeling. She stood up, walked over to the bedside chair and sat down, holding the boots in her lap.

"Really, my dear Miss Starlet, how can you possibly remember a set of old black boots? There must be thousands of that style all over London," I said.

"No. No. I am quite certain. On our belated honeymoon in Niagara Falls I saw the store of a Toronto merchant, a bootmaker. So, I put a pair of Brett's favorite shoes in my purse and for an hour excused myself claiming a need to purchase some feminine products. I had the bootmaker make two pairs of the highest quality boots for Brett using his shoes as the pattern. One set was for summer, one for winter. The Canadians you know are very good at making boots for winter, which our Atlanta cobblers, bless their hearts, simply are not. These are his winter boots. Look, here. Inside."

I looked. "Meyers, Toronto" was printed on the inside leather.

She continued to sit in the chair and stroked the boots as if they were a much-loved kitten. For a brief second, I saw her hold the open end of a boot to her nose, close her eyes and breathe in. Her lower lips began to tremble ever so slightly and her lovely mouth broadened into a warm smile. She clutched the boots closely to her bosom. I discretely examined the flower vases one more time.

The door to the hall opened and Holmes entered with Reggie-formerly-Theodore. Miss Starlet returned to the central room from the bedroom holding the boots. "He is here. What do we do now?"

"We sit and wait patiently for him to return," said Holmes, "which I expect he will very soon."

"If I may Mr. Holmes, sir," said Reggie. "How did you do it? I know from reading about your accomplishments in *The Strand* that you have used your methods of scientific deduction to lead us here, but please tell me how in the world you came to your conclusions."

"Very well, young man," Holmes replied, "finding your father was quite elementary and I fear will turn out to be the least dangerous portion of this quest we have embarked upon. His banking and legal records showed us that he had lived for a period in London many years ago and there was a reference to a Miss Victoria Cutler.

"Bonnie. That was the time when he took Bonnie Blue away from Atlanta and lived in London," said Starlet.

"Yes," nodded Holmes, "and he visited or lived in London many times after that. But over two years ago he ceased to conduct his affairs under his own name or initials. He used an assumed name or used someone else to act on his behalf. It would have been futile to look at all of London's hotels asking for Brett Cutler since he was not registered under that name.

"From 1893 until 1898 he was a resident at Brown's Hotel, an excellent establishment just around the corner from here in Mayfair. That was obvious from the letterhead he used. Both prior to those dates and afterwards he resided somewhere that supplied him with note paper that bore almost no trace of the name of the hotel, choosing thereby to assure its guests of the utmost in privacy and discretion. However, the new owners of this hotel, the Doily Carte family, are too commercially astute not to associate their name with their prestigious guests, so they altered the paper ever so slightly. Here, examine this."

Holmes pulled his glass from one inside pocket and one of the notes that had been sent under the initial "B" and handed them to Reggie. He looked it over closely first with plain eyesight and then using the glass, and looked up with a shake of his head and said, "I can't see anything that ties this note to this place."

"Look again," instructed Holmes, "very closely at the very edges of the paper. What do you see?"

"Aha!" cried the young man, "there is the tiniest embossed letter 'C' sitting inside a raised circle. The form is like that of the first letter 'C' on the hotel's sign on the street."

Ⓒ

"You discern correctly," said Holmes. "The next clue was the name in the register." He turned to Miss Starlet. "You read the list of names. Did not any one of them strike you as being unlike the rest?"

"Not really. Although there was one that struck me as odd." said Miss Starlet, "A 'Baron G. O'Halloran.' Odd only that it was the same last name as my maiden name, but it is a very common Irish name and there are thousands of them all over England."

"Ah", said Holmes, "but you will not find a single 'O'Halloran' in Debrett's Peerage. The good Queen, may she rest in peace while instructing God how to better manage the heavens, was not in the habit of bestowing titles of 'Baron' upon the Irish and never upon one of Catholic faith. So, permit me to ask you, was your husband fond of your father before his untimely death?"

"He barely knew Pa," replied Miss Starlet, "but he spoke of him with the greatest affection and honor."

"And," Holmes said, "he adopted his name as his own. A mark of respect no doubt. And finally, there was the very curious way that the porter gave several sideways glances to you, Reggie. You are reputed to look like your father and there was no doubt that the porter was familiar with your inherited profile but being discrete said nothing that would imperil the renting of rooms at a cost of more than £100 a month for the entire duration of your grand tour. Once you assemble all of these observations, you must then eliminate all of the alternative conclusions. Whatever explanation that you are left with, no matter how improbable, must be the truth. And so here we are. We will wait for Brett Cutler and I suspect that he will be along rather soon."

He had no sooner spoken these words than we heard the key turn in the door lock. The person who entered it was not Brett Cutler. It was not a man at all. It was a young woman who was holding her matching navy blue bonnet in one hand and examining some letters in the other. She was not as tall as Miss Starlet but still of significant height and bearing and uncommonly attractive. Her hair, released from her bonnet, fell in golden ringlets well below her shoulders. Her complexion was smooth and spoke of excellent health. I guessed that her age would be in her middle twenties.

She looked up and saw us. Her bright blue eyes widened and she made as if to turnaround and run from the room.

"Miss O'Brien," Holmes shouted, "we are here as friends to you and to Brett Cutler. My name is Sherlock Holmes and we are gravely concerned for your safety. Please enter and speak with us."

She looked intently at Holmes, appeared to recognize him, and walked directly toward him. She held out her hand and spoke. "I know of your reputation sir and while I have no idea as to how or why you found us I am grateful for your appearance. We are indeed in danger."

"Oh my, are *we* indeed," said Miss Starlet with a tone of sharp sarcasm. "Brett always did prefer his fillies on the young and tender side. Easier to break in and less likely to tire early."

The young woman looked at Miss Starlet. Her face quickly transformed from puzzled to surprised recognition, to a brief flash of a warm smile, and back to one of composed resolution. She strode over to the speaker. "Mrs. Cutler, I can assure you that your husband's actions toward me have never been anything but beyond reproach and unquestionably honorable. You may insult me if you wish but in doing so you dishonor your husband and your marriage to him. Brett Cutler has only been passionately attracted to one woman in his entire life and it most certainly is not me, Starlet O'Halloran."

This exchange was followed by a few seconds of intense staring into each other's eyes, which was graciously interrupted by young Reggie. "Excuse me miss, the other gentleman with Mr. Holmes is his partner, Dr. Watson, and I am Reginald Cutler. We apologise for being here unannounced and unsettling you."

The young woman turned toward Reggie and let out a short gasp. She recovered herself and said, "I'm sorry. I did not know that Captain Cutler had a son, which looking at you I can only conclude that you must be."

"Yes miss, I am. You could not know about me because my father is not aware of my existence. He never learned of my birth following his departure from Georgia and still knows nothing of my life in spite of the best efforts of my mother to inform him."

The young woman said nothing. She continued to look at Reggie. Her face evidenced a feeling of sorrow and I thought I saw a tear forming in her eye. She walked slowly over to one of the chairs, sat down, buried her head in her hands, and slowly shook it back and forth causing her lovely long golden tresses to sway.

A few moments later she raised her head and with a tone of confidence spoke to us. "Forgive me. The past few days have been very trying and I have been quite terrified. Three men with whom I have done business over the past several years have all been murdered and I am in fear of my life, and

Captain Cutler's. For reasons I cannot tell you I have not asked the police for their help and your presence is a godsend."

I had no doubt that the words she spoke to us were true, but there was also no doubt that her emotional collapse a few moments ago was occasioned by her being informed about the hitherto unknown son of Brett Cutler and not just her concern for safety.

"Perhaps you could tell us then how it is that you are connected to Captain Cutler," said Holmes, "but before doing so allow me to wish you a happy birthday which I gather is either today or tomorrow." The young woman stared in amazement at Sherlock Holmes with the same look as I have seen on the faces of countless women when they discovered that he knew far more about them than was humanly possible for any normal man to know.

"It would seem that the famous detective already knows more than I could have expected, so I will give you the briefest summary before Captain Cutler returns.

"My father, Connor O'Brien and Brett Cutler were fellow soldiers of fortune. They met in the Sudan and became great friends and comrades-in-arms. Both were men of unflinching principles who believed in fighting as they said..."

"For lost causes once they're really lost," interrupted Miss Starlet. "I remember hearing that line the night I watched the Old South disappear. Please continue miss."

"They consulted with kings and peasants, with bishops and prisoners of conscience, with all types so long as they believed them to be honorable and acting in the selfless pursuit of liberty and freedom. They provided them with the arms and ammunition they needed to fight their oppressors. Some of those they helped were victorious. Most were not. Many times, they came close to death themselves but always managed to use their wits and courage to escape, except for one time in India when, according to your husband, Mrs. Cutler, he was under fire and expected to die when my father came to his rescue.

"Sadly, my father was grievously wounded. Captain Cutler was able to get the two of them to safety and on board a ship back to England. My father did not survive and was buried at sea. Captain Cutler informed me that my father's last words to him were to tell him that he had a young daughter whose mother had died in childbirth while living under the Raj. My father beseeched his dearest friend to look after his Briany, for that is my name, and after his death I became an orphan. Captain Cutler made certain I was well looked after by the St. Andrew's Mission that was caring for orphans in Calcutta. Under the guidance of the sainted Rev. Dr. John Graham, the mission soon established a wonderful home for children in the village of Kalimpong, in the beauty of the Hill Country.

"Captain Cutler never failed to visit me once a term and always sent gifts at Christmas and for my birthday. Several times he took me on the little Darjeelng Railway down to Siliguri and back.

"I wanted to make him proud of me and so I worked very diligently at all my studies and at my sports. When I turned eighteen I graduated from the school, which we all affectionately called Dr. Graham's Homes, and came to live in England. He arranged for me to be tutored by his friends Beatrice and Sidney Webb at their newly founded school, the London School of Economics.

"Upon completion of my studies, Captain Cutler appointed me as his business manager and I carried out transactions in his name. Two years ago, events of which I cannot speak took place that forced him to become very secretive about his actions and whereabouts, and so I assumed responsibility for his affairs. That is my position today. My rooms are across the hall, however I work from here during business hours. And so here I am gentlemen, and madam."

With this she stopped. Holmes had listened intently in his familiar pose of pressing his fingertips together. After a moment's silence he spoke to her in a kindly manner. "Miss Briany, you are assured that we will do everything we can to protect you but if we are to be able to help, you must be willing to be forthright about your close relationship with Captain Cutler. It is well beyond that of his being your patron and now employer. You have left out an important point."

Briany looked at Sherlock Holmes, then at Miss Starlet and finally at Reggie. When she spoke, the volume was subdued and filled with quiet emotion, "My father asked his friend not only to look after his motherless daughter. He also implored him not to let me grow up as an orphan. Captain Cutler took the necessary legal steps and adopted me as his daughter. Since I was ten years of age, Brett Cutler has been my father." With this she stopped her narrative and took several deep breaths. "He has been the most loving and at the same time demanding father that I could ever ask God to give me.

"He spoke of you often, Miss Starlet, and has continued to be passionately in love with you but knew the two of you could never live together without, as he said, a re-enactment of the War Between the States. He had decided some time ago to return to Atlanta when he turned sixty-five years of age but the events to which I referred earlier took over and made that impossible. Once these current troubles are resolved I believe he would wish to come home.

"He refused to open and read your letters knowing that if he did he would be overcome with his feelings for you and come running back to Fayette County only to make life miserable for both of you. So, he instructed me to write "Whereabouts Unknown" on them and mail them back to you. It was for this reason, my returning of your letters, that he never learned that he had a son." With this she turned to Reggie and said, "I am so very sorry for depriving you of your father, and he of his son, and I pray for yours and God's forgiveness. It was not my intent." She returned her gaze to Miss Starlet.

"I am aware Mrs. Cutler that you and your husband had a daughter, Eugenia Victoria. You called her Bonnie Blue and she died so tragically. I did not in any way replace her in your husband's affections. If anything, my presence in his life was a constant and deeply painful reminder of your loss. He often said that I caused him to think about what your daughter might have been like had she not been taken from you. Our ages and physical attributes were, he said, quite similar. Although in the past few years he had often said that I have become so headstrong that I now remind him of you, Mrs. Cutler. I have considered that the most admiring and loving compliment he could ever give me.

"I trust with all my heart that you will be able to bear the news I have imparted and to make the best of things for the future, for it would appear that under the law you are now my mother, and I am your daughter. And you, young sir," she said turning to Reggie, "are my brother and I cannot begin to express the joy I am feeling in my heart having met you, and you, Miss Starlet, although I cannot hide from the pain I have caused you."

For a minute no one spoke as they took in this information.

"Well now," said Miss Starlet, "did not some writer say that unhappy families were all unhappy in their own way? I must say that ours will be truly one of a kind. So enough of the tears, my dear. Do not place any blame on yourself. Fiddle-dee-dee. Children are never the cause of family misfortune. It was Brett and I who brought all of this on ourselves and on you." Here she paused.

"As God is my witness, we shall do a better job from here on."

She paused again, lost it seemed in memory and reflection. "I do believe that the last time I spoke those words I was holding a carrot in my one hand and my other fist up to the sky. It was not my finest hour. But if I think too long about those days long I will go mad. So, let us get on with things. Should not father be coming home for lunch by now?"

She said these words and suddenly her eyes widened, as did those of Reggie and Briany. Holmes and I had our backs to the balcony doors and, as I turned to see what they were looking at, I found myself looking down the barrel of a revolver. A similar gun was held to the head of Sherlock Holmes. The holder of the guns was a tall man, impeccably dressed, broad shouldered and with silver hair. He had silently entered over the balcony and there was no escaping from his revolver. "Do not move a muscle or I will blow both of your brains out," he firmly told us.

Chapter Four

Brett

"**R**eally Brett, darling," spoke Miss Starlet from across the room, "you must try to be more welcoming and gracious to our guests. We have so few of them come to call these days. Please, my dear husband, allow me to introduce your newest business associates, Dr. John Watson and Mr. Sherlock Holmes. I have engaged their services for the protection of our family, and I have invited them to stay for lunch. We were all just waiting for you."

The look on our assailant's face was beyond description.

There was the shock of disbelief, followed by a warm and loving broad smile and a slow shaking of his head. The words came slowly from him.

"Starlet . . . O'Halloran," he said slowly and deliberately, "Starlet . . . O'Halloran, this is indeed a surprise, and you are even more ravishingly beautiful than I remember." He laid down his revolvers and walked slowly across the room, reached out for his wife's hand, dropped to one knee and lightly touched his lips to her fingers.

Brett rose to his feet and looked spellbound upon Miss Starlet. There was an awkwardness to them, such as a young man and woman might experience on their first outing without a chaperon, neither of them prepared to make the first move towards touching each other's bodies.

This embarrassed silence continued until Briany spoke up. "For goodness sakes, Father. She's your wife. She didn't cross the Atlantic to be stared at. Embrace her!" Both Brett and Miss Starlet smiled and threw their arms around each other. They stood there for some time with their eyes closed, lost in the intense feelings they still shared for each other.

Without letting go of Miss Starlet, Brett opened his eyes and raised his head. He smiled warmly at his daughter and then glanced at the other young person in the room. His eyes widened when they landed on Reggie, and he dropped his embrace of his wife. The young man walked up to his father, stopped a few feet away, snapped the heels of his boots together, stood at attention, and gave a salute. "Good morning, father. Reginald Gerald Cutler reporting for duty sir. I believe we are serving in the same regiment."

Brett was again stunned into silence. He looked at Reggie, seeing what was undeniably a version of himself fifty years ago. He looked at Miss Starlet, who smiled at him with forced sweetness, pointed a finger first at Reggie and then at Brett, and said, "He's . . .yours."

For what seemed an eternity no one spoke. Brett stood dumbly looking back and forth from Miss Starlet to Reggie. He turned and walked vacantly towards the balcony. As he approached the edge, he held out both his hands and placed them on the railing, lowering his head until we could only see his broad back. After several minutes, he raised his head and looked up into the cloudy sky. He turned and walked back into the room.

With a courtesy that was unfeigned, he said, "In my three-score and ten years on this earth, I have consistently followed my heart and my passion for causes that I believed to be righteous. Behind that bravado, I confess that I believed in Brett Cutler, the only cause I really knew. What was it you used to call me Starlet – 'a conceited, black-hearted varmint, a low-down, cowardly, nasty thing.' Perhaps you were right. But against all odds the good Lord has blessed me with a beautiful wife and now a son. I have badly neglected my duties as a father. I assure you that that will not happen again, and I will do my best, the good Lord willing, to make up for years that have been lost and cannot be lived over again. I do hope that you will join me, son, in doing so."

Reggie looked his father in the eye and replied, "Yes sir, it will be an honor, but only if you acknowledge that you have also neglected your duties as a husband and assure your wife that you will strive to make up for those years as well."

Brett looked at the young man who had just so firmly rebuked his father. He lifted his head as if to speak to the heavens, "Good Lord. I cannot escape divine retribution. My son has my ears and his mother's tongue. My seventy-year-old heart may not be up to this."

"Your seventy-year-old heart is just fine, father." This time it was his daughter that spoke. "You can still ride and run with men half your age. I've seen you. It's well past time you stopped chasing lost causes and that we all just got on with the business of being a family."

He looked steadfastly at Briany and sighed, "*Et tu, Bruté?* You are entirely correct, my dear.'

He gazed slowly at the three members of his family. "Once again I find that I have to ask for your forgiveness in the hope that we could give our life together another chance. And I seek no greater grace for my old age than being surrounded by those I love and will learn to love."

The warm smile faded from his face. "Unfortunately for all of us, those days will still have to be postponed, but perhaps only for a week. Events are quickly conspiring not only against us but against all that is good and decent in western civilization. Gentlemen," he said, turning to Holmes and me, "I thank you for your offer of protection and your diligent work in finding me. I had thought I had covered my tracks more successfully. Concerning my present situation, I can only say that Fortune, it now appears, is no longer on the side of the strongest battalion but on the side of the most utterly ruthless. I am afraid that I am involved in dangerous affairs to which you all cannot be privy."

"I assume," said Sherlock Holmes, "that you are referring to the nefarious plans of the Black Hand to assassinate the crown prince in conjunction with the coronation ceremony this Saturday?"

Brett stared severely at Holmes "Yes," he said, "that is precisely what I am referring to. And please tell me, sir, how it is that you came to know of this. The only other three men who knew about it are now all dead, their personal connection to me having somehow become known."

"In normal times," explained Holmes, "a gentleman would never read another gentleman's mail. But these are not normal times, and I read through the file your now-deceased solicitor kept for you, as well as the contents of his unreliable safe, and I managed to cross-question his staff and had them tell me all they knew about his and your undertakings. They did so knowing that they could not possibly do him any harm and with the hope and prayer that it might help to bring his murderers to justice."

"Well then," said Brett, "it would appear that we find ourselves fighting for the same cause." Brett graciously motioned for the group of us to be seated.

Sherlock Holmes spoke first. "While I have been able to synthesize much of the data, there are many facets of your story that I do not yet know, so pray you, sir, please enlighten us as to how it is we find you here and engaged in this most dangerous pursuit."

Brett began to speak in the manner that Americans refer to as the Charleston cadence, that slow and pleasant drawl that is so often associated with a gentleman of the South.

"For fifty years I have been a soldier of fortune, fighting for the Cause and for people I believed to be truly good. My doing so has had costs beyond what I ever could have imagined. Even now I am looking at my so recently restored family knowing that I have endangered the lives of another five people."

"Six, Brett darling," Miss Starlet interjected, "we cannot forget that Momma is with us."

Brett's face broke into a wide grin. "Momma? You mean to tell me that she is alive and well and here with you in London?"

"Yes, my dear. She is waiting for us at the hotel. She would not hear of my traveling abroad in search of you without her. She is quite ready to grab you firmly by the ear and march you back to the South where you belong," Miss Starlet said.

"Well now, I'll be . . . I do expect that will happen very soon. Very soon indeed. And she still won't like me. But let me finish a short version of my long story.

"As I helped to find fighters and get them organized in some sort of army, I, from time to time, would meet small groups of men and one or two women who had joined our ranks but who seemed woefully ignorant of who or why we were fighting or what we were dreaming of. They were fixing only to bring wrack and ruin to whatever dynasty was in power, no matter what the cost in lives lost and property.

"They weren't revolutionaries. They were just anarchists. They had all read their Marx, and Kropotkin and Bakunin, and they just wanted to smash the system. Some of them were all talk, but others were good mercenaries and brave fighters. And there were a few of them who were utterly ruthless, no conscience at all. They would sneak up behind enemy lines at night and murder and mutilate old men and women, mothers and children. They did so without a scrap of remorse, claiming that "sparing the nit breeds the louse." Whenever the opportunity arose they would check out the leaders of the other side – their politicians, their priests, and their generals – and assassinate them in the cruelest ways they could think of.

"Over the years, I began to see these men reappear in the ranks of the fighters that I had recruited. One year they would be in Hungary, the next year in Venezuela, the year after that in India. Most said little or nothing to me and didn't do much talking at all. But I befriended a few of them and over time they spilled the beans and told me their secrets.

"I got to know about the inner workings of an organization they called Black Hand." Here he paused and looked at Holmes.

"You appear to have become familiar with them, Mr. Holmes. In Holland and the Cape, they are *zwarte hand*, in Spain *mano neare,* in the Balkans they call themselves *oopa pika,* and in France *main noire*. They all know each other, and over time, I came to know many of their names and the forty or more cells of them that are scattered around the world. I made some records, and eventually I put together a list of most of their active members."

"Surely, "I asked, "you took that list to the Home Office or Whitehall and had them round these men up, did you not?"

"Ah, Doctor Watson, I regret to inform you that such a move does not come easily when you are *persona non gratia* to many of Her Majesty's civil servants. You see, I made a point of fighting for whichever side I believed in, not just the one with the friendliest flag. More than once that left me fighting against your Empire, not defending it. I went to the Cape thinking of helping the British Army overcome the guerilla tactics of the Boers. What I found was that Kitchener was violating all types of international law and basic human decency by rounding up the Boers' women and children, forcing them into concentration camps, and starving them to death. So, I changed sides and began to run the British naval blockades and provide arms to the Boers. You can guess that this did not endear me to either your politicians or your generals. So, I find myself in the rather unenviable position of now seeking to protect an Empire against the forces of anarchy even though that Empire dislikes me and I it."

"If," asked Holmes, "you bear no affection for the British Empire why, sir, are you risking your life to protect it?"

"Your Empire, Mr. Holmes, ain't worth a pitcher of warm piss," said Brett forcefully, "but the stability it brings to the world is a necessary evil. If it were to crumble and start fighting with the decaying French, Austro-Hungarian, Russian or Ottoman Empires, all of Europe and the colonies around the world would become one massive bloodbath, the likes of which history has never known, bigger than even the tragic losses of our war for the independence of the Confederate States.

"All it would take would be the assassination of some king or queen of one country that could be blamed on another, and your whole house of cards would come tumbling down. The Black Hand tried to kill the Prince a couple of years back in Belgium. Before that, they made attempts on the Czar. Thank heaven these failed.

"Now they have plans to kill the Prince of Wales either just before or after he is crowned this Saturday and make it look as if it were ordered by that silly young fool, Wilhelm, in Germany. If they succeed, it will unleash tragedy beyond belief. Scotland Yard and Whitehall will not listen to me. The only chance I have is to stop these evil bastards myself."

"I do understand, however," said Holmes, "that you have at least one significant person who has listened to you, whose coat of arms appeared often in your private correspondence."

"Quite right, Mr. Holmes. My dear old friend, Bertie, better known as the Prince of Wales and soon to be King, has been my confidant and drinking partner since I hauled him out of a whorehouse, sobered him up and got him back to Sandringham a couple of decades ago. But he is proud and pig-headed and refuses to cancel his ride to the coronation in an open carriage, where his subjects can cheer on their sovereign. He believes that he will be safe merely because he will be surrounded by thousands of ordinary blokes who would never let any harm come to him. He knows about the Black Hand but has no appreciation for their cunning and cold-blooded ruthlessness."

"Perhaps we can offer some reassurance," said Holmes. "While you may be on the outs with our constabulary I am not entirely. Even if I am far from their favorite consulting detective they have come to respect my work. If I were to suggest to them that not only might someone attempt to assassinate the King right under their noses but that their prized reputations would be trampled in the dust if even a failed attempt were to occur, they would start scampering about like mice very quickly. It might also be useful for you to know that my excellent regiment of spies has discovered the places where the five members of your cell of anarchists are staying. We may be able to round them up before they get to the spectacle on Saturday."

Brett looked intently at Holmes and gave a slow nod of appreciation. "Both of those actions would be very helpful, sir. If I could be assured that you could bring those to pass, I might even be able to relax for an hour or two and enjoy some time with my family."

"A well-deserved opportunity, I agree," said Holmes. "But I must caution you all to assume some sort of disguise before re-entering the Dorchester. Your enemies will have a lookout watching for you."

"Thank you, Sherlock," said Miss Starlet. "I have no doubt you will take whatever steps are needed for our safety and the preservation of your Empire. We will just hide ourselves at the Dorchester and, Lord willing, my family will book passage next week to return to a life together in America. Perhaps I am assuming too much," she added looking at Briany. "I do hope that my recently acquired daughter will be coming with us."

The young woman smiled at her. "I grew up in the warm, lush climate of Calcutta and the Hill Country. I would welcome the opportunity to live with my mother, father, and brother in the lovely warmth of Georgia. I have not seen the sun in the past two weeks. Have you?"

They chuckled, and Brett added, "Sweetheart, don't speak too soon; you have yet to meet Momma."

With that Miss Starlet and Reggie laughed, and the four of them all looked warmly at each other.

"Come, Watson," said Holmes, rising. "We have some business to do with Lestrade, and we are not needed at a family reunion."

With that, we rose and said our good-byes. Before he could exit the room, Miss Starlet threw her arms around Holmes's body, held him tightly for several moments and planted a kiss on his cheek, leaving a telltale mark of lipstick. I had never seen Holmes looking so utterly discomfited and could not wait to recount the incident to Mrs. Hudson.

Chapter Five

King's Lynn

We hailed a cab outside Claridge's, and Holmes gave the driver instructions for the route he wished to take to the Embankment and the offices of Scotland Yard. We backtracked several blocks so that we could ride down the length of The Mall from Buckingham Palace to Westminster Abbey, the route of the coronation procession on Saturday, and where any would-be assassin could be lurking amidst the throngs of Londoners, who, being English, would be sure to turn out regardless of whatever miserable weather might be visited upon them.

Holmes made notes as we went, jotting down the locations in which a sniper could hide himself, or those spots along the route where the curb was precariously close to the narrow roadway and where an attacker could come within a few feet of the passing open carriage. He seemed satisfied with his observations.

"Inspector Lestrade and his men may be lacking in imagination, Watson, but they are quite experienced in the management of crowds. He undoubtedly could have men in plain clothes scattered throughout. Even if we are not able to round up the evil bastards, as our Mr. Cutler calls them, there will be adequate protection from the Palace to the Abbey. Following the service, the King will be in a closed carriage and taken quickly to Windsor, so there is not much worry there."

The cab pulled into the new headquarters of Scotland Yard. Holmes and I entered and sought out our earnest if not always brilliant colleague, Inspector Lestrade.

He looked annoyed at us as we barged into his cluttered office. Its furnishings were Spartan, and one wall held floor-to-ceiling open shelves, all lined with filing folders of various degrees of bulging, some of which did not appear to have been touch by human hands in a decade. We sat ourselves down and began the meeting without seeking his consent. As he was wont to do, his first reaction was to dismiss Holmes's warning as yet another of his far-fetched imaginings.

"Really, Mr. Holmes," he protested, "you cannot expect me to lay on hundreds more constables, who were themselves looking forward to taking their children to view the parade, just because Mr. Sherlock Holmes has come up with yet another plot wherein an evil web of a few score people with revolvers are about to topple five empires and usher in Armageddon."

Holmes retained his patience, developed by many such similar encounters with Lestrade, and with firm evidence and undeniable logic laid out his case. As he did, I watched the smirk retreat from Lestrade's rat-like face and be replaced with a look of wide-eyed fear. His knuckles gripped the arms of his chair tightly. By the time Holmes was finished, Lestrade was on his feet and shouting orders out of his door for his lackeys and his lackeys' lackeys to hustle into his office.

"As you say that all of these men are armed and skilled in the use of weapons, Holmes, I will organize a raid upon the places you say they are boarding in the hours just before dawn. That is when we are most likely to find criminals sound asleep and the fewest bystanders in danger should we have to engage in an exchange of gunfire. However, I expect that by six o'clock in the morning, we shall have them all rounded up and securely locked up in the Old Bailey, waiting to appear before a judge."

Holmes nodded his consent and we departed. "I really see nothing else we can do, my dear Watson. Our client and her family will have to make accommodations with their multiple ferocious personalities if they are to get along. We brought them together and that was our task. Scotland Yard should be able to protect the King. As is standard with these cases no one shall hear about our efforts, and Lestrade will take all the credit for imprisoning the garrotters, but we shall know what we have done. And so I suggest that we visit Marcini's in Knightsbridge and reward ourselves with a little dinner. What say you, Watson?"

I heartily agreed. We enjoyed a long mealtime and took in a concert at the Royal Albert Hall, where a lovely contralto, one of Holmes's many former acquaintances, delivered an excellent Tosca, thrilling the audience before hurling herself from the parapet. Even Holmes was moved to his feet in sustained applause.

We retired to Baker Street and fell into bed with that feeling of tired satisfaction that comes from knowing that you have done your job well.

And all was well.

At least it was until five o'clock in the morning when there was an unholy pounding on the door of 221B Baker Street. "Mr. Holmes! Mr. Holmes!" we heard a boy's voice shouting. "Mr. Holmes! You must come!" The pounding was loud and desperate. I wrapped myself in my dressing gown and entered our parlor. Holmes appeared in his gown close behind me. We began down the stairs, only to see that the redoubtable Mrs. Hudson was already at the door and holding the young captain of the Irregulars by the back of his jacket to restrain him from bounding up the stairs.

"Let the lad up," said Holmes, whereupon he was released and leapt up the stairs, taking two or three at a time. We met him in the parlor.

He was gasping to catch his breath. He had no doubt run some distance at a very fast pace and was soaked to the skin from the never-ending rain, his pale skin all flushed from the exertion.

"Those men, those men you told us to watch Mr. Holmes. Those four blokes and the small boy. You told us never to let them out our sight, right, well we done that. But an hour ago they all got up an out their places. They was in four different inns, they were, and they walked through the night and all met up at Paddington, and they got themselves tickets and they left. My boys followed them all the way, and then they run back to me and wake me up, and then I come running to you, Mr. Holmes."

Holmes looked at the boy with grave concern, "Did your boys learn what train they were taking? What was the destination? Did anyone hear what tickets they asked for?"

"One of my boys, sir, Jimmy, the wee one that's not afraid of no one, he follows them right to the ticket office pretending to be a beggar, and he hears them asking for tickets to Norwich. All five of them. The four men and the boy with them. They got on the early train to Norwich. Jimmy and the rest, they waits until they see them board, and then they come running for me and then I come running for you, Mr. Holmes, sir."

"You and your boys have done well, Wiggins," said Holmes, clasping his hand on the lad's shoulder. "Better than you may ever know. Now I have another urgent task for you, and you must not fail. You are to run from here to the Dorchester Hotel. You know it, do you not? On Park Lane."

"Sure and I know it, sir. But they would never let me anywhere close to coming in. The maids would be chasing me with brooms all the way to Hyde Park Corner if I was to ever set foot in it."

"Master Wiggins, I do not care a fig how many maids there are with brooms, or what you have to do to get past them, and it would be best if you never tell me how you did it, but you must get a message to the guests in suite 615. Can you do that, Gordon Wiggins?"

A grin that, in other circumstances, I would only describe as mischievous bordering on wicked, spread over the lad's face. He nodded. "I can do that for sure, sir. Long as you don't never ask how I done it."

"Excellent. Tell the guests in that suite exactly what you have told me, and demand that both Mr. Cutler senior and his son be ready to be picked up at the front door in an hour. Tell them to make a quick run over to Mr. Cutler senior's residence and get his weapons. Do you have all that? Good. Now run like you had three bobbies on your tail."

Descending seventeen stairs in three steps is a skill that only the young can risk. Young Wiggins was off and out the door and on his way. I smiled at him, but Holmes was fearfully distraught.

"Dear God, Watson. How could I have not foreseen this? These villains are much too clever to try to shoot the King with thousands of onlookers and police throughout the crowd." He paused. "Either that or Lestrade has a spy in his troops. No matter. I should have known that this would happen."

"What is going to happen, Holmes? What!?" I came near to shouting back to him.

"Can't you see, Watson? They are not going to assassinate the King on the final leg of the coronation procession. They are going for the first leg. In Norfolk. As he leaves Sandringham. We have to get ourselves there to stop them. How could I not have seen this coming?"

Sandringham, on the grand estate in Norfolk, was one of the homes of the Royal Family. The Prince of Wales, soon to be the King, had lived there for the past four decades, from the time of his marriage to Alexandra when he was twenty-one until the present. He had held legendary parties, hunting outings, banquets and drinking bouts that lasted days and were rumored to have been attended by countless women whose morals were a matter of convenience. The Crown Prince, once called by his Christian names of Albert Edward and known by all as Bertie, was spending his last few days there before his coronation and his move to Buckingham Palace. He did not care for Buck Place for the simple reason that his mother did not care for him, and never forgave him for bringing about the untimely early death of his father, the Prince Consort. The Prince was said to have risen unwisely from his sick bed and hurried himself off to some seaside resort where young Bertie was cavorting openly with a married woman and threatening to bring shame upon the entire House of Hanover. The Consort took seriously ill after the stressful journey and passed away soon after. The Queen blamed Bertie for the next thirty years.

"Watson, we must move quickly," said Holmes as he studied the railway schedule. "There is not another train from London to Norwich until ten o'clock. That will be too late."

"Too late for what Holmes. What are they going to do?"

"Here. Look here!" he said handing me *The Times*. 'Read what is going on there today! Within a few hours!"

On the front page was a short piece that read:

Affectionate Send-off from Norfolk to be the First Stop of the Coronation Celebration

Citizens of King's Lynn in Norfolk all know that the coronation procession of King Edward VII will not begin at Buckingham Palace but rather at the train station in their village. For it is from there that the new King will begin the journey that will end with a crown being placed on his head in Westminster Abbey. For forty years the Prince of Wales was a much-loved favorite of this corner of the land. While his great gatherings and parties may have raised eyebrows at the Court of St. James, the townspeople knew that they brought well-heeled folks from around the world who needed food and lodging, carriage and horse rentals, and demands for all sorts of trades and medical attention. The Prince, Bertie to all and sundry, will be sorely missed.

They will not let him depart, however, without a "Royal Send-off" and have organized their own short coronation parade through the village in an open carriage, drawn by six of the Prince's glorious horses. Not only the merchants but also the many railway workers who serviced his private car for so many years, and the dock hands who made sure that his yacht was securely fastened and kept gleaming at its berth on the canal, will be there to give rousing best wishes to their loved and generous patron.

The carriage parade is scheduled to begin at noon at the north end of the village and end at the station twenty-five minutes after. The Prince and soon-to-be-King will then have a few moments in his private car before it pulls out on its journey to London at precisely 12:45 pm.

"That is where they are going to strike," said Holmes. "The chubby old chap will be an easy target for any assassin. The roads are narrow and there cannot be more than a few hundred people to line the route. The train will not get us there before the Black Hand. We shall have to find the fastest coach-and-four available and get there in time to stop them."

"Cannot we just send a telegram to the local police?" I asked.

"There is only one constable in a village that size. Reinforcements from London will need as much time as we will going by train. Mrs. Hudson! Mrs. Hudson!" Holmes had opened the door and shouted for our long-suffering landlady. She appeared in a moment still in her dressing gown but wide awake as a result of her effort restraining the nimble Wiggins.

"My dear Mrs. Hudson," began Holmes.

"Enough of the pleasantries, Mr. Holmes, I can see by the look on your face that something desperate is taking place. What do you need this time?"

"A coach-and-four. The fastest you can find. Immediately. And thank you."

"Very well," she said. She pulled her mackintosh on over her nightgown and off she went into the rain and early-morning gloom. I was somewhat concerned that she would catch cold on so foul a morning, but I had also learned that there were few things that so warmed her blood as being able to play an essential if small role in the adventures of her famous tenant.

Holmes pulled an atlas off the shelf and began to study the maps of Norfolk.

"Our villains are taking the train to Norwich and then will have to change and take the Great Eastern over to King's Lynn," he said. "We can ride hard, change horses at Newmarket, and then go due north, bypassing Norwich. That should give us a chance to gain at least an hour on them, maybe two. We shall have to try to pick up their trail from the King's Lynn station, which is the station that serves Sandringham. The locals should be willing to give us whatever information we need. Do you have your service revolver, Watson?"

"It is already in my pocket, and I have an ammunition pouch on my belt."

"Excellent. I shall do the same, and let us hope that our dear Mrs. Hudson is as efficient as she usually is."

Ten minutes later we heard the loud clatter of a large coach and the sounds of a team of horses, and then a shrill whistle. "They hardly have to whistle for us," objected an annoyed Holmes. "We are not deaf. Surely Mrs. Hudson could have stopped that unnecessary nonsense."

We descended the stairs. Mrs. Hudson held the door open for us, and as I passed her she opened her fist just enough for me to see a small whistle. She gave me a wink, and I daresay I felt her hand giving a firm pat to my backside as I moved through the door.

"Come, Watson, the game has become much more dangerous, and our adversaries are far more devious than I gave them credit for. Haste, driver! To the Dorchester and do not spare the horses."

It was only a few blocks from Baker Street to Park Lane and with the streets still deserted in the early-morning hours, we were there in a few minutes. Brett Cutler and his son, standing proudly beside his father, were waiting at the front door, with a wooden case of a foot square and five feet long on the pavement beside them. Together they hoisted it up to the top of the coach and with the help of the driver tied it down. Father and son may have not been present in each other's lives for the past seventeen years but there was a bond of blood between them and they moved like a well-trained team. They had already become comrades-in-arms and seemed beyond eager to enter battle shoulder-to-shoulder.

I felt exhilarated; the prospect of adventure and thrill of battle coursed through my veins, as only a man feels when he marches with his trusted fellow soldiers into the cannon's roar.

My lovely feeling vanished in an instant when to my shock and dismay Miss Starlet and Miss O'Brien emerged from the hotel lobby and climbed into the coach with me. I gasped and shouted to Brett, "You cannot possibly be allowing these women to come on this journey. We are up against highly trained and ruthless foes. This will be no place for a woman!"

Brett looked at me and gave me a warm smile, displaying his gleaming white teeth. "Yes, sir. They are coming along. Best soldiers I ever trained. I've always admired their spirits, especially when they're cornered. I wouldn't want to be in their sights at two hundred yards, and I for sure, would not want to be in the hand-to-hand combat zone with them, and neither would you if you value your life or your manhood."

I looked at Sherlock Holmes, desperate for some moral support. He just shrugged and said, "If the captain says so, then we can use the additional force. Let us be off."

Mrs. Hudson had found us an excellent coach. There was adequate room in the carriage, and it was well sprung. We moved as quickly as we could through the streets of London until we reach the Victoria Embankment. The road was clear along the Thames, and so we galloped all the way to Whitechapel, turned north and after working our way through the streets of the east end, we entered the open countryside where the driver gave the horses free rein.

The farms and the scattered houses flashed past us as we looked out the windows. We were constantly being jostled and from time to time would hit a bump in the road, and we would all take a jump into the air before landing back on our seats. Miss Starlet was seated beside her husband with her arm through his and I could hear snatches of a little ditty she was singing to herself:

> *She wept with delight at his smile*
> *And trembled with fear at his frown*

She seemed serenely happy.

On the opposite bench, Briany and Reggie were chattering away like long-lost brother and sister, all on fire to catch up on the years they had missed.

Holmes kept jotting notes and staring at maps. I had seen him this way before many times. His inscrutable mind was making sure that there was not one detail that would be missed. He had already been fooled once by this diabolical crew. He was resolute that it would not happen again.

By eight o'clock we were at Newmarket, and we stopped and changed horses. To my joy, the rain had finally ended, and the sun was shining. Holmes had no appreciation of nature at all, but the rest of us breathed in the beauty. The mists were rising off the fields, and the warmth of the sun on my face led me to think that perhaps the climate of our green and pleasant land was not entirely intolerable. And what a perfect day for the good people of King's Lynn to bid farewell to their favorite member of the Royal Family, or it would be if we could keep the man from being shot.

From Newmarket, we took the secondary road towards the north. The road was not as good and the ride much more rugged, but still we flew along. The conversations had died down. We knew we were approaching some highly treacherous waters. Within the next few hours either we would be dead along with the King, or some determined evildoers would be thwarted and either killed or in jail. There was no more laughter.

The coach pulled into the railway station at King's Lynn at just past ten o'clock. We had a mere two hours to find the killers and stop them.

Holmes immediately went to the station office, and we stood on the platform waiting for him. A few minutes later he returned to us. "Watson, I do apologize for the times I have accused you of exaggerating my exploits in your stories. Because of you, my dear friend, even the station master in King's Lynn has been reading them and was prepared to help in any way he could if it meant being part of a murderous mystery. He knows the men we are looking for. They have been staying in the village off and on for the past three months but not near the central square. They have rented a cottage a mile out that looks over the canal. There is no road to it, only a trail. So, we cannot take the coach. There is a liveryman in the village who is said to be a churlish piece of work but has excellent horses that he has rented for years to guests of the Prince and is quite happy to rent to anyone now that the Prince's sycophants have departed. We will have to unload our gun case and carry the weapons we need with us."

Brett and Reggie moved immediately and lifted down the heavy case. It had a strong metal handle on both ends and they each clasped one, lifted the case and began walking into the village. Upon arrival at the livery stable, Holmes approached a rather surly looking chap and enquired about horses to rent. His price was high, but the animals were very impressive and obviously well-cared for.

"It'll take me an hour to saddle up six of them. You can come back when I'm ready," he said.

I was ready to speak reasonably to the man, but before I could, young Reggie walked up to him and with a smile laid a hand on the much smaller man's shoulder and said, "Well now, sir, we just don't happen to have an hour, so I tell you what's going to happen. You're just going to stand aside, and we're going to get those saddles on those horses ourselves. I'm sure that's going to be real okay with you."

The gnarly little fellow looked up at the large young man but had no time to speak before Reggie was striding towards the tack room and saying to the rest of us, "We can all grab us a bridle, blanket, and saddle, it's all here. Let's get going." Brett stood beaming at him, and Miss Starlet stole a moment to slide her arm through Brett's and look proudly at her son.

Each of us marched into the tack room, took what we needed, chose ourselves a horse, and saddled up. I was surprised to see the two ladies firmly clasp the back of their horse's mouth, force it open and slide the bit into place. In England, a lady will normally wait for a groom to do that job for her, but then these were not normal ladies. They both chose men's saddles, placed their blankets on the horse's backs and swung the saddles up and into place. As Miss Starlet reached under her horse to grab the cinch belt her spirited beast gave her a firm bump with its haunches, causing her to land on her backside on the floor of the stable.

"Hey there, mother, you got yourself one who thinks she's in charge," said Reggie with a laugh. Miss Starlet got up and said, "We'll see about that." She took a step back and gave a swift, firm kick to the mare's midsection. The horse gave a whinny of pain. She then walked to the front of the horse, pulled on its bridle and looked the beast directly in the eye. "Do you want that again? Do you? Didn't think so." She cinched up the strap and pulled it tight.

Reggie, Brett, and Sherlock were already up on their mounts. "Sweetheart," Brett said to Briany, "would you mind handing us up the guns and rifles?" Briany opened the gun case and gave each of them a set of holstered pistols and a gleaming new Mauser 98 rifle. They fastened the holsters around their waists and slung the rifles over their shoulders. They looked like men who were not to be trifled with.

"We three shall go first to the small tavern that is closest to the rented cottage," said Holmes. "I will try to find out from the publican if our adversaries are in the cottage. We shall meet you there." Then they rode off. It was now already 10:30 am.

Briany, Miss Starlet, and I were about to lead our mounts out of the stable and into the courtyard when the surly livery man slouched towards the doorway, blocking our exit. "I must have made a mistake in the price I said you would have to pay. I will need one more sovereign from each of you, or I will not permit you to leave my property with my horses."

"Why, you miserable cheat and coward," I shouted at him. "We paid you a fair price and you have so little courage that you waited until those three men had departed before trying to swindle us. You will not have one penny more. Now move your miserable self and let us be on our way."

"You may call me what you wish, but you will not leave my premises with my horses until you pay me. I assure you that the law is on my side," he snarled back at me.

"Please, Doctor Watson." Miss Starlet spoke in what I detected as feigned sweetness. "What is one more sovereign to us? Besides, we are in a hurry. Sir, come, take your money and let us be on our way."

"Glad you sees things my way," the miserable cheat said as he walked toward Miss Starlet. She reached inside her jacket and withdrew her purse, and opened it. By this time the surly knave was just a few feet away from her. With a very fast move, Miss Starlet swung her leg forward and planted a hard kick in the man's groin. His mouth opened, and he let forth a roar of pain. His two hands immediately grasped his nether region, and he collapsed on the stable floor, writhing in pain. Instead of withdrawing sovereigns from her purse, Miss Starlet produced a small stiletto dagger and placed the end of it a short distance inside the blackguard's left nostril. The terror in his eyes was pitiable.

"We paid you a fair price, and I have no patience with cheats and liars," said Miss Starlet. "We will return within a few hours with your horses, and we thank you for your service."

As I walked past the wretch, I swear I heard him mutter something about "Bloody Americans. I should have known."

Chapter Six

The Black Hand

The two women mounted their mares, straddling them like a man and so unlike a proper English woman. We cantered through the village, retraced our path to the station, crossed the tracks, and began to gallop in the direction of the tavern and the cottage. About three hundred yards past the rail line, we crossed a swollen river that was moving with great force from all the rain. The bridge seemed firm, and I assumed that our three men had already crossed, so over we went and resumed our gallop.

As an officer in the medical corps in Afghanistan, I had been issued a horse and I was not unaware of how to ride. That was over thirty years ago, and I had forgotten what a beating your knees and legs take as you strive to keep your body from bouncing on a saddle. I cursed the Jezail bullet that had damaged my leg and forced me to grit my teeth against the pain, but I determined that there was no way under heaven that I would be outridden by two women.

To my shock and wounded pride was added the further humiliation that these two women could ride like cavalry officers. They leaned forward, gripped the flanks of their mounts with their knees, took all the weight and movement into their legs and appeared to be of one substance with their excellent mares. Even though the legs of the beast were flying, hooves thundering, and powerful bodies surging with each leap forward, the heads of these women hardly moved an inch out of the horizontal plane. Good Lord, was there anything these two could not do?

We approached the tavern, dismounted and entered. Our three men were already sitting at a table in the corner along with a portly man in an apron that I judged to be the barkeep. By their posture, I could see that both Brett and Reggie were extremely impatient and anxious, but they were unfamiliar with the deliberate methods of my friend, the marvelous detective, Sherlock Holmes. He knew that friendly chat and a generous tip were an infinitely better way to encourage people to divulge all sorts of information than threats and bombast, and it was proving to have its effect on the proprietor of the establishment. We three sat down at the table next to them, and Holmes introduced us with a comment on the excellent quality of the dark ale that had been served.

"Well, sir," said the barkeep, "as I was saying, sir, we saw those fellows off and on over the past three months, if you know what I mean. Right odd chaps they were. Foreigners they were. But not all from the same country, which we knew from listening to them, if you know what I mean. One, the youngest man, hardly more than a college-boy, was a sort of Frenchie. The father and his little fellow sounded like Russians but not quite, if you know what I mean. At first, we thought the little boy was only maybe a five-year-old, but the way he talked and acted, we thought he was maybe more like eight but just on the small side, if you know what I mean. One of the others, the one with the beard, he was a German for sure and the last one, well now I just don't know. Somewhere else in Europe, meaning that he weren't no Chinaman or such, but none of us here could place his accent. They sat themselves in that table over there in the corner and kept to themselves, not socializing at all with the others in the village. When they was talking, they did so real quiet like, if you know what I mean, so that no one could hear what they talked about. But my Bessie she says that when she served them their food and such, she heard them talking, and they was talking English and that seemed like the only language that all had in common like. The little fellow, his father kept calling him back to the table because he was wanting to wander around an I can't blame him, if you know what I mean. So, his father keeps calling him Gavrilo or something close to that. The young man, the Frenchie, they called him Jean-Baptiste. The one who sounded Russian but wasn't, they call him Ivan, but we didn't catch any other names.

"We ask them, being friendly an all, what they was doing in the village, and they say they is studying our farming an especially our fertilizers. Well, maybe that be true because they had some shipments of fertilizers shipped here, and they come an picked them up and took them up to the cottage, but they never looked like the farming type, if you know what I mean. Most of my customers here, they're farmers, and they got hands like meat hooks, and big arms and red faces, and strong shoulders from working all their lives, but these blokes they look more like the types that come around here from the government, or up from Cambridge. They were here up to a couple of weeks ago but then they left and we haven't seen hide nor hair of them since, but Freddie, he's the owner of the cottage, he says that they paid their rent all in advance, and their money's good enough for him, so he don't ask any questions and just lets sleeping dogs lie, if you know what I mean."

"My good man," said Holmes, "I think we understand exactly what you mean and we thank you for being so generous with the information on cottages to rent in the neighborhood. We shall just have to look for another one if that one is spoken for. And we thank you for your excellent ale and look forward to our next enjoyable visit to your fine tavern. And now we must take our leave and be on our way."

"Always happy to serve some gentlemen and ladies especially those who is friendly like as you are. Most welcome back here anytime."

We rose and departed and mounted our horses. "If the cottage is vacant," I said, "why are we going there? Should we not be trying to get to Bertie as quickly as we can?"

"Quite smart thinking, Watson," said Holmes, "except that the barkeep's reference to the fertilizer concerns me. There are many better ways to disguise their activities than pretending to be concerned with fertilizers and farming and certainly no need to have a shipment of it delivered, if that is what it was. So, we shall stop there for a quick inspection before trying to intercept the King's entourage on the way from Sandringham to the village. It has just gone eleven o'clock. We have sufficient time to stop them from shooting at him."

The cottage was a small private building with white walls and a thatched roof, a two-storied place with an old-fashioned porch and honeysuckle about it, well away from any other houses but pleasant and pretty enough. How galling that such a scenic location could be used to devise such demonic plans. The door was locked, but Holmes quickly took care of that hindrance.

As soon as we entered, I detected a strong smell, similar to the smell of a hospital ward after it had been cleaned and disinfected. Holmes smelt it too. He immediately, almost in a panic, began rifling through the detritus that was strewn through the cottage. Then he rushed outside, and we heard him out the back of the building. He rushed back inside and shouted to us, "Come, we have not a second to spare. They are not going to shoot at the King. They have been making bombs."

Once he said that, it was clear to me as well. What I had smelled was ammonia, the base for ammonium nitrate. Some called it the poor man's dynamite. In granular form, it is quite stable, but when crushed to powder and combined with fuel oil it becomes highly explosive. It was used in the coal mines in Wales where the mining firms were frugal and refused the additional expense of trinitrotoluene, the standard explosive of our wealthier English mines and our military sappers.

The scraps of paper had many sheets that had been waxed. They were using them to wrap the explosive and keep it from getting damp.

"Behind the building, Holmes, what was there? Were there barrels that were used for delivery of chemicals?"

"There was at least a dozen of them; enough for a score of powerful bombs. Any one of them could blow the Prince's landau to kingdom come. But let us divide and conquer. Watson, you stay here and inspect the cottage. Gather as much evidence as you can find that can be used when we drag these villains into court. Brett, Reggie and I will ride on and divert the King's procession. Fertilizer bombs are not like grenades that can be hurled. They are large and cumbersome and must be planted in place. If I can have the drivers change their route to the station, we will foil these murderers."

The three of them rode off to the north, along the route to Sandringham. Miss Starlet and Miss Briany did not at all like being left out of the action, and I had to remind them that more than half the time of a good detective or even a constable was always consumed with the paperwork. You could catch all the dastardly villains you wished, but without evidence enough to convince a judge or jury, they would never end up in a prison cell or swinging from the gallows. I said this, of course, to buoy up their spirits, but inwardly I had to admit to myself that I too was annoyed with being left behind to do the work of the clerks. My annoyance was very short-lived.

"Do not move, or we will kill you," said a voice from the doorway of the room. I turned quickly and saw two men, one of medium height with a swarthy beard, the other a tall youth with mere wisps of hair splotching across his pale face. Both were armed and pointing revolvers at us.

"You fools. You should not have interfered. You are too late to do anything to save your King or your monstrous Empire. Now you will die along with your King and your husband, Mrs. Cutler."

The sallow older man was speaking. He had a thick German accent. I had my service revolver in my pocket, but I could not reach for it quickly enough to do any good, and doing so would imperil the lives of Briany and Miss Starlet. Yet if I did nothing, I knew that these men had already killed and would not hesitate to do it, or worse, again. I gathered my wits and spoke back to them.

"Your plans are already foiled. Your bombs will go off on empty streets. You would be better to surrender and throw yourselves on the mercy of the courts, and since no one has died, you may be let off with just a few years in prison. Otherwise, you will face the gallows. Use your common sense."

Both of them laughed. "Non, m'sieur," said the younger one, "I already have been along that path. I am free only because I was too young to be convicted for trying to kill your fat prince. Now I am older and I would be hung no matter what happens. So non, m'sieur Doctor Watson, we will leave no witnesses who know too much, and this time with the help of my comrades, I will succeed."

I looked at him closely and remembered the face from the papers of three years ago. Jean-Baptiste Sapido was only fifteen years old when he tried to kill the Prince of Wales as he was traveling through Belgium. He missed, was immediately apprehended, and put in jail. Because he was underage, the Belgian courts let him walk free. He had returned, more ruthless, more fanatical than before, and had already helped to murder three men. My colleagues might be able to save the King, but if I did not do something quickly this vile young man and his partner would soon be murdering me and these two women.

"You think we are so stupid that we put our bombs on roads," said the older one with a sneer in his voice. "No, you fools. Roads can be so easily changed. Your railways cannot. In less than one hour the King of your greedy empire will have passed down the roadway to the cheers of your docile English peasants. He will then enter his lavish private railway car, and his adoring subjects will watch as his body is blown into a thousand prices and spread across your green and pleasant countryside."

"Mrs. Cutler, your husband and his friends have caused us a lot of problems. But we cannot thank you enough for coming to England and identifying his associates for us. You made our task much easier. Now we shall have to teach a lesson to people like your husband and your idiot detective. The King will die but so will you. If we cannot kill your husband and son they will find your bodies violated and mutilated, and no one will ever again doubt the determination of the Black Hand.

"Dr. Watson, sit in that chair." He motioned me towards a chair close to the table at the edge of the room. "Jean-Baptiste, give me your gun. I will keep two guns pointed at the breasts of these two women while you fasten Dr. Watson to the chair." Then the young man walked over to me, grabbed me by my shirt and pushed me forcefully into the chair. He picked up what I assumed was electrical wire that was used in making the caps for the bombs, forced my hands behind my back, lashed them painfully together and wound several strands of the wire around my torso. I was not able to move. Desperate despair had swept over me. Holmes would have ridiculed my prayer for divine intervention, but I could see no other possibility for our lives and that of the King. A dark cloud was about to sweep across the civilized world. What I heard next added to the depths of my grief.

The young man then turned to the older one and said, "M'sieur, you are the senior man; which one do you wish? You may, of course, ravish the pretty blonde if you prefer. I will take the older one."

The bearded killer gave a vile laugh, "No, J-B, this older one is a rare beauty who has had many years to learn how to look after a man when she is on her knees and has a gun pointed at her head."

He looked at Miss Starlet and advanced towards her. Sure enough, once he was within the hand-to-hand combat zone, the powerful leg and finely appointed boot rose rapidly and planted itself between his legs with an excruciating smack. Unlike the surly livery man, the bearded one did not shout; he did not grasp at his groin or fall to the ground. He did not lower his gun. He merely staggered back, his body shaking with pain, and stood still until the pain subsided. He had obviously endured pain in the past and had disciplined himself to absorb it and keep fighting.

"Mrs. Cutler, I admire your spirit. You are a fighter. So am I. As a professional courtesy I will kill you with my gun and not my knife. But while you are alive I will violate your body."

"Oh my," said Miss Starlet, "but you European men do disappoint me. All we hear in America is that you are supposed to be the masters of love. You are the ones that know that the greatest satisfaction a man can have is when the woman is driven to distraction by his manhood. Please, sir, slow down. If this is to be my last time, at least protect the reputation of your nation's men and make it an unforgettable one."

As she was speaking, she was slowly lifting her skirt and exposing her leg. Briany kept watching Miss Starlet out of the corner of her eyes and copied her every move. "You want this, don't you?" she was saying seductively to the younger killer. "You haven't seen a woman's leg before, have you?" Her skirts were likewise lifting and exposing a very shapely thigh.

I was thoroughly confused. These two women stood a very good chance of being murdered and could be standing before Almighty God in a few minutes. Instead of committing the souls to their Maker, they were behaving as if they were two-penny whores in the most disreputable of East-end brothels.

"You're having trouble restraining yourself, aren't you?" Miss Starlet was saying to the older one. "I can tell you are. You want to take me and ravish me, don't you?" A few feet away Briany had started to caress her thigh and was making such conjugal sounds as should only ever be heard by a woman's husband during the throes of their honeymoon. Then Miss Starlet began making similar sounds as she moved her hand under her skirt.

Both men dropped their eyes from the faces of the women and began to fumble with the fronts of their trousers. In that short instant, first Miss Starlet and, a second later, Briany, removed their hands from their under their skirts, raised them quickly towards the faces of their would-be violators.

I heard two pistol shots.

Both men staggered back, dropped to their knees and toppled to the floor. The older one had a dark, bloody hole where his nose had once been. The younger was staring at the ceiling with one lifeless eye as blood oozed out of the socket of the other one.

"Would you not agree, Doctor," said Miss Starlet, smiling in my direction, "that arousal of the animal spirit is truly one of the most dangerous reactions known to man." She walked over towards a trembling Briany holding out her gun in the palm of her hand.

"A Remington 41, double-shot derringer. And yours?"

Briany was gasping for breath and sputtered, "The same, with the pearl handle. The ladies' model."

"How surprising. Mine exactly. Let me guess. A present for your twenty-fifth birthday."

"What a coincidence," Briany replied with a nervous giggle. "You would think he could come up with some originality in the gifts he gives to the women in his life."

"So we might wish, my dear. But let us not forget that while he is an exceptional man, he is still . . ."

"*Just a man!*" they chorused in unison and then broke out into peals of girlish laughter.

"I do declare, honey child," said Miss Starlet, "I just might get to like having you as my daughter."

"Oh, now, wouldn't that be lovely . . . *mommy.,*" said Briany with a merry laugh.

Miss Starlet's face took on a look of mock rage. "But not if you ever call me that again!" she said wagging a finger in Briany's face.

"Sorry. Sorry. I promise. I promise. Miss Starlet. Miss Starlet," Briany sputtered in between laughter.

The two of them stopped laughing, looked intently at each other, and threw their arms around each other's shoulders.

"Ladies! Please!" I rebuked them. "We do not have time for this. Please. Untie me, and let us move quickly. We must find the three men and get on with the task at hand. We have only a matter of minutes left before the bombs will explode." I confess that while I was exasperated with their girlish behavior, I was also dumbfounded that two women could have dispatched a couple of vile men a moment ago and immediately begin to chortle about their birthday presents.

"Pardon us, Dr. Watson," said Briany, as she undid the wire that bound my hands and body. "It's not every day that a girl gets to have her first-ever adventure with her mother while dispatching a villain." In what was then an incongruous act of modesty, the two of them turned their backs to me, lifted their skirts and replaced their derringers in the holsters that were strapped to their upper thighs.

"Very well," said Miss Starlet, "let us be on our way before this whole silly world goes to pieces yet again." We left the wretched bodies on the floor, quickly mounted our horses, and started off at a gallop to find the three men. We had only ridden north for a few minutes when we saw them in the distance approaching us. They were cantering along and seemed in no great concern. We met up with them and Holmes spoke first. "Disaster has been averted. We caught up with the procession north of the village and diverted their route. I am surprised, my dear Watson, that you have curtailed your investigation of the evidence so quickly…"

Chapter Seven

Saving the Empire

"Holmes!" I shouted, but he ignored me and kept chattering away, so I screamed and got his attention. I quickly explained about the location of the bombs. The story of the method employed by the two women to save civilization would have to wait. Alarm spread over the faces of the three men. Holmes looked at his watch.

"Good Lord," he cried, "we have only moments to spare before the King enters his car. Ride!"

"Horse," said Brett to his mount, "make tracks."

The six of us galloped south along the pathway. Again, I cursed the Afghan sniper but I did my best to keep up with the rest. Brett and Reggie pulled out in front as they did not hesitate to give their mounts hard kicks with the heels of their boots to spur them on. We thundered past the cottage, and then a few minutes later past the tavern and the barkeep, who looked upon us with amazement from his doorway. Mentally, I was computing the vanishing time that was still available to us. If we could reach the bridge over the swollen river within the next five minutes, we should have a grace period of yet another ten to reach the rail yard and the King's car. Lord willing, we could do it. There was hope yet.

My moment of hope quickly vanished. Brett and Reggie had halted their horse in front of us and dismounted. The bridge was gone. The stream was over its banks; more than twenty yards separated us from the far side, and the waters were raging.

"No," I cried out, "it's been washed away. Yet it was firmly in place just an hour ago."

Holmes ran up to look at the remains of the structure. "It has not washed away. It has been destroyed by explosives. Yet again I have underestimated those evil men."

We could see the rail yard in the distance. It was no more than three hundred yards off. The King's car, the attached dining car, and the coach for his staff were all decked out with bunting and emblazoned with the coats of arms that only recently I could not recall. Hope of anyone hearing our shouts was beyond praying.

"The next bridge is a quarter mile to the south," said Holmes. 'It is made of concrete and will still be in place. It is our only hope." He ran back to his horse, but stopped before mounting and turned to Briany. "Young lady, I believe I read that you took a prize in swimming." He looked at her face, then deliberately turned his face towards the flooded river.

Briany looked puzzled for a brief moment and then turned towards Reggie.

"Hey! Little brother!" she shouted at Reggie. "Can you swim?"

Reggie looked at her, and then grinned. "I'll race you, big sister!"

With that, the two of them dropped their bodies to the grass and tugged off their boots. Briany stood up, ripped the buttons open on the bodice of her dress, shoved it back off her shoulders and let it fall to the ground. She stood before us in just her stocking feet, a white lace corset, and her undergarments. My inability to take my eyes off of her perfectly formed woman's body would demand an embarrassing time in confession.

Reggie took longer to strip out of his jacket, shirt and trousers, but a moment later he was standing before us in just his briefs and socks, his arms and torso rippling and the muscles in his powerful thighs and calves magnificently defined.

"Father!" Briany shouted to Brett. "Throw our boots across!" Then she turned to her brother. "Let's go!"

First she and then her brother sprinted to the edge of the flooded stream and with a running dive entered the water. The powerful current swept both of their bodies downstream, but with deliberate strokes each of them was moving steadily towards the far shore. We watched them, fearing for their safety until they were nearly fifty yards downstream but within a few feet of the distant bank.

Miss Starlet was watching them with a glow of parental pride. "Magnificent, aren't they, Doctor?"

While Miss Starlet gathered up her children's clothes, Brett picked up the two pairs of boots. Sherlock Holmes placed a hand on his arm and said, "Pardon me, sir. But there are a few things at which an English schoolboy excels."

He took one of the boots at the top of the upper, ran back about ten yards and with rapid strides ran towards the edge of the river. A few steps before reaching the bank, his long thin arm began to move in a full circle with the boot firmly in his grasp. As he reached the water's edge, the circle of his arm reached its apex, and he let the boot fly – as good of a cricket toss as I have ever seen. The boot soared through the air and landed in the grass well beyond the far edge of the river. He repeated the feat another three times, and all four boots were hurled to the other shore.

"I reckon that your game of cricket is not as useless as I thought," mused Brett.

"In my youth I dispatched many a batter and won my share of sticky wickets," said Holmes.

On the far shore, the young athletes had climbed out the water and run back to fetch their boots. Quickly, they dropped to the grass and tugged their boots back on to their feet. "Hey there! I won!" shouted Briany back at us. "Not fair!" shouted Reggie, "she had a head start!"

They rose, turned towards the rail yard and began sprinting down the gravel road at a speed that only the runners in our recent Olympic Games could have matched.

"Move it!" Brett shouted to us. "We have to ride to that next bridge try to get to the car before it blows."

We remounted and galloped hard to the south. The concrete bridge was still firm. We crossed it and turned back to the north. In the distance, we could see the rail yard, and the air above was still clear with no sign of smoke of flame. We had closed the distance to less than one hundred yards when an enormous explosion shook the earth. The horses halted and reared up on their back legs in fear. We struggled not to fall off and looked back at what had been the royal railway car. There were flames in many places. The superstructure of the King's private car was entirely gone. Debris was scatted for yards around and thick smoke was billowing from the site. We could hear screams of distress coming from the platform at the far end.

A sickening feeling crept over me. I looked at Holmes who looked back at me. "My dear friend," he said, "a prayer might be in order."

We dismounted and walked towards the chaos with our handkerchiefs covering our mouths to protect us from the acrid fumes. I placed my hand on Holmes's arm and we plodded our way forward, fearing the worst. Behind us were Brett and Miss Starlet. She had slipped her arm through his and was holding it tightly. They knew that their children had had more than enough time to reach the car before the explosion. They also knew that no life could have survived.

As we reached what was left of the car, we stepped over the pieces of furniture, partitions, and toilet fixtures that were strewn on the ground and down the embankment. Holmes moved back from the car and began to look into the debris that surrounded it. He did not have to tell me what he was doing. I knew that human bodies are dense and even in violent explosions do not move far from where they had been. Holmes had begun his search for what were the remains of our King and our children. Silently, I followed him. Brett and Miss Starlet followed me. She was still holding tightly to his arm.

From the base of the embankment, a familiar voice called out. "Yoohoo! Mommy! Daddy! Over here!" Thank God. They were alive. Staggering up the embankment were our two young heroes, clad only in their underwear and scratched and muddied flesh. Between them and being held on each side was a stout, bearded man in military trousers and a white shirt that was untucked at his ample waist.

Miss Starlet burst into tears of joy and relief. Brett Cutler handed her his handkerchief.

We met them as they reached to top of the hill. Holmes and I knew that British etiquette did not permit us to throw hugs and kisses on children in the presence of the King of England, but being Americans Brett and Miss Starlet practiced no such restraint. That being done, Brett turned to the disheveled man and said, "Hello there, Bertie. Thought I would drop in on your party. I see you have already met my family." He nodded in the direction of the scantily clothed young man and woman.

Prince Albert Edward, soon to be King Edward VII of England, looked at us without a word and then said, "Come and see me next week at Buckingham." Then he walked off toward the station, tucking his shirt back into his trousers as he went.

"Pardon me, Captain," said Holmes. "Could you look up to the top of the station? On the roof. Through the smoke."

We all looked up. Holmes pulled out his spyglass, looked again and handed it to Brett. He looked for a brief moment, gave the glass back and unslung his rifle from behind his back.

Through the smoke, we could make out three figures on the station roof. There were two men. One sat by himself. The other had a child sitting beside him. We watched them closely while the King made his way past the third railway car and rounded the far end of the staff coach. We heard a roar of cheers from the railway platform as the crowd of villagers discerned that it was the King and that he was safe and sound.

The man who was sitting alone quickly jumped to his feet. He appeared to be looking down into the crowd and then he bent over and picked up a rifle and lifted it to his shoulder.

"No, sir," said Brett quietly, "I don't think you're going to do that." He quickly sighted the gun and pulled the trigger.

The Mauser gave a sharp crack, and we could see the man fall back. The other man leapt to his feet and ran over to where the shooter had been standing, then immediately ran back, picked up the child and disappeared out of our sight over the back end of the roof.

"You are a superb shot, sir," said Holmes. "Well done."

"I did have some practice a few years back getting rid of Yankees," said Brett. "Some things you just don't forget."

"Nor, I suspect," responded Holmes, "shall that man and his son forget what they came to do. I fear we have not heard the last from little Gavrilo and his father."

"Well, sir, we have certainly heard the last of them today," said Starlet, "so we can put all this behind us until the next silly war breaks out. And, gentleman, I do declare, that riding has given me an appetite. I cannot imagine that this village serves barbecue and mint juleps, but I am sure our great detective can find us some place to relax ourselves."

"I believe that should be possible, Miss Starlet," said Holmes. "My notes tell me that there is a decent pub close by. It is reported to be spotless, and, if you can ignore the grumpy publican and condition of the WC's as a result of litigation with the next-door neighbor, acceptably convivial. If we make our way there quickly, we should be able to get served before the madding crowd descends on it."

Miss Starlet looked sternly at the nearly naked young man and woman, "Great balls of fire. What am I going to do with you two? Your clothes are back with the horses. If you will get dressed and promise to behave yourselves, your mother and father will treat you to lunch." She struggled to get the last few words out before breaking into a joyful laugh.

"Best offer I had all morning," said Reggie, "I'm hungry enough to eat a horse. How about you, father?"

"And wash it down with a cold beer, if only they had such a thing in this strange country," replied Brett.

Epilogue

In a corner of the *Crown and Mitre* we sat and talked in quiet tones, struggling to be heard over the boisterous voices of the patrons, who it seemed all had their own version of the events of the day and all had to repeat their stories to all their neighbors.

Reggie had dutifully made several trips to the bar and returned to our table bearing plates of hot battered cod, chips, and mushy peas, four ales, and two shandies for the ladies.

"So, let's hear you tell us," said Brett to his son and daughter, "how it was you managed to rescue my old pal, Bertie, the almost King of England."

"We ran," began Briany, "pell-mell towards the car. We knew by the station clock tower that the King was already inside it. We tried the doors on our side, but they were firmly locked. Reggie saw that one of the car windows was open and that the space was large enough for me to fit through, so he hoisted me up and into it. I ran back straightaway to the door and unlocked it so he could enter. We ran up and down through the car, but it was empty. We could see no one at all. But then my brother had a brilliant idea."

"I had heard," Reggie continued, "that the King was enormously fond of food and drink and, as any man knows, that means that he must also have to spend a lot of time on the loo. So, I ran towards one WC at the north end of the car while my sister ran to the other end. Mine was empty, but she…"

"I opened the door, and there he was. The almost king of England sitting on his throne. I shouted down the car to Reggie and then turned my attention to his Highness. I must say he was looking at me very oddly. 'Sir,' I said, 'you must get out of here at once!' and just laughed at me. 'Bloody hell!' he shouted, 'such a lovely parting gift from the villagers. But surely you can wait a moment until I have finished in here'. He has, it would appear, earned his reputation as a cad and a somewhat crude bon vivant. Then Reggie appeared and again the king laughed. 'One of each,' he shouted, 'God bless these villagers of King's Lynn. But, my dear boy, just wait for me in the bedchamber, and I will be there in three royal minutes.' 'Sir,' I said, 'you don't understand; your life is in danger. We have to get you out of here.' Reggie and I gave each other a look, and then he said to the King . . ."

"I said, 'Sorry, Bertie, old sport, but it's time to move.' So, I grabbed him under one arm, my sister grabbed the other and we manhandled him off the loo, out of the WC, and out of the door of the car. We all fell in a heap on the gravel beside the track. He was bellowing very nasty curses at us by this time, but we pulled him forward and pushed him down the embankment. He is fat and awkward, and so he rolled like a beer barrel to the bottom. We ran down and flattened our bodies on top of his."

"Then the car exploded," said Briany. "We were protected, being at the bottom of the embankment. The force and the projectiles flew over our heads. We stayed in place for a couple of minutes, but once we realized that there was going to be no secondary blast, we got up off of Bertie, helped him to his feet, pulled up his trousers, and made sure that he was unharmed. I looked up then and saw you. And here we are."

"Yes, my dears, here we are for sure," said Brett, "and unless I am sorely mistaken, the world will never hear of what you did unless Dr. Watson here tells them, and even then, they may not believe us."

"Ah, so true," said Holmes. "But you will know in your hearts that you have defeated the forces of unspeakable evil. But you must tell us, dear ladies, how you managed to shoot two very disciplined anarchists at close range."

"Fiddle-dee-dee, Sherlock," returned Miss Starlet, "there are some things that even the great detective is better off not knowing."

A week passed during which we all made our reports to Scotland Yard and Whitehall. The bodies of the three anarchists were removed from the cottage and the station, identified, and secretly buried. The name of the man who escaped remained unknown. We knew the child only by his Christian name of Gavrilo.

Another rail car was found for the King and he made his way first to Windsor, then Buckingham, and on Saturday, August 9, in the year of our Lord 1902, Albert Edward, the oldest son of Queen Victoria and the Prince

Consort, was crowned King of England, Sovereign of the British Empire, and Emperor of India. The crowds cheered.

On August the fifteenth, we gathered in a small room in the Palace for a private ceremony. His Highness said a very few perfunctory words of gratitude but then added, "As none of you are members of our Empire's armed forces, I cannot award you the Cross that bears my mother's name. But your valor is every bit deserving of it and shall not be forgotten." For a moment, he looked quite directly into the face of Briany. She raised her hand to her mouth and with her thumb and first finger gently pinched her lips together. The King gave a faint smile and nod and we were ushered out. Momma was waiting for us.

"About time y'all got done. So did that fat boy what was all trussed up in buttons and bows give you some trinkets, seeing as how y'all just about got yourselves all blown up saving him? But I suspect the angels was fighting on your side. But y'all know, don't you, that we got fat boys in Atlanta what'll give you trinkets. We call boys like that damn Yankees."

I believe I caught a quick flash of a brilliant red petticoat beneath her modest black skirt.

Over a celebratory tea at Claridge's, Miss Starlet announced, "We have sent telegrams to Atlanta, and have arranged to have a true Southern party on the fifteenth of September to celebrate our family reunion and to send Reggie off to the Citadel. We will be serving barbecue to all of the best and brightest of Atlanta and we simply must have you, Sherlock Holmes, and you, John Watson, with us to be part of it. We will arrange to book you first-class passage on Cunard's new steamship and entertain you as only those born, by the grace of God, in the South can do. I will not hear otherwise; you are coming to America."

"No, my dear Miss Starlet, we are doing no such thing," said Holmes kindly but firmly. "Evil men are still at large and planning unspeakable deeds, and I have no choice but to continue my singular pursuit and defeat of them. So, I must with gratitude decline your gracious offer."

"No, Sherlock."

"Yes, Starlet."

"No, Sherlock!"

"Yes, Starlet."

"But it just won't be a complete celebration without you. I shall be totally devastated. My feelings will be crushed. You will spoil my time eating barbecue. What will I do?" Her face assumed her famous pout.

Holmes gave her an imperious look and, with just the hint of a wink at Brett, responded,

"Frankly, my dear, I don't give a damn."

Dear Sherlockian Readers:

The magnificent novel by Margaret Mitchell, *Gone with the Wind,* is still under copyright protection. For that reason, it is necessary that you understand that while the character in this story named Starlet O'Halloran may remind you of a certain GOTW female heroine, it cannot actually be her. The same goes for Brett Cutler. Of course, if you chose to imagine otherwise, that is up to you.

On 22 January, 1901, Queen Victoria died after reigning over the British Empire since 1837. With her death, the Victorian Age passed into history and Edward VII became king. His coronation was scheduled for 26 June 1902, but was postponed until 9 August of that year. He began his journey to Westminster Cathedral the day before at his royal estate, Sandringham, in King's Lynn.

His waist measurement at the time of his becoming king was forty-eight inches. He was fat.

An attempted assassination of Edward VII took place in Belgium in 1900.

The *Black Hand* became active in the Balkan states in the early 1900s. It was one of their members, Gavrilo Princip, who assassinated Archduke Ferdinand in Sarajevo in June 1914, the event that led to the start of World War I. There is no record of the *Black Hand* ever being active in England. I made that up. Nor were there any subsequent attempts to kill Edward VII.

The names and locations of places in London, the state of Georgia, and Norfolk are more or less accurate for 1902. Claridge's was a fabulous hotel back then and still is.

Warm regards,

Craig

The Sign of the Tooth

A New Sherlock Holmes Mystery

Chapter One

The Bored Consultant

*Lizzie Borden took an ax
And gave her mother forty whacks.
When she saw what she had done,
She gave her father forty-one.*

"Holmes," I said one morning, "you must take a look at this latest on Lizzie."

The Illustrated Times had a ghastly sketch of the young Sunday School teacher hacking away at her mother's head with the caption "How She Might Have Done It." It was positively gruesome.

"Here, Holmes. Come take a look."

Sherlock Holmes glared across the room as I expected he would and in his surliest voice muttered, "You know perfectly well that I am not the least bit interested in lurid stories that the English press copies from the even more lurid American press. Kindly do not visit any more of those stories upon me."

"But Holmes," I continued. "If you will not look at the picture then read this. *The Telegraph* is saying that Miss Borden collapsed and fainted in the courtroom, and it was caused by the bringing of the severed heads of her mother and father as evidence. The story is utterly fascinating."

I was being deliberately provocative. My good friend, the brilliant detective whose mind never ceased its marvelous efforts once set upon the scent of a case, had been despondent for days. Nothing of interest had come across the doorstep of 221B Baker Street in several weeks, and I feared that he would resort yet again to his terrible dependence on pharmaceutical injections for no other reason than to relieve the boredom.

"Watson," he remonstrated. "Must I say again that I am not interested in the latest scandal from across the pond? That is entirely enough."

Like most Englishmen, including, I confess, yours truly, Holmes's could not find a single good word to say about America while all the time being inwardly envious and jealous of the opportunities that were enjoyed by all, even amateur detectives, in the colony that got away.

"Ahh," I said, ignoring him and continuing to read aloud. "The line to be taken by the defending attorney is unique and indeed quite daring. He is presenting several doctors and clergymen who will testify under oath that the female brain and indeed the female constitution as a whole is biologically – did you get that Holmes? *Biologically* – incapable of such a violent and bloody crime. What do you think of that, Holmes?"

He said nothing. He rose from his chair, approached me and removed the newspaper from my hands and read the story. As he did, he slowly shook his head.

"Oh what fools these mortals be, Watson," he muttered. "Have they completely forgotten the Amazons? Three thousand years ago they were impaling men on spears and hacking off their limbs. Our earnest suffragettes are telling us that women are equal to men in all possible ways, and they are entirely correct. This line of defense is pathetic. Even from the details given in the London press, I can see enormous gaping holes in the case presented by the prosecution. Had they any ability whatsoever in scientific deduction this woman would have been set free weeks ago."

"Oh. You don't say. I gather you have been following the story all along?"

"Only when I have felt the pain of utter mental stagnation, when I have been suffocated by the dull routine of existence. I created my role in society so that I could devote my mind to the solving of the most intricate problems and match wits with the most diabolical of criminals. And now I am faced with yet another empty day. So empty that even a banal item about Lizzie Borden brings a tiny serving of relief."

"Very well, Holmes," said I. "If you are going to be an unofficial detective…"

"A consulting detective. The only one in the world," he interjected.

"Fine. A consulting detective then. You are still dependent on cases walking across your threshold, but if the real detectives do their job halfways decently, there will be times when there are none left over for you."

"My dear friend," he said, and I sensed the annoyance in his voice, "I do not live on leftovers, as you suggest. I am consulted on cases when Lestrade, Gregson or Anderson find themselves to be in over their heads, which by the way happens rather often, and my peculiar powers are called for."

I had expected this protest to grow into a tirade, but suddenly his countenance softened as he looked out from our bay window down onto Baker Street.

"Speaking of Lestrade, he has just arrived in his private carriage."

"Really, Holmes. I did not know that Scotland Yard was now providing private carriages for their Inspectors."

"Of course, they are not, but the imbeciles over there decided that they wished to be secretive about their movements. So they purchased a dozen identical unmarked carriages with dark curtains. They are so bland and featureless that you can tell them from any other carriage in London a block away. Ahh … but that is not Lestrade's leg emerging. It is a fine and shapely leg of a young lady."

"Oh. Is it now?" I said as I pushed aside the curtain from the other end of the window.

"Yes. And she is walking directly toward our door which means that she is not yet another of those pitiful young things that have pathetic affairs of the heart, and who walk back and forth several times, trying to make up their little minds, before finally knocking on my door."

When he spoke like this, I instinctively responded in anger. "The affairs of a young woman's heart are neither pathetic nor pitiful Holmes! Have you no feeling in that brain of yours at all?"

He was a little taken back at my admonition. "Oh, very well then, doctor. But you cannot deny that they are frightfully boring."

I was about to make such a denial forcefully, but Mrs. Hudson entered the room and announced, "Miss Mary Morstan, gentlemen."

Miss Morstan entered the room with a firm step and an aura of quiet confidence. When she removed her bonnet, a cascade of flaxen tresses fell to her shoulders. She was well-dressed, and her clothes had the crisp freshness of having been recently purchased on the High Street. Her eyes were utterly arresting. With such light hair, one would never have expected such dark eyes. So dark that had they been all I had seen of her I would have judged her to be gypsy. Her features, though fair, were not the aquiline sharply cut ones of the British Isles but softer and more rounded, almost child-like, and perfectly balanced. I have never looked upon a face to which I was so immediately drawn. As she took the seat that Sherlock Holmes had motioned her to, I could see a faint tremble in her lip. In spite of her radiance and loveliness, she was inwardly upset, and I had to restrain my instinctive response to place my arm around her shoulders and assure her that she was among friends who would protect her.

Using two hands, she removed her handbag from her shoulder and put it on the floor. Before either Holmes or I could say a word, Mrs. Hudson walked over to the young woman and placed her hand on her back in a motherly fashion. "A cup of tea, dearie? It will help you relax. And don't be intimidated by these two oddballs. Their bark is much worse than their bite, and they are quite good at whatever it is they do."

Miss Morstan smiled at Mrs. Hudson. "Thank you. A spot of tea would help me compose myself. Thank you." Mrs. Hudson departed but not without first giving a hard look at both Holmes and me that promised a rap on our knuckles if we were less than considerate to the young woman.

Holmes began. "Allow me to offer my condolences first on having to endure a long interview with those fools over at Scotland Yard, but more so on your recent loss and bereavement. The pain of these things, though unbearable at the time, does eventually pass. The fact that you have come into a goodly inheritance as a result of your father's service under the Raj will help to improve the process. The recent increase in the price of gold will no doubt speed the rate of improvement, and you will likely to be able to say goodbye to your role as a governess, even though you adore your little charges and are loved joyfully in return."

Most young clients to whom Holmes delivered his practiced assessment react in shock and wonder. Miss Morstan did no such thing. She quietly accepted her tea from Mrs. Hudson, and then looked directly at Holmes and shrugged. "Inspector Lestrade certainly has you pegged Mr. Holmes."

"I beg your pardon, miss?" said Holmes. He was apparently not expecting this response.

"Inspector Lestrade told me on no uncertain terms that I was not to tell you that I had been meeting with him but that you would most likely know that all the same. He also said that you would tell me all sorts of things about myself but not to be surprised because it was your way of showing off. He said that you were the oddest bloke in town — but brilliant — and if I could live with your peculiarities that you could help me."

I could not resist asking her, "Did Lestrade indeed say that Sherlock Holmes was 'an odd bloke?'"

"No. Truthfully, he said 'Frankly miss, Sherlock Holmes is positively weird and endlessly annoying' but I did not want to be rude, so I softened his words because I need your help."

"But," I pressed, "did he actually admit that Sherlock Holmes was 'brilliant?'"

"No. Truthfully, he called him an *imbecile savant*. But he insisted that I meet with you all the same."

"Enough of Lestrade," said Holmes, who did not appear to be enjoying this exchange. "State your case."

I had had sufficient inward chuckles to last me the day and seeing that Holmes had returned to being a detective, a consulting detective I must not forget, I felt it appropriate for me to leave the room. "I assure you miss, that he is indeed truly brilliant, even if all those other things are true as well," I said, with a departing bow of my head.

"Oh, please no. Please stay. The Inspector said that I should ask you to help as well because even though you were not at all brilliant you were always kind and considerate and a necessary balance to Sherlock Holmes."

I smiled and took my seat in the empty chair, not entirely sure if I had been complemented or otherwise.

Chapter Two
The Statement of the Case

"I may as well start," she began, "with what you already know. As I entered this room, I saw you look at my shoes, and you no doubt observed that while they are brand new, they are black and plain and terribly unstylish, the sort that a young woman would buy only if she were required to participate in a funeral. I have come into some money very recently and, therefore, the new dress. And my handbag is extremely heavy; you could tell that from the way it bulged, the strain on the shoulder strap, and my needing two hands to lift it. So, you deduced that I have something very heavy in it, and as I am unlikely to be carrying rocks around London, it is more likely that there is gold therein.

"I am of mixed race as you observed by the color of my eyes and the shape of my features and yes, my father, Captain Robert Morstan, was in the Royal Engineers and served in Ceylon. My mother was Ceylonese. As to my being a governess, you are also correct, but I am not sure how you deduced that fact. I am an unmarried woman in my mid-twenties, and it is a reasonable guess to make as to my vocation, but there would be other possibilities, so I am not sure how you landed on governess."

"Ah," said Holmes, looking a little disappointed that his revelations had not exactly been considered miraculous. "On the left side of your skirt, you have a smudge with a spot of granular material. There is a similar one on the other side but a little lower down. Such residue is a telltale sign of a child's face, having climbed down from the breakfast table while still covered with milk and porridge, and giving an affectionate embrace to his or her much-loved governess. That there are two at different heights indicates two children, close in age. They appear to be very fond of you, in a sloppy sort of way."

She smiled. "Yes they are and I of them. I shall miss them. The reason for my departure from that service is related to the reason for my being here."

"Yes. Enough of wet-faced children," said Holmes. "You were stating your case."

"I am here because my father and his closest friend both died within the past three weeks and I believe that they were murdered."

"Indeed, and the dates?" queried Holmes.

"My father two weeks past. His dearest friend, Major John Sholto, a week ago. Both were elderly men in their eighties and had lived long and full lives, and no one seemed surprised when my father was found dead in his study. The doctor said it was a heart failure. No medical examination was performed since he was of advanced age. When the major died a week later, it was agreed that the stress of losing his friend had put a toll on his heart and he passed on as well."

"Those are reasonable explanations," I said. "When men are that old their hearts cannot last much longer. Why do you suspect foul play?"

"Both my father and Major Sholto were old but were still in robust health. There had been no signs of weak hearts in either of them. But that is not the reason for my suspicion. My father had finished his supper and had gone to his study. When the maid brought him his evening tea an hour later, she found him dead at his desk. She tried to shake him and reported that although his body was still warm, all his limbs had gone stiff as boards. Rigor mortis had completely set in."

"That is very unusual," I noted, "but there could be reasons for it. I am not aware of any, but strange things do happen especially with men who have served in the tropics. No telling what unknown pathogens might have entered their systems."

She nodded. "That is what the local doctor said. But a week later Major Sholto died, also in the evening after supper, also in his study, and also with immediate stiffening of his body."

Holmes was now sitting forward. His hands were held in front of his chin and his fingertips pressed together. "That is most certainly a very strange coincidence and although suspicious, does not demand that foul play is the only possible explanation."

"And then this, in yesterday's paper," she said, handing Holmes a clipping. He read it and gave it to me. It ran:

Death of a Student

Oxford. Local police report that the body of a Master Dharmarathna Gunawardhana, a medical student from Ceylon, who was studying at the University, was found in the library yesterday evening. No known cause has been given, and we are awaiting the report of the coroner. The library cleaning staff who found him shortly after the closing hour are reported to have said that he must have been dead for some time as rigor mortis had already set in. There is some confusion on this matter as a fellow student, Master Chandrarathna Wijekulaseriya, also from Ceylon, has been quoted as saying that he had chatted with the deceased just before the closing of the library. Two inspectors from Scotland Yard are investigating, but no report has yet been released. The University has stated that the lad will be greatly missed not only as he was a capable young man on his way to becoming a doctor, but also for his skills on the cricket field. He had excelled at the sport since his days as a scholar at Trinity College in Kandy. Messages of condolence may be sent care of the Central Telegraph in Kandy, Ceylon.

"This young man's father had been a friend of my father in Ceylon, and after his classes were over for the term, he had been helping my father and Major Sholto on their latest project."

Holmes had dropped his hands, and they were firmly clasping the arms of his chair. His eyes had become focused on the young woman's face. "When an unusual event happens once, it is happenstance. When it happens twice, it is a curious coincidence. When it happens a third time, it is a criminal conspiracy. You, my dear young lady, might also be in danger. I trust you are taking appropriate precautions."

"That is why I went to the police, sir. But that is not why they, as well as another party, sent me to see you. I believe, although they did not tell me outright, that it was because of the project on which my father, the Major, and young Dharmy were working."

"And what might that have been. Tell us," said Holmes impatiently.

She nodded. I noticed her hands twitching as she twisted her handkerchief. Had Holmes overbearing presence not been directly between us I would have placed my hand on top of hers and told her to take her time, but I refrained and withheld my annoyance with my friend.

"It might be best if I were to start back a few years ago," she said after composing herself. "My story requires some explaining."

"It is always good to have a complete set of data on which to make insights and judgments," said Holmes brusquely. "Please give us all the pertinent facts, miss, and do get on with it. We do not have all day."

"Holmes, honestly!" I sputtered. "The young lady is under duress. Have some consideration."

"Oh, very well. I correct myself. My colleague, Dr. Watson may have all day, but I do not. Please get on with it."

Instead of looking at him with a hurtful expression, she turned to me and gave a wan but warm smile.

"It is quite all right, doctor. The Inspector warned me about his behavior. He said 'Holmes would forget his manners in front of the Queen if his brain were already lost in the plot of the crime.' He said to take it as a good sign that he was already at work on my behalf."

Holmes harrumphed. She smiled at him and began her story.

"My father studied at the University of Edinburgh and upon graduation joined the Royal Engineers. He was posted to Ceylon and put to work building the railroad from the port of Trincomalee up to Kandy. His fellow engineer was John Sholto, also a Scotsman, who had done his studies in Glasgow, and they became good friends and worked alongside each other. Near to the end of his posting my father was injured and was released from the regiment with a small pension. He would have returned home, but he had no real family back in Scotland, and his friends were all in his regiment. He had also fallen in love with the island of Ceylon and particularly with the city of Kandy. He thought it a magical place. It happened that some missionaries from the Church of England had started a school there, Trinity College, and they were in need of someone to teach the boys their maths. They invited my father to join the staff of the college. He did and taught the boys for the next thirty years. He was enraptured with his calling, with the Spice Island, and with the art, history, and culture of Kandy. In addition to teaching, he coached the boys in cricket, and he became quite the scholar and published several books and monographs about the Kingdom of Kandy.

"John Sholto, who I called my Uncle John although we are not related, continued to serve in the Engineers and was promoted to the rank of major. He returned to England, married, and set up a small estate near Norwood. He had two sons, twins, and provided his family with a good life, but he continued his close friendship with Father. They wrote to each other every week. He came to visit every second year, and he also became an amateur expert on the religion and history of Kandy. The two of them became a little team of scholars and had a small reputation in the Royal Society, but they were highly esteemed by the Ceylonese who lived in Kandy. You may know that Kandy was the last independent kingdom to fall to the British Empire. The Kandians are very attached to their unique history and very fond of those foreigners who choose to live there and learn about their special corner of heaven on earth.

"While he was teaching, my father lived on the college grounds and lived very frugally. He remained single, set his military pension and most of his salary aside, and shrewdly invested in the new tea gardens that were being opened far up in the highlands near Nuwara Eliya. He convinced Uncle John to do the same. Over time, their shares grew, and they became very wealthy men. He never let on and thought it unseemly for a man to flaunt his money, so he continued to live in his cottage and teach the boys maths and cricket. When he turned fifty-five years of age, he retired. To everyone's surprise, and I gather to some shock and outrage, he married my mother, who was twenty-five years his junior, a native of the island, and the college's accountant."

"Oh my," said I. "That must have caused quite a stir."

She laughed. It was good to see that her distress had lessened. "Not as much as you might think it would, doctor. There are many, many English soldiers, civil servants, and missionaries who have, as they say, 'gone native' and become attached to a dark-skinned woman of the sub-continent. Some took Indian and Ceylonese girls as their wives and countless more as their mistresses.

"I was born the following year. We Anglo-Indians, as our mongrel race is known. There are several million of us now We are, in the words of my father, an everlasting biological monument to the adultery of the British Raj."

"That is very endearing," said Holmes. "It has nothing to do with any crime. Please get back to the essentials."

"Of course, sir," she said and flashed a beautiful sparkling smile back at Holmes. "Even though my father was an older man he was a vigorous man and, being retired, had the freedom to go on countless adventures with his little girl. My childhood in the highlands of Ceylon was a fairy tale. Once a week my father and mother and I would rise before dawn and drive our carriage all the way to Nuwara Eliya. As the morning sun came over the tops of the hills, I would watch the sunlight bounce off of scores of silver waterfalls. As the mist rose off the tea gardens, we would hear the voices, the singing of the Ceylonese women as they walked along the rows of the tea plants plucking the leaves and tossing them back over their shoulders into the wicker buckets that were strapped to their backs. Up to a dozen women would work together, each with her own row, but walking in unison through the gardens and singing. We would stop along the way at a tea house and drink the tea that had been picked and roasted the day before, and it was the finest elixir on earth. Father used to say that all the good tea was consumed in India and Ceylon, that the second rate leaves were sent to England, and that the grounds off the floor were swept up, put into tea bags and sent to America, where they were as likely to throw it into the harbor as brew it properly.

"I became a bit of a scholar and learned the ancient Sinhala alphabet and the language, and could read and speak it rather fluently. Father and I chatted in that tongue just for fun at times.

"On our winter break, he took me on his hunting trips, even on three tiger hunts in India. During the summers, we would take a vacation to the seaside in Galle, or over to the beautiful white beaches at Batticaloa. It was as wonderful a childhood as I could ever dream of. It lasted for the first ten years of my life and then, to everyone's surprise, my mom being forty and dad sixty-five, mother found herself expecting a child. I could tell that they were very worried and, sadly, the result was tragic. Both my mother and my baby sister, Anne, died in childbirth. My father was utterly heartbroken. He tried to keep being cheerful for my sake, but he was never the same.

"When I was twelve we came back to England and settled in London. Father and the Major spent a great deal of time together, most of it at the British Museum where they continued their scholarly study about the Kingdom of Kandy and founded the Society for Kandian Research. The center of all Kandian culture, art, and religion, as you may know, is the Sri Dalada Maligawa, the Temple of the Tooth. Over one thousand years ago Princess Hemamali brought to Kandy the tooth of the Buddha. It has been kept and venerated since that time in the great golden temple that sits by Bogambara Lake. It is the very beating heart of Kandy. Father and Uncle John are, or I must say were, the experts in all of England concerning the Tooth of the Buddha. Every year they spent two months back in Kandy pursuing their research. And that, sirs, is the project on which they were working when they died or, I must say, were killed."

"The Tooth," I cried out. "The Tooth of the Buddha? You have read about this, Holmes, have you not?"

The story had been all over the Press for weeks now. After months of negotiations, the Tooth had been brought it to London. The priests had refused to let it leave the temple until they were promised thousands of pounds worth of temple renovations, and agreed that temple priests would accompany it and never let it leave their sight. It would soon be on display at the British Museum, and thousands were expected to queue up to see it.

The special exhibit, *The Wisdom Tooth of the Buddha,* was scheduled to open in five days. The relic of Gautama Buddha was every bit as important to his followers as the Shroud of Turin was to the Catholics. While an old molar was in itself hardly anything to get all excited about, the Foreign Office had gone all out to assemble a magnificent display of the wealthy artifacts of the Raj. It mattered not that some were from Rajasthan, some from Bihar, and many from Bangalore, as long as they looked spectacular and drew a constant crowd. Photographs of the citizenry of London, having removed their shoes and looking up in worshipful awe at the sacred tooth, would be distributed all over the empire, proving that the heart of the Empire and the heart of the average Englishman beat in unison with all of the dark-skinned subjects of Her Gracious Majesty.

"Hmm. Yes. I do recall seeing some mention in the press," said Holmes. "Struck me as more an exceptional propaganda coup for the Empire than an effort of scholarship. Having countless English blokes and nannies all oooing and aahhhing over it makes the Empire look as if we actually respect the superstitions and handcrafts of the benighted heathen. When, if fact, we do nothing of the sort."

"Oh, come come, Holmes. Must you always be so cynical?"

"When it comes to political spectacle, cynicism is not only rational, it is imperative," he snapped back at me. "Nevertheless, Miss Morstan, do you have any knowledge of what your father, the major, and the young Mr. Wiji … Mr. … ahh, Master Dharmy were doing as regards this special exhibit?"

"No, I fear I do not. It was all rather secretive, and their conversations were very quiet. I do not live in the same house as my father any longer and only visited him on Saturdays. He generally did not work on those days and generously devoted the time to outings with me. Even though he was eighty years old, I was always his little girl." As she spoke, tears formed in her beautiful dark eyes and crept down her lovely face.

"It is unfortunate," said Holmes, "that your intellectual curiosity was non-existent and that you were content to be a governess, but it cannot be helped, and you will not be of much use along that line of investigation. Very well then, what have you brought in your bag?"

Again, instead of being offended, Miss Morstan smiled back at Holmes and sweetly replied, "I thought you would never ask."

She proceeded to reach into her large handbag and slowly extract and place on the table eight objects, all about the size of a fist. Each was wrapped in a black silk cloth, and she waited until the last one was on the table before returning to the first to untie the gold thread that held it together. I could see the vein in Holmes's left temple starting to throb as he waited in frustrated impatience for the ritual to be completed and the objects to be revealed. Miss Morstan went about her task with apparent unrelenting concentration, but I suspected that she was playing a game of wits with Holmes and, as far as I could see, was winning this round. I felt myself growing fonder of her by the minute.

One by one the artifacts were exposed. Every one of them was a small statuette of the sitting Buddha, and every one in gleaming gold, yet each in a slightly different pose.

"Would you like to look at one more closely?" she said, looking up demurely at Holmes. It was all I could do not to break out laughing and shout, "Of course he would. He is dying to look at it. You are torturing him."

To his credit Holmes, with delicious difficulty, refrained from being rude and brusque and snatching one off the table. He nodded politely and replied, "Yes, my dear. I would. If you would be so kind as to hand me the first one."

Holmes received the statuette and bounced it for a moment in his hand. It was clearly a heavy little fellow. "This is heavy enough to be solid gold." He removed his glass from his pocket and began a careful examination. "I could not say without taking it to a jeweler, but it appears to be of at least eighteen karat, if not twenty. The carving is exquisite. There are hundreds of fine details. It must have taken weeks of painstaking work from a master carver to make this.

"Are they all the same weight?" he asked Miss Morstan.

"Yes," she replied. "There is nothing other than the changes in the pose of the Buddha to differentiate them from each other. Each one represents one of the eight paths of noble enlightenment."

"Remarkable," said Holmes. "Every one of these must be worth hundreds of pounds for the gold alone. I have no expertise in the precious art of Ceylon, but I imagine that if these were to be auctioned by Sotheby's they would fetch well over a thousand pounds a piece, and many times that figure for the full set. So please, Miss Morstan, how is it that you have come to have these in your possession?"

"The first one arrived the day following my father's funeral. Then one each weekday after that. After the eighth, they stopped. Each was carefully enclosed in a small wooden case with protective wrapping."

"And were there any notes or instructions?"

"There was one with the first. And then another one with the last one and I have no idea from whom they came."

She reached into her handbag and handed two folded pieces of paper to Sherlock Holmes. He unfolded it, read it and handed it to me.

```
June 3, 1902
On this day, you begin to receive your
inheritance. Mine must wait another decade.
           With warmest regards,
```

ω

"Your inheritance, Miss Morstan?" said Holmes. "Were you expecting something following the death of your father?"

"Yes, but nothing until after the estate had cleared probate, and even then it would be the shares in the tea gardens, not a set of precious golden carvings."

"When did you say your father died?"

"A fortnight ago."

"But this note is dated before that time. It is very unlikely that whoever sent it could have known that your father was going to die. Was there any other significance to that date, Miss Morstan? To the third of June, 1902?"

"It was my twenty-fifth birthday."

Holmes said nothing for a moment and then held up the second note. "I suppose I am required to congratulate the writer on his good judgment." He then read the note.

```
My dear Mary Morstan:
Your life is now in danger. I beg you please
to seek the immediate protection of the
police. You should also contact Mr.
Sherlock Holmes at 221B Baker Street and
ask for his help.
                With deepest concern,
```

ω

Holmes sat in silence for a moment and then turned abruptly to the young lady. "Very well, miss. I will take on your case and expect to receive no payment unless it is resolved to your satisfaction. Take these figurines of Mr. Buddha and immediately put them into a safe box in a bank. The Capital and County Bank is close by on Oxford Street just a block east of Baker Street. I suggest you go there. Now get yourself out of here and back to your sloppy-faced children. I have work to do. Go. Now. And leave those notes with us."

Miss Morstan smiled back at Holmes, packed her Buddhas back into her handbag, rose and walked toward the door. I moved quickly to open it for her. "I will see you to the street and fetch a cab," I said.

"Oh, Doctor Watson," she replied, with a radiant smile. "That is entirely unnecessary, but I do thank you for your kindness." Then, lightly putting her hand on my forearm and with a hint of a twinkle in her eye, added, "I do believe the good Lord gave you not only a kind spirit but also a handsome face. It is a pity that you are covering so much of it with those silly mutton-chop whiskers and walrus's mustache." Then she turned and descended the stairs. I walked over to the window and watched until she had climbed safely into a cab.

Chapter Three

Mycroft

I then turned to Sherlock Holmes and in a firm voice said, "You really are an automaton — a calculating machine. There is something positively inhuman in you sometimes. Could you not display even a jot of consideration for the feelings of a young woman in distress."?

"My dear friend, I am considerate of my client's bank accounts, of keeping them from bankruptcy, prison, the gallows, and disastrous marriages. I am considerate of protecting their reputations even when they rightly deserved to be dragged through the mud. I am considerate of their property and even of rescuing their stupid children. I consider that those considerations are quite enough. I have neither the time nor the patience to consider their utterly unpredictable feelings."

"Holmes, you are wrong!" I said loudly in return. "I do not care if you were to save every soul on earth from the Tribulation and Armageddon, you are still an Englishman and rudeness to a young woman is simply not done, and you know that Holmes!"

For a moment, Holmes was taken aback by my rebuke, but then he turned as we heard a clatter of a carriage stopping at our door on Baker Street. Holmes looked out and then turned to me with a smile.

"My dear friend, I am about to be redeemed, if not on my own merits then by comparison. There is one, *the one,* coming up the stairs the laces of whose shoes I am not worthy to tie up when it comes to lacking feelings and being consumed only with facts."

"You don't mean…?"

"That is exactly who I mean. My brother Mycroft has departed from his *sanctum sanctorum* and is paying a most unusual visit to his little brother, conveyed here by another one of Lestrade's conspicuously inconspicuous carriages."

From my others stories about Sherlock Holmes the reader will remember that Mycroft Holmes did not merely work for the British Government, he *was* the British Government. His title was some nondescript assistant to some non-descript Secretary, but, in his head, he held the exact memory of everything that had taken place in Westminster, or Whitehall, or in every far-flung corner of the Empire for the past thirty years. He was the *eminence grise* behind every minister or prime minister. It mattered not which party was in power. He had memorized the dossier on every Member of Parliament of every party and knew far more about them than they could afford to have set free on the streets of London. He was paid well to know everything, to advise on all significant concerns, and to say nothing.

He never left his small office in a back corner of Westminster, and that he would come to Baker Street was a unique event, portending matters that must be of the gravest concern to the Empire.

"Your brother is here," said Mrs. Hudson, opening the door, and looking wide-eyed and close to panic.

"Do show the old boy in," said Holmes, remaining in his chair and rapidly lighting up a pipe.

If I ever wondered what Sherlock Holmes might look like in ten years, I had only to observe his older brother. Mycroft Holmes was as tall as Sherlock but carried twenty-five more pounds of flesh, equal parts muscle and fat. His hair had gone snowy white, but the eyes burned with the same intensity as his brother's. The fraternal resemblance was easily guessed even before they opened their mouths and removed all doubt.

"Ah," said Holmes the younger, refusing to rise, "how nice of you to drop by Mycroft. I assume you were in the neighborhood and stopped in for a cup of tea. Let me call for one."

"Stop the nonsense, Sherlock," the older brother thundered. "You know that I would never bother to come into this silly headquarters of yours were it not on matters of extreme importance to the Government. It is a state secret and cannot be discussed here. Now fetch your coat and hat and come with me to Westminster. At once!"

Sherlock Holmes did not budge an inch. Instead, he took a slow draft on his pipe and even more slowly exhaled it.

"My dear brother, May I suggest that rather than consulting me you call on one far more qualified than I to assist you."

"Who?! And do not be deliberately obtuse." Mycroft barked in response.

"Why the tooth-fairy of course. She is the one to whom missing teeth are entrusted. Alternatively, you might check the back of your upper jaw. Missing wisdom teeth do appear there from time to time."

The older fellow's face went red with anger. "Confound you, Sherlock!" Mycroft shouted, banging his walking stick harshly on the floor. "How in the devil do you know about that? It is the most sensitive matter the Government has faced in a decade. Who told you?!"

"Why, my dear brother, you did. What possible alternative is there? A woman, whose father was the expert on The Tooth and recently murdered, shows up in my rooms, sent by Scotland Yard. An hour later you do the same thing sent by the same incompetents. All other alternative explanations are impossible, and as I have said many times…"

"Blast you! I know what you have said," Mycroft replied. He glared for a moment at his younger brother and then slowly removed his overcoat and hat, laid them on the sofa, and dropped his large body into the chair that was recently vacated by a much more attractive one.

I stood up and said, "If state secrets are about to be discussed I really must excuse myself."

"Sit down," Mycroft snarled back at me. "All you ever write about are Sherlock's successes. His failures, and they have been legion, never appear in *The Strand*. Nobody will hear anything from Sherlock's simpering Boswell unless Sherlock succeeds, so stay where you are. You might be useful for something, which is why I assume Sherlock keeps you around."

I said nothing, fearful of poking the bear in our midst. Sherlock Holmes though was not about to give up a fraternal rivalry without at least one more lick at it.

"I'm dreadfully sorry, dear brother, but I have just accepted another case. My client may be in some danger, and I must act immediately to look after her protection."

"Stop it, Sherlock! Mary Morstan is being followed to the Capital and County Bank by two armed marines. Another three will be guarding her lodgings at Mrs. Cecil Forrester's around the clock. Your client is taken care of better than you ever could."

"Why thank you for that. However, there are other clients whose concerns are pressing on me. I do not see how I can neglect them."

"You do not have any other clients. You docket is empty. Now stop the foolishness."

"You have access to every police detective, military intelligence expert, or clairvoyant in the land that your heart might desire, all courtesy of Her Majesty's Treasury. I cannot see why I should take this on."

Here Mycroft leaned forward and glared at his brother. "You *will* take it on Sherlock. You will take it on because it is dangerous, perplexing and bound to be interesting. You know that it will be anything but boring. You already know that I have no idea how to solve it or I would not be here. So you will accept it because you cannot refuse it. Now just drop the pretense and get to work."

Sherlock Holmes sat back and drew again on his pipe. I gathered that I was witnessing a ritual that had taken place many times in the past between these siblings. For a moment, I allowed myself the delightfully wicked thought that they positively deserved each other.

"Well then Mycroft, since I am to be pressed into service without even having taken the Queen's shilling, please proceed and tell me all I need to know."

"The first thing you need to know," lectured Mycroft, "is that this is a matter of the greatest secrecy. If any word of this should get out, there will be hell to pay. It could be a disaster for the Empire."

"My dear brother," said Holmes, after yet another slow exhalation, "you know that I do not care a fig for your precious Empire. However, I have been engaged by a client who is closely connected to this matter, and you know that I would withstand torture before betraying the confidence of the young woman, or any other client for that matter."

"I suppose I do know that. Hmmm. Very well. The facts, in brief, are these — you can learn the details from Scotland Yard."

Sherlock Holmes interrupted his brother. "Scotland Yard has been informed? How many there know about this? Any others?"

"Due to its sensitivity, it has been confined to a very select few. Buckingham Palace, of course. Lestrade and two of his men. The Foreign Secretary and the Home Secretary and their private secretaries. That is all."

"Splendid," said the young brother. "That gives us three complete days to solve everything before it becomes headlines in every paper in the country. Four if we include the rest of the Empire."

"Enough sauciness, Sherlock," Mycroft muttered. "I have enough things trying my soul today without having to put up your jibes. Now then, here is what you need to know. The Tooth was placed in an ivory box, wrapped inside a padded shipping case and put into a small but new and secure safe before leaving the temple in Kandy. It was under guard as it was taken by rail to the harbor at Trincomalee. Then it was put on a cruiser and brought by the Royal Navy all the way to the Docklands, stopping only in Cape Town for resupply. It was unloaded under guard and taken to the British Museum, and again kept under guard. When the safe was opened so that the display could be set up, it was discovered that the box was empty. The Tooth was gone."

"Ahh, a tooth-napping. And the ransom demand?" said Holmes the younger.

"Not a word."

"You have interrogated all those who had access to it? The marines who were guarding it?"

Here, out of loyalty to her Majesty's forces, I had to interject. "The Royal Marines are sterling chaps of unquestioned loyalty. It is inconceivable that they would betray such a trust."

During the years that I have known Sherlock Holmes, I have been the victim many times of what I have called The Look. In its mildest form, one of supercilious condescension, it says to me, without a word being uttered, that I am behaving like a naïve schoolboy. In mid-range, it accuses me of being a pathetic dupe. The more severe variety announces that I am revealing to all that I am no more than an imbecilic moron. What I was faced with was the middling variety delivered, however, in unison by both of the grim Brothers Holmes.

Mycroft dismissively responded, "Everyman has his price, Watson. With a hundred pounds, you could turn one of the Queen's own Grenadiers. As to the marines guarding The Tooth, there were never less than four of them on any watch. Individually they might be suspect. However, while any one of them could have been bought off, they will never betray their fellow marine, and a collusion of that many just does not happen. They do have some principles."

Sherlock Holmes continued. "The Museum guards? They could be had for a fiver."

"They were not used. Only the marines and the monks."

"Very well, the monks then. Perhaps there is a fanatic amongst them. Have they been questioned? Surely someone in the Foreign Office could translate from Sinhala."

Here Holmes-the-elder shrugged. "It appears that the particular order of monks who guard The Tooth has taken a vow of silence, so we have not spoken to them. Demanding that they break their vow would be to them as offensive as putting the Archbishop in a whorehouse. So, no. But they are no more than a lot of dazed and doped-up fakirs who do nothing but burn incense and pray all day long and worship their deity's dentures. They would be confining their souls to hell, or whatever they have to serve the same purpose if they were to even touch the sacred relic. So we have ruled them out."

"If you have ruled out financial gain, as well as religious fervor, what then could be the motive?" asked Sherlock Holmes. "What theory have you reached?"

Mycroft Holmes sat in silence briefly and then spoke slowly. "To wreak absolute and desperate havoc upon the Empire. If the word goes out amongst the colonies that we have carelessly lost a most sacred relic of the Buddhist faith, it would be the greatest possible embarrassment to us. Utterly humiliating. But worse, there would be rioting in the streets from Banjul to Hong Kong. It would make the ruckus of 1857 or even the Boxer blow-up seem no more than a picnic by the Serpentine."

"But who on earth would want to embarrass the Queen and the British Empire?" I said and no sooner had the words left my mouth than The Look led me to regret them.

"Good Lord, Watson," said Mycroft Holmes. "I am sure that there could not be more than a five hundred million people on earth who would be of that persuasion. The Mohammedans, the Hindus, and the Buddhists would join forces overnight and start cutting our throats in the streets."

Here I felt myself on safer ground. "When I was in Afghanistan, I observed many of those faiths, and they rather did not like each other at all. If brought together, they could not agree on the time of day. How say you that they would collude against us?"

Yet again, The Look. In unison. This time, Sherlock Holmes took it upon himself to enlighten me. "My dear doctor, you are quite correct in your observation, but you cannot forget that while they do not like each other in the least, they dislike us even more. You might say 'The enemy of my enemy, and the enemy of his enemy are my friends.' There is nothing like a shared foe to unite the heathen."

I had to admit that he had a point there, and so said nothing else, but found myself worrying about what a dreadful and treacherous mess our young client had stumbled into. Neither Holmes spoke for a minute and to my relief sat and glared at each other, mercifully ignoring me.

"Very well, Mycroft," said Sherlock Holmes. "I will devote myself to your cause and do my bit for the Empire, and my very best for my client."

"Very good," the elder brother replied. "Keep me informed about any matter as it occurs. None of your grandiose saving everything for your *deus ex machina* at the end of the play. I have neither the time nor the patience for your theatrics." With this, he stood and departed. Holmes and I sat in silence until we heard the unmarked police carriage depart.

Chapter Four

In Quest of a Solution

"First things first, Watson," said Holmes rising from his chair. He descended the stairs and opened the door to Baker Street. I heard the distinct coded set of blasts on his whistle that he used to summon his beloved Baker Street Irregulars. Through the window, I could see about half a dozen of them assemble in front of him. I watched as he chatted with them for a few minutes and then sent them scattering off toward the center of the city. He then turned, climbed back up the stairs and entered the room.

"There are three matters upon which I would value your insights, my friend," he said.

"So far today my value appears to have been worthless," I said, not a little hurt by three visitations of The Look by the Brothers Holmes.

"Oh please, Watson. There is a sporting chance that, unlike those matters you commented on earlier, you might, in fact, know something about these items.

"The first matter," he continued, ignoring whatever damaged feelings I was still nursing. "You did indeed serve in Afghanistan. As you know, during the interval after my death at Reichenbach Falls I spent some time in Tibet.

Both of us have rubbed shoulders with scores of Buddhist monks, have we not?"

"Yes, I'm certain I did. I suppose you did as well."

"You suppose correctly. We have, but Mycroft has not. So did you ever come across any order of Buddhist monks that had taken a vow of silence? Or did you ever even hear of such an order?"

I paused, searching my memory. "Now that you mention it, never. They were all rather chatty and cheerful chaps. When they were done their shift in the temples, they would be on the sidewalks and in the local restaurants talking and laughing and enjoying their everlasting bowls of curried rice."

"My experience as well. Even in the most holy of temples in Tibet, they might have been quiet while on duty, but they erupted into pleasant conversation much as our English schoolboys do when let out of church. So our muffled monks are the first place for us to start our search for the missing molar."

"And the second?"

"You are a medical man, and a very learned one, I gratefully acknowledge. Have you ever known rigor mortis to set in within a few minutes? And how can you account for that in three men, within a period of two weeks?"

"Poison of some sort. Must be."

"My conclusion as well. Yet most poisons, such as strychnine, or arsenic, or even curare from South America, while they lead to paralysis take at least an hour, and the muscles do not stiffen for nearly two. How then the immediate effect?"

I searched my memory, frustrated that it was nowhere near to matching the prodigious capacity of Sherlock Holmes. I smiled when a name and an incident popped into it. "Did I not read of some case in the past two years involving a Dr. Thomas Cream? That nasty Canadian fellow who distilled the venom of the Russell's viper. He did in a number of prostitutes who were all found with bodies as hard as cement, were they not?"

"Yes. Thank you, my friend," he said and then walked to his bookshelf. "Ah, you have confirmed my research. Here it is."

He had his scrapbook, his *Encyclopedia of Crime,* as he insisted on calling it, opened to the reports on the notorious serial killer. "Just like the villainous

Dr. Cream, our murderer has used a means that, unlike a revolver, is completely silent, but unlike most poisons acts almost immediately, leaving the victim no time to call for help or to name the murderer in his dying breath. A diabolically clever killer indeed."

"Please, Holmes. Stop rubbing your hands in glee. If coming upon a fiendish killer makes your hardened heart go all pitter-pat, at least have the decency to keep your reaction hidden. Now, what was the third item?"

"These notes. What do you think of them?"

I looked at the two notes that Miss Morstan had received along with the golden statuettes. I observed to Holmes that the handwriting appeared to be either from a young hand or maybe from one that was not very experienced or educated, as the letters were uneven and jumped above and below the writing line. They were also distinctively and unusually wide and open letters. Women tend to make their letters rounder than men, but these were exaggerated, as if they were drawn rather than being written. Hard to say, since all I had to go on was the two short messages, but the tone was curiously intimate, as if the writer knew Miss Morstan. The sign used for the signature I could make nothing of.

"This sign looks like the number three pushed over on its side. Beyond that, I have no idea."

"Very good. Very good indeed Watson. The sign is, I believe, a letter in the Sinhalese alphabet." As he said this, he walked over to the bookcase and extracted a thick volume and turned the pages for several minutes.

"Ah ha. Here it is. One of the most artistically attractive and rounded ways of writing on earth. Look at this sample in the text."

ये धम्मा हेतुप्पभवा
तेसं हेतुं तथागतो आह
तेसञ्च यो निरोधो
एवं वादी महासमणो

"Whoever wrote this note most likely first learned to write in his native language, using its letters, not ours. Hence the wide rounding he gives cursive penmanship. And yes the message does betray some degree of acquaintance with Miss Morstan, most likely from her days in Ceylon. The first message is quite a pleasant one. The second one warns of danger. We may deduce that the writer learned of the death of Miss Morstan's father during the period of time between the first and the second. He appears to be very concerned about her. I must say, my friend, you may even find yourself facing a rival for her affections," he said giving me a mischievous smile.

"I beg your pardon, Holmes," said I. "You have no right to make such a remark. My feelings toward that woman, Miss Morstan, are honorable and nothing else."

"Oh ho," chuckled Holmes, "of course they are honorable. You are quite incapable of anything less. However, you have sat and watched as I have rudely offended countless clients and never leaped to their defense or rebuked me. I do detect something beyond the usual reaction of an English gentleman in your concern for her safety and feelings. Ah ha! Do I see just a hint of a blush, John Watson? I thought so."

He clapped his hand on my shoulder. I said nothing but could feel my face reddening in spite of my efforts to control my reaction.

"Do not let me interrupt your imaginings, my dear doctor. I have a copy on the shelf of Governor Hercules Robinson's *Days in Ceylon,* and I will read up on what he says about the Kingdom of Kandy and the Temple of the Tooth."

"Quite fine. I will take myself for a walk. It would do my constitution good."

"227 Lower Camberwell Road," said Holmes, shielding his face with the now opened volume.

"What are you talking about?"

"The address of Mrs. Cecil Forrester. You are trying to read it on Miss Morstan's card on the table without bending over. It's quite a hike from here, across the Vauxhall Bridge and past the Kennington Oval. But I am sure that in two hours you will have enough time to walk all the way, stand upon the sidewalk feeling lovelorn for as long as you need, and return in time for an outing this evening in search of the Lost Tooth."

I said nothing. I pulled the door smartly behind me. A walk along Grosvenor Street and down to the Thames would be just the thing for a summer evening. Perhaps even past the river.

Chapter Five
Where's the Curry?

I returned to Baker Street later in the afternoon. I was all prepared for Holmes to be poking fun at me again, but I was met instead with a somber look on his face.

"Is Mrs. Forrester's place well guarded? How many men were there?"

"I counted four. All in plain clothes. All strapping fellows. I would guess they were marines."

"Excellent. Those are Mycroft's men. Far better than the local bobbies. Trained to the top degree and armed to the hilt. Four of them could fight off an army and still break for tea if they had to. That's good. Our client may need them. And so may we this evening."

"Why are you saying that?" I asked, feeling alarmed by his words.

"We have two missions ahead of us this evening my friend. Please enjoy your supper quickly, and we will then have to be on our way."

I sat and ate the leg of chicken that Mrs. Hudson had prepared while Holmes brought me up-to-date on the case.

"This note arrived an hour ago from Miss Morstan."

I took the note in hand. It read as follows:

> Mr. Holmes and Dr. Watson: This message was waiting for me when I returned to Mrs. Forrester's. As it

> states that I may bring friends, may I
> beseech you to stand for me in that
> role?

It was signed: Mary Morstan. The message to which it referred read as follows:

> Be at the stage door of the Alhambra
> Theater tonight at seven o'clock. If
> you are distrustful, bring two
> friends. I have news concerning your
> father. We have met before. You will
> recognize me. I am an old friend.

"I know you well enough," I said to Holmes, "to be certain that you told her we would come."

"And I know you well enough to tell her that you, my dear friend, would be with me. Ah, there is a knock on our door, and I suspect that the captain of the Company of Irregulars is reporting."

Mrs. Hudson opened the door and in an exasperated voice announced, "One of your ruffians Mr. Holmes. Really."

In bounded a young lad whom I had met several times before. It was young Gordon Wiggins, the captain of the force. Had he had a better fortune and born to an upper-class family I am certain he would have been on his way to becoming the Lord of the Admiralty. Instead, he was destined to be confined to the streets of London.

"Yes, Captain Wigggins," said Holmes, cheerfully. "Stand forth and deliver your report. At attention now, young soldier."

The boy smiled back. "Mr. Holmes sir, we did what you told us to, sir, and we spied out the Museum looking for some fellows in orange dresses, we did sir. And sure enough, we spotted them, at least the Injin, he spotted them. He knew what to be looking for sir. They all had long coats on covering their dresses, sir, but the Injin, he saw four of them and says that they was wearing orange dresses underneath sir."

"*The Injin?*" queried Holmes. "I do not recall your having told me about him before."

"Aye. He's the new boy sir. Just off the boat from India and dark he is, sir. So we're calling him the Injin. He's real quiet like, sir, and just a skinny little fellow, but smart as a whip he is sir. Been with us now for a couple weeks, sir. Cleverest spy we got sir. And he speaks a whole lot of different tongues sir. Especially those from India sir."

"Very good, Gordon," said Holmes with a smile. "And what did you learn about my odd chaps in the orange dresses?"

"Seems, sir, that there's four of them and they're doing shifts every twelve hours. Twelve on and twelve off. They enters by the back door of the Museum and they goes right down to the basement where they sits around a bunch of cases and does nothing but burn their incense. Then when their shift relief comes they gets up and goes to their rooming house, right nice one it is sir, over near Saint P's, sir. Here's the address, sir. And they goes in there and they comes out again twelve hours later and changes places and does it all again. The local fellows over there, we asked them, and they been watching them now for a week sir. Real odd blokes they said they was, sir, wearing orange dresses and all."

"Thank you, Gordon. As always you have performed above and beyond the call of duty. You will let me know when you have additional news?"

"Right sir. We left the Injin over there, sir. He said he's going to be watching the house and waiting for anyone else to show up. He's reporting to me sir as soon as he does, sir."

"Excellent. Now then here is your soldier's pay. Two for you and one for every other lad who helped. And perhaps two for this Injin chap. We wouldn't want to lose a sharp new recruit would we?"

"Right sir. Will report back tomorrow morning sir." He bounded down the stairs and out onto Baker Street, slamming the door behind him with a bang that rattled the dishes. Mrs. Hudson entered and removed the supper dishes and gave Sherlock Holmes quite the glare. He smiled back at her serenely.

"Come, Watson, the game is afoot. I have asked your lovely young lady-friend to meet us in the middle of Leicester Square at half-past six o'clock. Between now and then we have enough time to take a cab over to Saint Paul's, see the rooming house of the monks, and learn what they are up to."

We hailed a hansom on Baker Street, and the driver hustled quickly along Marylebone Road to a pleasant residential area just north of the Saint Pancras station.

"I have no doubt, Holmes," said I, "that you have a plan in mind that will permit us to walk into a posh rooming house and demand information about their guests that is, by any decent standard of English manners, none of our business."

"That is exactly what we are going to do, doctor. So please remove your cravat and collar, leave your shirt open, take off your hat and put on this cap, and we will appear as the pinnacle of obnoxious busy-bodies who do nothing else but stick their noses into other people's business and repulsively invade their privacy."

"Aha! We are posing as members of the British Press. Splendid."

I took off my silk hat and donned the cheap, worn cap that Holmes had retrieved from a pocket in his jacket. By the time the cab had arrived at the address, we had done our best to look cheaply dressed and unkempt. We left our walking sticks and anything else that might identify us as gentlemen and asked the cabbie to wait around the corner.

Before approaching the front door, Holmes slid his body through the hedge, and I could catch glimpses of him staring intently at the lawn and garden. He returned looking puzzled and said, "There are footprints all over the paths. Some are of normal pairs of boots, and some are unshod, obviously the monks. But there is one set that is curious. There is only the print of the right foot and a deep circular indentation of about four inches in diameter and, not far away, a smaller circular indentation of only one inch."

"Captain Ahab perhaps," I said. "A wooden leg and supported by a crutch or a cane. The leg being bitten off by a great white whale."

Holmes smiled at my attempt at wit. "You are most likely correct, although there is no need to postulate a whale. Men lose legs for far more common reasons. In battle, for instance. I am sure you saw that in Afghanistan."

"Far too often, yes."

Holmes said no more but walked up to the steps and knocked repeatedly on the door.

A large Celtic-looking fellow opened it. "Jeeesus, Mary, and Joseph, you don't have to be waking the dead. Once is enough. And what is it you two blokes might be wanting? Sure as you aren't looking for decent lodging as we wouldn't be allowing the likes of you in here," he said with a look of disdain at our disheveled habits.

"Oswald Spengler's the name. *The Evening Star* of London's the paper, my good chap," said Holmes, forcing a card on the burly Irishman. "We learned from our sources that you are keeping in secret some foreigners who have come from the tropics, and they might be carrying Esmeralda fever after being in contact with the goblooks bird. This here is a doctor of medicine, and we are here to examine them and make sure they won't be spreading an epidemic amongst the good citizens of London."

Holmes began to walk into the house, but he was blocked by the large body of the housekeeper.

"Well now, isn't that a shame that those fellows just aren't going to able to meets with the likes of you. We do indeed have some very special visitors from overseas staying here. Right important chaps they are. But they're having their dinner now, so you will just have to say you tried but were not able to be seeing them."

"We must see them. If you will not permit us to do so, then we will have no choice but to report that you were afraid to do so for fear that the story of their contagious illness might become known to the public."

"And will it now? You don't say. Well now, me boys from the Fleet Street, it so happens that these gentlemen are not in secret at all. Every day they'll be walking from here to the British Museum in broad daylight. They will be, every twelve hours. So you can just wait until they do so again. But it won't be doing you any good seeing as they've all taken a vow of silence. You won't get a peep out of them. But you just wait for a few hours, and you can walk and talk all the way you wants to and see whats you gets."

"We have to file our story by six o'clock," snapped Holmes. "That will not give us enough time."

"Ah, dear me, so it won't. Well then, you'll just have to make one up like as you usually do. Here now, let me give you the first line. You can say, 'Soooo, it was a fine morning and I was out a walking along the Lethe…'"

With this, he let out a loud laugh and closed the door in our face.

"Well that was a waste of time," I said as we walked away.

"Not at all. Not at all," said Holmes. "A very small thing has told us much. Tell me, what did you smell coming from inside the house?"

I thought for a moment. "Nothing unusual. It smelled like supper was being served. Rather like a good Irish stew, just what you might expect to find in a rooming house kept by an Irishman."

"Exactly," said Holmes, beaming. "And when did you ever see a Buddhist monk eating Irish stew?"

"Cannot say as I ever did. They couldn't eat anything that was not drowned in curry."

"And did you smell curry wafting from the kitchen?"

"Not even a hint. You are telling me, are you Holmes, that whoever is having supper there is anything but a Buddhist monk."

"Exactly."

"So are we just going to leave them there now?"

"Of course, we are. They can do nothing but go back and forth to the Museum, and the house is being watched by Gordon's new boy, the one he calls the Injin, and who seems to be quite up to snuff for the task."

I turned and looked back at the house. From behind a lamppost, a slight brown-skinned figure wearing an oversized turban emerged and looked back at me. He raised his small hand and gave a timid wave.

Chapter Six

The Tragedy at the Alhambra

What though the spicy breezes blow soft o'er Ceylon's isle;
Though every prospect pleases, and only man is vile?

Another cab ride took us to Leicester Square. It was approaching half past six o'clock and, while there was still light in the sky on this summer evening, the dense drizzly fog lay low on the great city, rendering the entire atmosphere eerie and ghostlike. In the square, the crowds were already starting to gather for the evening theater performances. The show at the Alhambra was a popular one. A local troupe was doing a series of hilarious sketches making fun of the German Kaiser and his sidekick, Chancellor Otto von Bismarck, and the seats were all sold out. Hopefuls were lined up thinking that they could get last minute rush seats or a place in the stands. Carriages were rattling up discharging their cargoes of shirt-fronted men and beshawled, bediamonded women.

In the middle of the square, just after half past six, we found Mary Morstan. She was outfitted in a stunning royal blue long dress, with a black silk jacket, clasped by a fine string of pearls. She was looking absolutely beautiful. I could not help but remark on how well she was bearing up under such stress.

"I confess, Doctor Watson, that I am no longer pursuing the eight-fold path to enlightenment. It has been reduced to seven. I put seven of my Buddhas into the safe box at the bank and accepted a large deposit from Sotheby's for number eight. Then I visited Regent Street, and while it may make me seem like nothing more than a shallow, materialistic girl, it does wonders for the spirits to know that I look attractive, especially when I know I am going to be meeting a handsome man in the West End of London. I smiled at her and offered her my arm, which, to my joy, she accepted with a smile. The three of us walked over to the east side of the Square and stood before the front of the Alhambra.

Suddenly a cry went up. "FIRE!! FIRE!! The theater's on fire!" We watched in shock as hundreds streamed in panic out of the front doors. I could see more exiting at the side. I feared that someone would fall and be trampled. The panic that had set in was terrifying. A moment later I heard the fire wagons clanging and the thundering hoof beats of the horses. As the last of the patrons and staff were emerging, all coughing and gasping, the brave men of the fire department were running into the burning building pulling hoses behind them. Soon they had to retreat as the flames engulfed the front of the theater. A crowd had gathered, and the bobbies kept shouting at the people to stand back. When the façade of the building cracked and fell into the street, the crowd jumped back in fear. The heat from the flames could be felt, and I knew that had anyone been trapped inside they would by now have been either burned to death or overcome by the acrid smoke and fumes. It had been no more than ten minutes since the first cry went up and the old building was already a raging inferno.

"Come. Quickly," said Holmes. "It is not yet seven o'clock. The fire is confined to the front of the building. Our appointment may still be around at the stage door."

We pushed and shoved our way through the crowds, dodged the police and fire vehicles that were approaching by way of Cranborn and Bear Streets, and worked our way south on Charing Cross Road to the back of the Alhambra. The spectators there were fewer, but the fire wagons and the firemen and the bobbies were crowded around the doors. The firemen had dragged their hoses in through the back doors and were fighting the flames from the vantage point of the still untouched stage and backstage sections of the building. I could see Holmes scanning the doors and the crowd looking for anyone who might be looking for us. I could see no one.

"Stand back! Stand back!" a shout went up. "Stretcher coming through. Stand back."

From the stage door came two firemen each carrying an end of a canvas stretcher. On it was a man's body, dressed in a tweed suit. Sherlock Holmes pushed his way through the crowd until he was walking alongside the stretcher bearers. He reached for the arm of the man and attempted to place it on top of his body.

"Sir!" shouted one of the bearers. "Do not be touching him. He's dead already."

"Forgive me," said Holmes. "I was just trying to give him a little comfort."

"Too late for that, sir. Fumes must have got to him. He was just inside the back door but stiff as a board when we got to him. Poor bloke, almost made it out. Must have inhaled some poisonous gasses in there."

The stretcher bearers were walking toward Miss Morstan and me. Suddenly she let out a cry and covered her face with her hands. She buried her face into my chest, and I placed my hand on the back of her head and tried to comfort her. Between her sobs, I could hear her whispering, "I know him. I know him."

Sherlock Holmes led us up Charing Cross Road to a small pub, the Bear and Staff. The patrons had all vacated to watch the fire, and we were able to find a quiet table in the corner.

"I can see that you are in distress, Miss Morstan, but please, I beg you, compose yourself enough to tell me about this man. You said you knew him. Who was he?"

I wanted again to rebuke Holmes, but I recognized that he was devoted solely to stopping whoever was behind this rash of murders and protecting his distraught client from harm. I gave my handkerchief to Miss Morstan, and we waited until she had taken two or three deep breaths and looked up at Holmes.

"His name was Bartholomew Sholto. His father was Major John Sholto, my Uncle John."

"What was his connection to the project your father and the major were working on," pressed Holmes. "What did he have to do with the Tooth?"

"I don't know. I don't know," she gasped. "All I know is that he worked for the Foreign Office. He had the Ceylon Desk. He wasn't the scholar that Father and Uncle John were, but he read and spoke the ancient language. I had met him on three occasions on visits to my father. I don't know what he was doing with them. I'm sorry, but I just don't know."

To his credit, Holmes was decent and civil and even considerate in responding to her. He ordered a round of brandies for us, and we sipped them in silence. Upon finishing, he turned to Miss Morstan and said, "I am going to impose on my good friend, Dr. Watson, to see you back to your home. I'm sure he will not object, will you my good doctor?"

"Not at all. I was going to offer."

"That is very kind of you," she said. We walked out into the still drizzling evening. A street Arab offered us a large umbrella for a price that was close to banditry, but I paid him and we continued back to the Square to look for a cab.

Miss Morstan looked up into my eyes. "It really is quite a pleasant evening, and under this umbrella, the rain is not a bother. I think it would be good for me if we could just walk. It is a bit of a hike all the way across Vauxhall Bridge, would you mind, John? May I call you John? And would you mind awfully if I held on to your arm?"

The dark eyes were irresistible, and part of my heart melted inside me.

"By all means, you may, Mary." I did not admit that I knew precisely how far it was to her residence and the route to take, having walked it there and back already once earlier in the day.

I was vaguely aware of two large men walking a short distance behind us and humbly admitted to myself that this lovely young woman's safety was far better served by Mycroft's agents than by my right arm. A quick glimpse over my shoulder confirmed that they had not taken advantage of the thief bearing umbrellas and were most likely becoming soaked to the skin. But then Mycroft paid them well.

At the door of Mrs. Forrester's I bid her good night.

"Thank you, John. I do feel safe with you at my side." I mumbled some self-deprecating comment and turned to walk serenely back to Baker Street. At the first corner, I ran straight on into Mycroft's marines.

"Thank you, gentlemen," I said. "I am very grateful for your service."

"Right sir. Just doing our duty sir. Happy to oblige. We have the shift for the rest of the night and following a beautiful lady through the West End was a nice break, sir."

I gave them my umbrella and went looking for a cab.

Chapter Seven

Irish Stew

I felt somewhat like a schoolboy who has been kissed by a girl for the first time in his life. As I climbed the seventeen stairs back up from Baker Street to our rooms, I stopped on several of them for a moment and remembered each part of the evening: the terror of the fire, the thrill of holding a dear young woman as she trembled, and the joy of feeling her clinging to my arm as we walked through London on a damp and foggy evening.

I entered the room only to hear the voice of Sherlock Holmes from behind his latest document. "Having trouble with the stairs, sir? The old war wound acting up? Or perhaps some other part of the constitution?"

Holmes dropped the document into his lap and smiled at me. "Why don't you pour us both a brandy. I have a long night ahead of me, and I am guessing it may be quite some time before you fall asleep."

I took the bottle off the shelf and took two snifters out of the cabinet.

"You appear to be deep into something, Holmes. Mind my asking what else you have learned since we last were together?"

"Not at all. This case is tangled and puzzling, but there is one consolation, that being that Mycroft is getting no more sleep than I am. I keep sending him notes, and he keeps sending me back files and dossiers. He must have several of his bright young slaves at work around the clock, and since he is not present, I will concede that for a government officer he is exceptionally effective and efficient.

"I sent him the address of the house we visited near Saint P and, within the hour, this very official and terribly secret document came to our door. Would you like to know who we were visiting?"

"Indeed. I have been wondering all evening who was feeding Irish stew to Buddhist monks."

"My dear chap," said Holmes. "I am most certain that your mind was entirely occupied with other much more pleasant thoughts, but nevertheless, I will satisfy your feigned curiosity."

He opened a government file and laid out a small pile of papers.

"The house is known to both the Home and Foreign Offices. The title is registered to one Daniel Parnell." Here he stopped.

"And would that be a Parnell of the great clan of the recently departed Charles Parnell?"

"Indeed, it would," said Holmes. "Daniel is a younger cousin, every bit as dedicated to Home Rule as the remarkable Charles but much more inclined to violence and radical means. So far there have been no arrests, but he has been suspected in several mysterious deaths of Royalists and anti-Parnellites. He happened to be in Madrid at the same time as that miserable forger Piggott committed suicide. He had been overheard to have made threats because of the terrible damage done by the forgeries to the reputation of Charles, and the setback it brought to the movement towards Home Rule.

"The house is leased to one Michael Murphy at a rate far below what the market is bearing for comparable properties. Mr. Murphy is also known to the nameless, faceless bureaucrats that scamper before Mycroft's whip. He is known to have been closely associated with the Irish Republican Brotherhood and the Fenians. Whitehall considers his house to be the center of Fenian activity in London."

"So then, Holmes," I asked. "Have we landed into the middle of a Fenian competition with the Buddhists to see who can give the British the boots the quickest? I'm not sure I want to be on either side of that fight, nor on either side of the Home Rule battle."

"I, on the other hand," said Holmes, "consider Home Rule to be not only inevitable but an entirely just and good cause. Mycroft and I disagree strongly on that issue and have done battle royal several times over it. I fully supported the peaceful and legal means Charles Parnell was taking before his most unfortunate early death – I even believe that he had every right to divorce the woman he had not lived with for a decade and marry Kitty O'Shea – but that is beside the point. I have no sympathy whatsoever and find it repugnant with all my heart and soul that anyone would murder another human being to advance a political cause. If that is what we are dealing with, then we are fighting people who are no more to be respected than Jack the Ripper."

"But why would some radical Fenians want to steal The Tooth of The Buddha, of all things, Holmes? What possible good can come of that?"

"It is Mycroft's theory, and I must defer to him on this, that it is all tied to what he said earlier today about the enemy of my enemy. The loss of the Sacred Tooth will cause an uproar around the world. It will divert attention and troops from Ireland, and those troops would be sent off to the Malay States, Lahore, the Andaman Islands or any other corner of the Empire where the national people are agitating to have the Empire out. It would be an ideal opportunity to rebuild the Home Rule movement after it went off the rails with the divorce and death of Parnell."

"But where does that leave us in having to find the missing relic?" I said. "And what is the connection with that poor chap who died in the fire?"

"Ah yes. Thank you for reminding me. Mycroft sent a file on him as well. As Miss Morstan correctly informed us, Bartholomew Sholto, the son of Major Sholto, was an officer in the Foreign Office. He sat the Foreign Service Exam several years ago, had risen quickly through the ranks, and had been appointed to head the Ceylon desk because of his expertise on all aspects of the island, provided no doubt by his father, the major, and his close connection with Robert Morstan."

"It still makes no sense, Holmes. Hundreds of people knew about the Tooth and scores were involved in the negotiations, transport, and security. Why these four?"

"That, my friend, remains unknown, but we may learn a little more before daybreak. Until then I am going to keep reading and re-reading all these files until I turn into a listless, faceless, soulless bureaucrat. And I suggest that you, my dear doctor, go to bed."

I rose and would have followed his suggestion except that there was a familiar banging on the door of 221B Baker Street. I moved to descend the stairs, but Mrs. Hudson was there before me and blocking young Gordon Wiggins from entering.

"It is quite all right Mrs. Hudson. I will personally make sure that nothing is damaged and he will be gone in a few minutes."

Again, the much-tried lady gave me a glaring look and let the lad free. He bounded up the seventeen stairs in four steps and barged past me into the room.

"Mr. Holmes. Mr. Holmes, sir," that lad sputtered while catching his breath. "The Injin just reported to me, sir, an I brung his report directly to you, sir, like you asked me to sir."

"Excellent, Gordon," said Holmes. "And what did the Injin report to you."

"He said, sir, that he saw a nasty lookin' chap sir, a nasty lookin' chap with just one leg, sir. He comes and visits the house sir and then he takes a cab right all the way to Brixton, sir, an the Injin he hops on the back of the cab and seein' as he is just a wee fella no one sees him, sir, an he follows the one legged chap to Brixton an he gets off by Loughborough Road, sir, an then the Injin follows him to number 209 Cold Harbour Lane. An the Injin says it's a right frightful place sir with a very large and nasty dog sir. So, he couldn't be goin' and peekin' in the windows, sir, but he says that must be where the one-legger stays, sir, because he sees him leavin' in the mornin' sir, an goin' back to the first place and then back to Brixton again this afternoon, sir. An so he tells me this, an I'm bringin' the report to you, sir. Oh, an somethin' I forgots, sir. The Injin he says to tell you that the place smells to high heaven of curry, sir."

"Excellent Gordon," said Holmes giving the lad a friendly clasp on the shoulder. "Now then, just wait a minute and I will give you a message that must be delivered immediately."

Sherlock Holmes sat at his writing desk and wrote a lengthy note. He folded it, wrote the address on an envelope, placed the note inside and handed it to Gordon. The boy looked at the address and his eyes went wide.

"Oh sir, please, you can't be sendin' me there, sir. That place, sir, it has marines and Welch guards, and Gondoliers, an Calvary sir, an they would shoot the likes of me sir as soon as they saw me, sir. I can't go near that place, sir."

"Ahh, yes," said Holmes. "Now just wait another minute and I can look after that." He opened the drawer of his desk, pulled out a signet stamp and stick of sealing wax. He melted a few drops on the envelope and applied the stamp. "There you go, Gordon. That will get you past anyone who stands in your way. Now off you go. And on the double."

Gordon did not look at all convinced but took the envelope and proceeded down the stairs, slowly.

Chapter Eight

Your Service Revolver

No sooner had he departed than there was another knock on the door at Baker Street. This time, Mrs. Hudson sent up a young man dressed in a page's uniform. "Sherlock Holmes and Dr. John Watson?" he inquired politely as he entered the room. I nodded and took an envelope from his hand. Holmes paid him and sent him off.

The note read:

```
Dr. Watson and Mr. Holmes:Please, I beseech
you, provide constant guard for Miss Mary
Morstan. Her life is in danger. Jonathan
Small will kill her. He is very dangerous.
Your lives also are at risk.

                In loving concern,
```

ω

"Holmes," I said. "What do you make of this?"

"Someone else," he said, "in addition to you, my dear doctor, seems to be anxious about the well-being of your Miss Morstan. I do not know who it is, but he appears to be on our side. As we need friends, I welcome the help. Now I must read and re-read whatever data I have and wait for Mycroft to respond" said Holmes I suggest again, my dear Watson, that you get to sleep as quickly as possible as we will most likely be out and about on the streets of London well before dawn."

I appreciated his thoughtful suggestion and did as he advised. As it was not yet late in the evening, it took me some time to fall asleep but eventually I drifted off.

I was awakened by Holmes firmly shaking me by the shoulder. "Come, Watson, once again the game is afoot, and it promises to be an interesting night. Please get dressed as quickly as possible."

A glance at my watch told me it was four o'clock in the morning. I splashed some water on my face and pulled on an informal set of clothes. A surprise awaited me when I entered our sitting room. I stopped and stared, for in one chair sat Mycroft Holmes, dressed as he always was as if he were on his way to have tea with the Queen, and in the other chair sat the lovely Mary Morstan, dressed in a dark blue frock and holding a black hooded cloak.

"Good morning, John," she said with a warm and beautiful smile.

"What, in heaven's name ..." I began.

"I sent for her," said Holmes. "We needed someone on short notice who could speak the Sinhala language, and she was the logical choice. And, to my delight, she has brought some valuable data with her. Would you care to tell the good doctor and my brother what you discovered?"

"Certainly, sir," she answered. "I spent the past several hours going through my father's papers and found the file that dealt with the project of The Tooth. In it were many items of correspondence but also this one page that is headed *The Cognoscenti*." She handed it first to Mycroft Holmes, who then handed it to me. On it were five names, and they read:

```
Robert Morstan
John Sholto
Thaddeus Sholto
Bartholomew Sholto
Chandraratna Widjikulaseria
```

I looked up at Holmes. "Four of these men are now dead. Who is this fourth one, Thaddeus Sholto? What is his connection?"

Mycroft replied, "He is the son of Major Sholto and the twin brother of Bartholomew. He is also with the Foreign Office but stationed in Ceylon. He works out of Government House in Colombo but was the principle colonial contact on this Tooth thing."

"Well then," said I, "at least he is not likely to end up stiff and dead if he is half the world away."

"He arrives on board a naval vessel this morning. It is due to dock at the Greenwich Pier at seven o'clock," said Mycroft brusquely. "If someone were waiting for him he would be an easy target. There would be no time to warn him before he came down the gangplank."

"Do you believe our one-legged man is out to get him as well? Is he our killer?"

"Most likely," said Holmes. "His file is on the table, but Mycroft can tell you about him briefly."

"His name is Jonathan Small. He is the most radical Fenian at-large in the Empire. His father was hung some fifteen years ago, one of the Fenian Dynamiters. Five years ago he took a spray of grapeshot in his lower leg in a skirmish between British Troops and the Irish Invincibles. He may have been invincible, but his lower leg wasn't. After it was chopped off, he escaped from the hospital in Dublin and slipped away from us. Last we heard someone reported seeing him in Ceylon and we have a report, hearsay only, that he was a paid assassin and may have murdered a few plantation owners, Englishmen of course. This is the first we've heard of his being back in Britain, but if he is and he is involved in this plot to steal The Tooth, then we have a very nasty piece of work to deal with."

"If our reports are correct," said Holmes. "Our murderer should be asleep in his bed in his house in Brixton. Lord willing, we should be able to take him, and free the Kandian monks without a shot being fired. So let us be off, the carriages are waiting. Did you bring you service revolver, Watson?"

I patted the outside pocket of my jacket.

"Good," said Holmes. "Mind you Mycroft has done you one better and brought six of his Royal Marines. You should not need your weapon, but it is always good to have it with us. And Watson, would you be so kind as to bring that package on the table? And please, do keep it upright." He pointed to a small package wrapped in canvas. I picked it up and felt heat radiating from it.

"Miss Morstan," Holmes continued. "You are ready?"

"What!" I shouted. "Holmes, really! You cannot possibly be expecting to bring a young woman into a situation as dangerous as we are facing."

Holmes shrugged. "Can you speak Sinhala? No? Neither can I."

I turned to Mycroft. "As a senior officer in her Majesty's Service, surely you cannot allow a woman to be part of a mission like this."

Mycroft shrugged. "We use them all the time. As General Booth once said, 'Some of my best men are women.'"

Mary Morstan slipped her arm through mine and leaned toward my ear. "At ease, John. My father used to take me on tiger hunts. And … I loved them."

I shook my head in disbelief. Was I the only decent, civilized Englishman amongst us?

Chapter Nine

No Sign of the Tooth

There were two carriages waiting at the curb on Baker Street. The one in the rear was a large one and marked with military insignia. We boarded the smaller one and clattered off down Baker Street. In the pre-dawn darkness, the streets of London were deserted, and we were able to make good time running directly along Oxford Street, then down Regent Street and through Piccadilly Circus and on to the Embankment. We crossed at Blackfriar's and carried on into Brixton.

A block from our destination on Cold Harbour Lane we stopped and disembarked. Holmes gathered our little squad on the pavement. "Dr. Watson and I will make the first approach. Once you hear my signal, an owl's call, you may storm the door, disarm the guards and seize our killer. Be very careful as he is armed with some weapon that delivers poisoned darts. They are rather deadly."

"Please bring that canvas sack with you, Doctor," said Holmes. "As we walk perhaps you could untie the top of it."

I did and from within wafted the most delicious smell. "Holmes," said I. "This smells like Irish stew of all things. What in the name of all that is holy are you going to do with it?"

"Nothing more than neutralizing their first line of defense. Come now, the wind is blowing ever so gently from the north. We will approach the back garden gate with the wind behind us."

We made our way into the back lane and up to the gate. "Please remove the pot from the bag and hold it steady."

I did as Holmes directed. Within a minute, I saw a massive dog, an Irish Wolfhound, approach the gate. It gave a few soft barks but then stood still whimpering and wagging its tale.

Holmes dipped his fingers into the pot of stew and approached the gate. "Well, hello there Murphy, my big old boy. You smell some good Irish stew, don't you, old boy? They've been feeding you nothing but curried chicken for days haven't they, you old Irish fella, you. Now there, this is what you want isn't it?"

He held out his dripping fingers for the massive hound to lick. "There's a boy. You would like some more of that, wouldn't you?

"Watson, if you could slide that pot under the gate, I think that Murphy here, or whatever his name is, will ignore everything that happens for at least a few minutes."

I slid the pot forward, and the great hound eagerly began chomping away. His long hairy tail was swaying back and forth. Holmes put his hands in front of his mouth and let out an owl's call. "Come, we'll fall in behind the marines."

As we came around to the front of the house, I could hear a loud crash and the marines knocked down the door. There was a bit of yelling and shouting and by the time we were inside the soldiers were hustling several startled and not terribly effective guards out of the bedrooms. There was no sign of The Tooth and no sign of Jonathan Small.

Holmes took a dagger out from his pocket and approached one of the guards. "Sit him down," he said to the marine, who immediately forced the man onto a chair. Holmes placed his dagger against the man's left nostril and spoke quietly. "Where is The Tooth? If you do not tell me, I will do damage to you. Where is it?"

The fellow, who I had to admit, had more guts than brains, spat in the face of Sherlock Holmes. "I'm a citizen of the bloody Empire, and I don't have to tell you anything, and you cannot lay a hand on me." Holmes looked at the marines who in unison looked up at the ceiling and began to whistle.

Holmes drove the dagger two inches into the poor chap's leg. He let out a shriek of pain followed by a stream of curses.

"A matching pair is much more stylish, don't you think my good man?" said Holmes quietly to the writhing fellow. "Would you like to feel this in your other leg?"

"Small has it! He took it with him. He has it."

"Where has he gone?"

"I don't know."

"Tut, tut," said Holmes as he lifted the dagger in the air.

"No. Honest sir. In the Virgin's name. I don't know."

"Very well," said Holmes, turning to the rest of us. "The monks are most likely in the cellar."

Two of the marines made their way down the steps. Holmes, Mary Morstan and I followed. The big fellows had come prepared and using a large jemmy broke the door open. There was limited light, and I could hear voices speaking in a strange tongue. Mary Morstan pushed her way past me and spoke some words to the inmates of the room. Four men dressed in orange monk's robes, with shaved heads, came forward. Mary continued to speak to them, and they answered back to her.

She then turned to Holmes and I and said, "They are all safe and unharmed. They are distressed about The Tooth. They took a very sacred vow to protect it, but they were overpowered and taken captive."

"Please assure them that The Tooth will soon be back in their hands," said Holmes. "And ask them if they know what happened to the man with one leg."

She spoke to them. One of them replied to her. "He says that they know the man you refer to. They saw him when they were taken and imprisoned. They hear him arrive and leave every day, and can tell it is him by the sound of his cane and wooden leg. He departed from this house just over an hour ago."

"That is not good news," said Holmes. "Come, he is on his way to Greenwich. We have to get there before he strikes his next victim."

Holmes, Mary and I hurried from the house with two of the marines. The rest were left to tend to the prisoners and the monks. Holmes opened the door of the small carriage and pulled his brother by his coat sleeve out from within. I was quite sure that Her Majesty's senior civil servant was not accustomed to such treatment, at least, not since he had escaped the urgency inflicted upon him by his younger brother when both were still children.

The four of us and our marines climbed into the large military carriage, and the driver set off at breakneck speed through the streets that led out of Brixton. Then the horses were sent galloping along Rochester Way in the direction of the Naval Yard at Greenwich. It was well over five miles to the pier, and we were fortunate that the streets had not yet become crowded with the early morning hurly-burly of London.

We arrived at the Naval Yard as the morning light was breaking. I glanced at my watch and saw that it was approaching seven o'clock. Our troop made our way quickly out onto the Greenwich Pier where the naval vessel carrying Thaddeus Sholto was pulling into the berth.

"Holmes," said I. "Look. Out there by the edge of the pier."

In the glimmering light, I could discern two figures, both standing at the spot on the pier where the ship's gangplank would be lowered.

"Does one of them have a wooden leg?"

Holmes pulled his spyglass from his inner pocket and as we hastened along the pier put it to his eye.

"Yes. That's him. Marines, take those men up there on the pier. Beware; the chap with the wooden leg is armed."

The marines broke into a run and closed the distance between us and our target. One of them shouted, "Jonathan Small! Your hands in the air. Do not attempt to resist or you will be fired upon!"

The two men saw them coming, stood still for a moment and then darted to the far side of the long narrow pier and disappeared over the edge. I heard an engine start up and saw a small, narrow launch pull away from the pier's edge and into the open water of the Thames. Once it was away from the shore, it turned right and sped downstream.

"Where can they go?" I shouted at Holmes. He turned and looked at Mycroft, whose eyes were closed. I recognized the fraternal look of deep concentration on his face. "I read the arrivals and departure schedule looking for this one. Yes. The *Spirit of Derry* departed Canary Wharf just minutes ago. It should be about a quarter-mile farther down the river from us by now. It's on its way to Dublin. That would be his logical escape route would it not, Sherlock?"

"Precisely," replied Holmes. "But how can we get to him? Can you have men waiting in Dublin? But he could get off at anyone of a dozen places before that."

"Begging your pardon, sir," said the youngest of the marines, a massive strapping fellow who looked as if he would be as dangerous in a scrum as on the battlefield. He stepped up to the Brothers Holmes and gave a salute. "Begging your pardon, but sir we are marines and we do know how to pilot a boat, sir. And if it would not be too much against regulations sir, I happen to see a couple of fine fast launches tied up right beside us sir. If one of them were to be borrowed for a bit by Her Majesty, I would think the owner wouldn't mind too much, sir."

"Excellent," said Mycroft Holmes. "Very good indeed. Boys, cast off and full steam ahead."

We lowered ourselves into some good citizen's new launch. I marveled at how Mycroft could keep his walking stick in hand, his silk hat on his head and his cravat perfectly in place while lowering his heavy frame off of a pier.

Within five minutes the marines had the boat fired up and under way. We pulled away from the pier and opened the throttle and began to fly over the water. Once out in the current, there was a bit of a chop from the morning breeze, and we bounced and rose and dived over the waves. The damp wind struck against our skin and Mary clasped my arm tightly and buried her face into my shoulder to avoid the spray. I made a note in my mind to add this to my list of adventurous outings for a future date.

The marines stoked the engine. Sherlock Holmes leaned over the bow, peering through his spyglass. Mycroft Holmes sat with his back to the wind, his hat in his lap, and otherwise motionless — a veritable Buddha with a silk hat.

"I have spotted them," said Holmes. "They have pulled alongside that coaster. Yes, I can see a rope ladder being lowered. We should be upon them in a few minutes."

Some five minutes later our launch pulled up beside the coaster. "Customs inspection," shouted Holmes.

"Be gone with you," came a voice from the deck. "We're off to Ireland. It's still part of your bloody Empire. There's no customs inspections that can touch us."

"Allow us to board, sir," shouted Holmes, "or your vessel will be impounded."

I do not speak Gaelic, otherwise I am sure I would have understood some colorful curses directed our way. A rope ladder was tossed down, and one of the marines scampered up. The rest of us followed.

Once on the deck, Mycroft produced a badge and flashed it in front of the captain of the coaster. "On Her Majesty's Service, sir. These are Royal Marines. Now stand where you are as we search your vessel. Do not attempt to hinder us or you will be arrested."

Again, I heard some words in Gaelic, but the captain and his men stood aside and remained in the stern of the boat while we spread out. Under the salt-caked smoke stack, we worked our way past crates of Tyne coal, road rails, pig-iron, firewood, ironware and trays made of cheap tin destined to be sold at exploitive prices to the housewives of Dublin.

"He could be hiding in any one of these," I said. "We will need more help to search."

"I do not think that will be necessary," said Mary. "Mr. Small is not hiding."

She gestured toward the open section of the deck at the bow. There stood a one-legged man leaning on a cane with his right hand, and holding his left hand out over the railing.

Chapter Ten

On the Thames

We walked toward him. The marines had their pistols drawn and pointed. He continued to hold his hand over the railing, and when we were within five yards of him, he opened his fist, exposing a small box, such as one might use to hold a diamond ring.

"Come forward slowly," said Sherlock Holmes. "Hand over the box and surrender. If you do not, you will be shot."

Jonathan Small let out a quiet evil laugh. "And will I be? You don't say. Well now I have myself another idea, I do. This here, as for sure you know, is the third molar of old Buddha. And either it can go drown itself in the Thames, or you can let me pass. And while you would be at it, you will let me get back in my boat and take your boat too. So, what do you say, Sherlock Holmes, do you want your Empire to blow up on you or will you be a good cowardly Englishman and do what I says?"

With this, he gave the jewelry box a small toss into the air and caught it again. He opened it and swept his hand forward and back out again over the railing, giving a glimpse of a small gleaming white object. I heard Mycroft

Holmes gasp in horror behind me. "Let him pass," he gasped. "Let him pass. The cost is too high."

Sherlock Holmes looked in anger at his brother but slowly moved aside, as did the marines. I began to do the same when I felt a movement inside the pocket of my jacket. I looked in shock as Mary lifted my service revolver, cocked it and walked to within six feet of Jonathan Small.

"*On ne passé pas.* My name is Mary Morstan. You killed my father."

"Morstan's little mongrel has more courage than the officers of the Empire, does she?" shouted Small. "Well then, how about you prepares to die?" He raised his cane about his head as he shouted.

"The cane!" shouted Holmes. "It's poisoned!"

Small was not fast enough. Mary lowered the revolver a fraction and fired. A gush of blood and bone fragment exploded from Small's right knee. He collapsed on the deck.

He let out a stream of curses and looked up at us. "Your bloody British Empire can go to hell!" He hurled the box bearing the Sacred Tooth over the side and into the depths of the River Thames. One of the marines quickly jumped forward and put his foot firmly on Small's wrist, and yanked the cane from his grasp.

Mycroft Holmes raised his hands to either side of his head and fell back against one of the stack of crates. "Oh no. Dear God. Oh no."

Sherlock Holmes looked at Mary with a look that spoke the words of anger and condemnation.

Mary turned and looked at one Holmes brother and then the other.

"At ease, gentleman," she said merrily. "It was a fake. The true Tooth has never left the Temple in Kandy."

An hour later the four of us gathered for an English breakfast at the old Cutty Sark Tavern and looked out over the Thames, the watery resting place of the tooth that was not The Tooth.

"Really quite brave of you, my dear," said Holmes to Mary. "And quite an accurate shot. Where, may I ask, did you acquire such skills?"

"My father took me on several tiger hunts. A one-legged man with a cane is nowhere near as terrifying as an approaching Bengal Tiger. Father used to say that if you were afraid, your only shot was going to miss then you had better get closer until you were sure it couldn't."

"I suppose that is good advice for hunting," said Mycroft Holmes. "I wouldn't know. However, Miss Morstan, I do believe that you owe us some sort of explanation. The government of Great Britain, the entire civil service, and even Buckingham Palace have been under the belief that the authentic Tooth of the Buddha, the Tooth that has been on display for a millennium in Kandy, had been delivered to London and was to be the centerpiece of the magnificent exhibit at the British Museum, beginning in four days from today. Your information is rather startling."

"It *is* the tooth that has been displayed and venerated by the faithful," Mary replied. "But it is not the true Tooth of the Buddha. That one is kept in a vault in the depths of the Temple. The one that is displayed is only a polished ivory copy. They would never display the real one. Not only is it far too sacred and valuable to risk its being stolen, it is brown and mottled and not very attractive, as you would expect a fifteen-hundred-year-old molar to be.

"My father and his colleagues who handled all the negotiations for the loan of the tooth knew this of course. Father had the honor of seeing and touching the real one many years ago. But he and Uncle John, and the Sholto boys all knew that there would be no exhibit worth anything if the authenticity of the relic were known to be false. Now Father and the major were true and loyal soldiers of the Empire, but you must remember that they became Asian scholars, very attracted to the teaching of the Buddha, and by anyone's judgment, more than a little odd. They decided among themselves that they would just keep their knowledge to themselves and not rain on the parade of the Empire."

"Ah yes," said Sherlock Holmes. "The Fenians devised a very elaborate attempt to wreak havoc on the Empire. Then that whole plot would have been for naught as it would be revealed that the stolen tooth was only a replica. Mr. Small and his gang would have plotted for over a year only to have their dreams of uprisings from Hong Kong to Haifa vanish. That is why he sought to remove the five people who knew the truth."

"Hmm, yes indeed," added Mycroft. "Of course, the truth would eventually come out but not before anger had swept the world. I gather that Small learned of the planned exhibit and hatched his plot while in Ceylon. I have received a note saying that the phony monks were four Fenians who managed to overpower the real chaps and then impersonate them, giving them the opportunity to purloin the tooth. All very diabolically worked out, and it would have all been for nothing.

"Permit me to ask, Miss Morstan," continued Mycroft. "When and how did you become aware of this information?"

Mary looked straight back at him and replied, "Yesterday afternoon, as I read through Father's files. There were some confusing notes that suggested the truth, but I could not be sure until I saw the tooth itself as Small waved it in front of us. When I saw that it was gleaming white, I knew that it could not be the authentic relic."

"Hmm, very well then," muttered Mycroft. "If you will excuse me I have to go and rescue the British Museum and the Foreign Office from what is sure to be a very angry British public once they learn that they have been misled for six months and have bought tickets to see a scrap of ivory. And Sherlock you will have to come with me and help Scotland Yard discern what to do with Jonathan Small and his gang."

Sherlock and Mycroft Holmes rose and walked toward the door. Well before they arrived at the exit of the Cutty Sark I saw a slight young lad in a turban step inside, waive his small brown hand at me and then disappear back outside.

"The Injin has been quite persistent, has he not?" I said to Mary once we were alone. "Above and beyond the call of duty for just another one of the Baker Street Irregulars, especially for a new boy. Quite the young lad."

"Yes. Put himself in some danger as well no doubt. If you ever catch up with him do let him know that I am most grateful and would love to get to know him."

"Of course, my dear," I replied and then changed the subject to one that was giving me some distress.

"I simply have to ask you something," I said, in as kindly but serious voice as I could muster.

Mary smiled and nodded. "Ask anything, John."

"My dear, you suspected that the tooth that had arrived in London was not the authentic one. You knew the same thing your father and the major did about the real one's being kept in the vault and never taken out. Why did you not say something earlier after you knew that the only men who knew the truth were the ones that had been murdered?"

Mary said nothing and then took a slow sip of her tea.

"I fear that if I give a truthful answer, you will run away in horror and never want to marry me."

Had my intentions been that obvious? Oh dear. Nevertheless, I pressed on. "Then it is surely best that I know now before I ask you to marry me, rather than finding out afterward."

For several seconds, she gazed directly at me with her intense dark eyes.

"Revenge."

I waited to hear more, and on hearing nothing, said, "Revenge?"

"Yes, darling. Jonathan Small took the life of my father, my uncle, and two fine young men. I knew that the evidence against him for any of the murders would be weak and circumstantial and that he would most likely walk. There could not be much more than a petty fine for stealing a fake tooth worth no more than a few pounds. So, I took it upon myself to make sure that even if he lived, he would suffer for the rest of his life for what he did. If he does not swing from the gallows, then he will need two wooden legs until he dies and has to answer before God.

"So, John, that is why I shot him. If you want you can get up and walk away, and I shall only ever be thankful for your warm and caring friendship."

It took me less than a second to respond. "There is a pleasant chapel over at the Naval Yard. They probably have a priest on duty. Do you suppose he would marry us now if we asked him nicely?"

"He might, but I fancied something a little splashier than a hasty boring chapel wedding. I would look rather fetching in white, don't you think, dear?"

Chapter Eleven

Injin

I am not at all sure what Mycroft Holmes did within the government of Great Britain, or within the labyrinthine offices of the British Museum, but within twenty-four hours a sea-change came over London. Posters that for months had beckoned the citizens to "Come and View the Wisdom Tooth of The Buddha" suddenly disappeared and were replaced with ones enticing us all to "Share the Experience of The Tooth." In just the same way as the faithful in Ceylon sat before the display of the tooth, breathed the fragrant incense, were enchanted by the hypnotic *hevisi* sounds of drums and strange woodwind instruments, now Londoners, those hard-working families who would never have the opportunity to visit India and enjoy the exotic life under the Raj, could have that same experience in the intricately crafted display rooms, faithful to the smallest detail to the temples of the East.

The posters featured gorgeous young Ceylonese women in saris that exposed their mid-section, and rather more cleavage than any mother in Colombo would permit her daughter to flaunt. The pictures of the young men, all athletic and slender, were even more daring and had them all clad in sarongs with their torsos entirely bare.

The word "exotic" was used over and over again.

The Museum raided their vaults and other public or private holdings to bring out anything that came from the sub-continent. A gilded carriage, studded with gems that had belonged to some Maharajah was borrowed from some Duke. Select diamonds and rubies were borrowed from the Crown Jewels, and since they had been stolen fair and square from India, it was only decent that they should be put on display.

Overnight the Museum restaurant changed its menu and began offering several different varieties of curry with every known meat and vegetable that could be found in the summer in London. The spice-laden dishes ranged from the utterly and typically English bland to ones which would provide the patron with a near-death experience.

Upon arriving at the Museum, visitors were given the opportunity, for a small sum, of changing into a lovely, if daring, sari or a sarong. On young Britons, these looked almost attractive if you could get over the sickly pale skin. On older patrons, suffering from the effects of decades of over-eating and the ravages of gravity, they were embarrassing. But that did not stop them being enthusiastically attired and the wearers' pretending to be exotic.

In the room that held the tooth that was not The Tooth, all lights had been extinguished except for several score of candles that lit up the glass box with the pagoda roof in which the tooth was displayed, sitting serenely on a black velvet cloth. Visitors were required to remove their shoes before coming close and warned that it was a serious travesty to point their feet at the sacred relic. The good British public obeyed reverently.

About forty young people, whose only qualification for the role was their dark skin, were quickly recruited and dressed in sarongs and saris and served as guides. They greeted all visitors with a small bow, their hands held under their chins as if in prayer, and a distinct "ayubowan" that the visitor was encouraged to return.

It was rumored that some of the racier young members of England's nobility were going to host "Tooth Parties" on their estates where guests would parade around for the weekend in saris and sarongs. Overall everything that could be thought of that would heat the blood of the English people was laid on with the predictable result that no one bothered to notice that the real tooth was five thousand miles away.

On the day of the opening of the great exhibit, I rose early and spent a little more time shaving than usual, removing all non-essential facial hair from my face.

Holmes, Mary and I were given special passes to the Museum, courtesy of Mycroft. We gawked in wonder at the displays of jewels, gold, artifacts, ancient maps, models of temples and the like. The young guides recited the story of the Tooth of the Buddha and how it had been brought by the Princess Hemamali to Kandy over one thousand five hundred years ago.

We entered the room where the tooth was on display, not wanting to miss out on The Experience of The Tooth, even if we had already had enough of an experience of the tooth to last a lifetime. We stood at the back, behind several rows of worshipful Buddhists-for-a-day.

I gave a nudge to Holmes and pointed to a small person standing near the far wall. Although the room was dark, it appeared to be the same young fellow, the Injin, who I had seen a couple of days ago. Holmes nodded and quietly walked toward him, with Mary and me following behind. When the three of us were standing behind him, Holmes leaned forward and whispered, "Good morning, Injin."

Without moving, his eyes on the display of the tooth, the young lad replied, "Good morning sir."

"Thank you for the excellent work you did for us."

"Happy to help sir. It's my job as one of your Irregulars, sir."

Sherlock Holmes said nothing for the next minute, then he leaned forward again and whispered, "Good morning, Miss Anne Morstan."

Injin did not respond. I heard Mary gasp and felt her hand clamp like a vice on my arm. Then the three of us watched as a small pair of hands lifted the turban up and one by one removed combs that were holding a mass of black hair on top of the head. With a shake, the hair tumbled down until it was covering the shoulders. Injin turned to Holmes and said, "Good morning, Mr. Sherlock Holmes," and then turned toward me and said, "Good morning, Doctor Watson."

I was looking at an exquisitely beautiful face of a dark-skinned young woman in her mid-teens. Except for the color of her skin and hair, the shape and contour of her features and her dark eyes were almost identical to Mary's.

Finally, she looked at Mary and said, "Good morning, sister."

I felt Mary's two hands on my arm and holding me very tightly. She said nothing. Her eyes and indeed her mouth were open in shock and disbelief.

Holmes intervened and stretched his long arms out around several sets of shoulders. "Enough of gawking at a fake tooth. The Museum restaurant is serving some excellent curry, and I think eating some Indian for lunch would be a capital idea." With this, he steered us toward the door.

By the time we arrived at our table, the young person who was formerly known as Injin, now Miss Anne, had removed her street boy's jacket, revealing a spotless white dress shirt, such as might be worn to one of our finer public schools. She sat down beside Holmes and across from Mary and me. The girl was obviously very tense and embarrassed and avoided looking at Mary. To relieve the tension I asked Holmes, "Really Holmes. This is amazing. How in the world did you know who this young person was?"

Holmes smiled at me and then warmly at Miss Anne. "I would like to be able to say that it was a simple matter of deduction. The notes that accompanied the gold Buddhas were in a feminine hand and conveyed a strong sense of familial concern and affection. The only person who could possibly meet those criteria would be a sister. That is what I would like to be able to say, but I cannot. The truth is that Gordon snitched." The three of us chuckled in nervous laughter. Mary continued to stare at Miss Anne, and I detected tears forming in her eyes and creeping down her fair face.

"Anything else Gordon said," continued Holmes, "is subject to skeptical review, so, if you are able to, Miss Anne Morstan, we are depending on you to tell us how it is that you have ended up sitting here with us in the British Museum."

Miss Anne said nothing and continued to stare at the space where a bowl of curried lamb would soon be sitting. Finally, she looked up and began her story in an uncertain voice.

"My father ...I mean our father," she said, looking at Mary, "was a wonderful loving man, a very successful businessman, and a great scholar. But ... but even I could see since the time I began school that he was what the boys in the Irregulars would call a chap who had gone a long way down queer street."

Here Mary laughed spontaneously. "Oh that he was. That he was. Lovable, brilliant, but certainly a very odd duck." She smiled warmly at her newly discovered sister.

"When my mother died giving birth to me, Father was devastated, and it completely unsettled him. He said that he was so heartbroken that he could not continue to live in Ceylon, and that having to look upon me every day — it is said that I look very much like my mother — would be too much for him to bear, so he told everyone that I had died as well. He placed me in a children's home in the care of the church, fully expecting me to be adopted by a loving Ceylonese family."

"You do look like Mother," said Mary. "It is as if I were looking now at the woman my mother would have been in her teens." Again, the tears began to flow, and I handed her my handkerchief.

"After five years," Miss Anne said, "no one had adopted me. The Ceylonese families, all of them, the Tamils, the Sinhalese, and even the Burghers who wished to adopt a child all preferred those whose skin was fairer than mine. There were many Anglo-Indian children to choose from and so I was not taken. Father used to say that we millions of Anglo-Indians were an everlasting biological monument to the adultery of the British Raj.

"When I turned five and was still living in the children's home, Father accepted that I was not going to be taken by any other family and he assumed his role as my father. But having told everyone, including his family, that I had died, he could not face the censure he would experience if he admitted that he had deceived everyone. So he continued to be a father to me in Kandy and to you in London," she said looking up at Mary.

Mary gave a shrug of her shoulders and said, "As we have said, he truly was a bit of a strange bird."

"So Father enrolled me at Hillwood College, an excellent and caring place, the sister school to Trinity College for Boys, where he had taught for so many years. Twice a year he came back to Ceylon to visit me. While I was in classes, he would do research at the Temple. Sometimes I would wait for him there after classes finished for the day and I became very familiar with the Temple and the relic of the Sacred Tooth. On weekends and holidays, we would take trips up to the tea gardens in Nuwara Eliya, or to the beaches, and sometimes to the hill country in the north of India. He told me stories of taking my sister on tiger hunts but said that he was too old for any more of them.

"I had done very well in school, especially in my maths. Father had told me that Mother had been a qualified accountant, so I learned bookkeeping and accounting to be like her. Even though I am still quite young, Father put me in charge of looking after his banking and business interests. That is how

I came to be the agent for the trust that came to you," she said looking at Mary, "when you turned twenty-five.

"On his last visit this past spring he was quite excited about his role in the exhibit of The Tooth in London. He said that he would not be able to come back to Ceylon for at least a year. I was very upset with this, perhaps a bit angry, and perhaps a bit jealous that my sister would have my father all to herself. He was eighty-one years old on his last birthday, and I was terribly afraid that he would die before I ever got to see him again. I begged him to take me with him but he refused, so I decided that I would find my own way to London and I came here."

"How in heaven's name did you do that?" I asked. "Were you a stowaway?"

"Oh no," she answered. "I simply bribed one of the Royal Marines who was finished his posting. I paid him to say that I was his child and he took me on board the ship with him. That way I could bring my clothes and belongings and the set of golden Buddhas that I had to send to my sister. It was not difficult. There were several other dark-skinned children on board. No one asked any questions."

"How could you have found the Irregulars," I asked. "What would have brought you into contact with our beloved street urchins?"

"I had read all about Sherlock Holmes and his Company of Baker Street Irregulars in the stories in *The Strand,* and it seemed like such a splendid adventure. When I arrived here, I found a safe storage place for my property and then came right to Baker Street and asked Gordon if I could be an Irregular. I will have to behave like a lady for the rest of my life. This was my only chance to live a life I never would again. It truly was rather fun.

"I had planned to visit my father very soon, but then I had read the news of his death. I was very distressed, but I was also frightened. When I read that his body was found to be stiff already, I knew who had killed him. School girls in Ceylon had been warned about Mr. Jonathan Small. Several plantation owners had recently died, and their bodies had been found in the same condition. Kandy is a small place and rumors are plentiful. Stories of a one-legged man who murdered people by poisoning them with venom from vipers were well-known. I was terrified thinking that he had come to London. I was worried not for myself because I knew he would never know about me, but he would know about you, my sister."

"And so," said Holmes, "you told her to come to me, and you sent warnings, and sent information back to us through Gordon."

"Yes, sir. I did."

"All very well done, my dear," Holmes continued. "I do have one last question that I have not been able to discover the answer to."

"Sir?"

'Your notes were signed not with your name but with a letter of the Sinhalese alphabet. I have tried to discern the meaning but have not been able to deduce anything. Pray tell, why that sign?"

The young woman looked rather sheepish for a short moment and then smiled at Sherlock Holmes. "When I was just beginning school my father used to tell me stories about the legends of Ceylon and especially about Princess Hemamali, the beautiful and brave princess who smuggled the Sacred Tooth to Kandy. I loved to imagine that I was the Princess of the Tooth and so I began to sign my name with just that letter. My father began to call me Hemamali, and he kept doing so until the last time we were together."

"But that letter is not in any of the words that are used for The Tooth of the Princess," said Holmes.

Here Miss Anne giggled. "No, but look." She took a pencil from her pocket and drew her sign on the back of the menu.

ශ

"Can't you see?" She asked us. "It looks like a tooth. Like the third molar of the Buddha, his wisdom tooth, the one that for over one thousand years has been in the Temple in Kandy."

We all shook our heads bewildered by our inability to see what to a child had been so obvious.

"Ah, yes," said Holmes. "I see that I have been helped in my mission by the Tooth Princess. Splendid."

"In truth, sir," the young woman replied. "My father used to call me the Tooth Fairy. So I guess that is who assisted you."

"My dear girl," I said, "you are a wonder. And you have my utmost admiration. But you must permit me to ask just one more question."

"Sir?"

"Why did you not just come directly to your sister? Why hide from her?"

She dropped her eyes to the floor, looked at Mary and quietly replied, "I was afraid. I knew that you were beautiful and blonde and accomplished, and I was afraid that you would not want a darker-skinned younger sister intruding into your life."

Mary stared for a full minute at Miss Anne. No one spoke. Then Mary said, "I welcome the intrusion. You have just helped me solve an enormous problem."

Miss Anne said nothing for a moment, seeming too fearful to ask. Finally, in a quiet voice, she said, "What was that?"

"It is a problem that I will only have once in my lifetime, and you are the solution to it. I am in need of a maid-of-honor, and who better than my beautiful little sister to stand with me at my wedding."

Dear Sherlockian Readers:

On 4 August 1892, Lizzie Borden's parents were murdered with an axe. Her trial was news throughout the US and was also covered by the British press. She was eventually declared innocent and no one was ever convicted.

Fifteen hundred years ago (more or less) Princess Hemamali smuggled the tooth of the Buddha to Kandy, Sri Lanka. It continues to this day to be kept at the Sri Dalada Maligawa temple in Kandy and is one of the most sacred relics of the Buddhist religion. It has never been put out on loan.

The Fenian movement emerged in Ireland in the 1860s as part of the resistance to English rule. It had many offshoots including some who engaged in assassination and dynamiting. One American branch tried several times to invade Canada. One would have to assume that they had not bothered to read the reports about the Canadian climate.

In November of 1882, the splendid Alhambra Theatre and Music Hall in Leicester Square caught on fire. The patrons of the theatre escaped but two firefighters died. Some twenty-five steamer pumpers were brought to battle the blaze, but the entire building was gutted.

Poisons were favorite instruments of murder amongst the Victorians. Arsenic, curare, strychnine, and cyanide were all in use. There is no known viper's venom that induces immediate rigor mortis. I made that up.

The names and locations given for Sri Lanka and India are accurate and are based on my many wonderful visits to those places during the 1980s and 1990s. One of my most memorable experiences was staying at Dr. Graham's Homes and taking a walk to the edge of the ridge. From there I looked down into the valley of the Testa River, elevation about 1200 feet above sea level. Looking up the far side of the valley, you just keep looking until you see the summit of Mount Kangchenjunga, 28,169 feet above sea level. That's five vertical miles of the earth's crust.

The symbol used by Anne Morstan— ω — is a letter in the Singhalese alphabet.

Trinity College and Hillwood College in Kandy are excellent schools for boys and girls respectively and were founded by British missionaries in the 1800s. I have been privileged to have visited both.

To the best of my knowledge, the British Museum has never mounted a special exhibit that required attractive young men and woman from the Sub-continent to serves as guides while dressed in Sri Lankan saris exposing their mid-sections. It may still happen for reasons of marketing and would likely be every bit as effective today as it was in the late-Victorian era.

A Sandal from East Anglia

A New Sherlock Holmes Mystery

Chapter One

The Monk from Bury

To Sherlock Holmes, she is always The Nun. Although, strictly speaking, she was never ordained in any holy order, he mentioned her only by that name as a mark of the respect in which he held her. There were few women and no men that he believed to be more honorable or more determined. It was not that he held any emotional affection or any feelings generated by religious affinity towards Serena Eagle. Religious superstitions and all other persuasions, including irrational love for a member of the opposite sex that could not be supported by scientific evidence were to be eschewed as they would have impaired his ability to carry out his methods of analytical reasoning and deduction. He readily acknowledged the power of both spiritual beliefs and feelings of affection to cause actions of good as well as evil in men and women. But as a detached reasoner he could only see them as a distraction and never to be given a foothold in a nature such as his.

Yet, from time to time, he would quietly retire to his chair and his beloved pipe and reflect on that one woman, The Nun, and acknowledge that to this day Serena Eagle continues to defeat more evil and bring about more good than any unbelieving detective could dare to pray for.

I had not had much contact with Holmes in the past few months. Married life kept me busy with minor repairs and renovations to our pleasant flat in Marylebone and with those amorous interludes that are necessary if a man has any hope of founding his dynasty. Holmes, on the other hand, had no use for social intercourse and refused to move from our rooms at 221B Baker Street. He continued to provide services to Scotland Yard and other clients, both institutional and private, when the usual experts were befuddled and had given up. I heard stories and rumors of his adventures, some perhaps apocryphal. I read of his being called to Budapest to solve the murder of the sidewalk concertina player; of the tragedy in Bangalore that befell the would-be snake charmer from Tunbridge Wells; and finally of the assassination of the landlord in Albania by a band of his tenants. In all of these cases, Holmes used his powers to identify and capture the killers but allowed them to escape punishment, concluding that in each case there was an argument to be made for justifiable homicide, including for the snake. I really did not know much else of what my unusual friend had been up to.

One day in the spring of 1888, in that era when doctors still made house calls, I was returning from seeing a blind alpine guide when I found myself walking north on Baker Street from Oxford Street and chanced to see an open window in the rooms of my former and affectionately remembered abode. I observed the fumes of tobacco smoke wafting out. Even on the pavement below, I could smell the unmistakable scent of Holmes's favorite Turkish brand and I knew that my friend would be present and hard at work. I rang the bell and was greeted by a beaming Mrs. Hudson, who clasped my hand in hers, welcomed me warmly and showed me in unannounced to Sherlock Holmes.

He was pacing back and forth upon the carpet, apparently consumed with thought and concentration. He gazed up at me for a moment with a vacant look in his eye as if his mind were still in another realm, but then broke into a warm smile of friendly recognition.

"Watson, my dear chap. Welcome. I see that married life has been good for you. You have lost seven pounds."

"Eight," I insisted with a self-satisfied grin.

"As evidenced by your bulging stomach that mark was achieved before your full English breakfast and a full pound has now returned from whence it had been vanquished. And how is lovely young wife?"

We continued briefly to exchange some pleasant inconsequences, a social grace for which Holmes had little patience, and then he picked up a piece of fine linen paper and thrust it into my hands.

"The timing of your visit is most propitious. You have been a faithful adherent of the Church in a way that I have deliberately failed to be, and so I bow to what I hope will be your greater insight on this letter that arrived in yesterday's post. Please, Brother Watson, read it aloud."

The letter was not signed and bore neither signature nor address.

> To Brother Sherlock Holmes of Baker Street, who in times past and in divers manners has been the instrument of Divine Justice. Grace be to you and peace from God the Father, and from our Lord Jesus Christ, Who gave himself for our sins, that he might deliver us from this present evil world, according to the will of God and of our Father: To Whom be glory forever and forever. Amen
>
> On the morn of the twentieth day of March in the Year of Our Lord, Eighteen Hundred and Eighty-Eight, there will call upon you a humble servant of the Church who beseeches your succor in a matter that is of the deepest moment and of greatest consequence to all of the British Empire and the entirety of Christendom. Your recent services in the matter of the passing into glory of His Grace the Cardinal Tosca has revealed to the Church that you are a true servant of the Lord irrespective of your inability to acknowledge your calling. Kindly indulge us in this matter and be present in your sanctum sanctorum and do not be unduly troubled in your spirit if your visitor is forbidden to reveal his identity.

"What," asked Holmes, "can you make of this?"

"I fear I see only as through a glass, darkly," I answered. "The wording makes it clear that the matter is of an ecclesiastical nature. The quality of the paper suggests that it has been sent from a Diocese Office and not a local parish, and certainly not from one of the Reformist groups." I held the paper up to the light and noticed that in the upper right corner there was a watermark of a Gothic cross and, in Old English script, the letters BSE.

"I cannot identify the bishopric of these letters," I admitted. "But one of your atlases must display the various dioceses of the country."

"Correct you are," affirmed Holmes. "I have already consulted same and the note has been sent from the Cathedral of Saint Edmund in Bury St. Edmunds, Suffolk, a location of intense religious conviction and activities for the past thousand years. If nothing else, my friend, we may have our sins revealed and admonished to walk the straight and narrow at least until whatever the matter is has been resolved."

As he spoke a quiet tapping came to the door at the base of the stairs. Mrs. Hudson descended and opened the door, greeted the caller and returned to our sitting room.

"I must say," she began, "this one has to take the cake. I thought Hank the Eighth had abolished the monasteries five hundred years ago, but this one looks like he just walked out of one this morning. He's monk, or maybe an abbot for all I know. But he certainly is an odd one and he's all yours, Mr. Holmes." She retreated and fetched our holy visitor.

I heard him step up one step and then stop and say some words in Latin. He ascended to the second, and then stopped and said some more words.

"Ah, yes, Watson," said Holmes. "And do you know how many prayers in Latin we shall have to be subjected to before our visitor enters and resolves our doubts?"

"I have no idea."

"One for each of the steps on our stairs, so how many would that be? You have climbed those stairs hundreds of times. How many are there?"

"How many? I really don't know."

"There are seventeen and our friar is reciting a Benedictine blessing with each one."

The orisons continued until our visitor reached the final step and then he entered the sitting room. His tall, lean body was entirely covered in a monk's habit, the color of coffee with a generous portion of milk. A cincture was tied at his waist and a canvas bag such as a mendicant might have carried several centuries ago was slung across his shoulder. Even though it was far from the summer season, his feet were shod only in sandals. The hood covering his bowed head obscured his face.

He stopped in our doorway and made the sign of the cross and then entered. Without saying anything or waiting for us to greet him, he crossed our floor and seated himself on the settee across from Holmes. He raised his face, displaying a full beard and long locks of hair. Even covered in whiskers it was obvious that his face was gaunt, and his shining dark eyes deeply set. He slowly brought his hands together, interlaced his fingers, and placed them in his lap. He raised his head and stared without speaking at Sherlock Holmes.

Holmes stared back at him. "Whom do I have the honor to address?"

The holy man nodded his head slowly and spoke in a deliberate cadence. "You may address me as Brother Timothy. Forgive me, Mr. Holmes, but I do not know your colleague and I am only authorized to speak to you alone."

Holmes gestured with his eyes in my direction. "Dr. Watson is my assistant and most trusted friend. You may say anything in his presence and be assured of complete confidence."

"Ah ... yes ... your Boswell. Our vows do not encourage the reading of amusing detective stories, but I confess to a familiarity with a few of them." Here he paused, turned in my direction and gave me a slow look up and down.

"Forgive me, gentlemen, if I do not reveal my identity further, but the matter I am bringing to you requires the utmost confidence and discretion."

"You have both," said Holmes.

"The matter I bring to you is of a most serious nature and could have overwhelming implications for all of Christendom."

"So you said in your note," said Holmes. I could wickedly imagine that inside his head Holmes was about ready to shout "For God's sake, cut the nonsense and get on with it!" but he held his tongue. The monk spoke again, slowly.

"The matter that brings me to seek your counsel began nearly a decade ago. You may have heard that some ancient manuscripts were discovered in a library on the coast of France that pertained to the ruined abbey in Bury St. Edmunds."

"The story was in *The Times*. I read it when it was reported," said Holmes.

"Ah ... yes ... it was of some minor interest to the Press. The manuscript gave the locations of the burial places of the abbots who governed the monastery beginning back in the sixth century."

"So it was reported."

"Ah ... yes ... and recently a small group of scholars has been diligently excavating the graves and have discovered the remains of the abbots."

"That has also been reported," said Holmes, a note of impatience slipping into his voice.

"Ah ... yes ... that is the reason for my seeking your help."

"Very well then," snapped Holmes. "If His Grace, William Sidney Ormsby, Bishop of St. Edmunds would state his case I should be able to assist you."

The head of our visitor jerked upwards and his angered eyes glared at Holmes. He stood and walked quickly over to our bay window and remained there for almost an entire minute. Without turning back to face us, he slowly undid his cincture, pushed his habit off his shoulders and let it drop on the floor. He removed the beard and wig and dropped them on top of his monkish vestments. Then he turned back to face us and I could see that he was wearing a black suit with a dark purple shirt front and a clerical collar. The legs of his trousers had been rolled up to allow for his sandals. Without saying a word he returned to the settee carrying his mendicant sack in hand and sat down.

"Excuse me, gentlemen, while I get rid of these silly sandals. My feet are freezing in this weather. I have no idea how friars of olden times managed to wear them all year long. The country must have been warmer back then." From his bag, he extracted a polished pair of shoes and two thick socks and put his bare feet into them. Once his chilled toes had been safely looked after he sat back, crossed his arms and looked directly at Holmes.

"I am indeed the Bishop of St. Edmunds and my disguise appears to have been a foolish waste of my time."

"Not at all, Your Grace," said Holmes with a warm smile. "But a man's eyes do not lie. Your photograph has been in the Press on several occasions and your distinctive eyes are unmistakable. Otherwise, your disguise was excellent and I may copy it someday if the occasion requires. But please sir, enough of distractions, how may we be of help to you? Please, just state your case as clearly as possible."

"I am not accustomed to conducting meetings with detectives, but the matter is potentially so explosive that I had to come here myself. As I have already said, we have carried out excavations of graves in the ruined abbey."

"You have indeed already stated that."

"We found more than the bones of the ancient abbots."

"That is not surprising."

"What we did find, and have not made the public aware of, was indeed a surprise. In truth, it was a profound shock."

"And what was that?" asked Holmes. He had sat upright in his chair and brought his hands together.

"A sealed canister. It was in the casket of Hugh of Northwold, who led the monastery from the year 1215 to 1229. The wax seals had never been broken and the contents were in pristine condition."

"An archeological treasure," I exclaimed. "The scholars at the British Museum will be delighted."

"It is not a treasure," said the Bishop sharply. "It is a potential disaster. And no one, scholar or otherwise, is prepared for the contents. It would spell a sea-change in Christendom as we know it."

Holmes shrugged. "Voltaire made similar predictions and the churches of the land are still prospering. What could possibly do more harm than the Enlightenment?"

His Grace ignored Holmes's question and continued.

"You are aware, no doubt, that in the year 1215 King John had a meeting with his barons and earls in the field of Runnymede."

"Of course," I replied. "They forced him to sign the Magna Carta."

"Were you also aware that in the fall of the year before, in 1214, most of those same barons, earls, bishops and archbishops met in the Abbey of St.

Edmunds and prepared the first draft of the document they wished to place before the King?"

I searched my memory of my boyhood school days. "Vaguely I remember something about that. But it was not of any serious importance since the decisive event did not occur until the following year."

"That, sir, is what we all believed. It now appears that we have been quite wrong for these past seven centuries. What was found in the canister was an early copy of the document that had been prepared the previous year. It was much shorter, only some thirty clauses not sixty-three of them."

"Ah," I interjected, "then we had a Minor Carta before the Magna Carta." I was attempting to be light-hearted, but neither Holmes nor the Bishop seemed amused.

Ignoring my jest, His Grace continued. "We assume that many of the additional clauses in the Runnymede document were added in the intervening months. Those added were almost all somewhat frivolous ones about fish traps, confiscation of horses and carts and timber, debts owed to Jews, transport of Welsh prisoners and so forth. But the substantial clauses concerning due process, the consent of the governed, free movement of goods and people, taxation, the power of the council of barons and the like were all in place in 1214.

"Forgive my ignorance, Your Grace," said Holmes. "But wherein is the disastrous problem? If the additional clauses were added and agreed to by the nobles and King John, what does it matter if there was an earlier more concise version?"

The Bishop nodded in agreement with what Holmes had said. "The great tribulation that we are facing will not arise from what was added, sir, but from what was subtracted."

"You are saying," I offered, "that there were clauses in the original, concise version that were removed from what was presented at Runnymede."

"You have spoken correctly."

"But only the actual Magna Carta was signed by all the nobles and bishops and the King," I continued. "So it alone has the force of British Common Law. Any earlier document may be a splendid artifact, but the content only matters to scholars, and they never present that much of a problem to the country."

"Ah, that, my son, is where you err," replied the Bishop. "The original document is in an exceptional state of preservation and it clearly shows the marks of not only the barons, earls and bishops who were the representatives of the people of England, it also has the unmistakable seal of the King."

"But he wasn't there, was he?" I objected. "How could he possibly have signed and affixed his seal?"

"Again you are correct. He was not there but his appointee, Peter des Roches, the Chief Justicar at the time, was there as his designate, had the seal with him, and signed and sealed the document with the full authority of the King."

"Ah, so it is an official document and should have been part of Common Law for lo these many years. Is that what you are telling us?" I queried.

"That is again correct."

"Well then," said Holmes, "could Your Grace please enlighten me. What was in the original Charter that was removed and that is of such great concern to you?"

"Perhaps you are not familiar with the contents of the Magna Carta, my son?

"I am quite certain that I was compelled to read it as a child in school," replied Holmes a little testily. "I am equally certain that I have not looked at it since."

The Bishop smiled and nodded, and deliberately brought his hands together in front of his chest. "Then you will not be aware that there has been a longstanding debate amongst scholars concerning the hypothesis related to the seventh and eighth clauses, those that speak to the rights of widows. These clauses are not connected in content to the clauses that come before them and seem to have been truncated. It has been argued for many years, but particularly since the advent of the science of higher criticism, that we had only received a redacted version."

"And now?" said Holmes.

"Now we have the full original text. I do not have it in front of me, but the words have been seared into my memory from the hours I have sat staring at them in the past few weeks. The preamble references the Holy Scriptures, and in abbreviated but unmistakable Latin it says,

Autem, Scripturas docere non est Iudaeus neque Graecus non est servus neque liber non est masculus neque femina omnes enim vos unum estis in Christo Iesu."

The clergyman looked at Holmes and me. It was obvious that neither of us was about to attempt an extempore translation.

"Ah yes," he said, "I see that your Latin has receded along with your history. The words are from the third chapter of the Epistle of St. Paul to the Galatians. The introductory words mean simply 'Whereas the Holy Scriptures inform us' and then the words of scripture, as translated in the Authorized King James version say, 'There is neither Jew nor Greek: There is neither bond nor free: There is neither male nor female. For you are all one in Christ Jesus.'"

I nodded. "I am familiar with those words. They come around regularly in the readings from the New Testament, and are quite the favorites of clergy in their homilies. I have always thought that they described the dream world of the good St. Paul, and not one that the Church ever had any interest in seeing happen this side of Heaven."

"Yes, my dear doctor," the clergyman agreed. "Your insights are quite accurate. It is now almost nineteen hundred years since we were given those words and we have chosen consistently to fail to put them into practice. However, it appears that those who gathered at the Abbey in 1214 were quite serious about turning those words of exhortation into action. For the words of Scripture were followed first by a clause that forbade any discrimination against the Jews and accorded them the full rights and protection accorded to all Englishmen. Prior to that time, they had been specifically excluded the rights of protection by a Lord and were directly subject to the whims and taxes of the King."

"Did I not read somewhere," asked Holmes, "That a rather nasty massacre of them took place in Bury St. Edmunds not long before 1214? And then in 1290, we expelled the lot of them from Great Britain. I would have to say that regardless of whatever attempt was made at according them justice in your original Charter, the effort has a colossal failure."

"Sadly, sir, you are correct. Our history shames us, and it is only now, some six hundred years after expelling them that they have finally been accorded full rights within the British Empire. Tens of thousands of them have recently arrived on our shores seeking sanctuary from the pogroms of Russia. It has indeed taken us a long time to do what we should have done centuries ago."

"The second reference," I noted, "was to 'neither bond nor free.' Did the good folks who gathered in Bury also agree to free the slaves?"

The bishop smiled back at me. "That, sir, is precisely what they did. Instructions were included that would have immediately abolished slavery. Had those clauses been permitted to remain in the Charter, England would have been free of the abomination of slavery five hundred years before Mr. Wilberforce and his colleagues so pricked our consciences that we finally ended the practice. Had that happened there would have been no slave trade. Slavery could never have been started in America while it was still a British colony, and their terrible war between the States would not have been fought. Again, we continued in darkness for a long time but did eventually come to see the light. Now all men are free regardless of their color or creed."

"That leaves women," said Holmes. Then he waited for the bishop to respond.

"Indeed sir, it does. And the following words were written: *iura omnibus hominibus, eaodem omnuim iura mulierum sunt, aequiter et sine exceptionibus.* All the rights given to men are also given to women, equal and without exception."

"Oh my indeed," said Holmes smiling. "If that were to suddenly become the law of the land England would be a rather different place would it not? I rather suspect that we would be much better off."

"Please sir, this is not a matter for jest," said the bishop. "It would be a disaster if such a change were to sweep the Empire."

Holmes differed. "If half the population of the realm were immediately to be treated fairly and equitably, I can't see how that would be anything but an improvement."

"For goodness sakes, Mr. Holmes. We who try to care for the spiritual and other needs of the people have a hard enough time now trying to get men to take responsibility for their wives and children. The Christian faith makes it very clear that men are to protect and provide for their families. It is men who were told to toil in the fields and provide food by the sweat of their brow. It is men who labor in the mines and the factories to earn wages to bring home to their households. It is men who are pressed into service in our armies and navies to defend our country. Our entire way of life rests upon the moral responsibilities demanded of men.

"If all authority were taken away from men, if men were to be informed that women are to be their equals in all respects what hope would we ever have of keeping them faithful to their wives, of not deserting their posts, of not walking away from their employment? Perhaps some day, Mr. Holmes, our men will be prepared to accept women as completely equal and still behave responsibly but we are nowhere near to that today. If such a change were to become the law of the land overnight, total chaos would descend on all classes, from the greatest earl to the peasant farmer. It would apply not only to the women of England, which would be bad enough, but to all the women in India, and Africa, and even in Ireland. Sir, can you not see? It would be a disaster.

"Not only would it destroy the social fabric of the land, it would also apply to the Church of England, the third great branch of the universal holy and apostolic and catholic church. We would have to ordain women as priests and bishops. If that were to take place, then all hope of reunification with the Church in Rome would be lost forever."

Here he stopped. The poor old cleric was obviously deeply troubled. Holmes said nothing and just stared at the man for some time before he responded.

"Whatever happens to society and to the Church is none of my concern. The law is the law and even if it sometimes is an ass, it must be obeyed. If you are asking me to assist you in keeping this document secret then you are asking me to break the law and I refuse, and I must ask you to please leave and never to seek my services again." Holmes had a cold and stern look on his face and I could tell that he was struggling to control his temper.

The bishop dropped his head into his hands and said nothing. When he raised his head, there were tears in his eyes. "I am not asking you to break the law, Mr. Holmes. What you say is correct and, Lord willing, we will all have to find the strength to make the changes that will be brought upon us. What I am asking you to help me with is to recover the Charter. It's been stolen."

Holmes's countenance changed abruptly. A warm smile crept across his face. "Well now, for heaven's sake Your Grace, why didn't you say so at the outset? We could have avoided all that history and theology. Instead, we have a serious crime, a priceless historical document has been purloined." Holmes was involuntarily rubbing his hands together. "Now that is a matter in which I may be able to assist you. Please, my dear Bishop Ormsby, give us the facts of your case, as precisely and exactly as possible. Start with the discovery of the ancient sealed vessel."

The Bishop hesitated, perhaps nonplussed by the barely disguised glee of Sherlock Holmes when presented with a unique and interesting crime. Then he shrugged his shoulders and began his account.

"It took some time after the discovery of the document in France for the excavations at the Abbey to get underway, but by last summer, we had assembled a small team of scholars – three young graduates, all with impeccable academic records as well as unquestioned devotion to the Church. As students, they had joined the Franciscan Order of the Anglican Church and while not seeking ordination as priests or nuns, they have devoted themselves to scholarship and to service to the poor. They worked diligently all last summer and located the graves of many of the abbots and had begun a very careful program of excavation and preservation. They carried on through the winter snow chipping away at the frozen ground. Three months ago they opened the grave of Hugh of Northwold, the abbot who led the monastery at the time of the Magna Carta, and it was in his grave as I have told you that the sealed canister was found. It was carefully opened and the contents revealed. Within a day, they realized what had been discovered and within another two days, they had read and translated the Latin clauses. They are quite gifted young scholars and the Latin language has not changed since the thirteenth century. The discovery was brought to my attention. There was no attempt to keep it a secret. At first, I felt great excitement but it was soon replaced with deep concern about the implications of the contents. As you have discerned sir, it would affect Common Law and cause a sea-change within the Church and the Empire.

"The Charter was kept in a locked room in the chancery, but foolishly it was not guarded beyond that. Two weeks ago it vanished."

"Very well, then," said Holmes. "The ordinary course of thieves stealing artifacts is to demand a ransom for their safe return. Have you had such a demand?"

"None at all."

"Any demand that you take some course of action else the document would be destroyed?"

"No. Nothing at all like that."

"Any rumors that the thieves have approached other museums on the continent or in America and offered to sell it. It would be quite the coup if it could displayed in New York or St. Petersburg. Any such news?"

"Not a word."

"Very well then we shall have to start to solve the mystery by asking who could have access to it. Who could have had the opportunity of stealing it?"

"Oh, there is no mystery there at all, Mr. Holmes. We know who took it and it is still in her possession."

Holmes stared at the bishop in disbelief. "Then why on earth are you consulting me? Call in the police and have them arrest the thief."

"I have already told you, sir, that we cannot permit the contents of the document to become known in one fell swoop. Certainly it has to be made public, but it must be done gradually, decently and in order. If it were turned over to the police, then it would become public immediately. That sir, we must avoid at all costs."

"You said 'her.' Are you saying that some woman has taken it?"

"Ah yes, my son. It was indeed some woman, some exceptional woman who has taken it – Sister Serena Eagle. Are you familiar with her family? They are very wealthy and very well-connected."

"Kindly look her up in my index, Doctor," murmured Holmes. For many years, he had adopted a system of docketing all paragraphs concerning men and women, so that it was difficult to name a subject or a family on which he could not at once furnish information. In this case, I found the entry on the Eagle family sandwiched in between the Chief Rabbi of the Congregation Shearith Israel in Manhattan and that of a Naval Admiral, who had recently been reassigned to a post in Switzerland.

"Let me see," Holmes said. "Hum. Made their fortune in mining in Tanganyika. Came to England from Prussia a hundred years ago, anglicized their name, and have become one of the most successful mineral refining firms in the Empire. They still carry on operations in Germany under the name of *Adler Bergbauunternehmen* of Cologne. Where is our Sister Serena? Ah yes. Here she is. Last entry two years ago. Studying for her doctorate at

Cambridge. Active member in Anglican Order of Franciscans. Hum. Clearly a bright and dedicated young woman.

"Very well then," continued Holmes. "Go to her and get it. The Church of England has no shortage of money. Buy it back."

"Impossible. You have never met a young woman like her. She has the resolution of a Bismarck and the integrity of a saint. She is passionately committed to full and equal rights for women and believes that we want the contents of the Charter to remain unknown. Even if she did not have a farthing to her name, she would starve before accepting a bribe."

"Declare the document a forgery."

"Not a hope. It is so obviously authentic that there is not a scholar in the land who would challenge it."

"Send your best scholars and convince her of the error of her ways."

"We tried. She argued back every point and made us look like fools."

"Then hire some skilled thieves and rob her. It would not be the first time the Church has stooped to breaking the law."

The old bishop looked deeply hurt and ashamed. "We tried. We searched her room twice at the Abbey. She has secreted the Charter away somewhere. That is why I am here, Mr. Holmes. We have exhausted our options."

Sherlock Holmes first gave the old clergyman a hard stare and then closed his eyes for a full minute. When he opened them, he nodded, unsmiling, and said, "Very well then, Your Grace, I shall accept this case and will work diligently so that the stolen document can be returned to its rightful owner, in strictest confidentiality. I will use such methods as I consider appropriate and will report to you once I have succeeded. I will not have my task interfered with in any way and expect no more than my usual fee for my services. Is that agreeable to you, sir?"

"It is everything I hoped for sir. May the Lord bless you and keep you."

The Bishop rose and prepared to depart the room. He glanced at his monk's robe, sandals and hair pieces on the floor. "Could you be so kind as to ask your landlady to dispose of these for me? They were not my most useful investment."

Holmes nodded and smiled. The Bishop departed with no further words between him and the detective.

He looked at me and could see that I was giving him a bit of a sideways look. "Yes, Watson? I can almost hear you shaking your head."

"Frankly Homes, I am more than a little surprised that you took his case. You know perfectly well that there are powers not only within the Church but amongst the high and mighty who will make certain that the document will not become known to the public, ever. And yet you agreed to retrieve it and return it to him."

"My dear Doctor," said Holmes with a condescending smile. "I agreed to no such thing. I said that that I would find the document and return it to its rightful owners. Under English law, all such antiquities belong to the Crown. Once I have possession of it, I will deliver it to the British Museum and let them sort out how to resolve whatever problems arise. Now then, if you will excuse me, I have to prepare for a short journey to Bury St. Edmunds."

Chapter Two

The Saintly Sister

For the next two days, I heard nothing from Holmes. When a note arrived saying that he had returned to 221B Baker Street, I made haste to meet him and asked him about his investigation in Suffolk. He came as close to giggling as I have ever seen Sherlock Holmes. "Well, really," he cried and laughed heartily some more.

"What is it?" I demanded of Holmes

"It is quite too funny. I am sure you could never guess how I spent yesterday evening and this past night and what I discovered."

"I can't imagine. I suppose you were watching the habits and the actions of Sister Serena Eagle. "

"Quite so, but the sequel I observed, or I must say what I heard since I did not witness anything with my eyes, was most unexpected and puts our saintly sister in an entirely different light."

"Very well, Holmes. Get on with it."

"I disguised myself in the character of a solicitor by pasting on an oversize mustache and darkening my eyebrows, adding a little powder on my hair to look as if I had recently removed my wig, holding a cigarette under my eyes until they were acceptably bloodshot, and carrying a bulging valise. So of course, everyone in Bury spotted me as a member of the Inner Temple the moment I stepped off of the train.

"I went straightaway to the Cathedral's kitchen and caught the staff on their morning tea break. I apologized to the good ladies for interrupting them and informed them that I was in urgent need of their assistance in resolving a rather tricky legal question concerning the Abbey and Cathedral."

"That would most certainly attract their attention."

"Exactly. I informed them that a wealthy gentleman from The Cotswolds had recently died and that he had at one time been a pilgrim to St. Edmunds. He gave their dear saint full credit for his having become a successful and wealthy lawyer. He had returned annually and prayed to the saint for the continued expansion of his wealth and success in the courtroom and his prayers had been answered without fail every passing year."

"I rather suspect that the dear saint would not be thrilled to have such credit given to him."

"If it had been true no doubt dear old Eddy would be weeping in his grave. Nonetheless, with all solemnity, I informed them that in addition to a generous bequest to the Cathedral, the old lawyer also set a sum to be divided amongst the currently employed staff of the Cathedral and Abbey, who diligently cared for the property and made it such a green and pleasant place for him to visit.

"Now it wasn't a huge sum, only thirty pounds per individual or per family, but it was our duty as the solicitors for the estate to make sure it was distributed fairly and that no one was left out, or that no unjustified person became a beneficiary. And could the dear ladies please, since I knew that they were far more reliable authorities than whoever kept the payroll accounts, give me the names of all those who currently – at least from the first of March on – worked at looking after the Abbey and Cathedral.

"As I had expected I set the cat amongst the pigeons and didn't they have a good argument. They made all sorts of comments that were amusing and that I pretended to find very funny. As you know, my good doctor, people will go on telling you everything you need to know if they believe that they are entertaining you. So the ladies kept on being comediennes and I kept on laughing along with them. It was a more enjoyable tea break than I could ever have imagined. But in the end, I had a complete list of the working staff. And then I pointed out that I saw three young people working in the archeological excavation and asked if their names had been included.

"They muttered back and forth and then agreed that even if they were only new boys and a new girl they had been working since the previous summer and so, yes, all three of them: Brother Godfrey Norton, Brother Nathaniel Buddlesby, and Sister Serena Eagle, must be included as well. Then one of the ladies quietly asked if they should be considered as three individuals or as one individual and one family.

"Well didn't that sent them all into a titter. It was as if someone had told a rather off-color joke that all understood but knew that they really should not be laughing about. I gave them a look of exaggerated confusion, which sent them into further convulsions of stifled laughter. Then the head cook took charge of the situation and explained.

"She made it quite clear that they did not wish to speak uncharitably about anyone, least of all the two young people in question. All of the staff agreed that the young woman, Sister Serena, was not only the most beautiful thing under a bonnet in all of East Anglia, but had the kindest and most compassionate spirit of any young woman to have ever visited the Abbey, and goodness knows they had seen a few hundred young female visitors over the years. And the young gentleman, Brother Godfrey Norton, was as fine a young man as could be dreamed of by any mother in all of England, with the manners of a prince and the looks of an Adonis. The joke amongst the staff was tied to their observations that there was a surprising degree of familiarity between the two young people. Not that there was anything unseemly taking place, but only that the way they looked at and spoke to each other, the amount of time they seemed to be chatting together, and the way they held their bodies when in proximity to each other had been noticed. So much so that it had become a topic of gossip amongst the staff and the amusing source of the laughter. But the good cook went on to confirm that indeed the diggers, as they called them, truly were wonderful young people and as deserving of any share of benefit as the rest of them.

"With that information in hand, I thanked them profusely for their time, and the delightful conversation over tea and took my leave. I was now even more determined to find out whatever I could about our saintly sister, Miss Eagle. Throughout the remainder of the afternoon and from a distance I watched the diggers through my spyglass and even in that short period I could detect a level of friendly familiarity between Sister Serena and Brother Godfrey, which surpassed that which is normally appropriate for a brother and a sister. They were quite obviously romantically attracted to each other."

"Very interesting," I observed. "Please, Holmes, continue. This is becoming quite the adventure."

"I continued my vigil until darkness fell and watched until the two of them had parted for the night; he to a cottage, along with Brother Nathaniel, and she to a separate cottage, which she appeared to have all to herself. Now spying upon a young woman is not a particularly decorous aspect of being a detective but is sometimes necessary, so I hid in the bushes and waited for over an hour until she had extinguished the lamps in her bedroom. I assumed that she had gone to sleep for the night and prepared to depart when I saw the door of the cottage silently open and the lovely sister quietly emerge and walk quickly along the path that leads into the townsite. I followed her and to my surprise, she went directly to the Angel Hotel, the same one in which I had booked a room. So, being a guest, I followed her inside and watched as she asked for her key and made her way to a garden room suite on the first floor."

"Aha," I added pleasantly. "It appears that our lovely young sister has a bit of a double life going on does she?"

"She is of dubious and questionable character and does indeed have another life, and more than either you or I would have ever suspected. I exited the hotel again, telling the front desk that I was only going for some indulgence in fine tobacco and would return within the hour. I went immediately to the window of her room, which conveniently opened onto the back garden and had been left ajar by an inch or so, and seated myself in between some barberry bushes and prepared to listen. For the first twenty minutes, I heard only the sounds of the wardrobe opening and closing as the young lady was undressing and preparing for bed. I had concluded that there was nothing more to be learned beyond the fact that she had come from a wealthy family and understandably preferred the comforts of a good hotel to the spartan furnishings of her cottage at the Abbey.

"To my surprise, I then discerned that there were footsteps in the garden and that they were coming directly towards me. I had no path of escape but to push myself back into the barberry bushes and have my hands and face filled with prickles and thorns for my effort. Stepping right into the place where I had been sitting came none other than the handsome young Godfrey Norton. He tapped upon the window and a moment later it was swung open and he hoisted himself up and through and into the lady's bedroom."

"Goodness gracious," I exclaimed. "That is terribly indiscreet behavior for a young man and woman of any order, let alone those who wish to have futures in the affairs of the Church. There must have been some very pressing reason. The missing Charter perhaps?"

"That, and more," said Holmes. "As I listened in I heard them making some idle chit-chat about the day, as all couples do. Then he asked her quite directly if she was still sure about what she was doing with the Magna Carta. She responded by assuring him that it was hidden in her flat in London and then launched into a fairly short but impassioned speech about votes for women and the rights of women and so forth. He replied with 'That is just one of the many reasons I love you, darling.'"

" 'Darling?' He called her 'darling?'" I queried.

"His exact word. And then my dear doctor, the conversation ended and was replaced first with some warm and loving phrases, then progressed to the obvious sound of exchanges of physical affection, and a few minutes later to what were clearly the sounds of a conjugal relationship that was not only passionately romantic but well beyond wildly erotic, athletic, and of unlimited animal instincts."

For a minute I was speechless. "Holmes. I'm shocked, shocked. Are you really saying that this apparently pure and chaste young man and woman, servants of the Church, were carrying on an illicit relationship? That's … that's appalling."

"I confess, my dear Watson, that I was thoroughly surprised as well. Even for a professional detective, the continuing loud and earthy sounds were too much to be endured. I still am an Englishman and a gentleman, even if you sometimes think that I fail as both. I had to remove myself from the bushes, enduring another round of thorns, and retreat to my room. In the morning, I returned to the Abbey grounds and observed our not-so-chaste young devotees emerge from their respective cottages as if nothing whatsoever had transpired during the night."

"Well Holmes, you've walked yourself into a regular stunner here, haven't you?"

"Indeed, I have. But it has handed me a card to play that I never expected."

"And what card is that?" I asked.

"Why blackmail, of course. Perfectly legal, mind you. Tomorrow morning you and I will travel up to Bury and confront the would-be nun and demand that she either turn over the Charter to us or I would expose her scandalous behavior to her family, the Church and the Press."

"Why, if you did that her life would be ruined."

"Precisely. She will have no choice but to comply."

I thought for a moment and then gave my friend a hard look. "Sherlock Holmes, I know you. And I know perfectly well that you would never, indeed could never, make good on such a threat. It would be a violation of your moral principles, and you do have them in spite of your attempts to pretend they do not exist."

Holmes returned my look and then his face softened into a warm smile. "Ah, my dear, dear friend. You do know me, all too well. Of course, I would never expose a young women or a young man for nothing more than being overtaken by their understandable physical appetites. I could never do any such thing. However, the young couple in question does not know that. And they could never risk the consequences. So that card remains a good one to play."

I nodded my agreement and we parted for the evening, agreeing to an early meeting with each other on the next morning.

Chapter Three

Murder and More

At seven o'clock the following day, we met at the Bishopsgate Station on Liverpool Street and caught the early Great Eastern Railway train to Bury St. Edmunds. The powerful S69 4-6-0 locomotive pulled us speedily along. We arrived at the station in Bury by nine o'clock and made our way through the few blocks to the Abbey.

After rounding the final corner before the entrance to the grounds of Abbey, we stopped in our tracks and stared. Parked at the entrance was a large brougham bearing the markings of Scotland Yard. It was one of their special carriages, pulled by four horses and equipped with a bell and wind-up siren that they used only for truly serious situations.

"Good heavens," I gasped. "Do you suppose that the secret of the stolen document got out?"

"Stolen artifacts, no matter how precious, do not warrant four horses," replied Holmes. "Something much more sinister awaits us, I fear."

We entered the grounds and could see several men clustered around the door of the Cathedral. One I recognized immediately as our not-always-friendly colleague, Inspector Lestrade. We walked directly towards him. Upon seeing us, he first reacted with surprise and then gave a bemused shrug.

"Well, well. If it isn't Holmes and Watson. Holmes, you never cease to amaze me with the efficiency of your sources. We came racing here at breakneck speed as soon as we got the telegraph and then an hour later in strolls Sherlock Holmes. So, very well then, good morning Holmes. And what might I ask brings you to the Abbey of St. Edmunds on this fine spring morning?"

"We are simply paying a call on a client," replied Holmes with feigned nonchalance. "And permit me to ask in return what brings Scotland Yard up to Suffolk on this lovely early April day?"

"I am merely paying a call on a murder."

"A good reason to make a journey from London, I agree," replied Holmes, continuing the repartee. "Might I ask about the victim? Anyone, I would know?"

"Just a college boy from Cambridge. Name is Nathaniel Buddlesby. He's been here on some sort of a fellowship for the past year, digging up the bones of old abbots. And might I ask about your client? Who would hire Sherlock Holmes and have him come from London all the way to Bury so early in the morning?"

"His Grace, the Bishop Ormsby, has secured my services on what is an understandably private and confidential matter," said Holmes.

Lestrade nodded. "An important client indeed, Holmes. And since he is a man of God and servant of the Church I must assume that he is now communicating with you from the Great Beyond."

Holmes looked puzzled. "No. His communications so far have been personal and face-to-face."

"That's good," said Lestrade. "But from now on his communications will have to be by way of divine revelations seeing as how your client is in his room in the rectory with a bullet in his head. Victim number two."

Holmes's eyes widened involuntarily. Lestrade went on. "Sorry Holmes. That wasn't fair. Whoever killed the college boy also murdered your Bishop."

For a minute no one said anything. Then Lestrade spoke in a more friendly tone. "Since your client is dead and gone I really should tell you to get gone as well and not interfere in a police investigation. But I know you do have some good theories from time to time and right now this case is a complete puzzle. So since you are here anyway you might as well stay and help us. Mind you, I am not engaging your services, but I know full well that your strange brain is already running a mile a minute and you are not wanting to be left out. Am I right Holmes?"

"Yes, Inspector. I fear you know me all too well. Might I further impose upon your good graces to provide me with whatever details you and your men have determined so far?"

"Would be happy to do so. Let us walk over to the refectory and have the staff prepare a round of tea and some nourishment. We've been up for several hours now and I need something to help clear my head before listening to what Sherlock Holmes might have to say."

We walked past the ruins of the old abbey and into the dining building. The staff were obliging and obviously under terrible distress caused by the events of the past night. They said little to us, but one of them kept giving strange looks to Sherlock Holmes and then shaking her head before returning to the kitchen.

"This is all we know so far," began the inspector. "Somewhere close to eleven o'clock last night, after all the lights had gone out, some person or persons unknown, and we believe that there must have been at least two or maybe three of them, entered the grounds and proceeded first to the rooms of Bishop Ormsby. They wake up the old fellow – he was in his bed clothes when we found him – and beat him up pretty badly. We're assuming that they wanted him to reveal something. But he doesn't talk. So they gag him and tie him up and then turn his rooms upside down, obviously looking for something. Are you with me so far, Holmes?"

"Pray, continue," came the reply. "I will interrupt only if I fail to follow you."

"Right. So after they are finished and don't find anything as far as we can tell, instead of just leaving the old man securely bound and gagged they put a bullet in the back of his head from close range. Does that suggest something to you, Mr. Holmes?"

"Obviously, their motive was robbery but not restricted to that," replied Holmes. "They also carried out an execution. Did no one hear a gunshot?"

"No one yet that we've talked to. But that's not surprising. These old buildings are spread apart. They've got thick walls and it was a cool evening so the windows were closed. The staff live in the town, not on site. So no one hears anything. Well then after that they proceed to the room of the college boy. I guess he was more than a boy. He had already graduated with a handful of degrees and was here on some archeological fellowship. There's three of them here in fact. I'm not quite sure how they fit in and they may be candidates for being priests and a nun, but I don't have that one sorted out yet."

"If I may," said Holmes. "I believe you will find that all three, the two young men and the young woman, were members of the Anglican Order of Franciscans. It is a lay order of the Church of England for those who wish to give extensive service to the Church but still have other full-time vocations."

The inspector raised his eyebrows. "I see Mr. Holmes knows a bit about this case already. Very well then, permit me to continue. After doing in the Bishop, they enter the room of one Nathaniel Buddlesby and give him the same treatment. I mean they tear his room apart and then they shoot the poor chap in the back of the head. Another execution. Then, and again we're not sure of the timing or order of events, they head to the room of the other young man, a Mr. Godfrey Norbert, and then over to the cottage where the third student, Miss Serena Engel is living and they devastate their rooms as well."

Holmes interrupted. "I believe their names are Norton and Eagle, Inspector."

Lestrade gave Holmes a look and shook his head in disbelief. "I am sure that those are not the names in my notes, and I am equally sure that you are right and at some time in the very near future you will explain to me how it is that you are right. But for now, I will continue. Godfrey Norton is not in his room. Neither is Miss Eagle. Their not being in bed and asleep has made them a very lucky couple of young people. Otherwise, they would likely have been added to the victims. Either the murderers gave up after not finding what they were after or something scared them off, for it happens that not too long past midnight young Mr. Norton returns to his room and finds it in chaos and raises the alarm. He finds his friend, Mr. Buddlesby, dead and then runs to the Bishop, and then runs into town and wakes up the constable and he sends a wire down to Scotland Yard and the boys at the Embankment office come and rouse me and here we are. And so far Holmes, that is all we know."

"The young woman? queried Holmes. "What about her?"

"As far as we know, she is thrown into full terror and goes running into town and wakes up the livery office and has them drive her back into London. We don't know where to yet but we can find that out from the livery chap. I would have preferred that she had waited around, more convenient for us and all, but I can't blame her. Her friend and the Bishop are murdered and she barely escapes, so if I were her, I suppose I would run away from here as fast as I could too."

"You say you questioned the young man, Mr. Norton. Did he offer any explanation for his being away from his room at such an hour?"

"Oh yes, and a likely story indeed. He said that he and Sister Serena – that's what they call her – needed to have some serious discussions over the hypothesis and sub-hypotheses of the preliminary thesis they were forming about the bones of the old dead abbots and that walking through the town in the late hours of the night was the only isolated time available to them to have these discussions. I am sure Mr. Holmes, that you would agree that he gave us an entirely credible explanation."

Holmes gave a knowing smile. "Perhaps his memory was clouded by the weather."

"Must have been as it was bloody cold last night. Now we at the Yard have a rule that we never make accusations of hanky-panky without reasonable evidence, so all I can say is that I was young once and my fond memories of those days have not been lost, if you know what I mean. But it does not matter as it is not useful for the case as far as I can tell. If they were engaged in amorous pursuits, then they can thank their romantic souls for the fact that they're alive." Here he paused briefly and looked at Holmes. "So there Holmes is all we know so far. Any of your brilliant theories to offer to me?"

"It is obvious that the attackers were intent on finding some object, most likely an artifact of some sort of great value to them," said Holmes.

"Thank you indeed for that insight," said Lestrade sarcastically. "Any young bobby could have told me that."

"I am quite certain he could have," agreed Holmes. "And so we must move on to the next question, the one the ancient Cassius admonished us to ask, of *cui bono?*"

"Thank you again, Holmes, for offering a free lesson to school boys and I have to say that I think I could come up with over a thousand common thieves who would steal a valuable artifact and sell it to any one of a thousand pawn shops throughout the land. Your theories so far and not exactly what I would call enlightening."

Holmes nodded. "And just how many of your thousand common thieves would engage in premeditated cold-blooded murder and risk certain swinging from a gallows for something they could pawn at a local pawnshop?"

"Very well. That does narrow the field considerably."

"And of those who would take such a risk, how many would also have any knowledge of the local history or archeology of Bury St. Edmunds?" asked Holmes.

"Wonderful Holmes. The answer is 'none.' Now you have reduced the list to zero and left me no farther ahead."

"And now, back to *cui bono*. How many men, who are at one and the same time cognizant about the value not only of the object, and about the information related to the object, and are in a position to gain or lose massively in some way connected to it, and are such cold-blooded killers that they would execute a bishop and a young student without hesitation? Do any such men come to mind Inspector?"

"Can't say as they do," said Lestrade. "I could come up with a few who would might have the knowledge, but they wouldn't strike me as capable of these murders. And I can think of a few groups of killers, but none who have a farthing's worth of learning about ancient artifacts. There's none that would fit both camps."

"Precisely. Which leads to the inevitable conclusion that the former very likely hired the latter to do what they wanted but were unable to do themselves."

The inspector made no reply and then nodded. "I agree, Holmes. So we're looking for a small team of ruthless hired killers, no doubt going for a very high price, who are prepared to rob and murder without hesitation and they are in the temporary employ of some chaps who have an enormous amount at stake, so much that they are likewise willing to risk the gallows. Whatever it is they were looking for must be more important than I could ever imagine."

"Indeed Inspector, that is what you and the band of killers, and their employers are all now looking for. And its significance must be of earth-shaking importance."

"So what are you telling me, Holmes? That I'm off to find the one and only Holy Grail, and when I do there will a note scratched into the cup saying,

'Sorry boys. I've called our supper off because of the rain,' and it will be signed by J.C. Himself? Is that what I supposed to be looking for?"

Both Holmes and I laughed at Inspector Lestrade's suggestion. His sense of humor was, if anything, ever scarcer than that of Sherlock Holmes. His cynical suggestion struck us both as absurdly funny.

"Oh my, Inspector," sputtered Holmes between chuckles. "Forgive me. I truly underestimated your imagination. No, my good man, nothing quite of that magnitude, but I suspect not all that far behind and perhaps of the same order. And please, Watson, I do hope you wrote that one down. It surpasses anything I heard recently from Oscar Wilde."

I nodded and tapped my notebook with my pencil. "All duly recorded, sir."

Holmes then rose and smiled at Lestrade. "I fear that I have reached the limit of my theories so far, my good Inspector. May I ask you to excuse me from any further discussions until I have acquired more data and a greater degree of certainty? I assure you that I will report back to you in forty-eight hours at the most, and shall impart any and all information I have obtained at that time."

"Right, Holmes. As you wish. You have your methods I know and even if they are unorthodox, they do seem to work from time to time. So do as you will. The two murder scenes are guarded and undisturbed so you can go and crawl around them with your glass to your heart's content."

"That is very considerate of you Inspector," said Holmes with a gracious smile and nod. "However, my investigations are leading me back to London and I must decline your offer and be on my way."

Both the inspector and I looked at Holmes, as this was entirely out of character for him. He gave us both a blank look in return and rose from his place and began to walk towards the doorway. Inspector Lestrade and I caught each other's eye and both of us shrugged our shoulders. I rose and followed Holmes. I almost had to run to catch up with him as he made his way quickly over the grounds and towards the road into the town.

"Good heavens, Holmes. Where are you off to in such a mad dash?"

"To the livery station."

We continued our forced march past the houses and tradesmen's shops, across the High Street and, with the help of a local cabbie found the livery station in a lane just around the corner from the railway station. The sign proclaimed *BSE Livery: Deliveries to All of Suffolk*. Through the window, I could see a chap wearing his coat and scarf and sitting with his feet up on the desk. His eyes were closed.

Before entering, Holmes turned to me. "I will use the wager maneuver. Please play along."

He then knocked loudly as he opened the door. The poor fellow was obviously sound asleep and woke with a shock. He stumbled to his feet. "Oh. Good morning gentlemen. Sorry about that. Had a right early start this morning I did and I was just catching up on my forty winks. Sorry, there sirs. How can I be of assistance to you gentlemen this morning?"

"Terribly sorry ourselves to have disturbed you, sir," said Holmes with a touch of the theatrical. "My friend and I have gotten ourselves into a frightful argument and have ended up in a wager and we are both so sure of ourselves that we have five pounds riding on it. And you, my good man, are the one who can be the judge. May I appeal to you sir for your expert information?"

The chap smiled a toothy smile. It seemed that any good English workingman was always pleased to be called upon to settle a wager between gentlemen, and at five pounds this was most assuredly an important matter. "Happy to oblige in whatever manner I can, sirs. Must say you've caught my interest. Can't think of much here in Bury that would be worth a five pound bet on a weekday morning. What is the matter of the wager, sirs? Honored to provide a judgment if it is in my power to do so."

"My good man," continued Holmes. "It runs like this. My friend here is a hopeless romantic still living back in the days before steam power. He contends that a sturdy carriage with a strong pair of horses could get us to London faster than the Great Eastern. I told him that he was living in the past and that the train could get us there faster than even a galloping brace of stallions. We argued all the points of the matter and now have five pounds riding on it and when we saw your sign we knew we had found our judge. So sir. What say you? Which one of us is to be the richer man?"

The liveryman laughed pleasantly. "Oh my but you blokes will find anything to bet on won't you? So let me give you a clear and unequivocal answer to your question sir. The definitive answer is … it all depends." He laughed again.

Holmes returned the laugh. "And on what, my good chap, does it depend?"

"Well now it all depends on what you mean by 'London' doesn't it? It a rather big place London is. So if you mean somewhere in the far east end, almost out to Barking, that's one thing. But if you're talking about all the way across the town to Kew then that's another matter. Before I can pass judgment, sirs, you will just have to be a bit more specific, you will sirs."

"To our door," I stated in a playfully authoritative manner. "To our door."

"Well now sir," said the liveryman with a grin, "I suppose that helps you, but it doesn't do me any good seeing as how I have no idea where your door is."

"Baker Street," I said. "Close to the Marylebone Station."

"Well now, I just happen to know pretty much exactly then the answer to your question as I had a delivery to that same part of London town just this morning. It's on account of that I was napping when you entered. So yes, I can give you a definitive answer now to your bet."

He walked around from behind the desk, sidled up beside me and put his hand on my shoulder. "I thank you, sir, for bein' a lover of horses. Bein' in this business, my mares are my first love. Don't be tellin' my missus that, mind you. And it breaks my heart to say so sir, but your steam engine friend has the better of you. I just made a run a few hours ago straight from here to St' John's Wood and even with the roads clear and the mares runnin' it took me two minutes under four hours. The GER will get you to Bishopsgate in less than two hours and I don't believe that even the slowest cabbie in all of London, and there are some slow ones, would take much more than thirty minutes to get you home from there. I wish it were otherwise, sir, but you are a poorer man now than when you entered my establishment." He gave my shoulder another good clap and I responded with a pat on his back.

"Don't be troubled at all sir," I replied jovially. "I am quite sure we will have found something else to wager on before we leave Bury. I fully expect to recover from my loss." I repeated the pat on his back and turned to Holmes and pulled out my wallet. "Very well, this round is to you."

"Ah but one mustn't be too hasty to collect one's winnings. Bad luck you know," said Holmes. "Now five pounds is a serious wager and not that I, for a second, would doubt the word of our judge, but it is only the word of one witness and it was the middle of the night. Do you have any evidence, I don't know, your log perhaps, that would back up your memory? Always best to settle a wager in a manner that is irrefutable you know."

"I have just the thing." He reached into his coat pocket and pulled out his log book. "Here it is gentlemen. Most recent entry, made only a few hours ago."

Holmes and I looked at the penciled entry. It read:

1:00 am. Young woman. One bag. Direct to Briony Lodge, Serpentine Avenue, St. John's Wood. Delivery completed 4:58 am.

"There it is, gentlemen. In black and white. So no arguing about it. And better luck next round my friend," he said, directing his last words to me.

We bid the friendly fellow good day and began to walk towards his door when Holmes stopped and turned back to him. "I'm dreadfully sorry. This is inexcusably poor manners on my part, but my curiosity just will not let it go. It is none of my business of course, but what in heaven's name was going on that a young woman is running off to London in the middle of the night? Your log entry is altogether too intriguing to pass without asking about it. Could you explain just a little sir? Of course, it may be entirely a confidential matter and if so just say so."

The fellow pulled out his log and looked at his latest entry again and smiled. "I suppose you are right sir. An entry like that would set any imagination going. There's nothing confidential about it sir seein' as I don't know anything very much. But I'll tell you whatever I know and you'll just have to imagine the rest. It was a very unusual night it was, last night. The missus and I had had our tea and gone to bed and were sound asleep when about half past midnight there's a knockin' on the door. And there's this young woman, not really young mind you, about twenty-five, give or take, and just about the most beautiful young thing I have ever laid eyes on. So I open the door and she's all manners and gracious and terribly-sorry-to-have-bothered-you-sir but she has to get to London and it has to be right now. Well, I was all ready to send her on her way and tell her to wait at the station for the morning train and she offers me twice my standard fare. Now that would end up bein' more than I do in a whole week in and about Suffolk, so I agrees and gets myself dressed and goes and gets the horses harnessed up. The missus, she makes the young lass a pot of tea and puts a bit in a flask and gives her some biscuit and a blanket seein' as it was a wee bit nippy outside last night it was, and the lady gives me the address and makes sure I knows how to get there and she climbs into the carriage and we start to drive. She said she wanted fast so I set the mares at a steady gallop and we make a dash down to Chelmsford, and I stop there to let the horses get some water and oats. So I open the door and ask if you is havin' any problems and she says she's fine and on we go again. The roads are empty, the air is cold but the moon is shinin' down and it's just a sort of pleasant night that no one but a driver all by himself in the moonlight can know, and at just before five in the morning I arrive at her address. She thanks me, gives me another sovereign for my efforts and disappears. And that sir is all I know. Nothin' confidential there. Was it an affair of the heart? Maybe. Did her favorite auntie die? Perhaps. I will never know, sir. And it looks as if neither will you."

"You are quite right sir," replied Holmes. "My curiosity will never be satisfied. But it will have to do. I thank you again, sir. And here, for your troubles and being such an excellent judge." He tossed the man a sovereign.

"Oh, really sir. Not necessary. Pleasure talkin' to fun-lovin' chaps like you."

"Absolutely necessary," said Holmes with a wink. "A gambler must always be prepared to pay his dues to the judge. Only proper form, you know." We all laughed once more and then Holmes and I began to walk quickly down the street.

"Where to now, Holmes?"

"The fastest way back to London. Or did you wish to make a wager on what that way might be?"

"Hmm. My money is on the train."

Chapter Four

My Service Revolver in St. John's Wood

Once inside our cabin Holmes immediately closed his eyes, brought his hands together and pressed his fingertips against each other. He held that pose for a full half-hour.

Occasionally I could see his lips move almost imperceptibly. He briefly opened his eyes, adjusted his sitting position and looked out the window at the pleasant small farms and woodlots of Suffolk as they entered our vistas and then faded into the distance.

"I really must ask you, Holmes. You were given an opportunity to take a close look at two fresh murder sites and you turned it down. You have never turned down any such thing in my memory of working with you. Instead, we make a beeline back to London. Just what is going on?"

He looked at me in a not entirely sympathetic manner.

"Elementary, Watson. About how long did it take me to discover the address of the young nun, or whatever she is, Miss Eagle?"

"Oh about ten minutes. But that hardly answers my question."

"It answers it completely. If it took me that long, it will not take a band of killers much longer to find out the same information. They will be on their way to murder her in the very near future. Her paramour, Mr. Norton, is now surrounded by a dozen police officers and as long as he remains at the Abbey he is quite safe. She on the other hand, in understandable panic, has fled and in doing so has left any protection behind. She has made herself an easy target for whoever these killers are and I have to get to her before they do, else she will soon be dead."

He said no more, closed his eyes again and resumed his pose of intensity all the way to Bishopsgate Station. But now he was adding scowls and furrows of his forehead to the movement of his lips.

We hailed a cab at the station and Holmes gave the driver our address on Baker Street.

"Really Holmes? Do you not want to get to the young woman's address directly?"

"Perhaps I should, Watson. But I am on the horns of a dilemma. I have a pressing moral obligation to make sure this poor, fearful young nun is protected from a set of ruthless killers, but I also have an obligation to my client."

"But the Bishop is dead."

"True, he is. But he was acting on behalf of the Church of England or, at least, a certain set of offices within the Church, and so my obligation to them survives his passing. The young nun who is needing my protection is also the thief from whom I must retrieve the Charter if I am to fulfill my obligation to my client."

I nodded. "Yes, Holmes. You have yourself a dilemma. And how have you decided to solve it?" It was clear by the determined expression that had taken over his countenance that he had reached some sort of conclusion.

"If I were to appear on her doorstep as the detective, Sherlock Holmes, I am quite sure she would be very guarded in her conversation with me if she agreed to speak at all, suspecting the reason for my visit was tied to her possession of the Charter."

"I am sure she would. It would be a bit on the obvious side," I asserted.

"We have made good time from Suffolk so I shall take a few minutes to stop by Baker Street and assume a disguise. And I think I have an excellent one in mind, left behind by our dear departed Bishop."

At 221B Baker Street we stopped and asked the driver to wait for us. Holmes ascended the stairs, entered our rooms and disappeared into his bedroom. Mrs. Hudson, always considerate of us, brought in some tea and light lunch. When Holmes reappeared both Mrs. Hudson had to look three times and we laughed in amazement, for there in front of us was an ascetic monk, with full beard and shaggy hair. He was covered from shoulder to ankle in the same tattered cassock that the Bishop had worn. A hood covered his head and almost obscured his face. In his hand was a long walking stick. He looked as if he had stepped out of the pages of the medieval church.

"Well, Holmes," I said in between chuckles, "at least no one will mistake you for a detective."

"I think not. By the way, Doctor, I shall want your co-operation."

"I shall be delighted."

"You don't mind breaking the law?"

"Not in the least."

"Nor running the chance of arrest?"

"Not in a good cause."

"Oh, the cause is excellent. We have to save the life of a young nun and save the Church from a tidal wave of change."

"The first is sufficient, although not sure about the second."

"Neither am I, but as soon as I have eaten a very fast lunch we shall be on our way."

We ate and then descended the stairs and entered the waiting cab.

"We are going to meet Sister Serena in St. John's Wood," Holmes began. "I will present myself at her door as a servant of the Church, taking up collections for the poor in, oh I don't know, perhaps Calcutta and ask if she could spare me a cup of cold water. I am quite sure, given her affinity for the ministry that she will oblige. You will approach the house through the garden and stand unseen by the window. I expect it will be open as it is now a warm spring day. You should be able to see both of us sitting in the parlor. When I give you this signal …" Here he placed his chin into his hand with three fingers spread on the side of his cheek. "…you will toss one of these items in through the window."

He handed me a small sack. In it were several smoke-rockets.

"You will then raise the cry of 'Fire, fire!' and blow on your whistle. You do have it with you? And your service revolver? Good.

"It is common knowledge that when a fire or similar disaster is sprung upon a woman, she immediately seeks to save that thing which is most important to her. I am counting on the nun to show me where she has secreted the Charter. After that is all behind us, I shall remove my disguise and have a hard talk with her about her safety and about the unacceptable nature of taking things that do not belong to you, regardless of the nobility of your motives."

"And you believe this will work?"

"I am reasonably certain. Although you know as well as I that when dealing with young women there is always the chance for something totally unexpected by a rational man."

"Hmm. Yes. Quite so."

We had the driver hold the cab out on the St. John's Wood High Street and walked the half block to Briony Lodge. Holmes waited until I had found my way through the garden, secreted myself by the parlor window and sent off a signal that sounded like an owl with a head cold. Through the shrubbery, I could see Holmes, stooped over slightly, with staff in hand making his way to the door.

I assumed that he was greeted by the steward of the Lodge and subsequently by Sister Serena for it took a couple of minutes before he and the young woman appeared in the parlor. Had I been a younger man I might have gasped in delight and surprise. Sister Serena truly was an exceptionally beautiful woman. She wore not a speck of powder or paint on her face. None was necessary and would only have served to dull the radiance of her countenance. Mr. Godfrey Norton, her paramour, was indeed one of the most fortunate men on earth.

Holmes raised his hand, made the sign of the cross and uttered some words in Latin, which I could not make out. I was tempted to shout something like, "Come on Holmes. That's a bit much. Get on with it," but I held my tongue and inwardly chortled at the absurdity of the drama I was observing.

He sipped on his water and I expected his signal any moment.

That moment never arrived. Instead, I heard some loud words coming from the front door, and then a gunshot. The lodge steward came stumbling into the parlor and fell face first on the floor. Behind him were two tall, thin, rough looking men both holding pistols. Holmes gave a fearful look in the direction of the window. I already had my service revolver in hand and through the open window, I fired it at the lower body of the first man. He dropped to his knees. The second one jumped back as I fired again, but I must have hit him as well for he collapsed to the floor as well.

Holmes turned to the young woman and shouted at her. "Serena! Get out of here! They have come to kill you. Out the back. Now! I have a cab waiting on the High Street. Take and get yourself to safety. Now! Go!" He jumped towards the crumpled men, gave each a hard knock on the crown with his staff and snatched away their guns.

The woman jumped to her feet and ran through the parlor. Before running for the back door I saw her turn into the kitchen and heard a bit of a clatter, then she ran out again bearing a valise in her hand. As she was leaving, two more men came charging in from the street with pistols in hand.

Now a band of ruthless killers in London may be adept at running into a house, shooting unarmed victims and running away again, but they do lack even the most basic training in military strategy. Such training would advise even the greenest of recruits that it is not a good idea to run upright into a field of battle, fully exposing yourself to an enemy who his armed and has good cover. So no sooner had they entered the room than Holmes and I both fired, bringing them to the floor. Again Holmes put his staff to good use and there were now four wounded bodies on the carpet of the parlor. I began to blow sharply on my whistle, but the cry had already gone out for a constable from the neighbors and other residents of the lodge. I climbed through the window and approached Holmes. He was standing with a gun in each hand over the still groggy assailants.

I checked the men over for medical needs. I had deliberately aimed for their legs, not wanting to kill them. Dead men, as they say, tell no tales, and a dead criminal is not much use when it comes to information about his network of villains. Three of them were in no danger and other than putting a bandage on their wounds I let them be. The fourth one, however, was as white as a ghost, his eyes wide in fear. He was holding his hand to his sternum and breathing with some difficulty. The bullet had hit him in the chest and come perilously close to his heart, His pulse was still strong and his breathing, while short, did not seem to be impaired. The house steward was dead, shot at close range through the heart.

Holmes doffed his disguise. Several police officers appeared, and behind them came Lestrade's assistant, Inspector Anderson. He had the four assailants shackled and put into a wagon with instructions to take three of them to the holding cells at Scotland Yard, and the fourth, under close guard, to St. Bart's for medical attention. A hearse appeared shortly and the steward's body was removed.

He questioned us and the staff and then sent us on our way. Our waiting cab was gone as expected, taken I hoped by the fleeing nun. We hailed another cab and began the short route back to Baker Street.

"Holmes," I said as we drove. "I shot at both of the two men who first came into the room."

"Indeed, you did, my friend. And a good thing or neither I nor the nun would be alive."

"I aimed for their legs."

"Of course. Always the best thing to do when stopping a crime."

"You know, it may have been some time since my military training, but I am not at all a bad shot with a revolver."

"You are an excellent shot, Doctor. You just proved it again."

'I aimed for their legs."

"You have already said that."

"Holmes. The second man had no wound in his leg. He had a bullet in his chest."

"Very well, so you are not such a good shot after all. You can pride yourself on other accomplishments."

"The bullet wound in the man's chest was not from my revolver. It was far too small. It came from a gun that was of a smaller caliber."

Holmes said nothing and stared blankly ahead. He turned to me with a look of growing astonishment.

"The nun," he said slowly, "had a gun."

"She must have. She must have had it in her close possession all the time she was with you."

"And," he continued in a hushed voice, "she aimed right for the man's heart, and almost did him in."

Both of us said nothing for the next half block. Then Holmes smiled. "Well Watson, she most certainly is some nun."

"Most certainly she is."

By then we had arrived at 221B Baker Street. Our driver pulled up behind another cab that was standing directly in front of our door. As we were paying the driver, I heard the door of 221B close behind me. I turned around and was suddenly speechless. Exiting from our door was Sister Serena Eagle. She gave me a smile and walked quickly towards the waiting cab. As she stepped up into it, she shouted across.

"Good afternoon, Mr. Sherlock Holmes." The cab moved away and headed quickly down Baker Street.

Holmes was staring, speechless as well, at the back of the disappearing cab.

"She has been in our rooms," he said, stating what was rather irrefutable. "All the time we were meeting with the inspector she was sitting up there in our rooms," he said, again laboring over what was patently obvious.

He entered the building and ascended the stairs, shaking his head in disbelief as he climbed. Mrs. Hudson greeted us as we came into our sitting room. Her face was unusually florid, there were marks of tear drops on her cheeks and her eyes were reddened.

"My dear, Mrs. Hudson," I exclaimed. "What is the matter? Are you in distress? Was that young woman bothering you?"

She dropped her head back and laughed. "Oh no, Doctor, oh no. Not in distress at all. I just haven't laughed so much over tea with a stranger in my life. Whoever she was, the newest client of Sherlock Holmes I gather, she was a treat, an absolute treat to chat with, and a beautiful young woman. We laughed together like a couple of schoolgirls. Oh my, it was fun. Did my heart good to laugh like that. I'm so sorry you missed her. She left just a moment before you returned."

"And just what," asked Holmes, who was not smiling, "were you laughing about?"

"About you, Mr. Holmes, about you," she said and started laughing again. "I am sorry Mr. Holmes. I never thought of you, being so serious and all, as something funny, but that young woman made me see all sorts of things about you that gave us a good laugh."

I could sense that Holmes was not only not amused but becoming angry so I intervened.

"Really Mrs. Hudson, what is there that could be funny about Sherlock Holmes."

"Oh, my. Well, first she arrives at the door an hour or so ago and says that she does not have an appointment, but could she, please, wait until you get back. Well, she is such a beautiful and well-mannered young thing that I could not refuse and I offer her a cup of tea. And she asks, oh so politely if she could pose a few questions to me about Sherlock Holmes. No harm there so I tell her to ask away. Then she begins on all the disguises she has heard that you like to wear. So I start to tell her about the one you had just gone out in, and she laughs and says it sounds like a refugee from the Spanish Inquisition and we laugh and then I tell her about how you came by that disguise, how some bloke came in looking like a monk and departed being elevated to a bishop and she laughs at your ability to do miracles on monks, and on it goes. I said you had been a nonconformist gentleman and she wondered if such existed. And then I told her about the doubled up old bookseller and she gets up out of her chair and imitates you and, oh my, she was so funny. She kept laughing and so did I., Of course, it wasn't all nonsense. She asked about what you had been up to these past few days and I told her about the nasty business up in Bury St. Edmunds. It's in the papers today. No mention of you of course. And we just kept laughing about all those things about you that I never saw as funny but every time I'd say something she would find the humor in it. Oh, such a delightful young lady. I am so sorry you did not return in time to meet her, Mr. Holmes. You would have adored her."

Mrs. Hudson kept laughing as she left the room. Holmes walked slowly over to his arm chair. The anger had fled from his face and had been replaced by a look of friendly chagrin. He sat down and slowly shook his head.

"I have been bested, Watson. I have been bested by a nun. A totally remarkable, exceptional young nun. I have never run across anyone like her in my life. Truly remarkable."

He reached over for the Persian slipper and filled his pipe and sat quietly puffing on it. When finished just one pipe he extinguished it, laid it aside. There were some telegrams and letters waiting for him and he read these through. Then he drew up his legs, brought his hands together and entered the kingdom of his mind.

I let myself out of the rooms and returned to my home and wife.

Chapter Five

The Agony Column

Two days later I called in again on Sherlock Holmes. I must confess that my curiosity was eating at me and I could not wait to hear any news of the killers or the unusual nun.

Holmes was glad to see me and brought me up to date, although there was not much that was new. The nun had vanished without a trace. The killers were all now in jail and refusing to give the police any names regarding who had hired them. Holmes concluded that they must have been very well paid else they would have started singing. But once they see a gallows in front of them, he assured me, it is expected that they will cooperate. Then he changed the subject of conversation and made a request.

"My dear Watson, might I ask a favor of you on your way home? If I write a short note for the agony column could you drop it off at a telegraph office and send to every one of the major newspapers?"

"Happy to help."

Holmes rose and went over to the writing desk and wrote a short note. He handed it to me. It ran:

> Dear Boisterous Visitors to St. Edmunds: Willing to sell article you desire in return for substantial sum and pledge of safety. Contact may be made through Diogenes Club. Sister S.

"I will send this off right away," I said. "But would you mind telling me what it is about. I can see no sense in it whatsoever."

"It really is all rather elementary, my dear friend. You will recall my conversation with Lestrade when I invoked the famous question of Cassius."

"I do. *Cui bono?* Correct?"

"Exactly. So I have made some rather logical deductions and reached an inescapable conclusion. I began not with the bare question, but with a variant. Who would benefit ... most? I then inverted it and asked, who would lose the most? That answer should be quite obvious. Who, my dear Watson, would stand to lose the most if the right of male primogeniture were to be abolished?"

I thought for a minute. It was not a difficult question. "I suppose those eldest sons of the wealthiest families who might have older sisters. Today they stand to inherit everything. If the original Magna Carta were to be found and become Common Law then they would have nothing, at least not compared to what they would have had. It would mostly go to their sisters."

"Precisely. Since we know that the chaps that you and I immobilized ... or to be fair, you and I and the nun, were no more than hired thieves and killers, we also know that there is someone or some group of people who hired them. By logical deduction, we start with the group who would have the most to gain, or the obverse, the most to lose. And you have correctly identified who those would be. All we have to do is find them and see if they have been up to something sinister. If not then we move to the next most logical of suspects. If so, we arrest them."

"But Holmes, that is impossible. There are several thousand quite wealthy families in the country. Biological science informs us that the odds of having either a male first-born or a female first-born are evenly split. So half of our richest families would have sons that fit your description. That doesn't help us much does it?"

"As always, Doctor, you are accurate but as happens often you are only looking and not making logical deductions. The next question we have to ask is if there have been any reported meetings of eldest sons that have only been taking place in the past few weeks."

"Yes, yes. I can see that knowing that would help."

"Of course, my beloved Baker Street Irregulars have no access to that stratum of society so I will have to enlist my most reliable even if not my favorite source."

"You mean Mycroft."

"Exactly."

Readers of my accounts of the adventures of Sherlock Holmes will be familiar with Holmes's older brother, Mycroft Holmes. His official title indicated that he worked for the British government, but in truth, he *was* the British government. For many years, he had toiled away in an office in Westminster where he was called upon by every minister and Lord and senior mandarin to sort out the messes that they inevitably created. There was not a single file of any importance in the past thirty years that had not crossed his desk and been committed to his herculean memory. He relied on an extensive network of men and women throughout the country, the Empire, and indeed the world, to provide useful information of any and all plans and actions of significance to the government of Great Britain. He referred to these agents as his enlightened sources. There was a sibling rivalry between the two brothers that was born in their childhood and persisted to this day, not, however, diminishing their grudging but profound respect for each other.

"Ah," I said. "You are going to call in help from Mycroft's sources?"

"If you mean am I going to use his spies, you are correct," replied Holmes.

"Our remarkable nun," he continued, "and her document are safe, I assume, for the time being. The actual killers are behind bars. However, those who contracted with the killers are still walking the streets and must be apprehended to answer for the crimes they have already committed and stopped from carrying out any further actions. I fully suspect that Mycroft will know of any such recent gatherings of eldest sons and likely the names of all the participants. I have alerted him to the matter and expect reports within the day. The note you have kindly agreed to send off to the Press should provide a tantalizing bait for whoever these despicable rich boys may be."

I thought it as good a plan as any I could think of. "Excellent, then Holmes. I shall be on my way and will wire the note off before returning home. If I can be of any further assistance, I'm your man."

Holmes smiled warmly at me. "My dear friend, I would never be so unkind as to leave you out of an adventure in which you have already played such an important role. Besides, I know that your thinly concealed curiosity is burning and it would be my duty to satisfy it."

He was right. He always was. As much as I kept denying it to myself I had to admit that there was nothing else on earth that so brought my blood to life as assisting the county's finest detective in the pursuit of the nastiest of criminals. I smiled back at him and took my leave.

For the next two days, I heard nothing and it was only with a great exercise of concentration that I was able to devote my thoughts to my patients. My mind kept returning to the murders, the attack in St' John's Wood and, of course, the nun.

The headlines screamed about the murders in Bury St. Edmunds. Ordinary murders were a dime a dozen in London, but the assassination of a bishop was of a different order and led to all sorts of theories of nefarious conspiracies that were fully exploited by the newspapers. Most of the writers could not resist taking an arrogant poke at Scotland Yard for having not only having failed to apprehend the murderers but apparently not even made any progress at all on solving the case. Inspector Lestrade had, wisely, not disclosed the connection between the attempted armed robbery in St. John's Wood, and the murders in Bury, and so the Press was unaware that the killers were already behind bars while Holmes and Scotland Yard focused their efforts on trapping the criminal minds behind both events.

On the third day, a note came from Holmes asking if I could appear early the following morning at the Diogenes Club. My service revolver would not be needed, but my notebook would be required.

"The mice are sniffing at the bait," he informed me and the trap was ready to be sprung. I had no idea what his trap might consist of but, of course, I would not miss being present for the world, so I made sure that I was knocking at the door of the club before eight o'clock the following day.

The Diogenes Club is a small but highly exclusive club on Pall Mall. There is no name on the door and membership is tightly restricted. Talking amongst members is prohibited in the principle rooms but in the dining room and the small private conference rooms there have taken place meetings and conversations that have changed the course of world events. Enterprises of great pitch and moment have had their currents turned awry more than once as a result of a handshake in the Diogenes Club, and no member of the public, or for that matter most of the government, was ever the wiser.

Mycroft Holmes was a founding member of the Club and allowed his brother to make use of its splendid offices when the need arose. He had given my name to the front desk and I was welcomed by the porter.

"Good morning, Doctor Watson," the chap behind the desk said warmly. "Delighted to have you here. You didn't by any chance bring any extra copies of the latest *Strand* did you? The boys here won't admit it, but they are quite hopeless fans of your stories about Sherlock Holmes, and even though they are all awash in more money than they will ever need, the blighters keep pinching the Club's copies. We subscribe for ten copies now and there are only two left. It's a minor scandal you have brought about, doctor." He chuckled merrily as he teased me about my stories, and then he ushered me into a small meeting room in which were gathered Holmes, Inspectors Lestrade and Anderson, two other police officers and two ladies of a certain age bearing notebooks who, I assumed, were recording secretaries.

"Welcome, Watson," beamed Holmes when I entered. "Welcome to our lair. It looks like an elegant confidential conference room, but it has become nothing of the sort. The inspector has had carpenters toiling through the night making alterations. Please observe the panels in the closet doors."

I looked. Each of the lower panels in the doors of the two closets was filled with fine quality caning that had the look of having been present for at least a decade. I shrugged, obviously not understanding whatever it was that Holmes was expecting me to see.

He explained. "During the night, the solid panels were replaced by porous ones. Vision is somewhat obscured by the caning, but sound is not. When our mice come for the bait you and the secretaries and the inspectors shall be hearing and recording every word."

"And what are we going to hear?" I asked.

"Why their confessions of course," replied Holmes.

"Whose confessions?"

"Ah yes, allow me to bring you up to date on our machinations. Mycroft discovered, thanks to his spies, that there had indeed been some recent activity among the wealthy eldest sons of the realm. A call had gone out a month back specifically to about one hundred of them who stood to lose their fortunes if their older sisters took over the right of primogeniture. As far as we can tell, the great majority of them, being honorable young English Lords, would have nothing to do with what was being proposed, but a group of seventeen of them were prepared to take action. They formed themselves into the Order of Rightful Primogenitures and have held several meetings in some private clubs in Mayfair. Mycroft has even secured copies of the minutes of those meetings.

"Your note in the agony columns elicited a response and after a few exchanges, the executive members of the Order have agreed to meet with the solicitor for Sister Serena."

"Who is that?" I asked innocently.

"None other than yours truly."

"But you don't have the Charter and we have no idea where Sister Serena is."

He nodded. "Obviously. But they do not know that, and that is all that matters."

I looked at Holmes. His face was no longer open and friendly. I saw the look of steely determination in his eyes that I knew from so many times in the past when he was in hot pursuit of a criminal. I looked over at Inspector Lestrade as it was highly unusual for him to be involved in something so untypical of the pedestrian methods of Scotland Yard.

"I know," said the inspector. "It is highly unorthodox, but that is your Mr. Holmes for you. If it works, it will save us a month or more of slogging investigations. If it does not, then we'll carry on and slog. So welcome to the spies in the closet, doctor."

Chapter Six

Four Lords-a-Leaping

"Our villains are scheduled to arrive at nine o'clock, said Holmes. "I suggest that we all assume our places a few minutes in advance. There are chairs in the closets and your complete silence, of course, is necessary."

We all nodded, said little more to each other and polished off a final cup of tea accompanied by fresh biscuits that the Club had generously furnished. By ten minutes before the hour, we were secreted in our places, with Holmes sitting imperiously on the far side of a small conference table.

We sat in silence for over twenty minutes. When the quarter hour passed, I was beginning to doubt Holmes's plan and feared that our Primogenitures might have caught on to something. But no, their lateness was only due to their arrogance, not their intelligence. At twenty minutes past the hour the door opened and the porter ushered in our visitors. Through the partly obscured panel, I could make out four men, each of whom took a chair opposite Holmes.

"Identify yourselves!" barked Holmes.

"I beg your pardon," shot back one of the voices full of indignation.

"Are you deaf or merely stupid?" said Holmes. "I told you to identify yourselves. You are in a meeting in which a very substantial sum of money is possibly going to be exchanged. I have to know that I am not wasting my time with imposters. Now identify yourselves or get out."

There was silence for a moment, and then another voice, with a very proper Etonian accent, spoke. "Very well. But be advised that we will not endure a jot of disrespect. We are Lord Elderly, Lord Bottomere, Lord Sickert and Lord Camp. And who sir, are you?"

"Obviously your mommies and daddies, who have given you everything else you possess, failed to inform you that it is a violation of law to conduct business under assumed names. There are no such Lords listed in any directory of the peerage. Nevertheless, if you wish to risk that aspect of the law, it is up to you. I shall, however, address you by more appropriate names which shall be Lord Pimple-face, Lord Flab, Lord Bad Teeth and Lord Balding."

I could see one of the young Lords jump to his feet. "Just who do you think you are, sir?" he shouted at Holmes. "I said we would not endure any disrespect. Do you have any idea who you are dealing with?"

"I am dealing with four obnoxious little turds who stand to lose their fortunes to their sisters and, if there were any justice in the world, would be so deprived. Did you wish to enlighten me any further?"

The Lord brought his fist smashing down on the table and shouted, "I declare this meeting over until you learn your manners when speaking with men of our station. We will not be insulted by some pettifogging solicitor. We are leaving!"

"Teddy, shut up and sit down," came the voice of the one I thought Holmes had identified as Lord Pimple-face. "We need what this man has and that's why we're here. So what if he doesn't like us. Were you expecting a fan club? Now sit down." He then altered his voice and addressed Holmes. "We are here to purchase the document currently in the possession of a woman named Miss Serena Eagle; your client, I presume."

"That is good so far," said Holmes. "Let us proceed and I will give you my word as an Englishman that I will not repeat a word of whatever conversations we have. Do I have yours in return?"

"You do," said another one of them either Lord Flab or Lord Balding.

"My word as well," came from the other.

"And mine." "And mine," came from Lord Pimple-face and Lord Bad Teeth.

"Very well then. As solicitor for Miss Eagle, I am authorized to negotiate a fair price for the document you desire. What are you prepared to offer?"

Lord Flab spoke. "There is, of course, some question as to the authenticity of the document. We would have to have a full inspection of it first but, if you agree to that, then we are prepared to give you a note for five thousand pounds, which must be returned if the document fails to pass our tests."

"There will be no inspection period and no refund provisions," I heard Holmes say. "And you can take your note with you next time you use the loo and use it to wipe your flabby bottom."

"Bloody hell," came the sharp response from Lord Flab. "What sort of businessman are you? We do not carry out commercial dealings with those who insult us. That was a perfectly good offer. Now respond to it in a civil manner!"

"Nigel, shut up," came the muttered words of Lord Pimple-face. "We are here to get the document and close the deal. We're not housewives looking for bargains in a charity shop." He turned towards Holmes. "Please, sir. State your firm price."

"Forty thousand pounds," said Holmes, firmly as requested.

"That's bloody robbery," shouted Lord Balding. "There's not an artifact in the entire British Museum that would cost that much! Do you think we're complete fools?"

"Complete?" replied Holmes with a sneer in his voice. "Perhaps there is a part of you that is not a fool, but I have not yet seen any evidence of it."

Lord Balding stood and leaned over the table, bringing his face as close as he could to that of Holmes without toppling into the furniture. "If it were still permissible I would demand satisfaction from you for insulting my honor. I would love to blow your brains out from twenty paces."

"Teddy," came the exasperated voice of Lord Pimple-face. "Sit down and shut up. We have a deal. It is no more than you lost at the gambling tables last year. Now pull out your checkbook and write a note for ten thousand pounds. And you Nigel, and you Eustace. Ten thousand from each of us and the deal is done. Do it!"

Each of them grudgingly pulled a checkbook from their suit pockets and reached for the pens on the table. Holmes spoke.

"So there is no question about the purchase, kindly note that the funds are for the sale of the document found in the grave of Hugh of Northwold, in Bury St. Edmunds, and make the note payable to Miss Serena Eagle. No other wording or form of payment will be acceptable."

They complied and through the screen I could make out that each of them had slid their notes across the table to Holmes. He gathered them up and inspected them slowly.

Lord Balding now spoke. "You have our notes. Now where is the document?"

Holmes said nothing for a few seconds, then answered. "The purchase was only one part of the agreement. It was also stipulated that you must provide guarantees of safety and of no further attacks upon the person of Miss Eagle or any of her colleagues who have been part of this activity."

"Fine," snapped Lord Balding. "We promise to be good boys and not do nasty things to them anymore. What else do you want?" Bad Teeth and Flab laughed. Pimple-face said nothing.

Holmes continued quietly. "Two colleagues of my client were murdered. An attempt was made on her life. An inherent part of any deal is that she be guaranteed safety from here on. It is not enough for you to sit here and make childish promises and then giggle about them. How am I to know that you were the agents behind those attacks and that you have the power to now call them off? As far as I can tell not one of you has sufficient backbone to kick a puppy let alone engage in a contract with killers."

"Are you calling me a coward?" said Lord Balding, his voice elevated.

"How dare you call us cowards," added Lord Bad Teeth.

"Frankly," responded Holmes quietly. "You don't appear to have the backbone to do anything except run away from a fight with your nursemaid. No British regiment would want you anywhere close to them. You would turn you backs to a real enemy and run ... like cowards."

"That's crossing a line there Mr. Lawyer!" blaster Lord Flab. "If you think that we were not brave enough to order violence to our enemies, then you are about to be smartened up. What we did to them we can do to you."

"For God's sake, Nigel," said Lord Pimple-face. "Be quiet. You can't say things like that, you fool!"

"I'll say whatever I bloody well like to any stinking bloke who calls me a coward. I was a cadet first class at Eton and I am no coward." He came close to screaming.

"Nor I," chimed in Lord Bad Teeth. "Just what is it Mr. Pettifogger that you want us to prove? What?"

Holmes responded in a controlled voice. "Did you contract with a group of killers to murder the Bishop and the three students at Bury St. Edmonds, or are you just a pathetic group of juvenile poseurs who would pee your trousers before having the courage to take action?"

"Don't answer that, Nigel," shouted Pimple-face.

"I bloody well will answer it. We have his word that he won't repeat it. So, yes. That was us and we jolly well will do it again to your precious client and anyone else who tries to stop us."

"Prove it," said Holmes. "Prove to me that that was you behind those murders. Otherwise, there is no deal."

"No!" came from the agitated mouth of Pimple-face.

"What proof do you need lawyer-man?" sneered Balding.

"What were the names of the killers?" asked Holmes quietly.

"We don't know," said Pimple-face.

"Then there's no proof. Please get out of here. Take your money and go home," replied Holmes.

"Their names were Martin Smith, Eric Black, Tommy Stepleton, and Calvin Stout. All from Billingsgate. Is that what you want?" snapped Balding.

"How much did you pay them?" said Holmes.

"A thousand pounds each."

"You fool," hissed Pimple-face. "Stop it. You're hanging yourself."

"Prove it," said Holmes. "Prove you paid them."

"Here," said Lord Flab. He pulled his checkbook from his pocket and slammed it on the table with an oath. "Right there. Four thousand pounds. One thousand to each of them."

"You paid it all by yourself?" asked Holmes.

"Of course not. What type of fool do you take me for? My friends each paid in a thousand." He then turned to Lord Pimple-face. "Which reminds me, Derrick, you still owe me a thousand."

I could see through the screen that he was leaning over the table. In a voice that attempted to be menacing, which was not particularly effective as he was most likely a tenor, he spoke into Holmes's face. "We paid a thousand pounds each to get rid of those blighters, and we'll pay a thousand more to get rid of you. Now is there any more proof you want? Or do you want a bullet in your head? We weren't afraid to order a bishop killed and we certainly won't hesitate to get rid of a lawyer."

"No," said Holmes. I believe you have furnished sufficient proof that you are the only ones who can guarantee my client's future safety. So I agree, we have concluded our business. You may depart."

"Where's the document?" demanded Lord Balding.

"Yes," added Lord Bad Teeth. "Where's the bloody Magna Carta? Either we get that now or you get no money and no safety. Where's the document?"

"Oh yes, of course," said Holmes with bored nonchalance. "Yes, the document. Just a moment." He raised his head and looked towards one of the closets.

"Inspector, would you mind bringing whatever documents these chaps now need?"

The door to the other closet opened and Inspectors Lestrade and Anderson entered the room, followed by two police constables. I opened our door and followed the two secretaries into the room. Lestrade gave a short blast on his whistle and the door from the room to the corridor opened and two more officers appeared.

"You bloody bounder!" shouted Lord Flab, along with several oaths. "You gave you word as an Englishman. We trusted you."

"I gave my word," replied Holmes, "that I would not repeat anything that was said and I shan't. It will not be necessary. You have already hung yourself."

"You are all under arrest," announced Lestrade. "Hold out your hands and allow the constables to put handcuffs on them. Now do as you are told."

"This is an outrage!" shouted Lord Balding. "Don't you dare touch me." One of the officers, a rather portly chap, had grabbed his arm. Balding gave the officer a slap across the face. In a split second, it was returned with a hard smack of a nightstick across his nose and mouth. He fell to the floor, with blood gushing from his face. The portly officer reached down his hand. "Right mate. Bein' a good Christian, I suppose I should turn the other cheek. Want me to do that and see what happens?"

The shouting continued from three of the Lords.

"Do you know who my father is?" demanded Lord Bad Teeth of Lestrade.

"Can't say as I do for sure, but I rather suspect he's the rich earl who will be disinheriting his eldest son within a fortnight."

Within a couple of minutes, the officers had the three of those who were arguing in cuffs. The fourth, the one with the pimples and any show of common sense, remained in his chair his head buried in his hands. Holmes went over and sat beside him and placed a hand on his shoulder. The lad raised his face. Tears wear streaming down it.

"Derrick, you have made a foolish choice in your friends," Holmes said quietly, looking the pathetic fellow in the eye. "Now take my advice and don't be such as fool as to think that there is any honor in defending them. You will either have to sing or you will swing."

That lad nodded his head slowly. "Who are you?" he whispered.

"My name is Sherlock Holmes."

The lad's shoulders drooped then shrugged. "Of course. Who else?"

He rose slowly from his chair and walked towards a police officer, holding out his hands for the cuffs. The four of them were removed from the room. Anderson and the recording ladies followed. Lestrade remained behind.

"Must say, Holmes. That was quite the performance. Got them all. Hung by their own words, and I would guess it will not be long until we have the rest of these seventeen Primogenitures behind bars. Well done Holmes. Well done." He tipped his hat and departed.

I looked at Sherlock Holmes, yet again amazed at what I had observed. "Yes, my friend. Well done indeed."

Holmes shrugged. "*Dare homini satis funis* … give a man enough rope.

.

Chapter Seven

The Nun

Two days later the papers exploded with news of the arrests of seventeen young Lords, all charged with various crimes related to the murder of the Bishop of St. Edmunds and the student, the murder in St. John's Wood, and with dealing in stolen antiquities, and several other offenses that were not familiar to me. Praise was heaped upon Scotland Yard for its brilliant plot to trap the villains. The note to the agony columns was reprinted, with the explanation that Sister S, was a cryptic sign for Scotland Yard itself. The Diogenes Club was not identified, as its members would have no doubt insisted, as other than an exclusive club on Pall Mall. Holmes became "an expert interrogator from Scotland Yard whose identity cannot be revealed else it would endanger future investigations."

The four paid killers gave full evidence to the prosecution in the hope of saving their own skins. Their leader was most likely on his way to the gallows, but the other three might be given some clemency. The seventeen young Lords all came from very wealthy families and it was assumed that they would be defended by skilled barristers, although it had been rumored that one or two of them had been abandoned by their fathers and would be depending on a lawyer assigned by the courts.

The real motive behind the murders of course remained unknown, since the existence of the document, the original shorter draft of the Magna Carta, remained a secret known only by a very small handful of people, and its location known only to Sister Serena, who Holmes continued to refer to as The Nun, and whose forty thousand pounds in notes made out to her he guarded diligently.

No one had any idea where she was.

It was on a late May morning, two months after the events I have recounted above, that a note arrived from Sherlock Holmes.

```
Please, Watson. Come over at once. Something
you must see. Holmes.
```

Holmes had never yet summoned me for anything trivial or boring so I made my way immediately over to Baker Street. Mrs. Hudson welcomed me with a joyful smile and I sat down in my familiar chair, looking across the room at Holmes in his chair, pipe contentedly in his mouth.

"You must read this," he said and reached across the space between us, an envelope in his hand. I took it and read the address. It was in a woman's handwriting, addressed to Mr. Sherlock Holmes, but bearing stamps from India. In the top left corner was a coat of arms and the motto *Blood and Fire,* and an address in Calcutta. I opened the letter and read.

```
My dear Mr. Sherlock Holmes:

        Please forgive my terrible tardiness
in making contact with you. And please, Mr.
Holmes, be assured of my eternal gratitude
for your putting your own life at risk to
save mine. I shall be forever in your debt.
        I believe that I do owe you some
explanations and I pray that what I write
below will help to fill in the gaps in your
understanding of me and my actions.
        To begin with, I must admit that when
you appeared on my doorstep in St. John's
```

Wood I was immediately suspicious. You said that you were a member of the Beneficial Order of St. Anselm. I happened to know that the order had been dissolved over fifty years ago and that there were no members anywhere on earth still taking up collections. Then I saw the sandals you were wearing. They were the exact pair that had been for sale in a used clothing store in Bury St. Edmunds two months earlier and your lily white feet had obviously never spent a day in them. I was about to shoo you away when my spirit told me that you were not an enemy, but somehow a provision by the Divine for my protection and so I invited you in. Of course, I had a derringer tucked into my skirt and would have shot you on the spot had you attacked me, but I was quite sure you would not do any such thing.

    As we chatted briefly, I discerned that the texture and coloring of your eyebrows and the hairs that protrude from your nostrils did not match that of your beard or hair. Obviously, those features were theatrical props intended to disguise yourself from me. I was about to challenge you on these matters when the killers burst into the house. Your shout to me removed all doubt that you were any sort of monk and I fled, taking the Charter, which I had gathered you had come in search of, with me.

    I did as you instructed and ran to the cab that you had waiting and asked the driver to return me to the address from which he had come. He let me off at 221B Baker Street. At that point, I knew who you must be – the celebrated Mr. Sherlock Holmes – since I have been reading about your exploits in *The Strand* and the address has become familiar to all such readers.

Your lovely housekeeper let me in and on the premise that I was a potential new client of yours, we began to chat. Perhaps you are already aware of it, but it is proven fact that almost anyone will divulge almost anything, confidential or not, if they are met with joyful laughter and believe that their stories are giving the listener a round of soul-uplifting merriment. Your dear Mrs. Hudson responded accordingly and told me everything I needed to know about you.

One thing which you did not know about me, however, Mr. Holmes, is that my name is not Serena Eagle, nor has it been for several months. When I began my fellowship at the Abbey, I was introduced to my workmate, Mr. Godfrey Norton. As we worked and chatted together, it became inescapable to both of us that we shared the same devotion to the Church, to scholarship, to the compassionate mission to the poor, and to the complete equality of men and women. What began as a friendship deepened into a profound spiritual bond. However, by the fall of last year, we also had to confess that we had developed a burning physical desire for each other. St. Paul advised Christians that it is better to marry than to burn with lust and so we determined to marry as soon as possible. The problem we faced was that the terms of our fellowship required that only single students could apply. There was no restriction on becoming married during the term and likely it was never considered a possibility. However, we felt it best not to give rise to any offense and so we married in secret at Christmas and I have thoroughly enjoyed being Mrs. Godfrey Norton since that time.

As to the document which has brought about all of the terrible events of the recent past – please know that it is safe and protected and will be cared for as the priceless historical artifact that it is. I debated in my heart what to do with it and had determined to make it fully public, but, fortunately, had the opportunity to seek the counsel of two women whose wisdom I have come to rely on. My mentor, Commissioner Catherine Booth of the Salvation Army, and my dear friend, Miss Emily Pankhurst of the courageous suffragette movement, both listened to my thoughts. After prayerful consideration by Mrs. Booth and political reflection by Emily we agreed that the document should not become known to the public, at least not now. We realized that if all women in the Empire were suddenly given the gift of equality merely by way of the hands of dead men who had been in the grave for over seven hundred years then that equality would never be accepted by men as legitimate and would forever be the subject of attack in an effort to diminish it. We agreed that full and unquestioned equality for women would be far stronger if it were fought for inch by inch, with women demonstrating their irrefutable strength and bravery, scholarship and leadership, up to and surpassing that of men. One by one the barriers would have to be torn down. It might take many years but in the end, the argument would be won forever, and the complete emancipation of our daughters and their daughters would be secure. So the document will remain in secret and the struggle will continue.

Although both my husband, Godfrey, and I were raised in the Church of England and love its liturgy, history, architecture, and services, dearly we came to the conclusion that our convictions with regards to the complete equality of the sexes would no longer permit us to minister under its aegis. Therefore, we have joined the only Christian organization we know of that preaches and practices compassion for the poor and accords men and women full and equal rank and authority. We applied and have been accepted as officers in the Salvation Army. They have dispatched us to service in the Corps in Calcutta and we shall assume full responsibilities as officers as soon as Godfrey has mastered the trombone and I the cornet.

We know that we are in the place that the Lord wishes us to be. You too, Mr. Sherlock Holmes are likewise in such a place, even if you do not yet know it. May you be blessed in your pursuit of righteousness.

Yours in His Service

Lieutenant Mrs. Serena Norton

I put the letter down and looked over at Holmes. He had a far-away look in his eyes and puffed slowly on his beloved pipe.

"A remarkable nun," I said.

"Truly, the most remarkable," said Holmes.

And that is how a sweeping sea-change across the Empire and all of Christendom was postponed, but only temporarily, by the courage, determination, and wit of a brilliant and beautiful woman. Mr. Sherlock Holmes had been bested by a woman and he responded only with admiration. Whenever he speaks of Serena Eagle, as I will still call her, or when her name appears in the press in connection with her scholarship or her growing position of leadership in the Salvation Army, Sherlock Holmes always accords her the honorable title of The Nun.

… Dear Sherlockian Reader:

This new Sherlock Holmes Mystery is a tribute to *A Scandal in Bohemia* in The Canon. The BBC *Sherlock* series had already taken the similar-sounding *A Scandal in Belgravia*, so I could not use that idea. There are not all that many parts of England whose names end in *ia*. After poring over the map, I settled in *East Anglia* and then began to look for unusual incidents that had taken place there during the Holmesian era. That led me to the account of the unearthing of the caskets from the age of King John.

I learned that history records that a group of earls, barons and bishops gathered at the Abbey of St. Edmund in the fall of 1214 and came up with some sort of preliminary list of demands to be placed before King John at Runnymede the following spring. Unfortunately, there is no draft copy extant and we will never know if a medieval version of the Equal Rights Amendment ever crossed the minds of those who started the English-speaking world on the long road to democracy.

The references to the archeological work at the Abbey are accurate and so are some of the references to the peculiar doctrines of the Oxford Movement.

The Salvation Army was founded in London in 1865 by William and Catherine Booth. From that day until the present it has continued its mission to the poorest of the poor throughout the world and its commitment to the complete equality of men and women.

Dedicated Sherlockians will note that the name "Irene" is derived from the Greek word for "peace." "Serena" is the Latin equivalent. In the German tongue, the word "eagle' is, of course, translated as "adler." Many words and phrases have been borrowed directly from Arthur Conan Doyle, along with tributes to Shakespeare and Noel Coward.

Yet again, it was fun researching and writing this story. I hope you enjoy reading it as much as I did writing it.

Warm regards,

Craig

The Bald-Headed Trust

A New Sherlock Holmes Mystery

Chapter One

To Plymouth

The spring and summer of 1890 were quite tumultuous in London and on the continent. Some of these events led me to marvel at the scientific progress that was sweeping all of Western Civilization. Others left me with a deep sense of foreboding. The young emperor of Germany, Kaiser Bill as we called him, summarily fired the old chap, Bismarck, who had guided Germany through its unification. Great Britain, France, and Germany continued their scramble for Africa, claiming and swapping vast expanses of desert, shorelines, islands, and jungles.

The Scottish engineers opened the Firth of Forth Bridge in Edinburgh, the largest in the British Empire at that time. All over the world governments and companies were laying undersea telegraph cables. Several had been strung between North America and England, and Canada just announced a new link to Bermuda. The masses of London continued to flock to hear lectures by Henry Morton Stanley in Albert Hall. He had led a disastrous expedition into Egypt and had been roundly condemned by the Royal Society, but that did not stop Londoners, from the lowliest ostler all the way to the Queen herself, from marveling at his tales of Pygmies and cannibals and treks through Darkest Africa.

I had that spring, to some considerable acclaim, published in *Lippincott's* the second of my stories about the adventures of my friend and exceptional detective, Sherlock Holmes, and by the Fall, his name and reputation had become widely known throughout the country. I, or any reasonable man, might have thought that such recognition would have made him happy. It did not. He was quite the opposite. Since his rescuing of Violet Hunter and Alice Rucastle in March, he had not had a single case that demanded the application of his special province of logical deduction. I feared that he might again lapse into the use of his dangerous seven percent solution, and taxed my brain for some diversion that might occupy his imagination.

I settled on the idea of a short holiday to the seashore. I had not been to sea since returning from Afghanistan, and Holmes had little or no use for the beauty of the ocean or any other part of Nature for that matter. But I pointed out to him that a very high proportion of criminals and of his clients had spent some time at sea, and that it would be an excellent opportunity for him to learn more about seafarers and their ways if we were to spend a fortnight relaxing in the port city of Plymouth. The majestic Duke of Cornwall Hotel was advertising late-season rates and featuring excellent fresh seafood from the Grand Banks. After some exasperating negotiations Holmes finally agreed to a single week, and so began what turned into the *Mystery of the Bald-Headed Trust.*

On Monday, October 14 we rose early, took a cab to Paddington and boarded *The Flying Dutchman.* For several decades, it had made the journey along what some wags had called *God's Wonderful Railway* but which the rest of us knew as the Great Western. In just under five hours the powerful new *Royal Cornwall,* a sleek Dean Single 3031 Class locomotive thundered its way southwest to Plymouth. I made some attempt to draw Holmes into friendly conversation, but he was having none of it. He sat in silence, staring out the windows. He only spoke to me once and it was to say, in a grave voice, "My dear Watson, I know you are trying your best to be a good sport and make this a pleasant outing, and I can only ask that you forgive my melancholy mood. However my mind is consumed with the stories I have heard most recently about a syndicate of very evil men who are spreading their web through England, Europe, and America. They will stop at nothing: not murder, blackmail, nor treason to reap their ill-gotten gains. I fear it will be only a matter of time before I am called upon to lock horns with the mastermind of their nest of vipers. These few days respite may be the last I am able to indulge in for months, or perhaps years to come."

"Oh come, come, Holmes," I said with feigned cheerfulness, "we are going to be in sleepy old Plymouth. Nothing dastardly there ever happens except for an occasional sailor stealing a barrel of rum. Banish all evil doers from your mind and refresh your spirits. At least that way you will be physically and mentally restored to better fight your foes upon your return to London."

He smiled warmly at me. "Thank you, my good friend. You are very kind to look out for my well-being. You do a rather better job of it than I do myself. I will do my best to be a cheerful companion for the duration of our little holiday."

As I expected, he immediately returned to his quiet scowl and said nothing more until noon, when we arrived at the shabby shed of Millbay Station in Plymouth.

Having secured our suite of rooms at the Duke of Cornwall, I insisted on our taking a good brisk walk along the seashore and harbor. I guided him along the grand parade, past the historic Smeaton Lighthouse, around the curve of the Admiralty and gave a nod to the splendid Royal William Yard. Having read some of the Cooks guidebook concerning Plymouth, I chatted about each site and its place in history. "Just think Holmes," I remarked, "it was two hundred and seventy years ago that the *Mayflower* departed from this very harbor."

Holmes said nothing. The discovery and settling of America did not strike him as a historical event worth celebrating.

He stopped however at the Telegraph Wharf and looked upon the parade of shops that had recently been erected there. A smile of bemusement flicked at the corners of his mouth. I looked at the shops and noticed *The Jolly Jack Public House*, an office of the American firm, *Western Union*, a small store calling itself *The Little Flock Christian Book and Bible Shop*, the harbor branch of Baring's Bank, a vegetarian restaurant, and a carriage repair shop. I could see nothing at all that struck me as the least bit amusing.

"Pray tell, Holmes. What do you find to smile at when you look at what, as far as I can tell, is a very ordinary collection of new shops and services?"

"It is only my idle amusing of myself, Watson, but I am looking upon *damnation, communication, salvation, pecuniation, vegetation, and transportation* all in one row. Silly of me isn't it? But it is curious that all these enterprises manage to exist packed in together. What I found most striking was the proximity of the store selling Bibles to the pub. I rather fear that the effect of the one would be canceled out by the other."

"Oh, Holmes," I smiled back at him. "I had not thought of it that way, but I am sure you are quite right."

"Yes, Watson. This sleepy city of Plymouth has, if I remember correctly, quite a history as a haven of rowdy drunken sailors, side by side with the most intense religious revivals. That strikes me as an excellent formula for the fomenting of unusual criminal activities but, most regrettably, I have not been following the Plymouth press recently and so have heard of nothing. Very well, let us go and find our dinner and perhaps the library at the hotel will have some acceptable reading material."

With this, we left the harbor area and returned to the hotel for a pleasant howbeit entirely uneventful evening.

That night I slept that sleep that knits up the raveled sleeve of care and did not rise until well after eight o'clock. Holmes was already up and out of the hotel by the time I emerged from my room and so I contented myself with a late breakfast and settled in the sunny parlor to catch up on the past three volumes of *The Lancet*.

It was late morning before Sherlock Holmes returned, and what a change had come over him. He not only had some color in his cheeks from the morning sun and crisp seaside air, but there was once again that bounce in his step and his eyes were shining brightly between puckered lids. I recognized that look and knew straight away that it had nothing to do with the scenic vistas of the Atlantic Ocean.

"Good morning, Holmes," I said, a little slyly. "I see that your seaside holiday in the beauty of Nature is working wonders on your health and disposition."

"Oh, my good Doctor. You know perfectly well that I do not care a fig for the beauties of Nature. But you are totally correct in seeing that I am enjoying my holiday. However, I assure you that it is only because my holiday has ceased to be a holiday and has turned into a most interesting adventure."

"Jolly good for whatever reason. I am pleased for anything that has been such a tonic to you. But pray you, do tell what happened during the past four hours to dispel the melancholy."

"Very well," he said. "I slept rather poorly in a strange bed, alternately cursing the cacophony of squawking seagulls and the booming sound of the ships' horns as they made their way in and out of the harbor. So, at first light, I went for a walk through the town, if for no other reason than to acquire some additional knowledge of this uninspiring city. I found myself back at the Telegraph Wharf that I had thought to be amusing during our stroll last evening. I hoped, in vain it turned out, that the pub might be serving tea and breakfast, but on entering found only the cleaning staff and rather unpleasant odors of stale beer, urine and vomit from the night before — the smell that inhabits all pubs in the first hours of the morning after.

"The door to the shop selling religious books, however, was open, and having nothing better to do I entered and thought that, at the least, I could add to my knowledge of emerging spiritualist movements that have affected, or perhaps I should say afflicted, so many gullible folks of late. I entered and saw that the place was clean and orderly, and well-stocked with books, religious tracts, hymn books and various religious paraphernalia such as wall plaques bearing scripture verses, Bible knowledge quiz games, and paintings of the Lord as if he were the pilot of a ship, with a hand on the shoulder of a young man behind the ship's wheel.

"The proprietor was a youngish woman, I estimate in her late twenties. I can only describe her as plain but handsome. Tall and sturdy. She had the red hair of a Highland lass, but it was all bundled up into braids and wound about the top of her head. If ever it were to be let down and taken out of braids I imagine it would extend well down past the small of her back. Her skin was pale, as is common to redheads, but her complexion flawless, rendering her blue eyes quite striking. Her countenance was rather perfectly balanced, but she made no effort at all to enhance it. She had not a speck of powder or paint upon her, no jewelry, and no colorful or stylish clothing such as you would normally see on an attractive young woman. Her plain white dress covered her from her neck to her wrists and indicated an obsessive modesty.

"Assuming her to no more than a sad Reformist Protestant who was their equivalent of a nun, I ignored her and perused the bookshelves. The shop had some excellent works by St. Augustine, an entire set of Calvin's Institutes, the collected sermons of Dr. Spurgeon and a rather wide assortment of books by John Nelson Darby, Anthony Norris Groves, and George Mueller. Are you familiar with them?

"A very little," I replied. "Are they not some of the leading lights of one of the puritanical sects of evangelicals?"

"Yes. Precisely. And their movement has had particular popularity here in Plymouth. I confess that my indulgence in some of the pleasant vices that they condemn would exclude me forever from their ranks, as became abundantly obvious when I sat in one of their chairs to look through a volume of biography and prepared to enjoy at least one pipe of fine tobacco."

"Oh oh," I interjected. "I gather the good Christian shop lady was not pleased with that prospect."

"Not at all," Holmes replied. "But her words both surprised and annoyed me. She said, 'You do know, Mr. Sherlock Holmes, that your body is the temple of the Holy Spirit and you would be a healthier man and a better detective if you ceased breathing poisons into it.' Now, at first, I was a little annoyed, and not pleased with being deprived of the joy of tobacco. I also had some unkind thoughts about you, my dear friend, for publishing that story and giving me such notoriety that even shop ladies in Plymouth would recognize me. She continued giving me her little talking to and said, 'You are quite welcome to stay and read, but we will not allow our premises to be fouled by tobacco smoke.' Before I could think up some snide rejoinder, she then gave me a warm smile and proceeded to say, 'Please forgive my forwardness, sir, but my curiosity will not permit me to refrain from asking you how it is that London's famous detective is to be found in a Christian bookstore in Plymouth so early on a fall morning?'"

"So I gave her a less than entirely courteous but utterly truthful reply about being here on holiday, replaced the volume I had been looking into, and made a move towards the door.

"Well, didn't she give me quite the sideways look as if she did not believe a word I said, and then she posed a very interesting question about one of the details in your story."

"And which was that?" I asked.

"Oh, it matters not, for it was only the first question she asked. Then, without a trace of guile, she began to ask more. All along the line of 'Why did I not do this?' or 'Why had I failed to do that?' And when she was finished with the events recorded in *The Sign of the Four* she began in on other cases that had been reported in *The Times* in which I had some degree of involvement. And then she began on yet more cases on which I had not been consulted. Her interrogation of me was entirely without pretense, but I have never been so thoroughly taken to task. The woman had not only read every page of the reports in *The Times,* but she quite clearly had remembered every detail. And when she had exhausted the Crime Section she moved on and began asking me what I thought about the Germans and their new Chancellor, and the foreign policies of Lord Salisbury, and the Italians in Abyssinia, and the French in the Sudan, and the renunciation of polygamy by the Mormons in America. And if that were not enough she quizzed me further about the recent policy changes in the Bank of England, and trade with the Cape Colony, and if I believed that investing in shares of the company formed by W. B. Purvis to manufacture his newly patented fountain pen would be a wise choice or, given the topsy-turvy state of world affairs, should people just stick to gold.

"You can imagine that I was quite intrigued by this woman and eventually remarked to her that I had not expected a member of a devout sect to be so informed and concerned with the things of the world. She gave me a puzzled look and told me in quite a matter-of-fact way that to be an effective witness for the Lord one simply had to live with the Bible tucked under one arm and *The Times* under the other. I said that I was quite sure she was correct and I admit to you, Watson, that I refrained from saying that I might find occasional substitutes for Holy Writ. But then it was my turn to quiz this remarkable young woman.

"I asked her numerous questions about Plymouth, and about the harbor, and the shipments that moved in and out of here. Again she amazed me with her answers. She knew the names, schedules, and ports of call of every major trading vessel; of the shipments they were importing and exporting, and for which British firms they were intended. In passing, she noted that any astute investor should be looking into shares of the Armstrong Whitworth Co., who were sending armaments all over the Empire. She had bought a few shares of the company for her husband and herself, noting that while her faith would not permit her to invest in highly profitable manufacturers of whiskey and tobacco products, the provision of arms to those who were protecting the Empire was a calling ordained by the Lord Himself.

"So there you have it, Watson. If we invest our savings in armaments we shall be able to enjoy our retirement, for the dividends shall never cease as long as the Empire prevails and the rest of the world detests it.

"After over an hour of this delightful conversation I rose to leave and she gave me quite a hard look and said, 'This has been a wonderful opportunity for me, sir, as my chances to have the insights of such a well-informed gentleman are rare. However, I have to ask you, bold though it may seem, what your opinion is of the Telegraph Murders that took place here recently, as I assume that they are the true reason for your being on Telegraph Wharf and that your so-called holiday is merely a somewhat flimsy excuse.'"

"Ah yes, Holmes," I interjected. "I read of that event in the papers, but neither of us took any notice of it as it happened in the West and not in London."

"Exactly, Watson. I had to confess to the woman, that truthfully my visit to Plymouth had nothing to do with any crime at all, and that it was, quite frankly, only for a few days respite. And that furthermore, other than what I had read in the brief report in the Press I knew very little, but that I would be most eager if I could learn more, and would she be so kind as to enlighten me.

"She raised her eyebrows ever so slightly, but I gather that she discerned that I was being truthful and told me that she was quite concerned about it as she had been personally acquainted with the victims and that the crime had occurred only a few blocks away from her shop.

"The two men who had been murdered were family men from Glasgow. They were communications engineers who were under contract to the Western Union Company to assist in the installation of the new office that is adjacent to their bookstore. Both men were in their thirties and appeared to be dour, clean-living men who worked late into the evening, and then made their way directly back to their rooming house without stopping in at the *Jolly Jack* or any other public house for a pint before taking their dinner at their lodgings.

"On one or two occasions each of them had wandered into her shop but she felt it was out of boredom rather than any spiritual yearning. They had chatted briefly with her and her husband and left without buying anything. Then three weeks ago both were found lying dead in a lane off of Battery Street, not far from their rooming house. No one had heard any gunshots. No bands of thugs had been seen in the area. No one knew of anything these men could have been involved in that was in the least untoward. Their wallets had been emptied, but their watches left behind, leaving the police to assume that robbery was only a ruse to distract the investigation. To this day, the police continue to describe the event as 'By Persons Unknown' and 'For Causes Unknown.'

"It was terribly upsetting, she said, to the other merchants in the parade of stores along the Wharf. They had all recently set up shop, were all on good terms with each other, and had not had enough time to start to quarrel. The Western Union Company, being a very wealthy American firm and with a sincere sense of compassion, had looked after all funeral arrangements and set up a generous pension for the men's families even though, by law, they were not required to since the men had only been under contract and not employees. To this day, nothing more is known. My appearance in the lady's shop this morning was, she had assumed, connected to the murders and she concluded that I had been called upon to consult with the local constabulary.

"I acknowledged, somewhat apologetically, that I had not been and that the police did not know that I was here in Plymouth. I assured her, however, that I would avail myself of the opportunity and hoped that presently I would be asked to assist. I bid this fascinating woman good morning and promptly walked over to the police station. The local chaps there graciously welcomed me, repeated the details that the woman had already given me, and invited my participation.

"As a result, Watson, this holiday is not a useless waste of time at all. It has become an adventure that may keep us here for some time to come, and as long as you do not impose upon me any more hours of staring out to sea, my holiday may yet become memorable and enjoyable."

Chapter Two

The Telegraph Murders

Holmes said nothing more. When lunch was served, he ate quickly and I could see that the lust of the chase had overtaken him. His brilliant reasoning powers were being summoned and I knew that an evil time would soon be coming upon those whom he had set himself to hunt down.

He spent the next two hours poring over the reports that the police had given to him. He perused maps of the city and copies of the local newspaper from the days after the incident, which the front desk of *The Duke* has efficiently procured for him. On three occasions he set down the materials, lit a pipe, closed his eyes, pressed his fingertips together, and entered his familiar pose of burning concentration. I knew that he would snap back at me in anger if I were to disturb him and so left him alone, but in my heart, I was quite thrilled to see him back in his favorite role of the relentless sleuth-hound, the keen-witted, ready-handed consulting detective.

I was not paying sufficient attention, otherwise I would have cut off the young bell boy who had the misfortune to interrupt him. "Mr. Holmes," the lad announced, "a letter for you," and he placed a silver tray bearing an envelope in front of the detective, and had the further gall to place his young hand on Holmes's shoulder and give him a bit of a shake as one would give to a guest who had decided that the parlor of the hotel was an acceptable spot to take one's afternoon nap.

"Confound you!" Holmes exploded. "Cannot you see that I am working? Do not ever, ever disturb me like this again. Now get you gone and do not let me see your face again!"

The poor lad was visibly upset by Holmes's reaction. His face became distraught and I feared he would break into tears. I immediately interposed myself and took him by the arm and led him away a few steps to safety. "Please young man," I consoled him. "Do not worry about the reaction of my colleague. He has a very intense character. I will look after the letter. Now you get along and do not worry about it for another minute." I gave the boy two shillings, for which he thanked me and left, but not before giving a frightened glance back at Sherlock Holmes, who had once again retreated into his near trance. I rather suspected that no more letters would be hand-delivered by anyone on the attentive staff.

I sat down and took the liberty of opening the letter on Holmes's behalf. Upon finishing it, I sat up straight in my chair, took a deep breath and in a voice that is usually only heard from sergeant majors, announced, "Holmes! Wake up! This is urgent and you have to pay attention and listen at once."

His reaction was instant and predictable. However, I had been the recipient of his temper on more than one occasion in the past and knew that his bark would be far worse than his bite, particularly after he was forced to listen to the contents of the letter.

"Blast you, Watson!" he snapped. "You, of all people, should know that I am not to be disturbed!"

"And you, of all people, Sherlock Holmes," I snapped back, "should know that I would not do so if whatever I hold in my hand were not of critical importance to your case!"

That shut him up, or at least diminished his reaction to a glare.

"This letter is from the *Little Flock Christian Bookstore* and it bears on the Telegraph Murders. Do you wish me to read it to you, or shall I just send it up to our rooms and have it placed in your luggage?"

His glare softened. "Very well, Watson. I apologize for my rudeness and unkind words. Please, my friend, be so kind as to read the letter to me. I assume it is from the lady that I spoke with this morning."

"You assume wrongly," I said, with perhaps an unkind trace of smugness. "It is from her husband and both of them may be in some danger."

Now that got his attention and he gave it entirely to me and the piece of paper in my hand.

The letter ran as follows:

```
Dear Mr. Sherlock Holmes:
    This morning you visited our shop and
conversed with my wife, Mrs. Miriam Darby.
She wisely did not disclose all aspects of
the connection of our family to the
Telegraph Murders before committing it to
a short season of prayer and of discussing
it with me.
    My wife is a most remarkable woman and
in addition to having an exceptional
knowledge of history, commerce, and
commercial affairs, she has been given by
the Holy Ghost the spiritual gift of the
discerning of spirits . . .
```

Here I stopped. "I must say, Holmes, are you sure that this woman is not some sort of fanciful spiritualist? I am not familiar with any medical condition known as a gift for the discerning of spirits."

"In truth, my good Doctor, you are highly familiar with it and you have a rather good case of it yourself."

"I beg your pardon, Holmes. I have no such thing."

"Oh come now. If a man approaches you and tells you that he has a horse for sale, how do you decide whether to send him away or listen to him?"

"I do not know. I guess it would be based on whether or not I trusted the man; if he gave me a sense of being truthful, or of being a scoundrel."

"And on what would you draw to form such an immediate conclusion?" Holmes pressed me.

"I suppose on my years of working with a great many men in the army, as a medical doctor, and even from observing so many of your clients."

"Precisely. And if the horse were offered for sale to Mrs. Hudson, would she be taken in by a swindler?"

"Of course not. Her woman's intuition is highly refined and she would see through such a man in a moment."

"You are absolutely correct, Watson," Holmes continued. "And what if it were me? I have neither your vast experience of dealing with men, nor one ounce of woman's intuition. But still I would form a conclusion. How could that be?"

I shrugged my shoulders. "You would use you powers and processes of observation and scientific reason."

"Exactly, my good man. All these ways of reaching conclusions, that we call by different names, are the same thing. Some people have a well-developed sense of the motives of other people and some will be forever dupes. This very Christian lady gave me quite the going over this morning and I do not believe I could have deceived her even with my best disguise. She modestly attributes her gifts to supernatural forces. It matters not their origin, they are nonetheless present. Pray, continue reading."

I continued:

```
. . . of the discerning of spirits and
she knew in her heart that you had been
sent to us by God as an answer to our
prayers.
```

I stopped again, unable to resist. "My word, Holmes, did you sprout wings and a halo? I never knew. Why did you not tell me of your promotion?"

"Enough Watson. Get on with it."

```
. . . Her spirit has told her that our
family may be in danger and that the men who
committed the murders are known to us and
may do us harm. I beseech you to forgive our
intruding on your holiday, but I am
requesting a brief audience with you so that
we may ask for your advice.
    Yours sincerely,
    Jabez Nelson Darby,
    Owner,
    Little Flock Christian Bookstore,
    Telegraph Wharf, Plymouth.
```

"There is something quite strangely appealing about this whole affair, would you not agree, Watson? Please be so kind as to send a note off to Mr. Darby, asking him to come and see us here as soon as possible."

I took a moment at the writing desk in the bay window of the hotel, wrote the requested note, and went to find the bell boy, who, for good reason, had not returned to the part of the room in which we were sitting.

Within thirty minutes a young gentleman appeared in the entrance to the parlor. The bellboy pointed him in our direction. He was a pleasant-looking man of perhaps thirty years of age, with a thin frame and face and a bit of a stoop to his posture. He was dressed in a modest, but clean and well-pressed suit, such as one might expect of an earnest owner of a bookstore. Oddly, he had not removed his hat upon entering the premises of the grand hotel and approached Holmes and I with it still upon his head.

"Mr. Holmes, and Dr. Watson?" he asked politely.

"You have found us," I assured him. "May I ask the boy to bring us a cup of tea? You are looking a little concerned and I gather you have come here in haste."

"Why bless you, Doctor. That would be wonderful. Indeed, I did hurry and I beg you to forgive my intruding on your holidays. I gather it is a rather rare event in your busy lives."

"Fortunately, you are correct. They are rare," said Holmes. "And your intrusion and the reasons for it are the best thing to have happened in an otherwise tedious expedition. Please be seated and tell me, as frankly as you can, what it is that is besetting your good self and your remarkable wife."

He pulled up a chair, sat down, removed his hat and placed it in his lap. The eyes of both Holmes and I went immediately to the top of his head. There was not a single hair upon it. He was as completely bald as a newborn babe. He could see us staring and I felt embarrassed by our rude behavior. Holmes, who was never one to be overly tactful, ignored all manners and simply asked him, "What in the world happened to your hair?"

The young man blushed momentarily and I detected a flash of pain in his face. But he quickly recovered and smiled a little mischievously back at Sherlock Holmes and said, "You are the great detective. You tell me. I can't seem to find it anywhere. Perhaps you could track it down and return it to me."

Both Holmes and I laughed at his good natured and witty reply. "I deduce," said Holmes, continuing with the pleasant tone, "that you experienced a serious medical condition recently and that your fine head of hair vacated itself. You appear to have recovered from whatever it was that beset you, but your hair has not yet been so informed and still is in hiding."

The man laughed and smiled back. "You are entirely correct. For a period of over a year, I suffered from a terrible bout of brain fever. I lost weight, all my energy, any ability to laugh, and all my hair. My spirits have finally been restored."

Here he paused, and then continued, "But once again I find myself deeply troubled and fearful, as is my wife, and that is what brings me to speak with you. Again, I apologize for disturbing you but we have nowhere else to turn and your arrival in our shop this morning was indeed a godsend."

"I have been called few things any better," said Holmes, "and many things much worse. If I am to be of any use to you and your wife please tell me your story and whatever possible connection you might have with these terrible and inexplicable murders. Please. You have our complete attention."

"As you know from my note, my name is Jabez Nelson Darby. You may have heard of my grandfather, John Nelson Darby."

"Indeed," I said. "He was a rather distinguished Bible scholar and preacher. Did he not do a translation of the Bible from the original Hebrew and Greek entirely by himself? Is he still alive?"

"Yes. That is who he was, and sadly no, he passed on to glory two years ago, after a long a very fruitful life and ministry. He founded the movement that you may know as the Plymouth Brethren and one of the largest and most active assemblies of believers was started, under his oversight, here in Plymouth. Similar meetings have been formed throughout the world.

"He was a stern man in many ways, but he was a loving and devoted grandfather to me and, in his later years, became convinced that his mantle would fall on me as Elijah's had on Elisha. He fully expected me to take up his leadership position in the movement and devote myself to Biblical scholarship, and teaching and preaching of the Word of God. I loved him dearly and did everything I could to live up to his expectations but, alas, I just do not have the mind or the disposition of a scholar, and I quake with terror when I am in front of a crowd of people and expected to give a word.

"The best I could do was to open a small bookstore here in Plymouth with the hope and prayer that it would be a witness and ministry to the many seamen who are constantly making their way through our streets as they come on and off of scores of merchant ships that dock in our harbor. When my grandfather died, I was deeply saddened knowing that his wish to see me blessed in ministry was never fulfilled. It is hard to say why it had such an effect on my spirit, but I succumbed to a long bout of brain fever. For months after his death all my ambition, my cheerfulness, my desire for food and laughter all vanished. It was a daily struggle to get myself out of my bed in the morning, to try to show any attention and affection to my wonderful wife or our two small children. Many times I contemplated taking my own life and convinced myself that doing so would be the best favor I could bestow on my family so that they could be rid of me, and start over with someone who would not be such a burden to them.

"My wife, Miriam, who you met this morning, is an exceptional woman and I could not in my wildest dreams imagine having been blessed with so loving and caring and capable a helpmeet. She quite simply took over the business, looked after all the commercial affairs, managed the lives and schooling of the children and in short, carried me until my spirits slowly recovered. When she heard that there was to be new electrified building erected at Telegraph Wharf she immediately secured us one of the storefronts on the parade, knowing that it would not only give us a much more visible witness to the seamen, even those who were entering and leaving the *Jolly Jack,* but that a better location would cause our sales to rise and the book business, which is not lucrative at the best of times, to prosper. And indeed, it has. She was right. I have never in the seven years I have been married to her and the two years we courted, known her to be wrong.

"The events that my wife has discerned to have been connected to the murders began just over three months ago, on the first Sunday of July. As we do every Sunday, we came to meeting at the Gospel Hall for the service of the Lord's Supper and sat where we normally do every week, somewhat near to the back in case the children have to make an exit as children often have to do when required to sit still for over an hour.

"In front of us a few rows, I saw the strangest thing. There were two men, both dressed in dark suits, but whose heads were completely bald — exactly like mine. They did not stand and give a word or lead in prayer during the service, but they did partake of the elements, the bread and wine, as they were passed. When the service ended our leading elder stood to give the announcements and he acknowledged the presence of our visitors. They had brought with them a letter of commendation from an assembly in Brooklyn, New York, which the elder read aloud. These two men, Brother Ross Duncan and Brother Clayton Johns, were commended to our fellowship by the saints gathered in New York. After having been anointed with oil and prayed over, they had been miraculously cured of their severe medical condition. They experienced a call to missions and were given full-time commendation to ministry. They were on their way to help the work in the Faroe Islands but first would be spending a year in Plymouth where they would learn about the Brethren assembly movement and the truth of the dispensational understanding of the Word, as well as engage in a short task of Christian philanthropy to which they had also been called. And we were requested to receive them in the Lord and assist them in whatsoever business they had as becometh saints.

"As you might imagine their presence and their similarity to my condition was of intense interest to my wife, and she insisted that we wait at the back of the Hall after the service so that we could meet them. I had no desire to, as it was all I could manage to endure the service itself, and wanted to do nothing more than get back to my home and have a very long Sunday afternoon nap, but she prevailed.

"We met the two American men and had no more than introduced ourselves to each other and commented on the shared affliction of baldness, but one of the leading elders greeted us and insisted that we all come back to his home to enjoy Sunday dinner together. He was a very gracious and godly man and blessed by the Lord with material wealth, and it was his custom to invite visitors to the assembly back to his home. It was an invitation we could not refuse and so we went and enjoyed a pleasant dinner of roast beef and Yorkshire pudding that his lovely wife and the help had prepared. The children ate quickly and were given leave to play in the garden and we listened to the exceptional story of our visitors.

"They had both been dealt severe bouts of brain fever some three years ago and by chance, which they now acknowledged was divine providence, they met in the waiting room of the same doctor in the Gramercy area of Manhattan. They became friends, such as often happens among those who share similar afflictions, and would meet up from time to time for supper in the Greenwich Village part of the city. On one occasion, a Sunday evening, they were walking through the Bowery and heard the rousing joyful sounds of hymns being sung in one of the mission buildings. They entered, enjoyed the music and listened to the preaching of the Word of God. Having come under the sound of the Gospel, they were convicted in their hearts by the Holy Spirit and when the invitation was given to come forward and receive salvation, they both did so. Since getting saved they have been in fellowship in one of the Brethren assemblies in Brooklyn and have been blessed in all aspects of their lives, their health, and their income except, of course, for the restoration of their hair, which they claim as a badge of honor and note that it has become a surefire way to invite conversation, thus giving them an opportunity to share their testimonies.

"They had both felt the Macedonian call to mission work and were commended by the believers to do so, and were living by faith, depending on the Lord daily for their every need.

"Their reason for coming to Plymouth, they confided, was the result of a specific request from one of the men of the assembly. He had exceptional wealth and had, it turned out, suffered through a serious bout of brain fever himself many years ago. He felt a deep sympathy for men who were beset by this terrible sickness and had established a trust that aided medical research into the condition, along with the propagation of the gospel, so that men who were suffering so deeply might be cured in both their bodies and souls.

"My wife approved of this wise approach, combining as it did the most recent advances of medical science with the necessary ministry to the soul of man, and we had a friendly conversation. Twice that week they came to our home for tea and chatted further and they told us more about their work. They had been commissioned by the wealthy benefactor to register a similar charity here in England, to raise support for its work, and to get it started in its ministry to those men in need. They expected to have their work here finished within a year and then they would head on to the Faroe Islands.

"We wished them well and had a time of prayer together. Then the following week they came to me with looks of grave concern on their faces. It seems that the Office of the Public Trustee, the one that supervises British charities, does not permit those who are not British citizens to operate a charity. They particularly do not like it if Americans come across the pond, open a trust and assume that they can dictate its operations from Oshkosh, or some similar location. They had not expected to run into this roadblock. They had, they claimed, prayed about this issue and the Lord had given them the solution. They said that they would take over the temporary operations of my bookstore if I would serve as the founding general secretary of the charity. It would only be for a few months and I would have an office, which they had recently acquired, as well as a generous stipend of four pounds a week. They required no income for themselves since they were supported by the assemblies in Brooklyn.

"This appeared to us to be a gift from the Lord and we immediately accepted. In retrospect, it is a matter that we should have prayed over first. Had we done so, the events that followed might not have occurred.

"In mid-July, I presented myself to their new little office just off of Millbay Road. The sharp, bright sign on the door read *Gone Today, Hair Tomorrow – The Brain Fever Charitable Trust of England*. It was a witty and clever name and they put me to work writing out letters requesting gifts of funds from a long list of wealthy Christians throughout England. Each application was the same and I had to write it out over and over again with minor alternations depending on the relative wealth of the potential benefactor and any information they had secured on his previous gifts. They had quite a file and some excellent research on many wealthy people, and so I began to prepare the letters and submissions. They explained that I was engaging in what the American philanthropy industry called *grantsmanship*. I was unaware of the term or the practice but it was not difficult work and I felt that I was contributing to a good cause.

"The added benefit was that I was expected, as part of the letter and application, to include a personal word of testimony, sharing from my heart how I had suffered, and the ways in which both medicine and the blessings of the Lord were bringing about my healing. At first, it was quite a tribulation to me as I could not think of any good thing that had happened in my life recently. But as I persevered I acknowledged that my lovely wife had been a blessing from God, and so I wrote words to that effect in my testimony. But the next day I felt I could not just repeat what I had said the day before, and so I searched my soul for another small blessing in my life, and it became immediately clear to me that my beautiful children, my five-year-old son and three-year-old daughter, were an unmistakable sign of the Lord's blessing. And so it went.

"Each day I prayed and meditated and each day another blessing in my life was revealed to me, and so I wrote about it in the letters. I noted the blessings of my health, of my family, of my godly grandfather, of my loving parents, of the sunrise over the ocean, of living in the British Empire, and of our gracious Queen. There were so many truly wonderful things that had enriched my life and for which I was moved to be profoundly grateful. The result of all this was that the dark cloud that had come with my brain fever slowly lifted. In addition to counting my blessings every day, I was heeding the advice of our good doctors and taking a brisk daily walk, eating plenteous fruit and vegetables, curtailing my intake of red meats, and getting regular sleep. My body was healthier than it had been in years. My spirit was alive with joy. I was moved to loving intimacy with my long-suffering wife and enjoyed times of play with my children such as I had never experienced.

"And the two Americans were doing wondrous things in the bookstore. Our sales had increased threefold. They appeared to have a gift of closing the sale, as they say. The shop appeared to be clean and well managed. Every Friday afternoon they would meet me and take from me the applications I had carefully and prayerfully prepared, saying that they had arranged a private delivery service so that they could be handed to the potential benefactors in total confidence and privacy, which they claimed was critical for the success of philanthropy.

"By the middle of September, the store had made a clear profit of one hundred pounds. I had been paid over thirty pounds by the Trust. My astute wife invested the profits in some excellent public stock companies and we felt that we were enjoying the blessing of the Lord.

"Life could not have been better. But then, beginning about two weeks ago, some things started to change. It began one night as my dear wife and I were lying in bed prior to falling off to sleep. I sensed that she was awake, restless and upset. I asked her, 'What's wrong?' She responded, 'Nothing. It's nothing,' and rolled away from me and pretended to fall asleep. Such behavior, I gather, is common among wives. The next night I posed the same questions and added, firmly but lovingly, that it disturbed me when she refused to confide her feelings in me and feigned sleep. For a few minutes she said nothing, and then she rolled towards me and said, 'They are not bald and I do not trust them.'

"This took me by surprise and I demanded an explanation from her. She began by saying that she had no proof of anything but that her spirit told her things, and she had learned to trust what she heard from her spirit. She said that on two occasions she had heard each of them mutter rather vile oaths when they were frustrated with some simple task. I responded that they were still young in the Lord and that bad habits developed over years were the hardest to overcome. Then she said that twice for Clayton and once for

Ross she had sensed that they were looking at her not with the gentlemanly look of admiration that she felt from time to time from some of the older gentlemen in the assembly, but with the lascivious look of a sailor just off a ship. I asked, foolishly I gather, what the difference was. She said quite bluntly that it was something that every woman on earth understood even if no man would ever understand. I again stuck up for their side and reminded her that they were bachelors and that the demon of lust had had a long time to work on their souls, and that it was inevitable that it would occasionally rear its ugly and ungodly head.

"She then said that the store had become dirty and had not been dusted. I argued that she was most certainly wrong. The shelves were spotless. 'Only where you can see,' she cried. 'Behind the books and on the top of the volumes there is more dust and grit than we have ever had before. In the basement, the boxes of unopened books have thick layers of dust and dirt on them.' Now it is common among women to think that no one can keep a place as clean as they would have themselves, and such condemnation of maids, housekeepers, or tenants is quite a usual thing when the lady is no longer directly looking after the premises. I suggested this, as gently as I could. Then she rose up out of bed, kicked back the covers and stood to her feet. She looked back at me and said, 'Neither of them is bald. Three times now, for each of them, I had seen small dabs of shaving soap on their heads. They have used their feigned baldness to forge a friendship with you and it is fraudulent. They are using you and I know not what for. But I do not like it and I do not trust them.'

"This troubled me greatly. I have learned to respect my wife's insights and I know they come from the Lord. Yet I was happier now than I had been in several years. We were financially better off than ever before and I was loath to disturb my prosperous world. I promised to confront them, but I kept finding excuses, including the murder of the Scottish engineers that took place during those days, to postpone doing so. Then on Thursday, October 10th they did not open the store and did not again the following day. Neither did they appear at the usual time to retrieve all of the applications I had written. On Sunday they were not at our worship service and then yesterday, Monday, I went to the Trust office, but the door was shut and locked with a little square of cardboard hammered onto the middle of the panel with a tack. Here it is. You can read it for yourself."

He held up a sheet of cardboard, about the size of a sheet of notepaper. It read in this fashion:

THE BRAIN FEVER
CHARITABLE TRUST
IS DISSOLVED
OCTOBER 9, 1890

I was very disturbed and rushed over to their rooming house. There was no answer when I knocked on the door of their rooms. I asked the landlady if they had been seen, and she said that she had seen neither hide nor hair of them since Wednesday. I told her that I was concerned about them and she took her key and opened the door. The rooms were completely empty except for a number of objects left on the table."

"And what might those have been?" asked Holmes.

The man looked as if he were on the verge of tears. His lower lip began to tremble ever so slightly. With an effort, he regained his composure and said, "On the table was a stack of envelopes containing all of the applications and letters I had written. Every one of them. Not one had been sent anywhere. Beside them were well over one hundred books and other items. They corresponded almost exactly with the items they had sold from my store during the time they were looking after it. The whole business had been a fraud. They had deceived me."

"Yet you suffered no financial damage," countered Holmes. "From what you have told me you were not only in a much better cash position than you had ever been, but you now had all your inventory that you could turn around and sell again. The actions were bizarre but where is the crime? They stole nothing from you. They did not strike you or your wife in any way. They did no damage to your premise that a good dusting would not repair. Why are you here and telling me these things?"

Jabez Darby placed his elbows upon his knees and sunk his bald head into his hands. He slowly shook it back and forth and said, "I know. I know. You are right. There is no crime and I feel like a fool telling you all this. I am sure you think us just a couple of silly religious zealots. But we know. We know! In our hearts we know that something is evil. Yet I cannot explain what it is." He placed his hat back on his bald head and started to rise. "I am very sorry to have bothered you with this. I have wasted your time. I am very sorry."

Holmes reached out and firmly placed his hand on the young man's shoulder, stopping him from getting out of his chair. "You and your wife are no fools, my good man. You are entirely correct. It is undeniably true that something evil this way comes. I believe you. Will you take us at once to your shop? And Watson, might you by chance have your doctor's bag with you? Could you bring it along?"

I nodded and from long experience withheld my questioning of such a strange request.

Jabez looked at Holmes with wondering eyes and then nodded. "Thank you, sir. I am much indebted to you. Please. Come with me."

The three of us walked the few blocks from the hotel to the Telegraph Wharf. Jabez Darby unlocked the door, led us inside and, as evening had started to settle in, lighted a lamp. The store was orderly and spotless. "Take us to your basement," said Holmes. Once there Holmes reached up and ran his long fingers along the top of one of the stacks of cases, and asked me to do the same. Even without looking at my hand I could tell by what I felt that the surfaces were thick with grit and dust.

"Is this your usual arrangement for these cases," asked Holmes.

"No. We usually line the stacked cases up along the walls. They have been moved into the center of the room."

The walls of the room were lined with a wooden wainscoting. Holmes proceeded to strike the right-hand wall with his walking stick. He began at one end of the wall and struck regularly at small intervals. Each knock sounded as one would expect a knock against wood that was laid over brick. But as he reached the middle section, the sound changed and there was a distinctly hollow reverberation coming from the wood. A series of knocks indicated that there was a hole of about two feet round behind the wainscoting.

"Watson, I assume that you have a set of forceps in your bag. Forgive me, Doctor, but it is the only tool I could think of that would do the job and immediately available to us."

I opened the bag, withdrew my surgical forceps and used them to pry against the planks of wood. There were gaps between the planks where someone had previously inserted a pry bar. The planks peeled off the wall with little effort.

Behind the wood, there was a hole in the brickwork. The far side was covered by similar heavy planks.

"The adjacent building, Holmes," I began, "is it not the harbor branch of Barings?"

"Exactly, my dear Watson. I will wager that it is now several thousand pounds poorer than it was a few days ago. They must have large shipments of payrolls, bullion and negotiable securities moving in and out from the ships. I am surprised that they have not sounded an alarm yet."

Holmes turned to Jabez Darby and said, "You and your wife were correct in your apprehensions and most responsible in your actions. Please give her my warm regards and my admiration for her gifts of discernment."

"But we failed," he said. "The robbery is done. They have used me treacherously and gotten away with it."

"Now there," Holmes again putting his hand on the man's shoulder. "How difficult do you think it will be for Scotland Yard to track down two bald Americans? They will be apprehended in short order, I assure you. Now please, go home to your wife and children and know that you have played a most important role in the solving of a very devious crime."

"Thank you, sir," he said. He led us back up the stairs and we parted our ways; he to his unusually insightful wife and Holmes and me to the police station. We filed our report with the constable on duty and agreed to come back in the morning when the bank opened and a police inspector would be available.

"Well Holmes," I said as we walked back to our rooms, "how on earth did you deduce that they were robbing a bank and not selling Bibles?"

"Elementary, my dear friend. It was perfectly obvious from the first that the only possible object of this intricate deception must be to get the shop owner out of the way. It was a curious but brilliant way of managing it and no doubt suggested to the scoundrels' minds by their knowledge of Mr. Darby's religious convictions and the absence of his hair. The cost of his stipend at the Trust and the false profits they turned over were nothing to them, as they were playing for thousands. Their willingness to volunteer their services demonstrated that they had some strong motive in securing the situation."

"But how could you guess what the motive was?"

"Had any other woman been involved, I should have suspected a mere vulgar motive. However, Mrs. Darby is quite beyond reproach. There was nothing in the shop of any value, the cases of new Bibles notwithstanding. It must then be something out of the shop. The reference made to the accumulation of dust and grit indicated some sort of chiseling, and where could that possibly have taken place without being immediately discerned but in the basement. Remembering that the shop was adjacent to a bank and sharing a common wall led me to the only possible conclusion. Tapping on the wainscoting was all that was required to tell us where they had been chiseling and removing bricks from the basement wall. Those bald-headed villains put a great deal of effort and planning into their devious scheme, but, in the end, it was not really that much of a challenge to see through it."

"Splendid, Holmes," I exulted. "This case solved. Shall I begin to write it up? Or are there still some loose strings to tie up?"

Holmes stopped his walking and gave me that look that I have learned to dread. Without saying anything, his look accused me of being a hopeless fool.

"No, my friend whom I love but who sometimes disappoints me," he said, in a most controlled voice. "There are no loose strings; there are merely several gaping holes in this case. Two men are dead and we still have no way of linking them to the robbery other than what a court would have to consider to be the superstitious fantasies of a devout female member of an odd religious sect. This is far from over."

Chapter Three

A Wild Goose Chase

In the morning we made our way to the police station. An Inspector Johnson was there to meet us. To Holmes's considerable annoyance he had brought along a reporter and a photographer from the local newspaper.

"Thought it would be good to let our citizens know how we all work together to solve a crime," he said. Holmes said nothing. His scowl said it all.

Our little troop marched into Barings Bank and Inspector Johnson demanded to see the manager immediately. A tall, well-dressed gentleman in his mid-fifties came out of his office. "Good morning, Inspector, gentlemen, and to what do I owe the honor of this visit on an otherwise fine morning?"

"How does it feel," blurted out the reporter, "to know that Baring's Bank has been robbed blind?"

"I'm sure I wouldn't know," the manager replied coolly. "Perhaps you could suggest some way to feel since I have never had that experience?"

"Well, you're about to. When was the last time you looked in your vault? You been cleaned out and you don't even know it?" the reporter said loudly.

"Oh my," the manager said with a touch of sarcasm, "why don't we all go and take a look?"

"Please, sir. If you would be so kind to lead the way," said the inspector. The photographer shouted at us to all stop and turn around so he could get a photograph of our descending into the basement. Except for the reporter we kept on walking.

The manager came to a large, heavy iron gate and selected a key from the ring of them that were attached to his belt.

"Who else has a key to this gate?" asked the Inspector.

"Other than me, the only other key is held by Chubbs. They installed the gates."

"So you're saying that you believe Chubbs could have been an accomplice in this robbery, is that right? Can I quote you on that?" said the reporter.

"You most certainly may," said the manager. "In fact, since Chubbs was the only one to install this gate then perhaps it is I who is their accomplice. You may quote me."

"Huh?" said the reporter.

We passed through yet another heavy gate that the manager likewise unlocked. The reporter did not ask any questions.

The last barrier was a large metal door with a dial on the front of it. "Combination locks are being used by most banks today. We use the same type first used by Tiffany's in New York. If you will excuse me please." He turned his back to us. The inspector stood directly in front of the photographer who tried in vain to get a picture of the manager's fingers on the dial.

The door of the vault was opened and he led us into a small room and he activated the electric light bulb. We stood inside the vault room and tried to accustom our eyes to the poor light. Holmes began to knock on the wooden wall panels. He quickly found the one that sounded hollow and I helped him remove it. It came off with no resistance. It could only have been set in place and not nailed or screwed down since the thieves would have pulled it into place behind them as they made their escape.

Behind the panel, there was the same two-foot diameter hole as we had seen on the other side of the wall. Light from the basement of the bookstore shone through. The photographer pushed his way in front of us and took a picture.

"I regret to inform you, sir," said Holmes, "that your vault has been broken into by some very determined and clever thieves and they have robbed you."

"So Mister Bank Manager," demanded the reporter. "How much did they get? Ten thousand pounds, a hundred thousand? And please don't try to tell me you don't know. Every good bank manager knows how much is in his vault. How much did they get?"

"Let me see," said the manager, rubbing his chin. "Let me see. I would have to say that the total amount, in aggregate, net of any taxes would be somewhat less than a farthing. That's f-a-r-t-h . . ."

"I know how to spell *farthing*," the reporter said as he continued to write.

"I'm terribly sorry," said the manager with refined Oxbridgian sarcasm, "I was not aware that you had been to school."

The reporter kept on writing. Then he stopped. "What do you mean 'less than a farthing'? What's that supposed to mean?"

"A farthing, sir, is the smallest denomination in British currency."

"I know what a farthing is," the reporter shouted adding an oath for good measure. "What you're claiming is that they got nothing. That's impossible. I can see that the shelves here are bare. You've been completely cleaned out! Don't try to cover it up. Baring's has had a heist."

"I fear I must ask you to explain yourself a little less cryptically to us as well," said Holmes. "You appear to be saying that the thieves took nothing."

"That is precisely what I am saying. They took nothing because there was nothing for them to take. This vault was completely empty. Since the day this branch opened a few months ago not a single farthing has been stored here. Your clever thieves have robbed us of precisely nothing."

"What about your shipments to and from the boats?" asked the inspector.

"Nothing remains in this branch overnight. All deposits are kept under heavy guard in the safe upstairs and are loaded onto the London train every evening. They are guarded by no less than four private security men at all times. This vault was built with the intent that someday this branch might be more than a transfer point but so far has never been used. Not for a single farthing. The damaged wall will be repaired in due course, but it appears to have been breached by the world's stupidest bank robbers. They have led you on a chase of a wild goose."

The evening edition of *The Flying Post* had a front-page story under the headline:

World's Stupidest Bank Robbers
Famous London Detective Leads Plymouth Police on "Wild Goose Chase"

The story heaped endless ridicule on Sherlock Holmes. There were several pictures of the bank, the damaged vault, and the group of us who gathered inside of it. The manager was described as "imperious", which I had to admit was true, but since Baring's was a major advertiser, there were no accusations about its lack of a properly secured vault. Fortunately, there was little said about the Darby family, except to present them as a devout couple who had been victims of the ambitious detective from London.

I read the story as we traveled back to London on the same train that must have held the daily bank deposit. Our holiday had been cut short. Holmes said nothing at all and I knew not to attempt to engage him in conversation.

By the time we arrived back at Baker Street in the early hours of the morning a telegram was waiting for us.

```
Mr. Holmes:
My wife and I are devastated by all the
trouble we have brought upon you. Words
cannot express our apologies. We know, and
heaven knows, that your intentions were
solely for our protection and the righting
of wrong. Our prayers will continue to be
that the Lord will use this great
injustice to somehow work out His divine
plan and bring the light of truth to shine
upon this dark passage of evil doing. My
wife insists that I add to this note that
while there may be many words to describe
accurately the criminals who used the
names of Clayton Johns and Ross Duncan,
```

"stupid" is not one of them. May God bless you, sir, as He continues to use you as an instrument of righteousness.

Jabez Nelson Darby

Sherlock Holmes read it and spoke to me for the first time since we had departed the bank. "The lady is absolutely correct, Watson. These men spent nearly a year devising the most elaborate fraud and pulled it off almost perfectly for over two months. They were not fools and, if the good lady is correct, as I am quite sure she is, they had a hand in murder. Yet I cannot deduce the connecting links between their actions, the murders, and the nonsensical bank robbery."

He took the telegram with him and walked slowly towards his bedroom. "Good night, my dear friend. I am sorry that your well-intentioned holiday has been spoiled, and I am grateful for your consideration of my health. Good night."

"Good night, Holmes," I said and made my way home, with a heavy heart.

I did not call in on Sherlock Holmes for several weeks, and when I did one Sunday morning, he failed to answer his door. Mrs. Hudson kindly let me in and I found my friend lapsed into the dull stupor that he used his syringe to inflict upon himself during those times when he required his searing intelligence to cease its operations. He sat in his chair, staring out his window. His eyes were glazed over and a somewhat foolish smile was pasted across his face. I was deeply distressed. I had feared that the events in Plymouth would have this effect on him, and indeed, they had.

On his table was an unopened letter, dated the previous day. The return address indicated that it had been sent by the Little Flock Christian Book Store in Plymouth. It had been addressed both to Mr. Sherlock Holmes and Dr. John Watson and I took the liberty of opening it and reading it. As soon as I had finished it I laid it down and called for Mrs. Hudson.

"My dear lady, would you be so kind as to bring Mr. Holmes the strongest cup of coffee you are capable of brewing. Something that would induce heartburn in a Turk would be quite in order."

Mrs. Hudson looked at Sherlock Holmes. He gave her a silly smile in return. She then looked at me with a knowing nod and said, "I will fix a brew that will give him a strong jolt back to from Nirvana." Yet again I marveled at her loyalty.

It took some rather unpleasant barking of orders on my part to get Holmes to drink the brew but after an hour, it appeared to have had the desired effect. I then sternly told him to pay attention as I read the letter to him.

>Mr. Holmes and Dr. Watson:
>
>I hesitate to make contact with you knowing how terribly our last time together ended. Again we can only thank you for everything you did on our behalf and assure you of our fervent prayers on yours.
>
>I write again at the insistence of my most virtuous wife, whose worth is far above rubies. Neither of us has slept well these past several weeks and last night, at near to three o'clock, she woke me and said, "That man is part of it. I know he is. God has just revealed that to me." As I was only partly awake and entirely confused, I asked "What man?"
>
>She replied, "That evil man who came by the new shop months ago. You must remember him. You must remember how I felt about him."
>
>I did remember. In the early days of the previous summer, just after we had signed our lease on the new property and opened our doors, an unknown man walked into our shop. He was exceptionally well-dressed, with a fine silk hat and walking stick. He was around fifty years of age and greeted us in the most refined manner. He seemed surprisingly well-acquainted with our books and with the Plymouth

Brethren movement and he asked many insightful questions of us. As I was still in the depths of my bout of brain fever, I welcomed the distraction he brought to my gloom. I was most impressed with him and began to enjoy our conversation. My wife, who normally is most eager to engage with learned visitors, said nothing. As he departed, he asked if I could tell him about the new building and show him around it, as he was considering recommending it to one of his associates.

I took him outside and we walked around the entire structure. I pointed out the various merchants. Not all had fully set up their operations. He noted that the front section alone had been let out to merchants and that the back portion had only a few unmarked doors. I explained that the entire west side of the building had been leased by the Western Union Telegraph Company since this new building was the terminus of their transatlantic cable from New York, and that the back part held their many switches and rotors and whatever else was required to handle all the thousands of signals that would be received there, processed, and then sent on to London, or Paris, or other parts of the Continent.

As my shop was immediately adjacent to the Western Union office, he expressed concern that the activity and noise might be a problem to the atmosphere of a Christian bookstore, and he seemed genuinely concerned for our operations. I explained that a good thick masonry wall separated my shop from Western Union's operations and that much of the noisy machinery was in their basement and would not disturb us.

He asked if I would mind walking with him back to the Hotel – the same one in which I met with you – as he was not entirely sure of the way. I agreed and we chatted pleasantly about the doctrine of the Rapture, and the priesthood of all believers, and other such topics that are significant to our assemblies.

The route took us through a rather dodgy street alongside the harbor that is known to be the denizen of rough men. From time to time I have met such types in Plymouth and when they accost me and demand money I smile and quote the words of the Apostle Peter to them and I say, 'Silver and gold have I none, but such as I have, give I thee' whereupon I reach into my wallet and bring out a gospel tract and begin to show them the *Romans Road* to salvation. Not one of them has yet converted and been saved by my testimony, but I have been saved many times as they invariably roll their eyes, mutter a few curses, and leave me alone.

Two such men accosted my visitor and me, and I was about to respond in my usual fashion. He, however, made as if he were reaching into his wallet but then in a flurry of actions let fly with a left hook to the face of the one man and brought a dagger down on the extended wrist of the other. The first man grabbed his eye and I could see blood gushing from it. The second had his wrist firmly grasped and his arm twisted so forcefully behind him that I could hear his shoulder become dislocated. He screamed in horrific pain while his accomplice ran off in a panic with blood pouring from his face. The man, my visitor, forced the would-be thief to the sidewalk, placed his face right close and said to him, "Look at me, and remember this face. And do not ever attempt to rob me again or you and your entire family will die in miserable pain. Do you see me? Do you understand me?"

The ruffian had a look of terror upon him and as soon as he was released he ran away. The man composed himself and smiled at me and said, "I did a stint in the Royal Marines when I was young and they trained us to handle situations like this. Some things it has been wise not to have forgotten."

I have known several marines over the years and indeed a few have become part of our assembly of believers. They have all been highly trained, but I have never witnessed from any of them the violence and viciousness that I saw that day. But the man chatted on as if nothing had happened. We parted at the Hotel. He wished me great success and most graciously thanked me for my time. I returned to my shop and my wife.

Upon entering my shop, I heard my wife give a sharp cry and she ran towards me and threw her arms around me. She was sobbing violently. "Oh thank God, thank God" was all she could say and she kept saying it over and over. I had never seen her so sore distraught. It was a full five minutes before she calmed herself and was able to speak to me.

"I do not know who that man was," she said, "but he is as close to the devil himself as I could ever have imagined. The moment he walked in the door, I knew that he was evil. Did you not feel it? Could you not tell?" I confessed that I could not.

"He is a monster, whoever he is. You must promise me that you will never, never, have anything to do with him again. Never. I have been praying the shed blood of the Lord over you since you walked out of the door with him. I have never been so frightened. Promise me that you will have nothing whatsoever to do with him, ever."

My wife, sir, as you witnessed, is a very level-headed woman and I had never seen her so overcome with terror. Fortunately, the day ended and we have never heard from or seen that man again. We did not even speak of him until last night when my wife awoke, convinced that he was somehow connected with this whole evil business.

I know not if my sharing this experience with you will be of any use. It is my prayer that it would. About the man himself: he is extremely tall and thin. His forehead domed out in a white curve, and his two eyes were deeply sunken in his head. He was clean-shaven, pale and ascetic-looking. I can only remember that he had no card with him but said that his

```
name was James Morrison and that he was a
professor of something at Cambridge.
```

  ```
It is our hope and prayer that this
additional information may be of some use
to you. May God bless and protect you
always,
```

    ```
Jabez Nelson Darby
```

  I finished reading the letter and looked up at Holmes. The silly look of drugged stupor had vanished from his face. The look I expected to see, the look of brilliant and determined concentration and blazing eyes was also not present. What I saw in Holmes's eyes was something I had never seen in all the years I had known him. What I saw was fear.

  Holmes rose to his feet and began to pace back and forth across the room in vivid distress.

  "Dear God. Oh, dear God. He was there. We were right in his lair. Dear God, Watson. I had not expected this. That monster has laid out some terrible plot and we have walked into it by fate. That lovely family in Plymouth will be completely exterminated in the near future. Dear God, Watson."

  "Holmes," I cried, "what are you talking about? Who is this man? I have never seen you in such distress. What is it, my friend, what is it?"

  With a visible effort, he asserted control over his emotions and fears and quietly sat down in front of me.

  "You have probably never heard of Professor Moriarty?" said he.

  "Never."

  "He is the Napoleon of crime, Watson. He is the organizer of half that is evil and of nearly all that is undetected in this country. He is a genius. He sits motionless, like a spider in the center of its web, but that web has a thousand radiations, and he knows well every quiver of each of them. He is the central power which uses the agent but is himself never caught — never so much as suspected. This is the organization which I alluded to as we traveled to Plymouth, Watson, and to which I now must devote my whole energy to exposing and destroying."

  He leaned forward in his chair and looked directly into my eyes. "My dearest friend, you have never failed to support and care for me and I cannot thank you enough. The mystery in which I am now engaged is exceedingly dangerous and it is quite probable that both of us may be killed if we fail to stop this villain. I wish you to have no feelings whatsoever of obligation towards me. I do not expect you to accompany me any further. For the sake of yourself, your wife and the children you yet look forward to having, you are free to walk away and let me continue on my own. I will not love you any the less for doing so."

Sherlock Holmes is not moved to express feelings of the heart and has always spoken of them as weaknesses that have no place in the life of a man of science. Yet here he was affirming the intensity of our friendship in words that I never expected to hear from him.

I rose and affected a casual response. "Shall we meet on the platform of Paddington in an hour? I believe that I am at least entitled to pack my bags and obtain my service revolver before we catch the next train to Plymouth."

His somber look fled and he beamed a smile back at me. "My dear Watson, what's the rush? You may have a luxurious four hours. Forgive me for delaying you but I really must send off a few telegrams before we leave. Such data as we now have before us suggests that Professor Moriarty's interest was not in the bank at all, but in the telegraph office, and I must learn more about it."

We met at Paddington and took our seats in the front carriage. As *The Flying Dutchman* pulled away from the station, Holmes took out a handful of telegrams from his valise.

"Do not just sit there Holmes," I chided. "What have you learned?"

"The Plymouth Brethren sect claims to be free of all denominational administration, but they appear to know everything about every one of their locals churches from Auckland to Halifax. I contacted one of the Brethren that fellowships at a Gospel Hall in the West End and he provided me with the contact information for the Assembly of Believers Meeting on Union Street in Brooklyn, the local church which was claimed by Messrs Johns and Duncan to have been their sponsoring assembly. They confirmed that yes indeed they had commended two young Christians to the mission work in the Faroe Islands and that their names were Ross Duncan and Clayton Johns."

"So that part is true," I asked.

"No, that part is just further evidence of the extent that Moriarty and his ilk have gone to in setting up this crime. The good folks in Brooklyn also informed me that their men were already in the Faroes, had cashed the wire transfers of financial support that were sent, and most certainly have never been bald. Our two bank robbers assumed their identities as part of the pretense.

"But they also added that last year two other men had attended many of their services and had aroused some suspicion, particularly among the wives. These men gave their names as Isaac Proctor and Anthony Pistone. They had been most inquisitive about the beliefs and practices of the Brethren and asked innumerable questions but never took part in the Lord's Supper service that is restricted to confirmed believers. They had no visible means of support at the time but had ready access to all the funds they needed to live comfortably. Their idle chit chat with the church members led some to assume that they had worked in the telegraph business as they seemed to have quite extensive knowledge about its operations. I deduced that these two men were recruited by Moriarty and assumed the identities of the two missionaries.

"A late telegram to the personnel office of Western Union confirmed that men by these names had been previous employees of Western Union in America, had been highly skilled engineers, and had abruptly quit their employment in the summer of last year.

"The Office of the Public Trustee wired back that there was no such charity as *Here Today, Gone Tomorrow,* or some name like that. Our scoundrels fabricated that as well.

"I also sent a note to the Western Union office here in London. I had a prompt reply from the manager, a Colonel Thomas Sutherland. He was terribly disturbed by the murder of those two men who were working for him and has insisted on coming to Plymouth to speak with us and try to help. I had informed him that I was quite sure that some sort of scheme had been perpetrated upon their operations. He will join us and is bringing his head communications engineer with him."

"I spoke finally with Inspector Lestrade. He was quite up on the murders and welcomed my looking into them. He was not free to come himself but agreed to send one of his official agents, Peter Jones. You may remember him. He is an absolute imbecile in his profession, but he is as brave as a bulldog and as tenacious as a lobster if he gets his claws upon anyone."

"This is all very well, Holmes," I said. "But other than the murders for which you still have no clear motive, what crime was committed? What are we looking for?"

Holmes sighed, "My friend, I simply do not know. All the data I have has convinced me that Moriarty is behind this and that he has spent well over a year planning it, down to the smallest detail. As a result, I know beyond a shadow of a doubt that there is a very monstrous crime involved and that it will yield great ill-gotten gain to Moriarty and his syndicate. I am reasonably certain it is closely tied to the telegraph services of Western Union, but I do not yet know what it could possibly be that they have done, or are doing, or are about to do. That is what I hope to discover. And I am also very sure that once Moriarty learns that we are on his trail, he will take ruthless steps to stop us."

With this Holmes lapsed back into his near-trance of concentration. I read and re-read the telegrams and the letters from Mr. and Mrs. Darby and tried my best to see anything in them that Holmes had not, but after two hours I had to admit that I also failed to see anything new. We had victims of a crime, but we had no motive, and we did not even know what the crime had been.

Chapter Four

Arbitrage

We pulled into Millbay Station by the end of the day and made our way back to the Duke of Cornwall. The excellent chefs at the grand hotel provided us with a tasty supper, after which we rose to go to what I hoped would be a decent night's sleep.

"The chaps from Western Union and the man from Scotland Yard have agreed to meet up with us over breakfast," said Holmes. "Until the morrow, my good Doctor."

I came down early for breakfast. Holmes was already seated at the table. I noticed that there were six places set. "Is someone else joining us, Holmes?" I asked.

"Perhaps. I told the kitchen there might be one more. It does not matter."

Within a few more minutes Agent Jones had appeared and renewed his acquaintance with Holmes and me. Two other men approached the table. The older one, dressed in an American style business suit with a short jacket and long necktie, introduced himself to us, speaking the accent of a gentleman of The South. "Gentlemen, my name is Thomas Sutherland the Third, from Western Union in America, and I am in charge of our operations here in Europe. This here's my chief engineer, Donald Macquarrie. He's from Glasgow he talks kind of peculiar, but he's just as smart as a whip and we're powerful glad you all are taking an interest this tragedy. Right fine of you. Much appreciated."

As he and the young Scotsman seated themselves, a woman walked purposefully up to the table and sat down at the extra place. She was tall, broad-shouldered with a full head of red hair, and dressed smartly if modestly. "Good morning, gentlemen," she said. "I am Mrs. Jabez Darby and since Doctor Watson cannot be involved at one and the same time in apprehending criminals as well as being recording secretary for Sherlock Holmes I am taking over the secretarial tasks. I would not usually offer to work on the Sabbath, but matters cannot be helped. Is that not correct, Mr. Holmes?" she said with the confidence of a woman who is used to being right, and before the men could stand up to greet her took her place at the remaining table setting.

Sherlock Holmes looked intently at his new secretary, and even he could not conceal the traces of a smile at the corner of his mouth. "That is quite correct, Mrs. Darby, and now gentlemen and lady, let us get on with the matters at hand. Colonel Sutherland, we strongly suspect that there is something in the Western Union building that is the object of a criminal syndicate but we as yet do not know what it is. Could you please inform us about the structure and function of that office?"

"Sure. I can do that," said the Colonel with a deep voice and refined Southern cadence. "The Western Union Company is the world greatest provider of telegraph services. We now have well over a million miles of cables stretching around the earth and across every continent, except, of course, for the Antarctic, but when the day comes that the penguins need a telegraph cable, we'll just get one to them too."

"Of course," said Holmes, "but as we are in Plymouth and not in the Antarctic, perhaps you could restrict your information to our immediate location."

"Sure. I can do that. In 1865 our company invented and gave America the world first stock ticker machine."

"Don't you mean to say 1869," said Mrs. Darby, as she continued, using rapid shorthand, to take down every word spoken. "Your 1865 model was only a prototype. It did not appear on the floor of the New York Stock Exchange until 1869."

She said this in a matter-of-fact tone of voice that took the Colonel off-guard. He stared at her for a moment and seeing that she meant no offense nodded in a gentlemanly way and continued. "Right you are, Ma'am. Right you are. As I am sure you folks know, we have hundreds of wonderful companies in America, and many of them are public stock companies, and are traded on the various stock exchanges of the world. Not to make you English boys feel second fiddle or anything like that, but the stock exchange in London is the second largest now after New York. Kind of a distant second, but second nonetheless, and still a real important place. So we all decided over a decade ago that we needed to have one of our stock ticker units right there, right in the middle of your London Stock Exchange, so your firms could do the type of real fast up-to-the-minute trading that we've become accustomed to in New York City.

"Now, in order for that to happen, we decided that we needed our very own transatlantic telegraph cable that would run without interference from New York City to merry old England. So we strung one all the way across the ocean. Now most of the other cable fellows, they ran their cables from Nova Scotia or Newfoundland and ended up in Skewjack down by your Land's End. But that place was getting kind of crowded so we chose to go a few hundred miles more and run straight as a rifle shot from Long Island all the way to Plymouth, and then we could just follow the railway line right into what you folks call The City. And that cable is now up and running and working just fine and dedicated only to business. No happy birthday greetings or any of that family stuff, just business.

"That cable arrives at our new building on your Telegraph Wharf here in Plymouth and there we splice it up, boost it up, and send one branch line back over to Dover and on to Paris. A second and a third run cross-country then across the Channel to Amsterdam and Berlin, and then we run smaller branches back over to the Irish in Dublin and up to the Scots in Edinburgh. At two-thirty every afternoon — well now, that would be three-thirty on the Continent — all the opening prices from Wall Street come flooding through our cables. And that way everybody in Europe gets what's happening in New York at exactly the same time and so they can all do trades at the same time as we do in our Wall Street and everything is fair and square. And that's what our building here is for. Isn't that right, Donny? Did I miss anything?" he said, looking over at his chief engineer.

"No sir. I believe you covered it all," said the Scotsman.

"Please tell us about these two men who were murdered," said Holmes.

"Well sir, I have had just two days in my life that I consider to have been the worst that I could imagine. The first was the ninth of April in the year of

Our Lord, 1865. I don't suppose you English fellows know what took place on that terrible day?"

None of the other four men spoke up. Without lifting her head from her note-taking, Mrs. Darby said, "I believe that was the day when, having lost to the Northern Yankees, the Southern Rebels were forced to surrender at Appomattox and give up their slaves." She continued to make notes oblivious to the glare she was receiving from the Colonel. Ever the gentleman, he smiled courteously and said, "Well I suppose your facts are accurate even if we might not share the same perspective on them. The second worst day of my life was just a few weeks ago when two har-working young men were murdered just a couple of blocks from where we now sit. They were good family men with devoted wives and lovely children. I had hoped against hope that the police would come up with some reason other than their doing work for Western Union to explain why they were murdered, but there has been none. They got themselves killed just because they were doing a job that I had ordered and Donny here had designed. We have done everything we could for their families and they won't ever be in want, but their deaths are a very heavy burden on my heart."

I did not doubt his sincerity or the depth of his feelings. He ceased speaking and extracted his handkerchief from his pocket and wiped tears away from both eyes. "I am sorry gentlemen . . . and lady, but that was a very hard day for all of us and our being here today is because that event is far from over. We need to get to the bottom of this. And I would be most grateful if we can all somehow work together to get there."

"I hope so as well," said Holmes, "and could you please continue and tell us what these men were doing for you?"

The Colonel nodded. "These two men were independent engineers and had their own consulting firm somewhere in Scotland."

"In Glasgow, sir," said Donald.

"Right, in Glasgow. Well, they bid on the contract to do all the installation of the wiring and switching that I talked about earlier. And they gave a good bid, and had real good references, so we gave them the contract, and they came here and did it all. And they did real fine work, did they not, Donny?"

"Yes, sir. Their work was quite brilliant."

"It was the next to last day, the day when they had soldered in the last coupling of the secondary cables. The following day was to be the final inspection. Then we all were going to gather in the office and have a little celebration and bid them farewell, our employees having become rather fond of them. They went walking back to their rooming house and somebody shot them. Nobody heard the shot, but the autopsy said that someone must have put a revolver right close to their heads. Is that not right, Mr. Policeman?"

"Yes, sir. That is what I read as well in the reports," said Agent Jones.

"Thank you, Colonel Sutherland. May I suggest that we all now make our way to Telegraph Wharf," said Holmes. "It would be good if each of us could look at both the basement of the bookstore and the interior of the Western Union installation. There is something amiss somewhere and I believe that if we can find what has been done it should bring us closer to the killers and the reasons for the murder."

We made our way from the hotel over to the wharf and entered the bookstore. Jabez Darby led us down to the basement. I noticed that the dust and grime had all been cleaned away from the tops of the cases. Holmes repeated the task he had done a few weeks earlier but instead of knocking on the wooden panels of the right, he went up and down the wall on the left side of the basement. Again we heard the distinct sound of a hollow section behind a panel and he motioned to me. This time, I was prepared and had brought along a proper pry bar and I quickly removed the panels. Behind them, as Holmes had deduced, was another hole in the masonry, but rather larger than the one on the left that had so completely tricked us.

"Mr. Macquarrie," said Holmes, "addressing the Scottish engineer, "as you are the youngest and most limber of the lot of us, may I prevail upon you to crawl inside this hole and give a good push to whatever you find on the far side of it?"

The engineer got down on his hands and knees and moved his body into the hole. We heard a loud crash as panels on the other side fell into the basement room of Western Union."

"Thank you, sir, thank you," said Holmes. "We shall meet up with you on the other side of this wall in just a few minutes."

And so we did. After fetching Mr. Macquarrie out of the hole, the Colonel gave us a guided tour of the installation. It was rather impressive to a novice technician such as I. It was equipped with both steam tubes and electrical wires. There were many gleaming new machines humming, and clicking, and banging, and clanking. A team of workmen in overalls was tending to them, making sure that they were all oiled and kept in perfect running order. Donald Macquarrie had brought with him a roll of blueprints and he was looking at each unit as we passed, comparing it to what was shown on the drawings.

"They have been here, and they have changed something," said Holmes. "It may take us some time, but we must find out what they have done."

We began at the corner where the massive cable from the Atlantic Ocean entered the building. One by one we moved past the various machines following the path of the current. At each machine, the engineer compared what he saw on his blueprints to what existed in the reality of the building. Each time he shook his head and said, "No gentlemen. There is nothing amiss here. All according to plan."

We were approaching the far corner of the building where the cable was spliced before being run off to the various exchanges of Great Britain and Europe, and I began to worry that we might be yet again on a wild goose chase. The engineer stopped and looked at the Colonel. "Sir, I believe you said that we had auxiliary cables running to Amsterdam, Berlin, Paris, Dublin, Edinburgh, and London."

"That's right," affirmed the Colonel.

"Sir, that is only six stock exchanges. Are you sure that we are not serving any other locations?"

"Impossible. Those are our only offices. You know that, Donny. Why are you asking?"

"Because sir, there are eight auxiliary cables branching off of the main one and not six."

"That's plum crazy," said the Colonel. "Let me see."

Like a child counting toy blocks, the Colonel placed his hand on one auxiliary cable after the other, each separated by about eighteen inches as it was spliced off the main cable. "One . . . two . . . three . . . four. . . Yup. There's eight. Check these out will you, Donny. Are all of these wires real and working?"

The engineer removed a small instrument from his tool case. I recognized it as a recently patented current sensor with two protruding wires, both connected to a small electric bulb. He placed the ends of the wires on each of the auxiliary cables in turn. Each time the bulb glowed. "They're all live, sir. It may take us a few hours, but we can have our men follow each one of them after they leave the building and find out where they lead. Two of them have to be going someplace we don't know about. It looks as if someone is stealing our signals."

"Right. Get that done right away, Donny. And then rip out whichever of those cables isn't ours. We'll have those pirates put out of business in no time."

"May I suggest, sir," said Holmes, "that you might be much more helpful to the apprehending of those who murdered your men if you were not to do that quite so quickly."

"What do you mean?" asked the Colonel.

"Mr. Macquarrie, sir," said Holmes, "could I impose on you to use your sensor to test the main cable at each of the intervals between the auxiliary cables beginning at the far end?

"There has to be current all the way through the main cable, sir," replied the engineer, "otherwise the far auxiliary ones couldn't light up, and they all did."

"Nevertheless," said Holmes, "would you mind doing that for me? It can only take a moment."

The engineer shrugged his shoulders and placed his instrument on the sections of the main cable between each of the auxiliary cables. He began at the far end and, as expected, the current sensor lit up each time. The section between auxiliary cables seven and eight was alive, as was the section between six and seven, and on down the line.

The section of the main cable between auxiliaries one and two was dead. The sensor failed to glow.

The engineer immediately took his sensor away and looked closely at it. Then he tested it again on other sections and again it glowed. He returned to the portion of the main cable that showed no current. Again there was no reaction from the sensor.

"That's impossible!" said the engineer. "There cannot possibly be a part of the main cable that has no current otherwise the rest of it would all be dead. This is madness."

"No, my good man, it is not madness," said Holmes. "It is diabolical ingenuity. The only possible explanation for what you have just discovered with your current sensor is that auxiliary cables one and two are not auxiliary at all. They are nothing less than the main cable and form a detour loop. And I will assure you, sir, that somewhere along that loop someone is reading all your stock price information before sending it along to the exchanges."

"Why would they want to do that, Mr. Holmes?" asked the police agent. "It is an invasion of privacy, but it hardly constitutes a major crime and certainly nothing that might motivate a murder."

"It's arbitrage fraud and they stand to make millions of pounds every month," said Mrs. Darby.

"Pardon me, ma'am," said the Colonel. "But I am afraid I do not understand you."

The lady hesitated to answer but, after receiving a nod from Holmes, proceeded. "There have been several articles in *The Times* about it over the past few years, sir. This is how it works. Let us suppose that a shrewd financial investor were able to see the price of a stock, shall we say Imperial Oil, on both the New York and the Chicago stock exchanges at the very same time, and he observed that the New York price had just shot up by five and seven-eighths but that the Chicago price had not yet moved. What might he send in an immediate telegram to his broker in Chicago?"

"Well for sure he would tell him to buy a whole bunch of shares real fast because the price was for sure going up by a whole lot."

"Exactly sir. And that is what the traders call arbitrage. If I understand Mr. Holmes, he is suspecting that these villains have set up a scheme by which they can do that fraudulently. Is that correct, Mr. Holmes?"

"Correct," replied Holmes. "I will wager, Colonel Sutherland, that most of your messages about the opening prices on the New York Stock Exchange arrive in a timely manner, but that a select few of them are mysteriously delayed, arriving fifteen to thirty minutes late."

"How could they do that," queried the police agent.

"I would suspect," continued Holmes, "that somewhere not far away from here, and most likely quite close to the General Post and Telegraph Office, they have set up one of your stock ticker machines, with a teleprinter attached. They just remove their stock of choice until they have had an opportunity to send a wire to their broker, buy some shares, and then let the rest of the world catch up with them."

"But that's not like robbing a bank," said the Agent. "Where's the money in that?"

"Thousands of pounds every single day," said Mrs. Darby. "They can buy knowing that a stock is sure to rise, or they can short it, knowing that it is sure to fall. They would only have to trade a small handful of stocks every day to make a fortune, and, if I am not correct, Mr. Holmes, the people they rob do not even know that they have been swindled, and it is all done without having to fire a shot, or rob a bank."

"Robbing a bank is what they pretended to do," said Holmes. "And indeed, they fooled us and have, without a doubt, garnered several thousand pounds for their efforts already."

"Then why is it, sir, that you do not want us to put those varmints out of business right away?" asked the Colonel.

"Ah, because," said Holmes, his eyes sparkling, "because I believe that we can best them at their own game, do some rather nasty damage to their financial health, and entice them into our trap."

Chapter Five

The Noisy Nothing

The following morning was Monday and I ate breakfast alone at the hotel. Holmes had been up and out very early and had left a note for me asking that I join him at the bookstore around one o'clock in the afternoon. I did so and found the shop to be a hive of activity. The front room where the books and tracts were displayed was untouched, but the back office had been transformed. There were now two stock ticker machines, two teleprinters, and a web of wires and cables running back and forth every which way. Mr. Macquarrie, the engineer, and several of his men were scurrying to and fro with great energy.

I shuffled into the basement and observed another two workers huffing and puffing as they man-handled a strange looking machine through the still gaping hole in the right-hand wall and into the vault of the bank. They had also run a steam hose and an electrical cable from the Western Union cellar, clear across the cellar of the bookstore and into the vault.

"Come, Watson, the game is afoot," shouted Holmes from the top of the stairs.

"Good heavens, Holmes," I shouted back to him as I climbed back up. "What havoc are you wreaking on this gentle bookstore?"

Holmes, uncharacteristically standing without his suit coat, and with his shirtsleeves rolled part-way up, smiled, "We are going to hoist that villain

Moriarty on his own petard. And if we cannot put him away, we will do very nasty damage to his bank account."

"He is not going to be very happy, Holmes," I said with a smile at my devious friend, but had no idea how he intended to accomplish his plans.

"He will not be happy at all Watson, not at all. And that is the second part of our intrigue. I fully suspect that within a few days we will have an unfriendly visit from his henchmen, if not from the evil genius himself. He will be going mad wanting to know what has gone wrong. And we shall be lying in wait for them to come to us and enter our trap."

"And just where is this trap of yours, Holmes?"

"Why in the vault of the bank, of course. Our very industrious accomplice, Mr. Macquarrie, has adapted one of their machines and now it makes all sorts of wondrous clacking and banging and ringing sounds as it lights up and spits out printed tapes. It whistles and whirs and hums like no machine you have ever seen before. It will be inside the vault and will surely entice them to join it."

"But what does it *do* Holmes?" I had to ask.

"Oh, that's quite elementary, my dear friend. It does absolutely nothing. It will do naught but sit inside the vault and make all sorts of loud sounds and flashes. And we will just have to watch what happens next."

I knew better than to ask, although my curiosity was on fire. I had to be content to sit down beside Mrs. Darby and the Colonel, who were peering over the latest *Financial Times* and having quite the spirited conversation about the prospects of American companies that were listed on both the New York and London Stock Exchanges.

"Your Mr. Holmes has requested," Mrs. Darby said in response to my asking her what they were doing, "that we become familiar with those stocks that are considered volatile, ones that could quite reasonably either move up or down sharply on any given day. So we are familiarizing ourselves with their history and prospects."

"And, I might add," said the Colonel, "having just a real good time doing so. This here is a very well-informed young woman and I do believe she and I have missed our calling. We would of been smarter, the both of us, to do this for a living rather than selling Bibles and managing telegraphs. Do you not agree, Mrs. Darby?"

She laughed. "I never knew I had any such talent. I do not recall from my study of the scriptures that God gave insight into financial markets as one of the spiritual gifts. And I am quite certain that there is no such thing in all of the Bible, or in the entire history of the Church, called a *dead cat bounce.*"

A what!?" I stammered.

She and the Colonel both laughed. "Well now, Doctor," said the Colonel, "that's just an all-American way of describing a stock that used to be high and got low real fast and then looked as if it were coming back up. We call it that because when you drop anything from a high enough spot, even a dead cat, well, it's just going to bounce. So I was explaining that this here Electro-Steam Company of Pennsylvania only looks like it's going back up. But it ain't going anywheres but right back down. It ain't no better than a dead cat."

I smiled at the two of them. "But why are you doing this? Did Holmes explain what he was going to do with all your efforts?"

Both of them looked a little sheepish. "Well, now, sir, we got to admit that he wasn't all that clear. Maybe you can help us with that one. Is it us or does he sometimes not lay all his cards on the table? We're just not real sure what he has in mind. You got some idea?"

I sighed. "No, my friends. But I have lived with him long enough to be sure that he has his reasons that our lesser reason knows not of."

By two o'clock in the afternoon, everything appeared to be in place. Sherlock Holmes called our little troop together and warmly told us that he had christened us as the newest members of his Company of Irregulars. The Colonel, Mr. and Mrs. Darby, Mr. Macquarrie, and Police Agent Peter Jones were all quite pleased with his so doing. I did not have the heart to tell them that their senior officers in the Company were the urchins of Baker Street.

"We have had some useful data from Inspector Lestrade," said Holmes. "He has made inquiries at the London Stock Exchange and there has been some unusual trading going on there over the past few weeks. A certain Zurich Investments Company, a rather secretive firm out of Switzerland, has had a very lucky streak. They have made some large and bold trades on American stocks every day between two thirty and four thirty in the afternoon and regardless of whether they are buying or shorting, their trades are paying off handsomely."

"So that is Moriarty's syndicate?" I asked.

"You may be sure of it," replied Holmes. "And, if our little troop can perform cleverly on the field of battle, the syndicate is about to become distinctly impoverished."

We sat quietly in the back office of the Little Flock Bookstore watching the silent stock ticker machines. At a few seconds past two-thirty in the afternoon, at the same time as the exchanges opened in New York City, they sprang to life. There was a humming and clicking, and banging sound and the printed ticker tapes started to fly out of them. The Colonel was manning one and Mrs. Darby the other. They called out the results as they appeared.

"Dunlop Rubber down an eighth," announced the Colonel.

"Provident Financial up one and three-eighths," read Mrs. Darby, "But it trades at over one hundred dollars a share, so that is not much of a change."

And on they went reading the tapes. "Cable Piano down an eighth, Oneida up a quarter, Paine Webber down a quarter."

Then Mrs. Darby let out a short "Aha!" We looked at her and she announced, "Colorado Coal up three and a quarter. That's a jump of nearly twenty percent."

"Excellent," said Holmes as he rubbed his hands together. "Mr. Darby, please send it down by three and a quarter instead." Jabez Darby, on the teleprinter machine, typed in the instructions.

"Here's another!" called out the Colonel. "Carter's Little Liver Pills is down by two. They were trading at twelve. So that's quite the drop."

"Do you think," I asked, "that the American public finally woke up and stopped buying snake oil?"

"Sorry Doc," the Colonel rebuked me. "Those are just the greatest thing to come along. My Aunt Bessy swears by them. They aren't going out of business for a long time."

"Very well," interrupted Holmes, "the history of the medicinal choices of the American public is a monument to the resilience of the physical constitution of the average citizen. But that is none of our affair. Mr. Macquarrie, could you please send that stock up by two instead."

"Right sir. Done sir," said the engineer as he typed into his machine.

"Have any of you ever heard of something called *Coca-Cola?*" Mrs. Darby shouted to the group of us. "Their stock just keeps going up."

"It's a new tonic, a genuine elixir concocted a couple of years back by a real fine Southern pharmacist," said the Colonel. "Let the professor think it's going down and short it, 'cuz it ain't never going down. It's the real thing."

Professor Moriarty would soon be shorting Coca-Cola.

We kept up the intense pace for a full two hours and then Holmes abruptly called a stop. "It is four thirty and the Exchange has closed for the day. We shall return tomorrow and make more mischief for the professor." With this, we said our good-byes for the day and went to our several abodes. As Holmes sat down to dinner in the hotel, he looked positively gleeful. "Tut, tut, Holmes," I upbraided him. "We mustn't become over-confident."

"You are quite correct, Watson," he responded. "But so far it is all going swimmingly, is it not?"

"I am sure I would agree with you if I had any true understanding of what it is you have us doing."

"Ah, that will all become clear in a very short time. For now, you must trust me and be sure that we have turned the tables on scoundrels and are hurting them where they do not like to be hurt.

"For the rest of the evening perhaps I will go and enjoy the beauty of Nature looking over the seacoast. What do you say to that, Watson?"

"I would say you are either going mad or are annoyed with yourself that you forgot to bring your violin or any books along. You have no use or appreciation for Nature whatsoever."

"Oh my, you do know me far too well my friend. You are right, but the promenade along the coast is as good a place for a three pipe concentration as any in this provincial city and the good lady forbids me to smoke in our battle office. So allow me to bid you good evening. The Company of Irregulars assembles tomorrow at two o'clock."

The evening was uneventful, as was the following morning. At two o'clock, again a half hour before the opening of the exchanges in New York, the Irregulars gathered at their posts.

"Our assault on the enemy is working exactly as I had imagined," said Holmes to the members of the Company. "We are inflicting damage on them from which, if we can sustain the attack, they will not recover."

"Well now, that's real good, Mister Holmes," said the Colonel, "but ain't it past time when you explained just what it is we're doing to the enemy? I have been a soldier, sir, and any enemy I did damage to was standing there in front of me, and you'll just have to excuse me, but I just don't happen to be seeing no enemy round about here."

Like a grinning schoolboy showing off his model train set, Holmes explained his battle plan.

"As you have seen, at two-thirty every weekday afternoon the cables from New York City bring across the opening prices of their Exchange. Professor Moriarty devised a brilliant scheme to see the stock prices before anybody else on this side of the pond. He then runs in front of them, buying or shorting, knowing he cannot lose, and he pockets the profits. We are doing the exact same thing to Professor Moriarty. We have only two hours a day while the exchanges in London and New York are open simultaneously, and during which we are altering the stock price he sees. He now runs in front of the stocks and does exactly the wrong thing. He is doing precisely the opposite of what he hoped to do and is losing thousands of pounds within minutes."

In a way that copied the delaying loop that Moriarty had placed in front of the cables to the exchanges, Holmes had Mr. Macquarrie install a short delaying loop in Moriarty's cable. A chosen stock that opened higher on New York would be changed to opening lower, and those that opened down would be shown to Moriarty as having surged upwards. He would rush to buy the stocks that would fall, and to short the stocks that would rise.

"I have a telegram from Inspector Lestrade informing us that, most curiously, the winning streak of the mysterious Swiss firm came to a crashing halt yesterday. Lestrade's contact in the Exchange estimates that the poor dears lost nearly fifty thousand pounds yesterday."

"Bravo," we all cheered. "Right, back to our posts," chipped in the Police Agent, who did not, in fact, have a post, but stood ready to defend us against whatever danger might appear. Our bravado did not fully disguise our sense that our brilliant game could not continue unchallenged for very long.

Chapter Six

The Visitors

Yet the game did continue. Our routine of reading and altering stock prices went on uninterrupted through Tuesday, and again on Wednesday and Thursday. Each day before starting our tasks Holmes read us the telegrams from Lestrade and each day we cheered at the tens of thousands of pounds of financial causalities we had inflicted.

"He cannot let this go on much longer. I am surprised that he has not yet paid us a visit," said Holmes to his Irregulars as we gathered early Friday afternoon.

At four o'clock a boy appeared with a telegram and handed it to Holmes. He read it and looked up at us. "Cease operations, please troops. We are informed that as of twenty minutes ago our enemies have stopped making any trades on the London Exchange. They were being far more greedy than I had thought they would be and, overcome by their early success, had begun to trade on margin. Their creditors became alarmed and have called their loans. The scoundrels are now in debt by nearly one million pounds."

With this news, we broke into spontaneous applause and hoots and hollers. "My friends," said Holmes as his smile changed to a quite serious look, "our time of fun and games is over. We can expect some dangerous visitors before the weekend has passed."

It mattered not. We were elated and celebrated with a supper together at an elegant seafood restaurant. As we parted, Holmes once more admonished us, "We must all remain close to our residences. You may be called upon at any time to return to the bookstore post haste and come prepared for dangerous undertakings. Mr. Darby, I am sure that you do not own a revolver but, Colonel, I am equally sure that you do."

"Sir, the Second Amendment of the Constitution of the United States of America guarantees me that right. It says . . .," and he proceeded to quote it to us. I did not have the heart to remind him that he was in the Mother Country and not in the colony that got away. I fully expected him to show up when called bearing several revolvers and perhaps a Winchester rifle, or two, and silently thanked James Madison for his contribution to the security of a free Christian bookstore.

I retired to bed shortly after midnight. Holmes was still in our shared sitting room and pacing back and forth. I did not expect him to sleep again until this adventure was over.

Although I lay awake for what I was sure was well over an hour I finally fell into a deep sleep. At three-thirty in the early morning, Holmes shook me awake. "Get dressed Watson. They are here," he said urgently. I emerged into our sitting room and saw a young constable waiting for us. "Police Agent Jones," he said, "sent me on the double to tell you, gentlemen, that he had officers watching the station, and on the late train three rather suspicious looking strangers arrived and made their way to a rooming house near the General Post Office. He has several more constables waiting in the allies near Telegraph Wharf, sir. He wanted you to know that. He suggests that you should come at once, sir, if your plan is to work. Otherwise, he can't move against them as they haven't done anything yet."

"Thank you, Constable," Holmes said and gave the young chap a pat on the back. "You have done your job well and we are on our way."

In the darkness, we made our way to the bookstore and assembled our little troop in silence. To my surprise, Mrs. Darby had accompanied her husband. "Madam," I whispered, "this is no place for a woman. These are dangerous men we are dealing with. Mr. Darby, sir, I am shocked that you would permit your wife to be in such a situation."

"Doctor Watson," Mrs. Darby responded in a whisper, "I assure you that I have never, throughout our entire marriage, ever disobeyed my husband's instructions."

Jabez Darby gave me a gentle elbow in the ribs and whispered, "That's because I have never instructed her to do anything I knew she did not want to do. It's an excellent prescription for a happy marriage, Doctor. You might recommend it to your patients." I could detect the two of them restraining their laughter. I was not amused.

"Is your noisy nothing all set to be fired up, Mr. Macquarrie," asked Holmes.

"Aye, it is," the engineer replied. "And proud of it I am, sir."

We resumed our silence and sat in stillness for another hour. At first light, a constable silently entered the office and lowered his head to the police agent. "They're on their way, sir. There's five of them."

"There were only three on the train," countered Agent Jones. "Where did the other two come from?"

"They seem to have met at the rooming house sir," said the constable. "And sir, the other two are rather odd looking chaps."

"In what way?"

"Well sir, they're both bald as babies. Very strange sir."

"Hmm. Thank you, constable. Very well. To our posts," agent Jones whispered to us.

The men made their way down the stairs and into the basement. Mrs. Darby, not entirely pleased with being so, was assigned the post of sentry and would remain in the office. Once in the basement, the engineer worked his way through the hole in the left side wall and into the basement of Western Union. Holmes, the Colonel, Mr. Darby and I each secreted ourselves behind stacked cases marked "Oxford University Press - Scofield Bibles." Each stack had to be well over a hundredweight. Agent Jones stood in a small alcove, with his revolver drawn.

I jumped with a start as the most ungodly noise began from within the bank vault. There were intermittent flashes of light, bangs, and whistles, and clacking and clanging sounds all coming in a great cacophony through the hole in the basement wall.

"Good heavens," I whispered to Holmes, "What in the name of all that is holy is that?"

"He's is a Scot," said Holmes, "and I fear he was a little carried away demonstrating the superiority of Scottish engineers. It truly is the most fearsomely noisy machine I have ever seen, and it does absolutely nothing. I expect it will drive our scoundrels mad."

We said not another word. The light and the noise from the bank vault continued unabated. Some five minutes later we heard a series of quiet taps on the floor just above us. I dared not breathe.

Four men descended the stairs. I gave a nudge to Holmes and held up four fingers, followed by a questioning gesture, and then five fingers. He shrugged and then pointed up and towards the street, followed by raising a hand flat above his eyes, indicating a lookout. I nodded and waited.

Our visitors gathered in the center of the basement, all looking towards the hole in the brick wall from which the sounds and lights were coming. One of them crouched down and attempted to look inside. He cursed, and then he got to his hands and knees and made his way through the hole into the vault. We could hear him shout, "What the . . ." followed by a series of curse words.

A second man, one of the two with the bald heads, also crouched down and crawled into the vault. I could hear some loud banging sounds and I deduced that one of the scoundrels was striking the marvelous machine with his foot. The machine, in response, gave off a very loud whistle. It sounded as if a train were approaching. I smiled, knowing that behind the other wall Mr. Macquarrie had opened the steam hose and let it blast away.

The remaining two men had kept peering into the hole but with the whistle blast jumped back in fright, and then they quickly crawled through as well. "Now!" shouted Holmes, and one after the other we put our shoulders to our stacked cases of Bibles and completely blocked up the hole. Our villains were trapped inside the bank vault.

Again we heard loud cursing and could feel them pushing against the cases, but to no avail. It was not difficult to hold them back with the combined weight of our bodies and the cases. Then came the first revolver shot. I looked at Holmes and he calmly said, "Let them fire away. There is not a revolver ever made that is powerful enough to penetrate four feet of books."

Several more constables who had been watching the street came pounding down the stairs. There were more revolver shots. All were harmlessly absorbed by the books. I turned to Mr. Darby and with as close as I will ever come to gallows humor said, "No doubt we are being protected by the Word of God, but I'm afraid that they will be of little retail value after such a nasty attack upon them."

Mr. Darby, bracing his back against his stack of cases, gave me a thumbs-up signal. "If I can say they were damaged by bullets while protecting believers against evil doers then I shall be able to sell them at a premium. Some of my customers are rather fond of such items."

When the shots had ceased Agent Jones lowered his head towards the edge of the hole, pushed the cases back an inch, and shouted, "I am arresting you on suspicion of bank robbery, you do not have to say anything but it may harm your defense if you do not answer in question something you later rely on in court; anything you do say may be given in evidence. Now then, there are several police officers on the other side of this hole and all are armed. You cannot escape and you have trapped yourself in a bank vault. Be good chaps now and come out holding your hands in the air."

It did not occur to Agent Jones that it is rather difficult to crawl on your hands and knees while at the same time holding your hands in the air. Nevertheless, the four men, including those who had called themselves Ross Duncan and Clayton Jones emerged from the vault and were immediately handcuffed by Agent Jones and his band of constables.

"The paddy wagon is on its way, sir," said one of the young constables.

"Excellent," said Agent Jones. "Mr. Holmes, yet again you have proved your mettle. Your ways are passing strange but they have worked and we have got the rascals without having to fire a shot. Indeed, they have caught themselves." He chuckled at his own wit.

"Officer Jones," said the Colonel as we made our way up the stairs, "It may be that I have lost my ability to count. But I rather distinctly recall that there was a total of five rascals, and all I see now is four. I do believe that we still have a job to do to find number five."

"Quite right, sir. My men will scour the neighborhood and I am sure that the final villain shall be arrested forthwith."

"I thought my wife would have come out to join us," said Jabez Darby. "Let me fetch her and we can all go for a morning cup of tea to celebrate. He walked towards the back of the store and entered the office portion, the center of all of our operations. A moment later he came back out, but was alone.

"She is not here. Did she already come out? Did you or your men see her, Agent Jones?"

"No sir. I did not see her. Let me ask my men." He left us for a minute and returned looking perplexed, bordering on worry. "No sir. None of my men have seen her."

I could see a strange look coming over the face of Sherlock Holmes. It was the same look I had seen several weeks ago in Baker Street when he learned that Professor Moriarty was behind the grand scheme of fraud. "Agent Jones," he said. "Could you please summon every available constable at once and have them begin a thorough search of the neighborhood? Mrs. Darby may be in very grave danger."

The police agent was about to blow on his whistle to bring his men together when a boy ran up to us. "Is one of you Sherlock Holmes?" he asked. Holmes confirmed that it was he, and the lad gave him a note that Holmes read in the early light. The look of fear on his face deepened and I saw his lower lip begin to quiver ever so slightly.

"Dear God, Watson, he has her."

He read us the note:

```
Release the men immediately. Give them
safe passage back to the station and allow
them to board the London train.

If you do not heed these instructions,
your next search will be for Mrs. Darby's
dead and violated body. You have fifteen
minutes to comply.
```

"We have to release them, we have to!" cried out Jabez Darby. "You must let them go, Officer, you have to. She will be murdered!"

The young man was in a dreadful state of panic. He grabbed at the arm of the officer and pleaded with him.

"Jabez," said Holmes, "please believe me. If we release them he will only laugh at us, kidnap your wife and at some later time subject her to the most degrading and painful death. He is a monster. He is inhuman. And now that we have destroyed his diabolical scheme he will wreak revenge for no other reason than to assuage his anger."

"What can we do then?" shouted the young husband in distress.

"We must rely on the constables to cut off all of the roads and alleys, and guard the station. They will begin to do that straightaway. They will search all the buildings and hiding places within several blocks. He cannot have taken her far."

"That's not enough! He said he will kill her!" In a very quick motion, Jabez Darby grabbed one of the Colonel's revolvers out of its holster and turned and ran out of the office and into the street.

"Sir! Stop!" shouted the Police Agent. "You cannot run out alone. It is not safe." Agent Jones immediately ran after him. A few seconds later we heard the crack of a rifle shot from the street. Holmes and I looked at each other in panic and ran towards the door. The Colonel was already in front of us with a revolver in his hand. We entered the street and saw that Agent Jones was holding the ankles of Jabez Darby, having tackled him on the run. Neither appeared to be wounded.

I heard a scream, a man's voice, from across the road and looked up through the fog in time to see a flailing body fall from the third-floor balcony of the building and land in the street. The man landed feet first and must have injured himself badly as he struggled to get to his feet. He steadied himself and began to raise a rifle towards us. Agent Jones went after him like a tiger. In the short moment before he could take aim Jones was upon him, pushed the rifle away with his left hand and with the nightstick in his right hand laid a crack on the man's head that could be heard a block away. He crumbled into a sorry heap on the roadway. Three young constables were on him and handcuffed and removed his rifle and other arms.

Jabez Darby was standing in the middle of the street still in fear and terror. In the faint light and early morning fog, his gaze was moving wildly back and forth over the building from which the would-be killer had fallen.

From within the street level doorway, we heard a woman's voice call out. "Jabez, darling! It's alright. I am here. I am safe." Mrs. Miriam Darby came running out to the street and threw herself into her husband's arms. They held each other, trembling.

More constables and the paddy wagon had appeared out of the early morning light and fog. The four men were marched from the bank vault and into it. The injured rifleman was lifted up and laid on the floor.

"Holmes," I said *sotto voce*. "Look. Down the road."

In the gloomy light, we observed the figure of a tall, thin man, dressed in a black ulster and wearing a top hat. We could see that he was looking at us. Slowly he raised his walking stick high in the air above his head and then lowered it until it was pointing directly at us, as if he were a sorcerer casting an evil spell. He held that position for several seconds, and then turned to his right and vanished into an alleyway.

"Professor Moriarty is not a happy man," mused Sherlock Holmes. "However, it is unlikely that he will bother this family again. It is I who has become the object of his hatred."

With an air of affected nonchalance, Holmes looked at the group of us and said, "Might I treat my Company of Irregulars to a cup of morning tea? I do believe that we have all earned one."

We pasted on our brave faces and made our way back to The Duke. After some forced idle chit-chat, Agent Jones nodded respectfully towards Mrs. Darby and said, "Madam Darby, I know that what happened was very trying and although it should not be necessary to have a sworn statement given at the police station, I must ask you to tell me what happened to you and the nature of your fortunate escape."

Miriam Darby took a slow sip of her tea, drew a deep breath and began her story.

"As soon as all of the noise and commotion began in the basement, I, unwisely it now seems, but not wanting to miss out on what was happening, came out of the back office and into the store. I was met there by an unknown man who immediately grabbed my arm and placed a revolver under my chin. He commanded me to be silent and come with him, and I had no doubt he would kill me if I refused. I did as he ordered, commending my soul to my Maker and giving a desperate prayer for my husband and children who I feared might never see me again.

"He led me into the building across the way. As it was still before daybreak and a Saturday morning, it was empty. He forced me up two flights of stairs and into a room that looked out over the street. He stood by the window and every so often looked back at me and waved his revolver in my direction. We could hear the goings on from the bookstore and I heard my husband cry out and the Police Agent's shout to him.

"At that instant, the villain put down his revolver and quickly removed his rifle from his back. I heard him say, 'Lovely, a bright bald head gleaming through the fog. A perfect target.'

"I was petrified by fear, but the Lord intervened and I found the strength to rush towards him."

Here she stopped and took another slow sip of tea.

"Yes madam," said Peter Jones. "Pray continue."

She looked at him and quietly said, "Sir, as you can see, I am not a small woman, and the villain who was shooting at my husband was not a very large man."

For a moment, no one spoke as it became clear to us that this devout Christian lady had tossed an armed man off of a balcony and into the street. I sensed that this act, although frightfully brave, was not one that she wished to be attached to her reputation for the rest of her life.

Holmes had reached the same conclusion and turned to Agent Jones. "It is a common characteristic of the criminal class, is it not sir, that they try to brace themselves with copious amounts of alcohol before engaging in a dastardly crime?"

The agent looked at Holmes curiously for a moment and then broke into a smile. "Right you are, Mr. Holmes. I swear that nasty blackguard stunk to high heaven of gin. Drunken sot he was. Couldn't even fire a shot from a balcony without toppling off. That's the way it is with drink. It will bring you down every time, if you know what I mean. It will bring you down." He laughed loudly at his witticism.

Epilogue

The rest of the fall of 1890 passed peacefully. The winter was one of the coldest on record. I began to publish stories about Sherlock Holmes in *The Strand,* a practice I would continue for many years thereafter. The first station of the Underground was opened by the Prince of Wales. So many men, women, and children were fleeing the hard life of Europe for America that the Americans opened a special receiving center on Ellis Island. It was destined to become the gateway to a new life, the American dream, for millions who would follow. February of the following year brought England one of its worst blizzards ever and it was weeks before the snow finally melted and the warmth of spring returned.

On a lovely Sunday in April, I received a note from Sherlock Holmes asking if I would join him in the early afternoon as he was expecting visitors and thought I might wish to greet them as well. I came with no idea who he was expecting and sat down beside Holmes in the comfortable and familiar room at 221B Baker Street. Mrs. Hudson had prepared us a delicious lunch, after which we sat in our traditional chairs and Holmes lit up his pipe.

It was at that moment that Mrs. Hudson entered and said, "There is a family down on the sidewalk, sir. I asked them to come up, but they declined and asked only that you might take a moment to say hello as they passed."

Holmes rose, pipe in hand, and descended that stairs. I followed close behind.

On Baker Street, we were greeted by an attractive and stylishly dressed young family. A mother, father and two adorable children smiled and addressed us by name. The young husband tipped his hat towards us, displaying as thick a head of chestnut hair as I have ever seen.

"Goodness gracious, Jabez Darby!" I blurted out joyfully. "You look wonderful. All of you. Magnificent." Mrs. Miriam Darby introduced us to her beautiful children who politely extended their hands to both Sherlock Holmes and me.

"This is a delight," I said. "What has brought you and your lovely family to London?"

"We moved here last week, Doctor Watson," Jabez replied. "We attended services this morning at the Gospel Hall by Marylebone and knew that we just had to call upon you on our way back to our new home.

"At the time we met you, Mr. Holmes," he continued, "we could not have known that you would be like an angel of light in our lives. You were truly an answer to our prayers and the instrument used by the Lord to deliver us from evil. We thank God every night for you."

This was a bit too much for me and I made as if I were looking at Holmes's back and above his head for the wings and halo. Holmes gave me a bit of a look and I confess that I struggled to conceal a smirk.

Holmes responded to his visitors graciously. "And what of your bookstore. How is The Little Flock managing without its shepherds?"

"I gave the management of it over to one of our elders who had recently retired, and had a decent pension from the government on which to live. He is as happy as a clam sitting and reading and chatting with the occasional customer, and his wife has thanked me a hundred times over for getting him out of the house.

"And this, thanks to you and the mysterious ways of the Lord, is what I am now doing."

He handed his card to Holmes, who smiled and gave it to me.

> **The Brain Fever Trust**
>
> Jabez Nelson Darby
> General Secretary
>
> Bedford Row, London

"It gave me such satisfaction when I was working every day for a good cause that did not even exist, that I went ahead and set up the Trust on my own. Then I sent out all those letters and applications I had prepared, and many of them were returned with generous donations. With the help of a learned group of doctors we are providing the money needed for medical research, and at the same time giving help and encouragement to those who are suffering.

"My medical advisors have suggested that we change the name since they are starting to call the malady from which I suffered *clinical depression,* but that can wait until we are better established. I am enjoying my life and career as never before, gentlemen, and I cannot thank you often enough."

"The smiles on your face and those of you wife and children," said Holmes with authentic grace, "are all the thanks we shall ever need." He gave the young gentleman a pat on the shoulder, all the while continuing to puff on his beloved pipe.

"And you my good lady," he said with a twinkle in his eye as he warmly regarded Mrs. Miriam Darby. "What might you be up to when you are no longer escorting drunken villains off of balconies?"

She gave a peal of delighted laughter and handed us her card.

> **Miriam Darby (Mrs.)**
>
> **Private Investment Consultant**
> **Bond Court, City of London**

"After our adventure, the Colonel and I became great friends and formed a business partnership. It turned out that he is a devoted Southern Baptist gentleman, and their beliefs are not that much distant from ours as to have me unequally yoked. So, he quit Western Union and we went into business together. He has become an honorary grandfather to my children."

"And your new business, if I may ask?" said Holmes.

"The Lord is blessing us beyond all we could ask or imagine," she replied. "We have rather quickly acquired a reputation for expertise concerning firms that are traded both in New York and in The City and are quite sought after."

"Some three thousand years ago," said Jabez Darby, "my namesake in the Bible – you will find his story in the First Book of Chronicles – prayed to the God of Israel, "Oh that thou wouldest bless me indeed and enlarge my coast, and that thine hand might be with me, and that thou wouldest keep me from evil." That prayer has been answered many times over in my life. We are blessed with friends and family and with fearless protectors, sir."

Miriam Darby looked up at Holmes and asked, "And you sir? And you, our wonderful Doctor? We trust and pray that you are well."

Holmes took a slow draw on his pipe and exhaled it even more slowly. "Other than continuing to defile my 'temple of the Holy Spirit' as you called it, we could not be happier. You would agree, Doctor Watson?"

"Most assuredly."

"In that case," said Mrs. Darby, "all you have to do is stop putting that dreadful poison into your body." With this she quickly snatched the pipe right out of Holmes's mouth, gave the bowl of it a smart rap on the heel of her boot, and handed it back, empty and extinguished, to the nonplused Holmes and said, "Then you will be a healthier man and, as a result, a better detective, Mr. Sherlock Holmes."

With a beaming smile, she threw her arms around Holmes's neck and planted a kiss firmly on his face.

I could never be so sure as to swear to it in a court of law, but I am quite certain that I saw a trace of lipstick on the cheek of Sherlock Holmes.

Dear Sherlockian Readers:

The plot device of this story was inspired by the 2014 book by Michael Lewis, *Flash Boys*. That story revealed the milli-second electronic version of what once was called *frontrunning*, the illegal practice by a stockbroker upon receiving a large buy order to purchase the same stock himself just before placing the order, knowing that the large order would drive up the stock. *Arbitrage,* as explained in the story, is the practice of knowing what happens on one stock exchange and buying or shorting a stock on another exchange immediately before the second exchange adjusts its price based on information from the first. The first practice is illegal, the second best left to experts. I suggest that we amateurs just buy and hold.

In 1900, Western Union Atlantic Service laid a telegraph cable from the New York Stock Exchange, through Nova Scotia to Plymouth, England. From there it continued overland to the London Stock exchange. It entered the port of Plymouth at the place still called Telegraph Wharf. To the best of my knowledge, nobody ever hacked into it, but who knows.

The names and locations of place in Plymouth are more or less accurate for 1900, except for the bar and bookstore that Holmes visited. I made them up.

I was privileged to grow up in a very conservative fundamentalist sect known variously as the Plymouth Brethren, or Brethren Assemblies, or Christian Brethren or the Gospel Halls. As a separate people, they were overwhelmingly honest, industrious, generous, moralistic, and caring, regardless of their very odd beliefs and practices. Although I am now a long way removed from those days of my past, I remember them fondly and continue to have great respect and admiration for the many wonderful individuals I knew.

The references to the individuals and writings of the Brethren in this story are accurate, although they may not be the most interesting to readers today.

A Case of Identity Theft

A New Sherlock Holmes Mystery

Chapter One

The Hat

On one mid-November afternoon in the year 1888 Sherlock Holmes sat in his armchair, absently smoking on his pipe, and reading the weekend copies of London's newspapers. "Watson," he said, speaking my name but not looking up, "what is your opinion of this chap over there in America who claims he has discovered some sort of ray of light that can penetrate solid objects? He lacks sufficient imagination to even come up with a name for them, so they are being called 'X-rays?' You are a man of science, is there anything to them?"

"I believe that the chap you are reading about, Nicola Tesla, is a very clever fellow, but as far as there being a way for humans to see through walls, well, as they tell us up in Glasgow, I hae me doots."

"But just think," said Holmes. "If we could peer through the walls of all of these homes and buildings in London would we not be in wonder at the infinitely unique; those things that are beyond the imagination that people, even Londoners, say and do to themselves and to each other when they are certain that they cannot be seen or heard by any outsider?

"It is precisely these tiny details of their lives that betray their motives and their machinations, and which I have trained myself to look for. Such a pity that all I am permitted to observe is what takes place outside of those impenetrable walls. If they ever do manage to make these wondrous new rays effective then you will find me standing on the pavements of London gazing into the most mundane of English houses."

"And," I countered with a chuckle, "about to be arrested by the local constable for being a Peeping Tom."

'Ah," said Holmes, still not looking up from the newspaper, "But I would be more than satisfied by restricting my observations to those who were fully clothed. Even to see and listen to them would solve a host of riddles and permit me to deduce answers to an endless list of unsolved crimes."

"If it unsolved crimes you are seeking," I said, "why are you not devoting yourself to solving the one the Press has been screaming about for the past three months?"

"And what might that be?" said the voice from behind the newspaper.

"Really Holmes," I protested. "You know perfectly well what it would be. I'm speaking of Jack the Ripper. Why has the nation's most accomplished detective not been involved in the case?"

Holmes uncharacteristically made no reply. This surprised me and I said nothing until a small light went on inside my head.

"Aha! You are involved in it. You are. I can tell."

"My dear friend," said the hidden voice, with just a small hint of impatience, "even to you, who I trust with my very life, I can say nothing. I will neither confirm nor deny any assertions you care to make. Although I would ask you to move on to other matters, as that case has been the subject of so much frenzied speculation that I am finding the entire matter tiring and tedious."

For a moment I said nothing, inwardly gloating. "Then you are involved. I knew it. But Mycroft must have recruited you and threatened to rap your knuckles if you ever let on to anybody. Admit it, old boy. I've got you on that one," I said triumphantly.

Holmes said nothing but he slowly lowered the newspaper, looked at me with just the barest hint of a smile, and then lifted it once again. "My good doctor," came the voice. "Do try your best to indulge me and stop commenting on the matter."

I ignored this request. "Well then, would the greatest detective mind in the Empire then offer his enlightened opinion on the matter? What is your scientific analysis of Mr. Jack the Ripper?"

"He does not exist."

"Nonsense Holmes. Five women have been murdered in the same manner and near the same location. How can you say the killer does not exist?"

"I did not say, my dear Watson, that there is no killer. I only said that Jack the Ripper does not exist."

"But of course, he does," I protested. "He has sent taunting letters to the newspaper, *The Evening Star*. He is daring the police to find him."

"The letters are a complete fabrication," replied Holmes.

"Oh, really Holmes? Who would be so twisted and indecent as to impersonate a demented murderer and send a letter to the newspaper?"

"The newspaper."

"Yes, the newspaper. Did you not see it? You must have."

Holmes still had not looked directly at me. "My good man, you asked me a question and I answered it."

"I beg your pardon? Oh, so you are saying that the newspaper itself wrote a letter to itself? That's preposterous. The Press may be obnoxious and ill-mannered, but you cannot possibly be saying that they would entirely fabricate something and use it to deceive their readers?"

With this Holmes lowered the newspaper and looked steadfastly at me.

Readers of my stories recounting the adventures of Sherlock Holmes will recall that I have stated that from time to time something I have said has been responded to with The Look. In its mildest form, one of kindly but supercilious condescension, it says to me, without a word being uttered, that I am behaving like a naïve schoolboy. In mid-range, it accuses me of being a pathetic dupe. The more severe variety, the third degree, announces that I am revealing to all that I am no more than an imbecilic moron. To my relief, my question occasioned only the first degree.

"Very well then Holmes. The Press cannot be trusted on every single instance, but what purpose would they have in forging a letter and making up a clever name for a perverted murderer?"

"I would have thought that the answer was obvious. The *Evening Star* is a fairly new venture and needs to increase its circulation, thereby improving its profits and enriching its owners. Had the real murderer not come along they might have invented him if it were not for their utter lack of imagination. To them, he was not sent "from Hell" but was as close to a godsend as could be hoped for. I imagine they even thanked the good Lord for sending him their way."

"My dear chap," I rebuked him. "You really are crossing the border from cynicism to blasphemy with that one. It is no doubt a good thing that you are not officially involved or Mr. Ripper might now be knocking on our door instead of the much less interesting one who is about to," I said, looking out of our window down to the pavement of Baker Street.

On that note, Holmes finally put down the newspaper and stood and joined me at the window.

Wandering back and forth in front of the door to 221B Baker Street was what I concluded must have been a woman. My bewilderment resulted from my being unable to see anything except the top of a preposterously large hat. It not only obscured the bearer's head and shoulders but also the entire body, including the feet. All that could be seen from our vantage point was the hat's top side.

The hat approached our door, stayed there for a few seconds and then rotated counter-clockwise and bobbed several yards in the direction of Oxford Street. Then it stopped, rotated clockwise one hundred and eighty degrees, and returned to the door. Then another ninety degrees clockwise and flopped its way toward Marylebone before a final ninety degrees counter-clockwise and returning to our door and ringing the bell.

"Spare us," said Holmes. "Yet another young woman who is in love and confused. Were she a victim of a crime or a breach of promise, she would have marched resolutely to the door, but being in love with the object of your quest renders the brain paralyzed and incapable of clear and logical deduction. Yet another reason, Watson, why I have found it best to avoid such disastrous entanglements."

"Mrs. Mary Angel," said Billy, the young page that Mrs. Hudson had recently hired to assist her in dealing with the endless stream of odd persons who crossed our threshold.

"How divine," I replied in response and congratulated myself on my outburst of quick wit by chuckling. Holmes did not even smile and I was left on my own to enjoy my droll humor.

The hat appeared behind Billy. As the hat was of short stature and Billy somewhat tall for his age, his body and head obscured the rest of the client and all either Holmes or I could see was the massive hat flopping on the top of the page's pill box like a great set of wings.

"Please enter and be seated," said Holmes to the hat that having been circumnavigated by a backward-leaning page boy had now become a young woman in her early twenties. She sat and removed her hat, placing it in her lap.

"And," Holmes continued, "welcome back to London from your time in New Zealand and Australia, where you enjoyed writing stories about the tour of our English Footballers rugby team."

"Yes, Mrs. Angel," I added. "I quite enjoyed reading all about the triumphs of our boys out there in the Antipodes."

"Why thank you," replied the young woman as she seated herself on our sofa. "I had not expected that as a professional detective you would enjoy reading *Rugby News*."

In truth Sherlock Holmes not only did not enjoy reading this publication, he never read it at all, and never would. He had formed his conclusions, I was sure, by his observation of the lady's appearance and clothing and was, I was sure, mildly disappointed by the lack of any surprise from the would-be client.

I, on the other hand, as a sportsman who occasionally indulged in a small wager on the outcome of matches of all sorts, was a regular reader of the sporting newspaper that Mrs. Angel worked for, and had seen her byline attached to the reports of the recent tour of a British national rugby team to New Zealand and Australia.

"Indeed," I responded cheerfully, "it was a delight to read that our boys consistently trounced those upstarts in the colonies. Although you must have gotten a little weary writing the same thing every time. Twenty-two matches to just one for the local chaps, was it not?"

"Oh yes," she replied, looking at ease and smiling back at me. "It was quite the splendid time for our team as well as for my husband and me. We saw every match and journeyed up and down …"

"And he," interjected Holmes brusquely, not at all interested in letting any discussion of sporting events become the topic of conversation, "is, I gather, the reason for your being her today."

The smile vanished from her face and was replaced with a look of pained concern.

"Yes, sir," she answered. "He is. He has vanished." She brought her hands together as she spoke in an effort to stop the shaking that had begun in them. I could also see that she was biting on her lower lip to control the trembling that had set in.

"The facts, please madam," said Holmes. "When and where did you last see him? What communication have you had from him? What makes you sure that he is missing? And having told me all those matters do not forget to tell me his name, occupation, and family connections."

Mrs. Angel closed her eyes briefly and took a deep breath. "Of course sir. I will try my best to tell you everything I can. If it can help you to find him, I would be most grateful."

"I make no promises, madam. I have not yet agreed to take on this case, if indeed it amounts to a case at all. Please get on with it."

Chapter Two

On a Wild Goose Chase

Holmes lack of manners and consideration for young women in distress constantly vexed me, but I had learned over the years of watching him that he had a very soft place in his well-protected heart for the fairer sex, especially those who had been wronged and damaged by the men to whom they had given their trust. I could have told Mrs. Angel at that moment to relax and that Sherlock Holmes would ride to her rescue but doing so would have angered England's finest detective beyond what I was willing to endure on an otherwise pleasant morning.

"My maiden name was Mary Sutherland. I grew up in the village of Coldfield, just outside Birmingham, as did my husband, Mr. Hosmer Angel. Our families were close friends and we, that is my husband and I, have been companions since we were children, and we were betrothed to each other, we liked to think, since we were ten years old. For the past several years we yearned to get married but our mothers — both of our fathers had passed away while we were children, but I do have a stepfather — they all insisted that we should be established and earning at least a modest income before doing so. That was a sensible thing to do and so we waited until we had both turned twenty-one, had secured gainful employment and had some prospects in front of us, and then were married following Michaelmas last year. Our first anniversary has just passed."

At this point, tears began to appear in her eyes and her lower lip started to tremble. I leaned toward her and offered her the use of a clean handkerchief. Holmes did not move.

"Take another deep breath and keep going," he said. "Was your marriage pleasant or did the two of you make each other miserable?"

"Oh sir," she sputtered, "we could not have been happier. We had found very pleasant lodgings in Camberwell. Hosmer, my husband that is, had secured employment at Thomas Cook's Travel Service, and I, being a skilled typist, had set up a business offering stenographical services to many of our local shop owners. I charged the going rate of twenty pence a page and was bringing in a steady income. Indeed, I could scarcely handle any more. We were setting money aside, sensibly you know, and planned that in a year's time we would be able to start a family." Here she stopped and took another deep breath.

"Our only indulgence was that once a week, on the weekend, during the season, we would go and take our place in the stands and watch the rugby matches. We never missed one when our home boys, Birmingham and Solihull, were playing and we could cheer them on. After the match, we would treat ourselves to a pleasant supper down at Denmark Hill. We had a simple life, sir, but we could not have been happier."

"Of course. So what happened?" asked Holmes.

"You will recall, sir, you being a fan of rugby and all, that last winter it was announced that a national rugby team would take a tour of New Zealand and Australia."

Holmes said nothing as he had no use for any such recollection. I responded pleasantly instead. "Of course, that was all through the sporting news. Quite the exciting opportunity for our boys, and for their loyal fans."

"Indeed, it was sir," she returned with a look that was not quite a smile but, at least, she was no longer crying. "Cook's had been given the contract to make all the bookings and because Hosmer, my husband that is, was such a rugby fan, and of course because he was a diligent clerk, he was given the assignment of being the guide and managing the tour. He was quite over the moon about it but would not agree to do so unless I could accompany him. Well then, the managers at Cook's sent a word over to the *Rugby News* and then sent me to speak to them, and as I was a strong typist and had some skills as a story-teller, they hired me to be their reporter for the tour."

"And congratulations on getting the job and sending back such excellent reports," I said with unfeigned enthusiasm.

"Oh, thank you sir, but I must admit that much of the reason was that the newspaper would be able to claim that they had a reporter on the spot and have their stories sent back, but it would cost them a pittance as my travel and lodgings were already paid for by the team tour. But it was unusual to have a young woman report on rugby sir. Some of the older chaps were quite jealous. I would like to think that the editors were enlightened and supporters of universal suffrage, but I have to confess that they were merely pinching their pennies."

"Keep going," said Holmes. He gave me a bit of a look that said that I was becoming a distraction. However, as a loyal fan of the great sport of rugby, I accepted that there are rebukes that cannot be avoided and have to be endured.

"Of course, sir," she said. "The tour was like the honeymoon that folks in our station in life can only dream about. The ocean journey on the Steamship Kaikoura was glorious even if the cabin we were assigned was not what you could call posh. But the food and the music — the rugby boys are great singers you know. Welsh many of them. Some of the songs were a little rude, but that's just the way they are, especially after a few rounds of ale. We laughed and danced all the way to the far side of the world and back. And the matches were glorious. We won all but one, as you have noted doctor. But there was nothing at stake except the fun of the game. The Kiwis, as the New Zealanders like to call themselves, were wonderfully hospitable, and even if we beat them on the field they always joined us afterward in the pubs.

"Their players brought along their wives and girlfriends, who were all refined young women. We in England do them a great disservice by lumping them in with the Australians, you know. The New Zealanders are really much more, well, civilized I guess you could say. And since many of our boys are still bachelors we were joined by a number of quite attractive young ladies in search of a sturdy young gentleman who had good prospects as a husband. Rugby players are not well-known for acting like gentlemen, of course, sir, but most of our lads came from good families. Two young women did manage to land a couple of our lads, and they were married by the ship's captain and returned to England with us. And, all in all, the tour was just a great success and we, my husband and I that is, could not have been happier."

"And then when you returned to England he disappeared?" said Holmes.

"No. Well, yes, but not immediately," she replied. "When we arrived back in London I had to return to our lodgings in Camberwell and work very hard to get my business back, as I had neglected it for five months. But Hosmer was called immediately to Cardiff. The Welsh national team had observed the success of our tour and wanted one of their own next year. Cook's sent my husband to meet with them and he was not only to be the tour guide, but he had been selected to manage all the negotiations and business arrangements. It was quite the feather in his cap. So we were apart from each other for over a week. But we were both so busy that we hardly had time to miss each other. And then . . ." Here she paused.

"Yes?" said Holmes.

"And then this letter arrived in the post." She reached into her purse and produced an envelope and handed it to Holmes. He read it and handed it to me. It was typed on plain paper and ran:

```
My dearest:

     Unbelievably good news! We are to return
to New Zealand at once. The Kiwis are
sending a rugby team made up entirely of
native Maoris to England. It will be a
sport and exotic culture tour combined.
Cook's has the travel contract and I have
been chosen to manage it. My salary has
been doubled. I said I could not go unless
you came as well and they had already
spoken to the News, who were so pleased
with your work, and made that arrangement.
I cannot believe our good fortune.
     My dearest, we must make arrangements
very quickly. The next steamer for the
Antipodes departs on October the twenty-
fourth, just three days from now my
dearest. I will have to meet you on board.
Please, dearest, re-pack and get ready to
go. Your ticket is enclosed. I shall not
need to pack as I have enough with me
already. I will board at the last minute
and then will be all tied up with meetings
```

```
until dinner. But I will see you for dinner
and dancing at our table at six o'clock
after our ship is out to sea.
    My dearest, how could we be luckier?
Another honeymoon! See you on board.
    Your happy husband,
    Hosmer
```

Enclosed with the letter were the stubs and receipts from Mrs. Angel's ticket.

"I was in ecstasy," the young woman whispered. "It seemed that my life had been transformed into a fairy tale. I did not sleep for the next two days what with laundry and packing. I took a cab to the Union Pier and boarded the Oceana two days later. Our cabin was two decks higher than the last trip and the help very accommodating. I imagined myself lifted into the noble classes. I enjoyed walking the promenade as we pulled away from the shore and bade goodbye to England. Just before six o'clock I dressed and made my way to the dining room and took my place at our table, and it was such a good table, and I waited."

Here she again paused. "I waited, and he did not arrive at the table. At first, I thought nothing of it and assumed that his meetings had run overtime. But he did not show up that evening and at ten o'clock I went searching for him. I asked about meetings being held and no one on the crew knew anything about any such meetings. I waited in the cabin. I was awake all night long. He did not arrive. First thing in the morning I asked to speak to the captain and at noon had an appointment with him. He said he was sorry for everything that had happened to me, but he checked the list of passengers and although my name was listed my husband's was not. He was quite kindly, but he clearly saw in me an abandoned wife who had been deceived by a wayward husband. I gathered that it happens often on such journeys."

"You were not the first, I regret to inform you, Mrs. Angel, and you will not be the last," said Holmes.

"Sir," she pleaded. "You must not believe that I was abandoned. Hosmer would not do that to me. I have known him since we were children. I know his heart. He has a good heart. He would never do anything to hurt me so terribly. Something dreadful has happened to him. I know it has. You have to help me. You have to help me find him."

"First things first," said Holmes. "Please continue your story."

"Yes, of course, sir," she said. "By this time, we were had rounded Gibraltar and into the Mediterranean. There was a stop scheduled for Marseille the next day and I got off the ship there. What little money I had with me I used to have my baggage transported to a small hotel near the docklands where I found cheap lodgings. A woman alone was not at all safe and I was fearful of walking on my own. However, I said a prayer and made my way to the nearest British bank and arranged to have funds transferred from our saving account in London.

"The money arrived two days later. With that, I purchased train fare back to Calais and booked passage across the Channel and home. A week had passed since I had boarded the Oceana. I contacted my mother in the Midlands and she immediately called her friend, Hosmer's mother, Mrs. Angel, Mrs. Angel senior that is, as I am now also Mrs. Angel. She was very disturbed as Hosmer had sent her word that he was meeting me on the ship and we were returning to New Zealand."

"Ah," said Holmes. "That is material. Your husband had also sent word that he intended to travel with you?"

"Yes sir, and he does not lie. He does not lie to me and he would never lie to his mother. Even if he ever wanted to, he never could lie to his mom. So he must have been telling the truth when he said he was to meet me on the ship and sail to New Zealand."

"Hmm," said Holmes. His telltale sign was giving him away. He had placed his hands in front of his body, his fingertips touching each other. He was staring quite intensely at Mrs. Angel.

"Please, miss. Do continue," he said.

"There was no sign of his having been in our rooms recently. So I contacted his employer, Cook's travel. They were very courteous as all travel service providers are, but they informed me that Hosmer had completed his assignment in Cardiff and had given his notice, all very rushed and all because he was leaving for New Zealand because of the position I had been offered by *Rugby News*. They had wished him well and told him to try and secure the travel contract to bring the native rugby players to England, as they thought it might be awarded to a local firm in Auckland. But they had given him no assignment and were quite firm in saying that they had not issued tickets, good tickets they were, for my husband and I to travel half around the world and back."

"Your story has a certain symmetry to it," said Holmes, now with his eyes closed. "Quite interesting."

"Then sir, I went to speak to the men at *Rugby News*. They had been very nice to me, even if they had been penny pinchers. I told them my story, including the parts about talking to the people at Thomas Cook's. They were sympathetic, they rather liked me a little I like to think, but they floored me when they said that no offer of any sort had been made to me, and that they had never spoken to the people at Thomas Cook's, and that they had no plans to sponsor any part of the native Maori rugby team for they were of the belief that rugby should only be played by gentlemen, and only then by amateurs, and that there had been rumors that some of the New Zealand natives were receiving cash secretly to come and play in England and they would not be part of any such arrangement. No, sir.

"I was utterly shamed in front of them, but they were still courteous to me and one of the older chaps — I wouldn't have expected it of him since he was one of the old boys who had objected to my being given the assignment with our national team — he took me aside and asked me a few more question, in private like and all. He said he would help me because he had read my stories and thought they were so good that no one could have known they were written by a woman had my name not been attached to them; and he thought I was a right good rugby fan, for a woman that is, and that I knew the game quite well, for a woman, of course, and had a right good passion for it in my soul, at least as much could ever hope for from a woman. So, he gave me your name and address, Mr. Holmes, and sent me to see you straightaway, and he even offered to loan me the money to pay your fee if I needed it, which was kind of him as he is far from wealthy himself, and I thought that was about as kind and generous as I could ever hope to expect, from a man that is."

"And now you are here," said Holmes. "Remind me please Watson to send a note of thanks to the right good gentleman at the *News*.

"Now madam," said Holmes. "About this letter you received from your husband. Was he in the habit of writing letters to you?"

"Oh yes, sir. He and I wrote to each other since we were ten years old whenever we could not see each other for more than three days. He always wrote such beautiful letters, sir. They were always full of affection and sometimes even a bit naughty, if you know what I mean sir, but I believe that it is not a bad thing between a husband and wife is it, sir?"

Holmes wisely did not attempt an answer to the question but carried on with questions of his own.

"This letter has been typed. Was your husband a typist?"

"Oh no, sir. I wouldn't let him near my typewriter sir. He was all thumbs as they say. But I thought that with him being promoted to a manager level almost at Thomas Cook's that he must have been given a secretary to help him, which made me quite proud of him and all. So I thought it most unusual to receive a letter like that but I made sense of it and then thought nothing of it."

"He addressed you as 'dearest,' more than once I believe," said Holmes. "Was that his usual term of endearment for you? If not, what did he used to call you? Please just be frank in your answer. Doctor Watson and I observe the strictest confidence with all clients."

I thought of adding 'and especially with young women having troubles in their love lives' but I refrained.

"No sir," said Mrs. Angel. Then she looked at the floor and I could see a blush rising into her face. For a moment she said nothing, and then shrugged her shoulders and spoke. "He always called me his heaven-sent little heifer, and I called him my bully-boy. We were raised in a farming village, sir, and I will have to let you take things from there and please do not ask me to say more on that sir."

Here I spoke up for fear, knowing Holmes, that he was quite likely to do the opposite of what she had just asked. "Mrs. Angel, you may be sure that we understand and will not pursue that line any further. And may I, as a doctor, tell you that you are a fortunate young woman to have such a warm and playful relationship with your young husband."

She looked up, still blushing, "Thank you, Doctor. You are being very considerate."

"Fortunately, I am not the same way inclined," said Holmes, "or I would never get to the end of my questions. So just one last item with regards to your letter. He was not only uncharacteristically discreet, but he did not even sign his name to it. Had that ever happened before?"

"No sir, but as I said, sir, I assumed that he must have dictated it to a secretary and, therefore, he had to be very proper and all, and that the secretary had just typed his name because that is what secretaries do when they are in a hurry, or, at least, that is what I concluded must have happened, sir."

Holmes said nothing in response. He closed his eyes and folded his long legs under his body, brought his hands together, fingertips pointing up, and held that pose for a full two minutes. Mrs. Angel stared at him and then looked at me with bewilderment all over her face. I reached out my hand and laid it on her forearm, then lifted it in a silent gesture that told her to just wait. She must have thought Sherlock Holmes a very queer bird indeed, but he returned from his imaginary flight to who knows where and spoke.

"I will accept this case, madam. I cannot promise anything except that you will have my utmost effort and my complete confidence. Kindly leave your card behind and we will be in contact with you as soon as we have anything to report. In the meantime, I suggest that you resume your typing business as it may be financially necessary as well as distracting. And may I wish you good day, Mrs. Angel." With this he unfolded his legs, rose and gestured toward the door. The young woman stood, the look of bewilderment still on her face, and made her exit.

"Thank you Mr. Holmes, and thank you, doctor," she said as she replaced her monstrous hat on her head and walked down the stairs. I watched from the window as she stood on the pavement on Baker Street, but I quickly jumped back when she turned and looked up. Fortunately, her line of sight was blocked by the hat. When I looked back down, I saw the hat climb into a cab.

"Very well then Holmes," I began. "Even if your newest client was not surprised at what you knew about her I was, so do tell how you deduced all you did. I am sure you are itching to enlghten me. You always are."

He looked a little miffed as he took his scientific observations and deductions quite seriously, but he deigned to enlighten me all the same.

"Her fingernails were clipped short rather than being allowed to grow to a fashionable length, and the fleece on the cuffs of her sleeves has two parallel lines marked on them. Together a sure sign of a typist. Her face was sunburned sometime in the past three weeks as could be seen by the faint peeling still on her forehead. As there is no sunshine capable of giving a sunburn anywhere in the British Isles she must have been abroad to someplace much warmer and only recently returned; obviously an ocean voyage to the tropics. Her boots and her dress were quite new and of good quality but two years out of style indicating that she had bought them in one of the colonies where our merchants send all of their fashions after they have gone out of style here since the colonists do not know any better and rush to buy them. Why would an earnest young typist be returning from a warm colony at this time of year as it is not reasonable to think she would have gone there to seek employment? The colonies are chock full of cheap labor. Therefore, she must have been sent, and who would send a typist on an ocean voyage other than a newspaper? And what newspaper could possibly have sent someone in the recent past except for that miserable little *Rugby News*, of which I am most certainly not a reader, but the news of the tour was mentioned in *The Times*. As to her being worried about her husband the obvious clue was the wedding ring. I could see that her finger was red and swollen on both sides of the ring — an obvious indication that she had been grasping and twisting it quite desperately, as do so many women who are distraught concerning their wayward husbands. All put together it was more than enough to come to the conclusions I did."

"Remarkable as always, Holmes," said I. "Of course I knew all that, except the husband part, as soon as Billy gave the name since I do read the *Rugby News* and had read all of her stories. Quite a good way to keep up on what is happening, you know. I might recommend it to your reading list."

Holmes scowled, sat down, and lit his pipe.

"What I do not understand," I said, "is why you accepted this case. You generally do not give those with affairs of the heart the time of day. Why this one?"

"Aha, because this is not a case of a lovesick wife and a wandering husband. There is something behind this, Watson. A return ticket to Auckland, 'and a good ticket it was.' Someone has invested at least a hundred pounds to get her out of the country. The letter is not from her husband but some other party. From what little we know the husband may have been similarly deceived. There is no hint of another romantic interest, and no longstanding passions or hatreds. So the only other motive must be financial gain. And it must be significant for someone to have made such an extensive and expensive plan to get the poor thing out of the way."

"And you are quite sure," I returned, "that the young husband could not have had another love interest. It does happen you know. Especially amongst the young athletic crowd."

"Quite right you are. I thought that at first when I looked at her, did you not? What did you make of her?"

"Well," I said. "She is no beauty that would turn heads in Trafalgar Square, but she seems pleasant enough."

"Oh, my dear doctor. You are entirely too kind. She was not the least bit attractive. Her face was vacuous if not bovine. Of late we have been quite fortunate to have been blessed with clients from such splendid places as Goa, or Trinidad where the mongrel races are loveliest on earth. Even the Scots and Irish lasses who have come through our door have been more than comely. We forget that the English, we English I will admit, are a singularly unattractive race. I had fully expected that Mr. Hosmer Angel had been bewitched by some Maori maiden, but her confession of their terms of endearment disabused me of that notion. Any young husband who joyfully takes his wife to rugby games, and refers to her as his ... what inane thing did he call her? 'My heaven-sent little heifer'— good lord what romantic notions will do to addle the brain — is quite obviously besotted with affection. That, sir, was what led me to conclude that there was a mystery to be solved, robbery of some sort to bring to justice, and quite likely foul play to be avoided. It has the promise of a fascinating case. Would you not agree, Watson?"

"If you say so, Holmes," I nodded in agreement, although not altogether comfortable with his inconsiderate observations about the English race.

Chapter Three

The Wayward Husband

I saw little of Sherlock Holmes for the next three days. He came in late in the evening, caught three or four hours sleep at most, and then departed at first light in the morning. On Thursday in the late afternoon, he appeared looking tired but smiling.

"You have solved your case," I exulted. "Well done. Are we to celebrate?"

"Ah, not quite so quick to the final conclusion, my dear Watson. A part of it has been solved. The young husband has been at least located and is, I fully expect, on his way back to his forlorn young wife. That is all good. The mystery behind what took place still remains, and I am still in a fog about it. But I can do no more sleuthing about this evening so I suggest dinner. Marcini's?"

"Delighted to join you. Let me alert Mrs. Hudson that she need not prepare anything for us."

Over an excellent Italian dinner and a generous decanter of Chianti, Holmes explained his progress to date.

"My real interest in this case is the mystery behind it. However, I have to discipline myself and put first things first. My priority must always be the safety and well-being of my client, and that meant that before doing anything else I had to locate and return to Mrs. Angel her husband. It took some basic detective work, but I visited every steamship company's office and asked to review their recent passenger lists. It is fortunate that they keep such records, unlike the railroads. It makes finding lost husbands so much easier.

"They are however rather protective of their passengers' privacy and not all that eager to reveal their lists, so it took some time to find a way to be able to review them in detail. I shan't explain how except to say that several disguises, even to the point of becoming a repellant masher and preying upon the foolishness of a young bookkeeper were put to good use. I did discover that on the Cunard vessel, the S.S. Aurania, there was a passenger named Mr. Hosmer Angel and that it departed from the India Pier at half past six on the same date as the Union line's Oceana did."

"And to where was it destined," I asked, quite curious.

"Also to the Antipodes, with stops in both Sydney and Auckland. More than coincidence, is it not Watson?"

"Indeed, it is."

"I then removed my disguise and returned and asked to speak to the office manager. I told him who I was and that I had been retained by the wife of one of their passengers who was very concerned for her husband's safety. The young chap gave me an odd look and asked if I could come with him immediately to the office of their director of security. The director, a fellow I remembered from his having worked for Scotland Yard in the past and now having sought greener and more lucrative pastures, or I suppose I should say 'waters' with Cunard, sat me down and in a most solemn voice told me a remarkable story that the captain of the Aurania had wired back from Cairo.

"He said that yes indeed Mr. Hosmer Angel had boarded at India pier on the twenty-fourth of October. Late in the evening, after the ship was well into the Channel, he came banging on the captain's door very distraught demanding that a search be started immediately for his wife, as he could not locate her. Well didn't the captain just order up a crew and they did a thorough search from stem to gudgeon and found nothing and feared she might have fallen overboard or some such awful fate. But one of the clerks thought to check the passenger manifest and reported to the captain that only Mister Angel's name was on the list, but not his wife.

"On showing this to Mr. Angel, the poor man became extremely disturbed, in an outright panic. First he demanded that the ship be turned around and sailed back to London. The captain, of course, could not comply. And then he demanded that they let him off at the nearest port of call. Again the captain had to decline as they were not scheduled to call at any port before Alexandria. The captain, having commanded many passenger vessels, was not unfamiliar with distraught husbands or wives looking for their respective spouses and becoming highly disturbed. It took several days before they reached their first port and stopped there prior to entering the Suez. All the while this poor chap paced the decks and asked the other passengers repeatedly if they had seen his wife at the pier, or on the boat, or anywhere. As soon as the gangplank was lowered he scampered down, carrying what little baggage he had brought on board, and has not been heard from since.

"Now Cunard is a respected line and they do not like it at all when passengers disappear, especially a few miles from Cairo where goodness only knows what could happen to them. The director chap asked me if I had heard anything and I informed him that while I had not I was reasonably sure that he could relax and the young Mr. Angel would find his way by hook or by crook back to London and would re-appear within a few more days. And that, my dear friend, is what I am quite confident will happen."

"Well now, I suppose that is some good news. Mrs. Mary Angel will be very relieved."

"And after making my report to her tomorrow after breakfast, I shall be able to turn my mind to whatever the very strange mystery is behind our travelers."

Two days later we were enjoying a sumptuous English breakfast when there was a furious banging on our door. Young Billy answered it and all we heard next was his shouting, "Sir! Really sir! You cannot just charge in here, sir!" His shouts were accompanied by heavy footsteps as our newest visitor scaled the seventeen steps in a few bounds. He burst into our room, dropped his valise with a thud, and shouted at us, "Which of you is Sherlock Holmes?"

He was young and slender, with an athletic physique. His suit and his entire appearance were a complete mess. He had not shaved in several days, nor, it appeared, had he slept. His clothes were terribly disheveled and even in the cool of the early autumn morning, he was sweating profusely and gasping for breath.

Holmes rose from our table. "Good morning, Mr. Hosmer Angel, we have been expecting you, but forgive us, we were not expecting you quite so early. I am Sherlock Holmes and I hope that your journey by tramp steamer across the Mediterranean was not overly stressful. I assume that the train from Milan was a little more comfortable. I assure you that your lovely wife is quite safe and before I direct you to her, please tell me how it is that I find you at 221B Baker Street so early this morning?"

The poor Mr. Angel looked at Holmes as if he were the opposite of anything angelic. He spoke hesitantly.

"I do not know how you knew all these things. Yes, I took a tramp steamer from the port of Alexandria to Genoa. On the dock there a stranger met me and spoke in perfect English. He handed me a card with your name and address and a generous amount of cash with which I was able to purchase a train ticket, and told me to come directly to you as soon as I returned to London. I have no explanation for anything that has taken place in my life for the past ten days sir. Please tell me, where is my wife?"

"Of course, young man. Mrs. Angel is now waiting for you at Number 31 Lyon Place in Camberwell. I believe you are familiar with that address?"

"That is where I live sir. She is there and waiting for me? Are you sure?"

"Absolutely positive. So please be on your way post haste. Ah, but I have two requests. Please leave behind the letter you received from your wife telling you about her assignment and the departure time of the ship, and please be so kind that you and your good wife make an appointment to see me within the next two days. There are some matters that must be cleared up."

Hosmer Angel did not answer. He reached into the pocket of his suit and retrieved an envelope, somewhat the worse for wear and having been assaulted by several days' sweat. He handed it to Holmes all the while looking at him as if he were viewing an apparition. Then he picked up his valise and bounded back down the stairs. The last I saw of him he was running pell-mell down Baker Street and shouting at a cabbie.

"I would have preferred to have questioned him at length," said Holmes, "but breakfast is getting cold, and it is in the interest of my client that her husband return to her without delay. So we shall just have to wait for two days. Meanwhile, Watson, relax and enjoy your breakfast and I will do the same. After which I will resume my efforts to discern what is behind this most peculiar case."

"Not so quickly, Holmes," I protested. "How in the name of heaven did that poor fellow happen to run into somebody on the docks of Genoa who knew who he was, gave him your name, and sent him back to London? You were behind that, I am sure. But how did you do it?"

"Elementary, my dear Watson. It was a spot too far to send my Irregulars so I had to borrow some of Mycroft's."

"Mycroft, your brother? He has street urchins working for him in Europe? That's unimaginable!"

"Not at all. Except he does not call them Irregulars. I believe that his usual word for them is 'spies.' He has a network all over the continent and he sent out the alert. He would never have acted had it only been a case of yet another philandering husband but when I told him the details and imparted my thoughts he just said that this was not the first case he had heard about. Something similar and much nastier had taken place recently in Oslo. Beyond that he said no more but clearly he put his not insignificant network to work. We appear to be on to something Watson. This endearing if not altogether attractive young couple are likely only pawns in a much wider web and I must address whatever faculties I have to understanding it, and, Lord willing, vanquishing it."

He said no more, but finished his breakfast in silence, then donned his hat and cape and left the room. I watched as he climbed into a cab and proceeded south toward Marble Arch.

Chapter Four

The Mothers

Two days passed and there was no return visit of Mr. and Mrs. Angel. I asked about them in passing and Holmes responded, "They had a rather traumatic experience and if they are like most your married couples, and I fear they are, they will take several days before re-engaging with the civilized world."

Then the third day passed and then the fourth. Holmes was showing some signs of concern.

"I sent them a note, late yesterday asking them to come and see me, but I have heard nothing," he answered in response to my query.

Late on the fourth day, we heard the bell on Baker Street. Billy appeared at our door shortly afterward bearing a visitor's card. "A Mrs. Angel," he began, but he got no further before Holmes interrupted.

"Show the young lady up right away," he said, restraining his obvious desire to shout at the lad.

"Begging you pardon, Mr. Holmes, sir," the boy replied with well-taught manners under duress. "There are in fact two ladies, and I have been taught never to say that a lady is old, sir. But neither of these are what I could ever call young, sir."

Holmes glared at the poor lad. I responded, "Quite alright, there Billy. Do show up whoever it is that is waiting at our door and don't leave them out in the cold." Then I turned and beckoned for Mrs. Hudson. "Mrs. Hudson, we have some ladies of your vintage joining us. Would you mind awfully organizing a bit of tea?"

"Right, Doctor. Be there soon," came the reply from our ever-indulgent landlady.

Coming up the stairs were two women of a certain age, old enough to have adult children but not yet old enough for a brood of grandchildren. They were not so much conversing as they climbed the stairs as nattering back and forth. I tried to listen for a complete sentence but heard none.

They entered our parlor. Both were attired in sensible dark dresses and overcoats such as might be seen in the Midlands last winter or in London ten years ago. They were each about five foot and two or three inches in height and wore sensible-looking flat shoes. Both had hair that had gone a little gray with shades of blonde left behind in the one and of a darker chestnut in the other.

The first one to come through the door advanced toward Sherlock Holmes and extended her hand. "Good morning, Mr. Holmes. I am Bedelia Windibank and this is my good friend Mrs. Angel." Whereupon the second came forward extending her hand and said, "Good morning Mr. Holmes. I am Gertrude Angel and this is my dear friend Mrs. Windibank."

This little ritual was then repeated for my benefit. Holmes had been mannered enough to stand but said nothing. I acknowledged their greeting. "Honored to make your acquaintance, aren't we Mr. Holmes. Please be seated and enjoy a cup of tea. I gather you have come some distance to London."

Holmes said nothing and continued to stare at them.

"Oh yes, some distance," said Mrs. Windibank.

"Yes quite a ways," said Mrs. Angel.

The reader will forgive me if, for reasons that become obvious, I cease to give full attribution to what was said by whom in the minutes that followed as the alternated their comments to us.

"We came down from just outside Birmingham last evening."

"We started from Coldfield, a mile north of Birmingham, yes."

"We are quite concerned about our children."

"Very worried we are about my daughter and Mrs. Angel's son."

"We heard all about their very strange and trying escapades on the high seas."

"And then they told us about the way you helped them, Mr. Holmes."

"They both said quite emphatically that the famous detective, Sherlock Holmes, had aided them. Indeed, that is what they said."

"That was three days ago."

"Going on four."

"You can imagine that we were greatly relieved as we had not heard from either of them for over a week prior to that."

"That was the week when they were on their wild goose chase of each other in the steamships."

"So we made our way from Coldfield to London, and paid a visit to their lodgings."

"We paid a visit this afternoon. And what do think we found?"

"Nothing. Not a trace of them."

"They were gone."

"Completely."

"Vanished."

"Not a trace."

"You already said that."

"Indeed, I did. I already said that."

At this point Sherlock Holmes interrupted. "My dear ladies. Are you telling me that your children, Mr. and Mrs. Angel, are missing."

"Only the younger Mrs. Angel. Mrs. Angel senior has not vanished."

"I am sitting right here. Obviously I have not vanished. Only Mrs. Angel Junior."

"That younger one."

"That's what I just said."

"Actually my dear, you said 'Junior' which is an appellation used by Americans, not the English."

"Ladies! Please! Where have your children gone?" shouted Holmes.

That shut up our visitors, but not for long.

"Mr. Holmes, that is why we are here."

"Why do you think we came to see you?"

"If we knew where they were we wouldn't need to ask you. We are trying to be sensible about this, you know sir."

"Why would we have come to England's most famous detective if we knew where they were? That would make no sense at all. You see, we don't know where they are."

"They've vanished."

"Without a trace."

"They were supposed to come and see me two days ago," Holmes said rather more loudly than necessary. "Do you have any idea why they did not do so?"

"Oh yes. They told us that Uncle Peter had arrived in town."

"That's my daughter's Uncle Peter, not Mr. Angel's."

"But he calls him Uncle Peter as well, of course. Very dear to both families he is."

"He just arrived from New Zealand and sent for both of them."

"He wanted to see them right away. He's rather old and not in good health."

"Might not be with us much longer. So he wanted to see them immediately."

"He just arrived all the way from New Zealand."

"He's been there since he was a boy, he had. He's come all the way around the world to see the two of them."

"Said he had to see them now they were married."

"Pity he could not have come sooner and been at the wedding."

"Oh yes. It was a very pretty wedding. Pity he could not have been there."

"But he did get to see them, all the same. Sent me a note saying he was glad he did. But now they're gone missing."

"Vanished."

"Without a trace."

At this point, I took pity upon Sherlock Holmes. I noticed Mrs. Hudson standing in the doorway trying very hard not to burst out in uncontrolled laughter. So I summoned her to my side.

"My dear Mrs. Hudson, could you perhaps bring these ladies another cup of tea. I do believe they have run dry."

"Of course, I will doctor. And ladies you will have to enjoy it quickly before it gets cold. Nothing to ruin the taste of good tea like letting it get cold you know."

She filled up their cups and they devoted themselves to their tea. This gave Sherlock Holmes an opportunity to clear his mind from the recent onslaught and speak.

"This is deadfully serious, Mrs. Angel, and Mrs. Windibank," he said nodding to them respectively. Having done so he immediately looked up at Mrs. Hudson with a pleading look, seeking assurance that he had remembered which was which. She smiled and nodded. Holmes continued. "I will not keep you any longer here. You must be tired and the shock of what you have discovered has been very upsetting. I will assure you that I will do everything in my power to solve this mystery and find your children."

He again looked at Mrs. Hudson, and if begging for her intervention.

She responded perfectly on cue. "Let me see you ladies to the door and order you up a cab. Don't worry my dears, Mr. Holmes will look after the fare. Come please and let these two get to the task at hand of finding your children. Oh, and do leave me your address in London. Mr. Holmes will be getting back to you very soon and he will have to know where to find you."

With a talent I had not seen in her previously Mrs. Hudson kept chatting, not letting either Mrs. A or Mrs. W get a word in until they were up out of their chairs, out the door, down the stairs, and dispatched into a cab.

Holmes smiled as he gazed out of the window. "I do rather expect that there may be a surcharge on our rent next month. Do you agree, Watson?"

"If it is less than fifty pounds I would say you got off lightly."

Silence returned to the room as Mrs. Hudson cleared away the tea service.

"This is dreadful," said Holmes. "Those two who we reunited just days ago are now missing."

"Hmm, yes," I said. "Vanished."

"Indeed," added Mrs. Hudson, "without a trace."

Holmes looked up and glared at the two of us. I returned his look with the smile of a thousand-year-old Buddha. Mrs. Watson assumed the face of the Sphinx. I could not wait for Holmes to leave and for the good lady and me to have a not-to-be-drinking-tea-at-the-same-time jolly laugh about it.

Sherlock Holmes was not amused. "If you two comedians will excuse me for an hour, I must send my Baker Street Irregulars to work. I may have to send Mycroft's as well. There is something very sinister going on here and I fear their children are not at all safe." He then put on his ulster and hat and departed.

I do not know at what hour Holmes returned to 221B Baker Street. I had retired for the night before he did so. My years, however, with the BEF in Afghanistan had forced me to be a light sleeper and I was awakened by the ringing of our bell at close to five o'clock on a Saturday morning. I jumped out of bed and pulled on my dressing gown and made my way to the stairs. Mrs. Hudson was already at the door and admitting Inspector Lestrade. He ascended the stairs and greeted me with a sullen nod. "Doctor Watson, would be so kind as to wake Holmes? I need both of you come with me at once."

Holmes appeared in the parlor, also in his gown. Both of us quickly dressed and returned to meet with the Inspector.

"Good morning, Inspector," said Holmes. "And what brings you to Baker Street at this early hour. I'm afraid I am already quite consumed with another case that may have significant implications to the nation." Sherlock Holmes usually took some subtle pleasure when Scotland Yard turned to him in desperation, but there was no hint of *sangfroid* in his voice. The grim look on Lestrade's face made such a reaction unwelcome.

"We wouldn't be here if we didn't need you, Holmes," said Lestrade. "You bloody well know that. There's been a murder. Two of them in fact. A young man and woman. Over by Fenchurch Street. It's a ghastly site. Very nasty."

"All murder is nasty," came Holmes's rejoinder. "What is it about this one?"

"They were decapitated. He cut their heads off and just left the bodies. There's no blood around so it must have happened elsewhere and then the bodies were dumped in the lane."

"That's terrible," I blurted. "Another Jack the Ripper attack?"

"No. Impossible," said Lestrade.

"How can you say that?" I challenged. "That fellow has not hit for awhile. He may have wanted to do something a little different this time around."

The heads of both Lestrade and Holmes turned to me at the same time and their voices came in unison. "He's dead."

The tone of the voice and the look I was given told me to be silent and not ask any more questions.

"Oh," was all I said.

"Very well," said Holmes. "Tell me more. What else did you see? Have you kept your men away from the bodies?"

"Of course. We're not completely incompetent, as much as you would like to believe we are. I searched their bodies for any papers, any type of identification. I have their names, but nothing else yet."

"Very well," said Holmes. "Who are they?"

"They're a young married couple. Names are Mary and Hosmer Angel. They had travel tickets in their pockets. Here," Lestrade said. Holmes did not reach out his hand to take them. He did not reply. I looked at him and saw the blood drain from his face. I have observed Sherlock Holmes in many situations where his life was in danger, but I had never seen him look as if he were about to faint. He put his hand on the back of a chair for support and then with some awkwardness sat down. He lowered his head into his hands and shook it slowly.

"Good heavens Holmes; what's the problem?" said Lestrade.

Holmes looked up and stood up slowly. "They were my clients, Inspector. They had come to me and it was my duty to protect them."

"Well then, they won't be needing your protection anymore Holmes," said Lestrade brusquely. "Ours neither. We're Scotland Yard, Holmes, and we're supposed to be protecting all of Great Britain. Every day one of our clients gets killed. It's called failure, Holmes. Welcome to the club."

Holmes looked at Lestrade and then reached for a card on the side table. In a voice just above a whisper, he said, "Their mothers are both staying at this address. They will be able to give firm identification. Please have one of your men go and bring them to the scene. And please send one who has, at least, a modicum of sensitivity and tack. It will be a painful mission."

As we descended the stairs and entered on to Baker Street, I saw something that again I had never seen in Sherlock Holmes. There was a tear, several tears in fact, trickling down his face.

"Lestrade," said Holmes, "please have your driver take a short detour via Westminster. There is someone else who must be told."

Lestrade looked at Holmes. "This is bigger than a crazy head-chopper is what I believe you are telling me."

"Possibly much bigger," said Holmes.

The police carriage hurried through the deserted streets of London. In the late Fall, there was a bitter cold dampness to the air. I could imagine two mothers being told that their children were dead and being brought through the miserable, chilly streets of London to identify their headless bodies. A part of my heart died that moment in sympathy with them.

At Westminster Holmes descended from the carriage and walked slowly toward the entry. After being cleared by the guard he entered. It was a full fifteen minutes before he returned.

"I am sorry to have delayed you, Inspector," he said humbly. "But that had to be done. Mycroft had to know."

Lestrade said nothing and just gave a small nod.

Fenchurch is all the way across the City and past St. Paul's. With the streets empty we arrived in less than twenty minutes. Holmes and Lestrade and a couple of his men began walking toward a laneway. I followed. I looked into the lane and froze. The two mothers were coming out, holding on to each other for support.

Holmes stiffened and then walked toward them resolutely, knowing that he had failed to protect their children. "Mrs. Windibank, and Mrs. Angel, I cannot tell you how deeply sorry I am..." That was as far as he got in his words of condolence that I was sure he had been rehearsing all the way since Westminster.

"Mr. Holmes," interrupted Mrs. Angel, "may we have a word with you. And please, you too, Doctor Watson."

"Yes, please," said Mrs. Windibank. "We must speak with you."

One of these country ladies grabbed Holmes by the sleeve of his coat, and the other grabbed me and led us back out onto the pavement by Fenwick Street.

Mrs. Angel looked directly into the face of Sherlock Holmes. "Mr. Holmes," she said, "what we saw back in the lane was terrible and horrible to look at and my heart goes out to whoever will be affected by it, but those are not our children."

For once Mrs. Windibank did not repeat what had just been said even though Holmes waited for her to do so. Hearing nothing from her, he spoke in the low and gentle voice that he is capable of summoning when tragedy and necessity require it. "My dear ladies, what you saw was beyond doubt a devastating blow to both of you. I am deeply sorry, and I know that you must be in shock ... " Again he was not allowed to finish his sentence.

"Mr. Holmes," said Mrs. Windibank. "Please listen to us. We are the mothers of our children. We know what their bodies look like head or not. Those are not our children. We are in deep shock at what we saw but we and not so far gone that we cannot tell that whoever those poor souls are they are not related to us."

Holmes looked intently at both of him and they looked just as intently back at him. "Please permit me to ask," he said respectfully. "How it is that you are so sure of what you have just said?"

"Their hands," said Mrs. Angel.

"Yes, their hands," repeated Mrs. Windibank. "My daughter was fair-skinned. You have seen her. There is not a freckle on her body. That young woman, whoever she may be and my heart goes out to her mother, is covered with them."

"My son," continued Mrs. Angel, "has long slender fingers. That young man has hands like bear paws and fingers like sausages. Bratwurst. And he is far heavier and larger than my son. The man, bless his soul, is not my son."

Holmes nodded at both of them. "If you will excuse me, ladies, I must go and confirm what you have just told me. And you have my assurance that I will not rest until your children are safely restored to you." He turned and entered the laneway. I followed

Chapter Five

The Rugby Head-Couple

Holmes approached the bodies and knelt beside them while a constable held a torch to provide light. The pieces of canvas covering the tops of the bodies were removed and the gory sight of their bloody necks was revealed. The heads had been severed quite cleanly, indicating either a sword or an ax and a powerful single blow. As Lestrade had told us, there was little blood on the ground around them. There was also little blood on their clothes. They were both dressed in evening wear, not of the most expensive kind but acceptably fashionable. Holmes gently prodded at various parts of the body, managing as he always did to show complete respect to the corpse yet at the same time working to discern any possible clues that might be gleaned.

"Please," he said. "You may take them to the morgue. There is nothing more that can be learned here. Thank you, Inspector. I expect that by noon hour we should be able to identify those two poor unfortunate souls."

"You are quite certain, Holmes," said Lestrade," that they are not the Angels. They were most certainly carrying the identification papers of Mary and Hosmer Angel."

"There are many things I do not yet know about this case," Holmes answered. "But of that, I am very sure. These poor souls, whoever they were, have been gruesomely murdered by some fiend who obviously intends to deceive and to lead us to believe that Mr. and Mrs. Angel are dead. The ghastly decapitation is intended to make it appear as if it is the work of Jack the Ripper, which we know it cannot possibly be. Why these events have taken place, I do not yet know but am determined to discover. I met both Mr. and Mrs. Angel howbeit briefly but I am positive that these two are not they. So are the mothers of Mr. and Mrs. Angel. That should be sufficient evidence for you, Inspector."

"If you say so, Mr. Holmes," returned Lestrade. "At the moment, however, the names on their documents are all we have and that is what I must release. If you could let us know as soon as you deduce who they really are, we will give the rightful ones. Of course, if you could find the real Mr. and Mrs. Angel that would help us as well. Good-day Mr. Holmes, Doctor Watson." Lestrade turned and left Holmes and me on the pavement of Fenchurch Street.

"Bodies usually require heads in order to be positively identified, Holmes. How are you going to go about discerning who these two are?"

"Elementary, my dear Watson. They were both wearing matching wedding rings so it is almost certain that they were married to each other. The male is an enormous, athletic young man. Sixteen or maybe even seventeen stone and not a bit of fat on his body. His lower legs show recent signs of small cuts, abrasions, and bruising. His hands are heavily calloused. A gentleman who plays sports may have large powerful hands but the palms remain soft. A workingman's become hardened. There is only one place, or should I say one position, that a man that athletic and large could have acquired those physical attributes. And with your knowledge of the sporting world, I am quite sure that even you could come to a logical conclusion once you had observed those facts."

I thought for a moment. "He is too large to be a footballer, and much too that way for cricket. I would guess he is a rugby player. Most likely a forward, one who plays prop in the scrum. That reduces our possible candidates to a few thousand; maybe a few hundred if we think he is a member of a registered rugby team."

"Excellent, my good doctor," said Holmes. "Now, we add to that that his skin, those parts that might have been exposed to the sun, was still bearing a tan. Players in England never get a tan in our miserable wet climate so he has been somewhere recently where it was warm and the sun was shining."

"One of the team who just came back from Australia and New Zealand? That would make sense."

"Ah, yes it would. And the only one who will not be showing up for practice today. Now then, how difficult will it be to establish his identity?"

"We should have his identity by supper time," said I.

"I was rather hoping to have it before finishing lunch," replied Holmes. "I suggest that we just locate the team captain and ask him about his players."

"Very sorry, Holmes, but that cannot be done," I answered.

"And why not?" he queried me, a touch imperiously.

"He's dead. Robert Seddon was the chap's name. Drowned while on the tour. Fell out of a boat and couldn't swim."

"Very well then, can we locate the manager? Please do not tell me that he also drowned."

"No. He's fine. His name is Alfred Shaw. In fact, he spends most of his time playing cricket and took on the national rugby team tour as a special venture. But I have a hunch where we might be able to find him."

"Very good, Watson. And just where, pray tell would we find an enthusiastic cricket player who has just returned from the Antipodes with a national rugby team?"

"Lord's Cricket Ground would be a good place to start," I replied. I had been to the place many times as it was only a few minute's walk from Baker Street. Holmes had never been there but with his encyclopedic knowledge of London he certainly knew where it was.

Alfred Shaw had often been described by the sporting press as "larger than life." Whether this was true or not it was undeniable that he was louder than life. By mid-morning we had found him in the clubhouse at Lord's. Like many sporting men, he was also an avid reader of my stories in *The Strand* and quite pleased to meet Sherlock Holmes in person and to know that he might have a part to play in solving a mystery.

Our conversation began with some idle chat about the recent tour of the team. I had to carry this part of our meeting since other than knowing that there had been a tour, Sherlock Holmes had not bothered to read anything at all about it as he considered all sporting pastimes to have little relevance to intriguing and diabolical crime. On all other occasions in the past, he had been right. Today, however, was different and I was pleased — very well, I will admit that I might have felt a little bit smug — that he had to depend on me. Holmes sat in silence for the first short while and tried to look interested as Mr. Shaw and I chatted about the highlights of the tour.

To my relief Shaw turned to Sherlock Holmes after a mercifully short few minutes and said, "Right. Now I could sit here and talk rugby, or cricket, or football all day long, gentlemen, but I rather suspect that Mr. Sherlock Holmes did not come here for that reason. I would suspect that you, Mr. Holmes, sir, must be investigating something untoward about our tour. Were some of the lads taking money under the table? We were very strict about all members being amateurs, and not a one could take a farthing. No? Well then, I will wager it was the wagering. Thousands of pounds were bet on the games and it would not be the first time that a player or two took a bit on the side and deliberately let the other side win so as to please the gamblers. Mind you, that would be much more likely to have been some of the New Zealand lads, since our boys beat them every time, except for the Auckland squad. Or do you believe that one of my lads threw that game? Can't say as I saw anything that would have led me to think that. Far as I could see those sheep herders were just lucky, that's all. Right from the start … "

I am quite sure that Mr. Shaw would have recounted in detail every play of the game had we permitted him to carry on down that track. Holmes respectfully but effectively cut him off.

"Not at all sir. Not at all. We are here for a much more serious reason than the fixing of a rugby match."

"Really, Mr. Holmes. For the life of me, I cannot think of much that could be more serious than fixing an honest sporting match. I remember in 1847 we had three rascals … "

"Murder," interrupted Holmes. "There has been a murder. That is why we are here."

Alfred Shaw stopped speaking. The voluble gentleman stared at Holmes in open-mouthed shock.

"Not one of my boys, sir? Please do not say that one of my fellows has been killed. Please, sir."

"Was there," queried Holmes, "a member of your squad who played, ah, what was it, Watson?"

329

"A prop. Big fellow."

"Yes, a prop," continued Holmes. "A working man, with dark hair, and he was married to a red-haired woman who accompanied him on the tour."

"Why that would be Oswald and Roberta Whineray. Wonderful chap. His wife too. Couldn't find a nicer couple. And no, he was not from the gentlemen class, sir. He was a working class bloke that had a position down on the docks. Spent all day there when he wasn't on the field, lifting sacks and pallets. Strong as an ox it made him. Just a bull in a scrum. You're not saying that something has happened to him, has it? That would be terrible. He and Roberta were not married all that long and talking about starting a family and all. Is she alright? Does Roberta know that something might have happened to Ozzie?"

"The situation is terribly serious," said Holmes. "I am terribly sorry to be the bearer of tragic news, but it appears that they may both have been the victims of foul play. I know that such news will be very disturbing to you, sir, but I beg you, please compose yourself and tell me everything you possibly can about what may have taken place in the lives of this unfortunate young couple in the past few weeks. If you could manage to do that, sir, it will be a great help to me, and to Scotland Yard, and to their families."

The sportsman said nothing and I could see that the color had gone out of his face. Twice he tried to speak and could not get the words out. He stood and in a whisper excused himself, saying that he would come back to us in a few minutes. I watched as he walked toward the door of the clubhouse and then stood outside, looking out on to the cricket pitch, alone.

Mr. Shaw remained alone on the edge of the field for a full five minutes. I knew that Sherlock Holmes was impatient to extract every possible bit of data from him as quickly as possible. Yet I had also observed in Sherlock Holmes a rigid discipline in dealing with people. Friendliness and compassion, he had often said, along with generosity loosened more tongues than demands and orders ever did. Holmes waited and said nothing until Mr. Shaw returned.

He sat down across from Holmes and spoke quietly. "Ozzie Whineray was a lad from the east end of London. Just a big, happy boy. Not the brightest star in the sky but just a large convivial boy who was always ready to laugh and sing over a pint at the pub. He met Roberta — as far as I know she was a barmaid in Whitechapel — and they were married two years ago.

The majority of our team were young gentlemen who came from wealthy families and could easily afford to come on a tour for five months.

"Ozzie and Roberta had no money at all, but they decided to come anyway for the love of the game and knowing that they would most likely never again have such an opportunity. I tried to arrange to give them what we call broken-time payment to replace the wages he would lose from being on the team, but the directors of our sport are very strict. No payment whatsoever is allowed. Everyone must remain strictly amateur. That wasn't a problem on the tour. Some of the wealthier lads were true gentlemen and they made sure that any bills at the pub or in the restaurants were discreetly looked after. No one talked about it; it was just what was done. The captain, Bob Seddon, he was as fine a young gentleman as I have ever met. God bless him. He quietly put the arm on some of the other young gents who had ample funds and they made sure that the working lads were looked after.

"Of course, when we all got back to London a few weeks ago the boys from working class homes were in a very tight spot as they had not been able to earn their wages for months on end, so they were all scrambling to find something to do to earn a quick quid or two. I had thought that Ozzie would just ask for more hours on the docks since he was not opposed to doing a double shift for a week or two, and get himself back on their feet that way, but he had a different opportunity.

"He came to me a few days back and told me about a strange meeting he had with some chap who had offered him a hundred quid. Said this fellow came and told him he was acting on behalf of the family of Mrs. Hosmer Angel. She and her husband were on the tour as well. Not as part of the team but she was the writer for the *Rugby News* and Hosmer worked for Thomas Cook's and did all the travel arrangements. The two couples had become somewhat friendly with each other on the tour."

"That is quite understandable," said Holmes. "What was this offer? Please tell me as much about it as you can remember."

"Well sir, I thought it a bit odd but there was good money in it and goodness knows Ozzie and Bobbie needed it. Ozzie told me that this chap told him that some aged great-uncle of Mary's, Mrs. Angel that is, had just arrived in London from New Zealand and wanted to see his grandniece before he passed on. He was over eighty years old and had no other family. Not in good health and pretty much blind. But then Hosmer and Mary had just missed him because both of them had just taken assignments to return to New Zealand and were already on their way. The chap tells Ozzie that it would break the old man's heart if he couldn't see his niece before he died, seeing as he had come this way and it would be terrible if he had come to England from Auckland to see her, only to have her be on a boat headed out the day before he arrives.

"So he said that as a friend of the family he thought it would be a responsible thing to do to have someone, another couple that is, pretend that they were Hosmer and Mary and spend some time with the old fellow and that it would bring just a lot of joy into his life before he passed on to the other side, as they say.

"Well now Ozzie was a bit of a humble fellow and he didn't know if he could pull that off but the chap says he wants him and Bobbie to do it because they were just on the tour with Hosmer and Mary and would be able to talk about it realistically. And besides, the old fellow's real interest was in his niece and Bobbie, having been a barmaid, had lots of practice pretending as barmaids have to do with all sorts of blokes they would prefer to throw their ale at and kick them out the door.

"So Ozzie and Bobbie pretended they were Hosmer and Mary and they went and visited this gent, and they had a nice little meeting and the old boy was happy and Ozzie had a hundred quid and could pay their back rent and everything is just fine. At least for awhile."

"Ah, and then something happened?" queried Holmes.

"Well now, Ozzie is such a friendly lad that he would never suspect anyone of not being on the up and up with him. But Bobbie, she's been working in the pub serving men since she was sixteen years old and, well, as they say, she's been around. She's a fun lass and friendly, but you wouldn't be able to pull the wool over her eyes, as they say. She gets it in her head that something is not right about this whole arrangement and she doesn't quite trust this chap who says he's a friend of Mary's family. She and Mary, they got pretty close as two young married women will do when they're traveling on tour with their husbands, and something about the whole thing didn't sit right with her.

"So Ozzie came to me. I gather he sort of thought of me as a father type advisor as I am quite a few years older and managed the tour and all. And he asks me what he should do. And I ask him what is it that was upsetting Bobbie. He says that during this meeting they had together with the old man, Mary's great Uncle Peter, Peter Sutherland his name was, that the old fellow puts a stack of papers on the table and says that these are for Mary. He has no other family and so he is handing over his wealth to her. And then he has a document in his pocket and he gives it to her to sign saying as she has received them. Well now, Bobbie wasn't expecting anything like that and was caught off guard and so she signs it, writing Mary's name. And then the old boy puts the document back in his pocket without bothering to look at it seeing as he is nearly blind, and smiles and says that he had a great load off his mind and that all of his affairs are now in order. And he can go to his eternal reward in peace.

"When they get out of the meeting, the chap who hired them to pretend they were Hosmer and Mary is waiting for them and he takes the papers they were given saying that he will look after them for the family and he pays them their hundred quid and throws in another twenty for good measure and assures them that Hosmer and Mary will be so grateful to them for standing in for them and would have been so very disappointed when they learned that Uncle Peter had come to London to see them and they missed him. And everything seems just fine.

"Well now, Bobbie, she doesn't mind acting and pretending but she knows that it is against the law to sign another person's name. She knows that it's forgery, and she gets more and more uncomfortable about it as the day goes by. She also had a bit of a look at the papers they were given and she knows that they are certificates for stocks and bonds and bank deposits and such. Now Ozzie, he wouldn't know a stock certificate from a score card, but Bobbie has seen a lot of them passed back and forth between gentlemen who do their business in the pub as many do. So she thinks that there may be something a bit on the sketchy side going on here. She tells Ozzie that she is ready to go and talk to someone at Scotland Yard about it because she's an honest lass and doesn't want anyone to think she was a forger and such.

"Ozzie, he tells her not to do anything yet. He doesn't want to risk the hundred and twenty pounds he's just been paid for an hour's work. So he says he'll go and find the chap that hired them and ask about it and get it all sorted out. That's what he told me he had decided when we talked just a couple of days back. So I have to suppose that's what he did and that was the last I saw of him, Mr. Holmes."

"That has been very helpful. Thank you, Mr. Shaw," said Holmes in return. "May I ask about this chap who said he was a friend of the family?

What else might young Mr. Oswald have said concerning him? Please try to remember and tell me exactly as you can, sir."

Mr. Shaw looked thoughtful for a minute. "I cannot say much as I never met or saw the man. Ozzie said he was older than I am, so I would think maybe in his fifties. Tall. Came across as intelligent, very knowledgeable, and very polished. Perfectly dressed, with a very expensive coat, suit and hat and all. Very charming. But there was one incident that Ozzie thought rather odd."

"And what, pray tell was that?" said Holmes.

"Well now, at the entrance to the rugby field where we practice; that was where the chap met with Ozzie the first time; there's a big old friendly mongrel dog, Punch we call him, that has staked out his territory near to the gate. He's been there for several years. Just a big old friendly cur that comes up to you and nuzzles you as dogs do. And we all give the old fellow a friendly pat and rub his head as we go by and if we have a treat, a bit of lunch leftover and such, we give it to him.

"Ozzie said he watched as this chap walked out of the gate Punch comes up and nuzzles him and doesn't the man raise his stick and brings it down terrible hard on the old dog's front leg and breaks it. The poor old mongrel is in pain and whining and the man just walks on. We learn later that the leg is shattered and that the old thing has to be put own. It was very sad. The rest of us didn't know what had happened, but Ozzie saw it and it troubled him. Said he couldn't imagine anyone connected to Mary's family being so cruel and heartless in that way."

""Yes, that was a surprisingly cruel thing to do," said Holmes. "Did this man have a name that he gave to Ozzie?"

"Oh I am sure he did, but not one that Ozzie told me. Said he was some sort of professor at Cambridge or something like that. But that's all he said, to me at least."

"Is there anything else, anything else at all you can remember, Mr. Shaw? Please, it is frightfully important," asked Holmes.

"No. If I do I will send a note back to you straightaway," said Shaw. "It is sad, you know. Such a triumphal tour it was and we should all be celebrating. What with Bob Seddon drowning and now this, it's become something tragic. The rest of the boys will be very upset when they hear about this."

"It is only to be expected that they will," said Holmes. "They have lost a friend. Please tell them not to believe anything they read about it in the press."

Alfred Shaw gave a questioning look to Sherlock Holmes. "I will tell them that sir. By your words, I suspect that there is a deeper story to all this than you have told me."

"Indeed, there is," said Holmes. "In due time it will be revealed and, if it is at all within my power, justice will be done."

We thanked the affable sportsman and, as Baker Street was close by, we started our return there on foot.

""Alright, Holmes," I said. "Out with it. Who is this mysterious professor that appears to be behind all this?"

"At the moment," he replied. "I am not at all certain. I have heard through my contacts that a man fitting the description has emerged as a very powerful figure in the network of crime that has crept over the Continent and all of England. Very little is known about him and he has never been so much as brought in for questioning by Scotland Yard. However, I will contact all of my agents, and set my Irregulars to work to find out whatever can be known. I may even have to ask Mycroft to help by using his spies. However, there is nothing else I can do concerning him presently, so we will follow the path that is open to us and try to find this old Uncle Peter."

"And just how do you plan to do that," I asked.

Holmes stopped walking and gave his head a bit of a sideways nod. "If I can tolerate it, we shall have to meet with the mothers again. They very likely could tell us immediately."

Chapter Six

Uncle Peter

We did not return to Baker Street but hailed a cab and made our way to Number 31 Lyon Place in Camberwell where the mothers had taken over the rooms of their missing children. We had had a very early start on the morning and it had just gone half-past ten when we arrived there. It was a modest rooming house and the landlady ushered us into the sitting room while she went to fetch the mothers.

When they appeared, I immediately offered our apologies as it was evident that they had gone back to their beds after such an early and shocking start to their morning.

"It is not a problem at all, Dr. Watson. We are eager to hear if you have any news of our children."

"Yes. Have you found out anything this morning, Mr. Holmes?"

"We have made just a little progress," said Holmes. "I will not give you false comfort. I am deeply concerned that your children may be in peril. However, we will not cease to search for them until they are found. We have again disturbed you this morning as I believe you may have some additional information that will be useful to us in our quest."

"What is it you wish to know, Mr. Holmes?"

"If there is any way at all that we can Mr. Holmes, just ask us."

"They are, after all, our children."

"We are their mothers."

"Ah yes, you are indeed," said Holmes. "I need to know about this man, Uncle Peter. Who is he and what brought him to London? It would be perhaps a bit more efficient if just one of you were to tell me the whole story. Please."

"Oh yes, well then Mrs. Angel should tell you. She has more schooling than I do and is quite the gifted story-teller."

"Goodness gracious, Mrs. Windibank, you are the one who is the relative of Uncle Peter, not I. It is incumbent on you to tell Mr. Holmes what you know, not me."

"Oh, well thank you my dear, but you really are far better suited . . ."

"Ladies," interrupted Holmes. "Mrs. Windibank, Mrs. Angel is quite correct. As you are the relative to Uncle Peter I would ask you to pass on the information."

"Oh very well. But I am not a blood relative, you know, only by marriage and twice removed."

"That, I assure you," countered Holmes, "still makes you a relative. Please. Proceed."

"Uncle Peter as we call him is Mr. Peter Sutherland. He is the uncle of my first husband, Russell Sutherland, who, bless his soul, was a wonderful husband and father to my daughter Mary but he has been dead these past five years and I have remarried, to Mr. Windibank, which is why my name is now Mrs. Windibank. He is somewhat younger than me, but that is another story. Younger husbands can be useful from time to time. But that is most likely not the information you are interested in is it, Mr. Holmes? Very well. Peter Sutherland left England as a young man nearly sixty years ago and immigrated to Australia and a few years later to New Zealand.

"Now I do not know all that much about what all he did overseas, but he became a very wealthy man. And then when he was over seventy years old, he was the first to invest in shipping frozen beef and lamb from New Zealand. As you know, that business is growing by leaps and bounds every day. Last year he turned eighty years old and he sold all of his interests and he came back to London to put his final affairs in order. So yes, we hear that Uncle Peter Sutherland is one of the richest men in the Antipodes. His estate, what with the shipping business mind you, might be worth at least half a million pounds, we really do not know, but he is very wealthy indeed."

"You said that he put his affairs in order," said Holmes. "Why was it necessary to come to London to do that?"

"Oh, because my daughter, Mary, is his only living relative. He was a bachelor all his life. I gather that is why he ended up so wealthy. Married to his business, he was. I had corresponded with him quite faithfully and had told him that Mary had grown up to be a responsible young woman and was now married and, along with her husband, Hosmer, was doing quite well for herself. He was pleased to hear that and wrote that he felt quite at peace in leaving his estate to the two of them. It was always in his will to leave his estate to Mary, but now he declared he was at peace about it, yes. He was at peace."

"They will be one of the richest young couples in England," I exclaimed. "I am amazed that they were just living as they were and seeking to establish careers. They have a life of leisure ahead of them."

"Doctor Watson," Mrs. Windibank said a bit sharply. "My dear friend Mrs. Angel and I are sensible, God-fearing women and we were not about to let our children become spoiled, lazy toffs like all those sons and daughters of the dukes and earls. We expected them to earn their own living and do a decent days work for a fair wage. Did we not, Mrs. Angel?"

"Indeed, we did. No children of ours were going to be parasites, living off the backs of the working people. The two of them will come into money soon enough. We wanted to be certain, before God we did, that our children were not raised to be idle layabouts."

"Are you telling me then that Mrs. and Mrs. Angel had no idea that they were the sole recipients of Mr. Sutherland's fortune?" asked Holmes.

"That is quite correct sir. Mary, my daughter that is, had been led to believe that he had left his estate to the New Zealand Society for the Protection of the Kiwi Bird and other such charities and that he had become highly patriotic toward New Zealand and so all his money would remain there. She expected nothing and yet had warm feelings toward him as he was her father's uncle and part of her family."

"Yet she was in New Zealand earlier this year. Did she not see him at that time?" asked Holmes.

"It was unusual and most unfortunate, but no, she did not," replied the girl's mother. "It had been planned and hoped for, but Uncle Peter had taken ill and had been sent over to Melbourne to convalesce. She tried to take time off while the team was in Sydney, but he had to undergo some minor surgery and her visit had to be canceled. It was just one disappointment after another and so they never met. That was also part of the reason he came to London. But then she and Hosmer took off on their strange journeys back to New Zealand just before he arrived. Fortunately, with your help Mr. Holmes, they found each other and we reached them by post and told them about Uncle Peter's arrival, and they arranged to go and see him. I assume that the meeting took place but as we have not heard from them I do not know for sure."

Sherlock Holmes stood up and abruptly ended the conversation.

"Excuse me, ladies," he said. "I am sure that there is much more I could learn, but time has become very pressing. It is of vital importance that we locate and speak to this Uncle Peter immediately. Could you please tell me where he can be found?"

"Oh, he spends much of his day at the Reform Club. It's on Pall Mall I believe."

"Do you know the Reform Club, Mr. Holmes? It's the place that Mr. Phineas Fogg began his adventurous journey from. The one Mr. Dickens told us all about."

"No, my dear. That was not Mr. Dickens. It was that Frenchie fellow, Mr. Jules Verne."

"Oh yes. The Frenchie. But it was that club all the same."

"Yes. The Reform Club on Pall Mall. I believe it is near Buckingham Palace."

"Ah, yes," said Holmes. "Pall Mall is near the Palace. Thank you for helping us with that." He then turned to me and said, "Come Watson. There is no time to waste."

We hailed a cab in Camberwell and Holmes offered the driver a generous enhancement to the fare if he would break every regulation of the streets of London. He obliged and did so.

"We certainly now have a motive for murder," said Holmes and we bounced along over Vauxhall Bridge. "Half a million pounds has been the cause of minor wars between nations. Some very patient criminal or a syndicate of criminals has been plotting this enormous theft for some time. Watson, you and I must now divide and conquer. May I impose upon you my good doctor to carry on to the Reform Club and see if you can locate this Uncle Peter chap? I am willing to wager that if he left England for Australia at a young age that he may have done so as a prisoner and will have an interesting story to tell. I will be dropped off at Westminster and pay a visit to Mycroft. When half a million pounds worth of negotiable securities is about to be circulating through London, I must, even if not altogether willingly, call in reinforcements."

The driver stopped on Abingdon and Sherlock Holmes alighted and crossed over into Westminster. I continued on to Pall Mall. The porter at the door of the Reform Club greeted me and on learning that I was Dr. Watson, the author of all those wonderful detective stories about Sherlock Holmes and that I was making a visit on a Saturday morning, was quite pleased to show me in. The General Secretary of the Club was called and he led me into one of the sitting rooms. "It is a delight to have such an interesting visitor, Dr. Watson. We subscribe to *The Strand* and the men enjoy reading all your splendid stories. In fact, we have ten subscriptions to *The Strand* and we can never keep the copies on hand. Our members keep pinching them. And you, my good man, are entirely to blame. Our staff are about to serve a lovely luncheon. It is quite a popular event on a Saturday you know. The wives are only too eager to shoo the husbands out of the house and the men are only too happy to oblige. It would be most interesting if you could join us. It would just the type of event that the chaps would thoroughly enjoy. It would make their day, I dare say."

"Ah, you are very kind to offer," I said graciously. "However I must decline. I am in the midst of helping Mr. Holmes with some research on the criminal temperament and there is a visiting guest at the Club, who he has asked me to interview. It is a rather confidential matter. The dear old fellow may once a guest of Her Majesty in Botany Bay but seems to have had an upright and prosperous life ever since he paid his debt to society. I'm sure that it would not do to alert your regular members to that. Would you not agree?"

"Most understandable," said the Secretary. "No doubt you are referring to old Mr. Peter Sutherland. He arrived in London just a few weeks ago and has been quite the entertaining story teller since then. Not at all ashamed of his time in Botany Bay all those years ago. Been regaling the chaps here with all sorts of fabulous tales. Although I must confess to you sir," he said lowering his voice to *sotto voce*, "that there are quite of few of our chaps who have seen the inside of one of Her Majesty's special residences and have gone on to earn their fortune. The other clubs up and down Pall Mall are far too snobbish to allow them in, but we at the Reform Club rather enjoy the spirit of the adventure that they bring. A bit on the non-conformist side we are. Quite the lot of lovable old rascals we have here, if you know what I mean."

"And for that reason," I replied, "among many others, you have the reputation as the liveliest Club on the Mall. So would it be possible for you to arrange a place for Mr. Sutherland and me to have a private chat? And perhaps your staff could bring a little refreshment?"

"Of course sir," he replied. "Please come this way."

He led me to a comfortable but small sitting room. A few minutes later he re-appeared followed by an elderly gentleman who was supported by a cane in one hand and the arm of one of the young stewards on the other. He was stooped over, thin and gaunt. His face looked a bit on the pasty side and his eyes somewhat clouded, but he beamed a smile at me, friendly even if his teeth had long since ceased to gleam or even be entirely present.

After being introduced by the porter, the old chap sat down and in a voice still quite loud, as is common among those whose hearing is failing, said, "So you're the one who has been writing all those stories about that Sherlock Holmes fellow. Can't read them anymore. Can't see well enough. But there's always some young lad around who will read them to me. For a shilling or two mind you. But they're a welcome change from having to listen to some poor lad read lawyers letters and yet another miserable bond perspective. Wonderful stories, sir. Right glad to meet you, Doctor."

"Well thank you, Mr. Sutherland. Sherlock Holmes had heard of you and that you were in London, and he is most interested to learn about you, sir. You had a bit of a rough start to your life, but you have done wonderfully well ever since. Mr. Holmes, as you may know, sir, is quite the expert on criminal justice as well as being England's finest consulting detective. He's writing a bit of a monograph on the effectiveness of our prison systems. Not much good coming out of them these days but everyone has an opinion on how to better the system. But as he is of a scientific bent, sir, he wants evidence of what has and has not worked. Your life is a stellar example of what did work. So he is most anxious that he learn about Mr. Peter Sutherland."

"Ha. Indeed. Right, now I am flattered, doctor. So you ask away. At this point in my life, I have nothing more to gain nor lose. We Kiwis don't put much store in past reputations, as many of us have some skeletons in the closet. So you just go ask away and if I live long enough to make it into one of your stories I would be right proud. Trying to put my affairs in order I am now and knowing that I might end up in a story about Sherlock Holmes would give me just a little something more to present to St. Peter when I arrive at the pearly gates."

"Oh good heavens, sir," I replied with a chuckle. "I don't believe that being connected to Sherlock Holmes is going to do any of us any good in the great beyond. But do tell me your story all the same. I don't think it will do you any harm at least. I have my pencil and notepad at the ready."

The old fellow smiled. "Shall I 'Begin at the beginning and go on till you come to the end: then stop?' That's what the King demanded of the White Rabbit. Would that do for Sherlock Holmes?"

"Most assuredly, sir."

"Right then. All the chaps here already know that I was once a guest of Her Gracious Majesty in Botany Bay. They know because I now wear that as a badge of honor. Didn't feel that way about it sixty years ago, mind you. It was a right bad thing back then. But when I was just nineteen years old I relieved a gentleman's house of some of his silverware. He had more than he needed and I was on the hungry side. Course I didn't know what to do with it after I'd taken it so I tried to sell it to a pawn shop and the pawnbroker tells me to come back the next day and he'll have the money for me. So I go back the next day and takes the money and two constables are waiting there and next thing I know I'm in the jail, and then in front of the judge, and then on a ship to Botany Bay where I have to spend the next seven years wondering how I could have been so stupid. Are you with me so far, doctor?"

I was scribbling furiously. "Yes. Yes. Off to Australia to join the convicts you were. Please, go on."

"Right. Well now, first thing I learned is that if you're going to survive in that miserable place, you can't do it all by yourself. A man has to have a mate and you have to look out for each other. So I found another young lad who had done something as stupid as I had, George Windibank was his name, and he and I became great mates. We put our backs together and fought off any blighters who crossed us and after seven years we were out of the convict zone and free.

"Now the second thing I learned was that you can live a life of crime and make a fair pile of quid without working and without paying taxes, or you can sleep in your own bed at night and be at peace. But you can't do both. So Georgie and I we decided that we would make our fortune all honest like and so we tried every opportunity that the Aussies offered us. We joined a whaling ship and darned if it did not nearly kill us both several times over. If it wasn't by drowning it was by freezing, and if it wasn't that then it was by getting crushed between a whale and a dinghy, or a dinghy and the ship. Right terrible work it was, sir. Compared to it the convict zone was Mayfair. We worked in fear of our lives every day thinking that we were going to get a handsome payment at the end, but because we were the lowest fellows on the ladder our share was a miserable one sixty-fourth of the profits and we had no more than would be gone in a month even if we near-starved ourselves. So we had had enough of that.

"We heard that there was good work in New Zealand. They were still fighting the natives over there and a couple of blokes who were willing to work hard could make a fortune or so we were told. So over we went and found work right away helping to herd sheep we did. Now I suppose you've heard that story from the Holy Writ about there being ninety-nine sheep what came safely home to the fold and one was lost. Well now sir, that story's a lie. Sheep are the stupidest animals on God's green earth. The true story is that ninety-nine got lost and only one was smart enough to find its way home. Georgie and I we chased those stupid things from the north of Hawk's Bay to the south. We set aside a little money though and bought our own land and stock but after a few years of that we looked at each other and we said 'Chasing these stupid things may be alright if you're a Scot or an Irish man, but we're Englishmen, and there is no way under Providence that we're going to spend our lives with this nonsense.' So we sold out, at a tidy profit mind you. And then we went looking for gold for we heard that some bloke had found it near Westport in the Buller River. So off we went and blimey if we didn't find some and made a few quid, or I suppose I should say a few hundred quid, enough to walk back into Auckland and pretend we were gentlemen. In the colonies you know, of course, no one cares who your great-grandsire was, if you have money then you're a gentleman.

"Then Georgie, he wants to start being friendly with the city toffs who do nothing but sit in clubs all day, like you see all up and down Pall Mall here. And the next thing he's been collared by some comely young lass who sees his money. So he gets married and heads back to England. And I lost my mate. Right sad I was about that, but no use crying over spilled milk, so on I go. As for me, never had a wife and never wanted one. Always said that those who love children should have them, and us who have no use for the little blighters should never get married.

"I looked all up and down the islands. The Scots had established themselves in Dunedin and were raising sheep. I thought they were much too dour for me in those days. But did you hear that just this year past they built themselves a statue to Robbie Burns, that miserable drunken philandering poet of theirs? And did you hear that no sooner had they unveiled the blessed thing that some bloke all full of his Scotch looks and says, "Ooo, look will ye. Hasn't our Robbie goot hees back to tha Kirk an hees face to tha poob?' Did you hear about that Doctor Watson?" He was laughing as he told me this.

I had heard about it. It was just the type of story that the English loved to tell about the Scots.

"Right, now I could see that from the harbor in Dunedin, and from Wellington, and from Christchurch, and from Auckland there were ships coming and going and they were sending out wool and bringing in all the refined clothes and goods from England. And I knew from being a sheep rancher that I got a pittance selling my wool compared to what I paid for my suitings. I could see that somebody was making money and I learned that it was the fellow they called the middle man, the chap that controlled all the coming and going.

"He didn't do any of the real work; he just passed things from one poor bloke who was working all day making things or growing things, to another poor bloke who was working all day selling things. So I decided to be a middle man. I used my savings from the gold fields and bought the licenses to control all the wool leaving the port of Dunedin, and then every other harbor. And then I added to that all the lumber. And then all the freight coming in. And then I bought some interests in the gold fields, and in the new foundries and machine works. And then I expanded across the ditch and added all sorts of things coming and going from Australia.

"Ten years ago now we sent the first refrigerated ships bearing beef and lamb from Sydney and Auckland all the way to London. Those shipments have expanded fifty-fold since that time and are continuing to grow. My only regret is that I am now over eighty years of age and I will not be around long enough to see the transport of frozen beef and lamb and fish help move good food all over the globe, from those places that have it in abundance to those who need it. There is more than enough food in the world to feed the world's people several times over. But the food and the people who need it are not in the same place, but we are on our way Dr. Watson to ending the hunger of every soul on earth."

With this, the old man sighed and paused. "But I have to be content that I have done my part. Others who are younger and healthier than me will have to pick up the torch. My run has been a good one, but it has come to an end. I was very ill earlier this year and speaking frankly, Doctor, I do not expect to be around this time next year. So starting a few months back, I liquidated almost all my properties, my contracts, my licenses, my patents and turned them into cash and negotiable shares.

"Right. I was so grateful that I could do that before I died. Had I not my estate would have been tied up in the courts and those barracudas, those sharks, those greedy lawyers, and judges would have eaten everything they could and held matters up for years. Did you ever read Dickens's *Bleak House,* doctor? He didn't exaggerate. No sir, he did not.

"Well now doctor," he said and then paused. "That's my story, short and simple. I came to England to meet my only remaining blood relative, my great niece, Mrs. Mary Angel. She and her husband were in New Zealand and Australia from May until September and try as we might we could not arrange for our paths to cross. So I have come back home to England for the first time since I was removed from its shores sixty years ago so that I could meet her and pass on my assets for her to look after. Blood, they say, is thicker than water and my brother always stood by me when I was in trouble so it's only fair that I should do the same for his grandchildren now that I'm in a position to do so.

"I met the young lady and her husband here a couple of weeks back. Had a nice chat about rugby and their visit to New Zealand. They were a little coarser than I imagined they might have been, bit then so was I and more so when I was their age. The young fellow is supposed to come by again later this afternoon."

"You say," I asked, "that you met your niece and her husband recently?" Holmes had told me not to reveal anything to the old man that would upset him, so I said nothing about his visitors' being imposters. I could only hope that this bizarre case would be solved and that the dear old chap could end his days in the peace he sought. "And how did they look upon your not-so-illustrious early life and subsequent success?"

"Oh, they were right proud of me. Shipping young convicts off to Australia isn't done anymore. Hasn't been for a long time. Many of the early blokes died. But there were some of us who stayed on and prospered. Some began schools, another chap wrote novels, and one fellow started a theater. So for some of us the punishment worked. But then who is to say if we might not have done far better in a prison in England. No one really knows nor can they, doctor. Although that does not help your research or Mr. Holmes's monograph if I say that no one really knows what works and doesn't when it comes to criminal justice."

"Even knowing that much is important," I assured him. "And on behalf of Sherlock Holmes I cannot thank you enough for imparting your story and your insights. I have no doubt it will appear, at least in summary form, in his monograph."

There was one very queer item that he mentioned in passing that I had to find some way to uncover further. "Your mate, George Windibank, how did he make out once he returned t England? Did he prosper in the same way you did?"

"Georgie? No, not at all. His wife spent all his money and in their later years they lived very modestly. He had a son quite late on. Called him George after his father. But by the time Georgie died about ten years back, there was no money at all. Just debts to leave to his wife and son. Rather sad, it was. But 'twas his own fault and no one else's. His son sent me some rather harsh letters a few years back saying that I had an obligation to him and his mother seeing as his father was my mate and had a role in helping me build up my fortune. But I was having none of that. George Windibank took his half of everything we had when we parted. If his widow was poor, it was her own fault. And if the boy was poor, then he could do what his father and I had done and get out and work and stop being poor and then he could look after his mother. So I gave the lad a firm rebuke. I did not hear back, but I am sure he did not like what I told him."

"I'm sure he did not," I ventured. "And do you have any knowledge as to what happened to young George and his mother?"

"The mother died in penury," he answered. "It was most peculiar, but young George ended up marrying my nephew's widow. Must have kept in contact somehow. I hope he's happy. She is a bit of a tough mother, she is. Doesn't give the time of day to those she thinks lazy. She'll be kicking his backside and putting him to work she will. Has no use for layabouts. No not her."

"She would have been quite a few years older than young George, would she not?" I asked. "You said that George did not have any children until much later in his life."

"Oh no," he replied and I could see a bit of a smile curling the corners of his mouth. "My nephew's widow was well into her forties. Getting close to fifty. But a healthy widow is often happy to have a much younger man around the house, or at least around the bedroom, if you know what I mean."

"Well now," I said, not wishing to pursue that line of conversation. "I hope they are getting on. And again please let me thank you on behalf of Sherlock Holmes."

"Right. Well now, you tell Mr. Sherlock Holmes that I was happy to oblige. But you better make haste and get your study published Doctor Watson. I wouldn't want to get old while waiting for it."

I gave a hearty laugh and he responded in kind. I held out my hand before remembering that, in his near blindness, he could not see what I was doing. So I gave him a friendly clap on his boney, shrunken shoulder and bid him good day. Then I made my way as quickly as possible back to Baker Street.

I was dismayed but not surprised to hear the newspaper vendors shouting at the top of their lungs "JACK THE RIPPER STRIKES AGAIN!" The early editions of the Saturday papers were on the streets. The posters read "JACK IS BACK," "JACK GETS AHEAD" and similar sensational claims. *The Times,* to its credit, ran a headline claiming only that a gruesome murder had taken place in Fenchurch. *The Evening Star* and the other barbarians of Fleet Street all were claiming that Jack the Ripper had reappeared. I glanced through a copy that we were handed as we crossed Piccadilly. On the interior page, there was a note, buried near the end of the story, stating that Scotland Yard had claimed that there was no possibility that Jack had done the deed. But that did not stop the editors from misleading their readers and doing everything possible to panic the public and sell more newspapers.

To my frustration, Holmes did not return to Baker Street until supper time, whereupon I told him all I had learned in my visit with the aged Mr. Peter Sutherland.

"What did you learn of the papers, the asset ownerships and negotiable securities he handed over to our headless imposters?" queried Holmes.

"Nothing," I responded. "My pretense was the issue of criminal justice and penal reform, not the managing of inheritances."

"All the same," rebuked Holmes, "you might have found some way to discern more. It would not have taken overly much imagination."

My short-lived pride at what I had been able to accomplish was crushed, yet again. Perhaps noticing my now sullen face Holmes added, "Ahh, but persisting in the matter of the Windibank father and son was most ingenious. Well done, Watson. Although I am not at all sure how this new data fits into our puzzle. I have no doubt that it does in some way, but all I see is a fog when I try to discern its relevance."

Having finished supper, Holmes returned to his chair and lit a pipe. He said nothing. Then he let a second pipe and again said nothing. Only when the second pipe was exhausted did he turn to me and said, "I fear that tomorrow morning we will have to return to the Reform Club and meet again with Mr. Peter Sutherland. He will be horrified to learn that the people to whom he gave over several hundred thousand pounds were imposters, but we need to know as exactly as possible what was transferred. If we have that information we may, or I should say Mycroft may be able to halt any transactions of those securities. I assume that he will show up at the Club sometime following breakfast. It will be Sunday but from what you have said, Watson, I do not assume that he would be attending church services."

"Most unlikely. I am quite sure he will be back in the club by ten o'clock."

I did not sleep well. It had been a long day that had started with the gruesome headless bodies of two young people. I could only hope and pray that the other young couple, the ones whose identities had been stolen by the deceased, would not meet the same fate.

I slept late on Sunday morning, exhausted from the long hours of the previous day. On entering our parlor, I saw Sherlock Holmes already sitting and reading some documents. I did not ask, but I assumed that he had not slept at all, as was the usual situation when his burning intellect and his hot determination were combined against whoever was engaging in brutal villainy.

"Any news?" I asked.

Holmes looked up and nodded. "Lestrade sent over some reports. He and his men are not complete imbeciles all of the time. They are devoid of imagination and deductive capacity but when it comes to plodding police work and the asking of endless questions they can be quite effective. He is telling me that he is close to identifying the killer of the young prop and barmaid."

"How has he managed to do that?"

"The couple was seen last in the pub where the girl had worked. She has friends there and they remembered seeing her. The two of them were chatting with some big chap who had a mustache, a red scar across his left cheek beginning in the corner of his mouth. And he spoke with a distinct Cornish accent. More questioning led to the chap's name. He calls himself Bill Sykes, but I have to assume that it is a false name. Lestrade's men were able to find out where he lived — a boarding house on Hayward Street in the East End. When they arrived there was not a trace of the Cornishman but there was a mass of dried blood on the floor, and in the bins behind the house they discovered the severed heads of our unfortunate young rugby couple."

"Do you think that some scarred chap from Cornwall is behind this whole scheme?"

"Of course not," said Holmes. "He is nothing more than a paid killer doing what he was told. No, if Mycroft is right, and I have no reason to believe he is not, this is the work of a newly formed criminal syndicate that not only commit crimes in their own interests but will undertake murders, extortion, and fraud for hire for anyone willing to pay their exorbitant fee. It is all headed up by this mysterious professor that no one can ever find and who keeps himself far removed from the actual criminal acts that he directs.

"His syndicate is now in the possession, we must conclude, of an exceptionally valuable bundle of securities. They will attempt to transfer these into cash as quickly but as stealthily as possible. If we can spot them doing so and follow them, it should lead us back to the center of the web. For that reason, we must return to the Reform Club tomorrow morning and see what we can learn from Uncle Peter about the documents he handed over."

Chapter Seven

Reform and Claridges

We departed Baker Street and as it was a clear Sunday morning walked over to Pall Mall. London on a Sunday morning in November can be a pleasant place, what with church bells pealing out hymns and Londoners dressed in their finery coming and going to religious services. We arrived at the Reform Club at an hour that we thought appropriate for finding the old man and chatting with him. The porter smiled at us when the name of Sherlock Holmes was given and asked us to wait briefly while he summoned the General Secretary of the Club.

"Welcome back the Reform Club," said the Secretary. "Now you have returned and brought the famous Mr. Sherlock Holmes with you. Splendid. May I introduce you to some of our members? They are a rather adventurous lot and would love to be able to go home to their wives and boast that they had had a conversation with Sherlock Holmes."

"Thank you, but no," said Holmes. "I am working not only on a monograph but in truth on a case that involves Mr. Peter Sutherland, and his safety and that of his family may be at risk. So if you would be so kind, do not show us around the Club. Please just arrange for a meeting with Mr. Sutherland."

"Yes, yes, indeed," said the Secretary, who had suddenly stopped beaming at Sherlock Holmes. "Perhaps you could step into my office to discuss the matter in private. Maintaining confidential matters regarding our members is of utmost importance to the Club."

We entered the oak-paneled office of the Secretary. It was festooned with maps and carvings and artifacts from all corners of the world, gifts to the Club from those many members who came and went to the far reaches of the Empire and beyond.

"It is very kind of you to welcome is, sir," said Holmes. "However it is rather urgent that we meet and speak with Mr. Peter Sutherland. If he is present may we speak with him? Now please sir."

The Secretary frowned. "Certainly you could Mr. Holmes. He has been here every day for the past three weeks. But it so happens that he has not yet arrived this morning. Rather surprising as he usually shows up by half past eight. Never fails. Did not give us any notice of a change in his plans and had registered for the luncheon. Maybe there is a problem with the old fellow. He is getting on. Over eighty I understand."

Holmes looked worried and then asked, "Has he had any unusual visitors call on him in the past two weeks?"

"Ah, yes, an interesting question. Not surprising you ask it. I thought you might, Mr. Holmes. And yes, a couple of weeks back a young couple appeared at the door. Pleasant types they were but not of the sort we normally have visit the Club. They were accompanied by an older man, exceptionally well-dressed. He did not give his name but just waited in the foyer. The young fellow, big young lad he was, gave their names to the porter and said they had an appointment to meet Mr. Sutherland and that the young woman was his great niece. They were listed in the appointment book and so we showed them in and set them up with Mr. Sutherland in one of our private rooms. I know all this because the porter came straight away to my office and had a very puzzled look on his face. He asked if I would mind just doing a quick look in on Mr. Sutherland and his guests because he thought there was something very odd about them. So I did and just pretended that it was a normal sort of welcome-to-the-club kind of thing, and I got a good look at the young man.

"Now sir we don't admit this publically, but as you are a detective, then I assume you must know that our members are not like the stuffed-shirt types from the City, who belong to some of the more snobbish clubs up and down Pall Mall. Our fellows are more the sporting types, travelers and all. So as you might be aware, and I sure you are, there is a fair bit of wagering goes on here especially on our sporting events."

I could not resist commenting on this and added, "Mr. Secretary, I would say it is more than a fair bit. The Reform Club is the liveliest place in London for a sporting man to place a wager. A place loved by all true sportsmen."

"Ah, thank you, doctor. You are very tactful in your phrasing. Because of this activity, our staff have to be up on all the leagues and games and team members. They know all the odds being offered and give our members no end of smart, reliable tips for their bets. So when I looked in on Mr. Sutherland's guests, I had a bit of a surprise. Now, of course, I did not let on but the large young man sitting there, who had given his name as Mr. Hosmer Angel, was none other than Oswald Whinery, the bull of a forward and indomitable prop of the team that just returned from overseas. Now it is not unknown for some athletes to use other names to avoid publicity, nor for our members to be met by people using false names so as to avoid possible embarrassment, but was Ozzie Whineray that notorious that he would have to be secretive? I thought not. And he has a reputation as a fine young man and there would be no reason for either him or Mr. Sutherland to hide his identity. So it was very puzzling.

"When they departed, as I am told by the porter and the doorman, they were carrying a file of papers, and they entered into a very elegant carriage with the older fellow who had been waiting for them. I might have just let the whole thing go and not thought about it again, but three days ago another young man comes by and gives his name to the porter and says that he is Mr. Hosmer Angel and he registers an appointment to meet with Mr. Peter Sutherland yesterday afternoon, just a couple of hours after your meeting had ended, doctor. So as soon as he has departed the porter comes to my office and tells me that a second Mr. Angel is coming to meet Mr. Sutherland. As that was very peculiar, I made a point of being at the front desk when the young fellow was expected yesterday."

"Yes, and what happened," asked Holmes.

"He never came. Old Peter Sutherland kept asking if he had arrived, but he never did. The old man was quite put out. He left after tea time and returned to his hotel."

"And which hotel might that be," asked Holmes.

"Claridge's. But before you go running off there, as I sure you want to do, there is one other piece of information that might be of use to you."

"Please, sir."

"Immediately after the visit of the first young couple, the one where I am quite sure the young man was Ozzie Whineray, Mr. Sutherland called one of our stewards and gave him an envelope and asked to have it sent to his box in Lloyds Bank. If you can give me a minute, I am sure we can find the details in our record book. Not that it will do you any good on a Sunday. But come Monday morning you could follow up if need be."

"That would be very helpful, sir. If you could do that, sir."

The Secretary of the Club checked the recent record book and wrote the address of the bank and the box number on a slip of paper and handed it to us.

"Mr. Holmes, I can tell by the look on your face that something quite unpleasant is taking place. We've become quite fond of old Mr. Sutherland even though we have only recently gotten to know him. If there is anything we can do, you know where to find us."

"Quite so," replied Holmes. "You have been very generous with your time and your information. We thank you, sir."

Before leaving Holmes sat at a writing desk and wrote out a note. He took a stub of sealing wax, lit a match and with a signet ring sealed it. On the pavement alongside the door of the club, there were three boys in page uniforms standing by their bicycles. Holmes approached the first of them and gave him the note and a shilling. The lad looked at it and his mouth opened widely. He showed the address to his fellows and they let out a whoop or two. Then he jumped on his bicycle and sped off in the direction of Westminster.

We hailed a cab. "To Claridge's," shouted Holmes.

It was not far to Mayfair, and the route took us through some of the most elegant urban neighborhoods in London. By now it was past noon and the gentlefolk from Mayfair and Belgravia were out on the streets in their finest winter fashions. By the time we reached Brook Street the crowds on the pavements had vanished and we made our way into the fashionable lobby of Claridge's. Holmes walked up to the young man on the front desk, most likely a member of the weekend staff, and announced his name and stated that we were here to see Mr. Peter Sutherland. The lad looked as if panic had struck. He immediately turned and entered the offices of the hotel. A minute later an older gentleman in a tailored suit and trousers, and who I assumed to be the manager, emerged.

"Mr. Holmes, Dr. Watson, will you please join me in my office for just a minute.

"Please, gentlemen, be seated. I understand that you have asked to see our guest, Mr. Peter Sutherland, is that correct?"

"Thank you, sir," said Holmes as he remained standing. "We are here to see your guest. We have already informed your man at the front desk of that fact and he has informed you. I am quite sure that you do not need to have it confirmed. Please, sir, you are wasting my time and yours. Kindly have the desk call on Mr. Sutherland and inform him that we are here and need to speak to him."

"I am terribly sorry, Mr. Holmes, that will not be possible."

"Do not be ridiculous, sir," said Holmes quite sharply. "I have called on many guests at this hotel. Messages are sent immediately. There is no reason for your obstructing this visit. Please announce our visit to Mr. Sutherland."

"It will not be possible, Mr. Holmes, because Mr. Sutherland is dead."

Sherlock Holmes said nothing in reply but I watched him and saw his shoulders fall and heard a quiet sigh.

I spoke to the manager. "My name is Doctor John Watson. We are friends of Mr. Sutherland's family. Could you kindly tell us what happened?"

"All I can say, gentlemen, is that the old man died last night in his sleep. He took his supper here last evening and entered his rooms sometime shortly after nine o'clock. He did not come down for breakfast. The housekeeping maid knocked on his room at nine o'clock this morning and there was no answer. She knocked again at ten. Then at eleven, she unlocked the door and entered and found the old fellow dead in his bed. A funeral director and doctor have been sent for. I expect they will arrive very soon."

"Have you notified his next of kin," I asked.

"We had an address for his great niece but were unable to locate her. I have just received word that another niece is visiting London and staying in Camberwell and she has been sent for. And gentlemen as you are not members of the family I cannot say more nor allow you any access to see the deceased. I must bid you good-day and ask you now to leave Claridge's.

Thank you, gentlemen and good-day." He opened his door and gestured to us to exit.

"You know who I am sir," said Holmes. "You know that I would not be here unless there were something untoward taking place. I am sure I could expedite whatever processes are required and save you a visit by a squad from Scotland Yard if you would grant us access to Mr. Sutherland's rooms."

"I am quite sure, sir, that you could not," answered the manager firmly. "Please, gentlemen." Again he gestured for us to exit and again Sherlock Holmes did not move.

"Sir, if I may be blunt. I strongly suspect foul play in the death of your guest. To be forewarned is t be forearmed and any information I am able to secure would be fully disclosed to you."

"I am sufficiently forearmed, sir, as I know that foul play could not have taken place. Our guest was inside his room alone from the time he entered it until the time the maid found him late this morning. This hotel is secured by the most advanced locks available. They were all set at nine o'clock last night. No one passed the front desk and it would have been impossible for anyone to approach his room without our knowing. I am sorry to disappoint you, Mr. Holmes, but there is no mystery except for our doctor to discern whether the cause of death was heart failure or some other regular event that overtakes elderly people. Please, gentlemen."

Standing out in the cold air on Brook Street I looked at Sherlock Holmes and noticed the signs of anger in his face. He did not take kindly to having his work obstructed, particularly when he believed that his clients were in peril, but then I saw a brief smile at the corners of his mouth.

"Come, Watson," he said. "We are about to offer this excellent hotel our services, gratis."

"And what, Holmes, are you planning to do?"

"Why, to test their security services and give them a full report as to how they should be upgraded so that their guests may be even better served."

I followed him around to the back of the hotel. There was a door to the go-down leading into the furnace room. Holmes pulled out a small set of tools from his coat pocket and in about fifteen seconds picked the lock and opened the door. The furnace room door took him about ten seconds.

"The servants' stairway is this way," he said walking through the basement. "Only the weekend staff are on duty. If we encounter any, we will tell the truth and say we are doing a security check."

"But we have no idea what floor or what room he is in," I protested in a loud whisper.

"Of course, we do. A top-drawer hotel does not put wealthy elderly gentlemen on the higher floors. More than one flight of stairs can be a killer. He will be on the first floor, as there are no suites on the ground floor."

"But what room? There are at least forty of them. We can't go breaking into every one of them. How can you possibly know what door is his?"

Holmes gave me a quick form of The Look. First degree only, thankfully.

"The cold one."

Hmm, I thought. That does make sense. The last thing a reputable hotel wants is the smell of a decomposing body in a warm room. The management would have turned down the heat and thrown open the windows, turning an elegant bedroom into a makeshift refrigerated morgue.

We met no one on the servants' staircase. As we walked quickly along the hallway of the first floor I took one side and Holmes the other and we held our hands to the keyholes. After about my tenth door I stopped and gave a low whistle to Holmes, then beckoned him to come over.

"Excellent, my dear doctor. There is a steady stream of quite cold air coming through the keyhole. Now please, allow me." Yet again it took about ten seconds and Holmes turned the handle and opened the door.

We entered a large and beautifully furnished sitting room. Holmes put his hand on my arm and bade me stand still. "Give me just a few minutes to inspect. I should be much more thorough, but time is being pressed."

He walked first toward the writing desk and looked it over carefully. Then he got down on his hands and knees, pulled his glass from his pocket and crawled slowly toward the bedroom. When he reached the door, he stood up and waved at me to follow him.

"There is cigar ash in the ash tray. It is of a brand from a rather cheap cheroot that is seldom sold in London but quite popular in the southwest. It is certainly not available in New Zealand. The writing paper is fresh," he said, "but the inkwell has been left open. The numerous marks on the carpet by the desk chair indicate that significant activity took place there, most likely a struggle. There are parallel scuff marks in lines leading from the desk all the way to the bed."

"The body was moved into the bedroom with the heels dragging," I offered. "Excellent, Watson. Now please sir, do be a doctor and take a look at the deceased."

In the bed was the body of an elderly gentleman. It had turned blue with death and the cold temperature.

"There are distinct marks on his neck. Some sort of ligature. I would have to say he has been strangled."

"Ah yes. My thoughts as well. What do you see that he is wearing?"

"His dressing gown."

"And underneath?"

"Why his evening clothes except for his suit jacket."

"And on his feet?"

I pulled back the covers. "He still has his shoes on."

"Precisely. Whoever entered this room came up quickly behind the old man, strangled him, dragged him to the bedroom and threw him in bed all in haste. So much so that he did not even take the time to remove the old man's shoes. Then he left and locked the door behind him. Not a sound was heard. A very efficient murder."

I was about to say something but stopped when I heard the door to the hallway open in the sitting room. I could hear the voice of the manager as he entered.

"This way ladies, please. I know that this is terribly distressing to you. But your uncle, madam, was an elderly gentleman and we all have to bid farewell to this life at some time. I can assure you that his last moments on this earth were a time of a delicious meal and a warm, comfortable bed. He could not have departed in a more serene way than in the comfort and security of a dinner and bedroom at Claridge's. Please, the bedroom is this way and try not to be alarmed at the appearance of the body. Your uncle is now in an even more splendid place than the finest hotel in London."

Mrs. Angel and Mrs. Windibank entered the bedroom. Holmes and I were standing on either side of the bed with the deceased between us. On seeing us, they both gasped.

"Oh no."

"Oh dear."

I thought the hotel manager was about to burst in apoplexy. His face went red with anger. He strode immediately over to Sherlock Holmes and placed his face less than two inches away from the detective's.

"Get out of this hotel in an instant or I will call our security officers and they will forcibly throw you out! And if you are injured it will be on your own head."

"I'm quite certain, sir," replied Holmes, coolly, "that with a modicum of effort you could do better than that and call Scotland Yard and inform them that one of your guests has been murdered."

Then turning to Mrs. Angel and Mrs. Windibank he said in a gracious manner, "My dear ladies I am so sorry to have to be the bearer of such tragic news. Your Uncle Peter did not pass away peaceably in his sleep last night. Someone entered his room, strangled him and placed him in bed still wearing his clothes and his shoes. The only consolation I can offer is that his death came very quickly and he was not in pain for more than a minute or two before passing out."

The manager was speechless. I walked up to him and quietly spoke close to his ear. "There are obvious marks of strangulation on his neck. Your own doctors will confirm this as will the coroner. It would be good to call Scotland Yard as quickly as possible."

He persisted. "No one could have entered his room. The doors were locked."

"Oh my," said Holmes sarcastically. "And how is it you suppose we entered. Are we fairies who flew in through the window? And if I may, sir, I would advise you to replace all of your locks with the most recent offering from the chaps at Chubb. They are far from foolproof but vastly better than your present ones."

I then turned to the two ladies. "Ladies, this is yet another tragedy to befall you here in London. May I suggest that a cup of tea in the hotel's parlor might help to calm your spirits."

"Do they not serve brandy?"

"I could use a bit of whiskey, doctor. Shouldn't they have some at a place this posh?"

Over brandy and whiskey, we sat as Sherlock Holmes enlightened the mothers concerning what he had discerned so far.

"Your Uncle was an exceptionally wealthy man who knew he was not long for this earth. In order to avoid outrageous taxes, unconscionable delays, and ridiculous fees paid to solicitors he sought to transfer ownership to his beneficiaries, your children, by way of outright gift while he was yet alive. A very nasty criminal syndicate must have heard about this plan and laid a very intricate plot to intercept the documents. The foolish young couple who impersonated your children has been gruesomely murdered. All of the documents are now in the possession of the syndicate. That is all we know at this time. I can assure you that I, along with Scotland Yard and the special services of Her Majesty's government, will do everything in own power to thwart their plans and bring these monsters to justice.

"I regret that I cannot explain more at this time. And now please, ladies, if you will excuse Doctor Watson and me we must continue in our pursuit. I would not be at all surprised however that this excellent hotel would be willing to offer you a complimentary room for the remainder of your stay here in London."

"Oh my, that wouldn't that be lovely."

"Oh yes. Lovely. A shame we cannot thank Uncle Peter for making the arrangements."

A cab from Claridge's took us to the front door of Lloyds Bank in the City. I had muttered something about it being impossible to gain entry on a Sunday, but Holmes had just given me The Look and muttered, "Mycroft," in return.

On the pavement in front of the door was a gaunt middle-aged man in a gray suit, gray hat, gray whiskers, and gray hair. He nodded at us and said only, "Holmes and Watson?"

We nodded, whereupon he unlocked the door of the bank and we entered. He locked it again from the inside immediately behind us. Five more doors and locks were passed in the same manner until we were in a secure room where the bank served those who wished to examine the contents of their private boxes. The gray man left us there for several minutes. Holmes and I sat in silence waiting for his return. He reappeared bearing a small security box which he placed in front of us. From another pocket, he withdrew yet another key and opened the box.

"Gentlemen," he said." You may take the contents with you or examine them here. What is your wish gentlemen?"

"We will take these with us and we thank you for your extraordinary service on a Sunday afternoon. It has been very good of you sir," said Holmes.

"Goodness had nothing to do with it sir," he responded. "Please follow me and I will see you back out."

Yet another cab ride took us to Westminster. As we traveled, Holmes looked through the small stack of papers that were in Mr. Sutherland's box at Lloyds. "Ah ha!" he let out with a grim smile. "Exactly what I was hoping the old boy would have put here."

"Come Holmes. What is it?"

"A list bearing the titles and the registered numbers of all of the securities that were given to the now departed couple. And look, he had her sign it acknowledging acceptance."

I was looking at a page bearing a list of names and numbers. At the bottom was a brief paragraph acknowledging that the signer had received them. It was signed with the name 'Marie Angle'.

I looked at the name and then at Holmes. He said, "It would appear that the departed Mrs. Whineray suspected something was rotten in the state of Denmark and deliberately signed with a falsified name. She is helping us from beyond the grave. I am quite sure that she must have been an excellent barmaid."

I said nothing, pained again at the loss of a sporting young couple whose only fault had been their gullibility.

At Westminster Holmes alighted and disappeared behind a gate. Twenty minutes later he re-appeared.

"By tomorrow morning," he said, "any bank or brokerage house in the nation that is capable of exchanging securities for cash will be telling their customers that due to recent problems with the telegraph system any transactions involving securities that had previously been registered in Australia or New Zealand will, with deep regret, take four days to settle. So could the customer please return on Thursday? Thank you very much. We appreciate your patience and value your business."

"Really Homes. Can Mycroft just issue such an order to every financial house in the land?"

"Of course, he cannot. He never orders. He only requests. Those houses that do not happily honor his requests will be met with a never-ending line of bank inspectors, several a day, for the next year. It is always much to their benefit to honor his request, happily of course. No matter which financial house our villains present themselves to they will be met with the same story."

"But there are several hundred such houses in south England, "I protested. "Even Mycroft can't be watching all of them. How can you possibly know which ones they will come to?"

"We can't, my dear friend. We only have to know which ones they will come back to in four days. I would imagine that our master villain will not be so foolish as to try to sell all of the securities at once. He will trickle them out but his men will have to return to the first test locations on Thursday and we, or at least I should say, Mycroft's boys, with some help from Lestrade, will be there to follow them back to the center of the web."

"You are truly a genius Holmes." He smiled. He secretly enjoyed having his brilliance acknowledged. I continued. "Did you come up with this plan entirely by yourself?"

Holmes said nothing for a moment. Then, "Mycroft made some contribution." Then a moment later. "As did Lestrade." And finally, "As did Mrs. Windibank and Mrs. Angel."

"The mothers? What in heaven's name were they doing there?"

"Mycroft had sent for them. Cut short their whiskey and brandy. He had wrung more information out of them than I ever could. He is exceptionally methodical. Mrs. Windibank was the one who suggested making them wait to get their money. She suggested that we make them wait a year, but Mycroft assured her that would not be realistic."

"And Mrs. Angel?"

"She agreed."

"Of course. And what will you do until Thursday?"

"Most regrettably I will not be able to lull my brain for fear that something untoward might happen before Thursday, so I am quite sure, my good doctor, that I will go partially insane with the waiting."

I was quite sure he was right.

Chapter Eight

My Wrong Right

Fortunately, I had the benefit of having patients waiting for me to attend to who had managed to remain healthy all weekend and then to take ill on Monday. The English are rather good at doing that. Malingering is, I fear, becoming a national epidemic, rearing its ugly head every Monday morning. The epidemic is unknown in Ireland. They are far more honest and just claim to be too hung over to work.

At supper time, I returned to Baker Street.

"Well Holmes, any news?"

"Our little scheme is working, Watson. Two men appeared at brokerage houses in the City seeking to exchange a few of our listed securities for cash. Another entered a bank on Oxford Street, and another, but matching the description of one of the chaps who appeared in the City, entered a small branch in Hampstead Heath just before closing hour. All were told exactly the same thing — that the telegraph system between London and the Antipodes was having some delays and could they please return on Thursday."

"And you Holmes? How goes the battle, my friend?"

"Under the circumstances, I am in reasonable health. I made some effort since you had initiated the idea, of writing a monograph on the effectiveness of various forms of imprisonment and a rationale for prison reform."

"Wonderful. That should keep you busy looking for the correct answer to that problem for, I would say, about the next fifty years. Well done."

He said nothing. Tuesday was a repeat of the previous day except that six visits had been made to financial houses. Four were in the City, one in a branch just off Regent Street, and again one late in the afternoon in another small bank in Hampstead Heath. There were only three individuals involved however and Lestrade had secured detailed descriptions of all of them. One had a scar on his cheek and spoke with a Cornish accent.

"They are trying various houses," Holmes observed. "They are receiving the same consistent response. There is no reason for them to suspect that we are on to them."

Wednesday was the same. Four new houses were visited and a larger institution in the City that was visited on Monday had a repeat visit. There was no attempt in Hampstead Heath. I thought it unlikely that there would be more than two bank branches in that small village that would deal with securities and I assumed our villains have come to the same conclusion.

I arrived back at Baker Street early on Thursday afternoon, all eager to hear if the plan was working.

"Have we found our blackguards?" I shouted as I quickly climbed the stairs.

There was no answer. I entered and found Holmes quietly smoking his pipe.

"Holmes. An answer. Out with it."

"There was no action at all today. No one visited a brokerage and no one came to collect," he replied calmly.

I was alarmed. "What is the meaning? Have they seen through us? Will they run off to America and try to cash the certificates there? Is all lost?"

"Oh, my dear doctor," he responded. "Not at all. Lestrade believes he has found the house that appears to be the center of this criminal web, and I have concluded that we are dealing with a serious and professional criminal. Haste and greed are the downfall of the lower criminal classes. Whoever is behind this scheme is content to wait a day, perhaps a week or more. He knows that his funds will eventually be in his hands and that anything that is precipitous would create suspicion. And I confess, my dear Watson, I trust you will not think it vain of me, but I am secretly rather pleased that a new and professional class of criminal has emerged in London. I was getting frightfully bored of the commonplace, especially since we did away with Mr. Ripper."

I did think it a little vain of Holmes but was relieved to know that if indeed a new professional level of criminality was about to spread like a disease through London that it would be met by the scourge of justice administered by Sherlock Holmes. As to Jack, I knew better than to ask.

"So what do we do now?"

"We wait until tomorrow. And tomorrow. And tomorrow."

"Holmes. Stop it. If I wish to hear Macbeth whining, I am sure I could go to the Lyceum for a better rendition."

"Ah, well then, if you will not appreciate my drama I trust you will my musicianship." He picked up his violin and began to play a short piece of his own composing. I would have to wait until tomorrow.

I sent word to my medical office that all appointments for the day were to be canceled and put over until Monday and I waited in Baker Street. He pretended to work on his monograph, and I to reading the latest *Lancet*.

At three o'clock there was a polite knock on the door. Mrs. Hudson opened it and, with a sideways look at first Holmes then me, said, "Constable Mactavish to see you." I knew that the dear lady was not in the least surprised and only dying of curiosity.

"My dear Mrs. Hudson," I assured her. "If all goes well you will learn all about it in *The Strand*. Mind you it might not appear there for a year, but just be patient." She gave me a glare and I am quite sure that were I within arm's reach I might have had a pinch on the cheek and accused of being saucy.

The constable was all business. "Mr. Holmes and Doctor Watson, could you please come with me now. We have a carriage waiting around the corner." Holmes gave me a questioning look and held his hand with his finger pointing like a gun. I nodded and patted the pocket of my jacket. He, in turn, patted the pocket of his and I nodded in return.

Holmes, the constable and I climbed into a closed four-seater, drawn by a brace of powerful horses. There was another man seated already. He put his head out the window and spoke to the driver. "Hampstead Heath. Back door of the inn."

I recognized the chap as an inspector from Scotland Yard but could not remember his name. We bounced along Marylebone Road for several blocks, making slow progress in the busy Friday afternoon. No one spoke. After we had turned left on Eversholt and cleared some of the mayhem of London, the constable leaned over to the inspector and I heard him say, "What's the reason for sending in the Royal Marines. We have enough boys to handle it without them."

Without turning to answer him, the inspector quietly replied, "Lestrade arranged it. Says there could be some fireworks and better the marines taking it than us. They're paid for combat."

"Hmm," said the constable and that was the end of the conversation. As we started to climb Haverstock Hill the inspector chap reached into his pocket and handed over a sealed letter to Holmes. "You appear to have some important friends, sir," he said. I could just make out the seal and knew that it came from somewhere deep within Westminster.

Holmes read the letter slowly, finishing it just before we reached the village adjacent to Hampstead Heath. "We are to wait at the inn. There will be no action until midnight. They have traced three men who tried to cash the certificates to a small estate house just outside the village. I assume that my clients are inside. However, we have no way of knowing how many men our enemy has beyond the three. Lestrade has a dozen of his boys and Mycroft has sent as many marines. They are taking this affair very seriously, I must say."

We entered the inn, arranged for a room for the night, and sat in the dining area and ordered a brandy, but only one each. There was a score of other guests and the conversation was lively as is common on a Friday afternoon once folks are done work for the week.

"Do you observe that fellow by the window?" asked Holmes nodding toward the far wall.

"With the tweed jacket and cap. Yes, what about him? He looks a little distressed."

"Very. Can you discern who he is?"

I looked intently at the man. He was of average height and weight and around thirty years of age I guessed. He was quite fidgety and read and re-read a note in his hands, and kept looking toward the entrance of the room.

"Beyond that he is disconcerted and expecting someone, no I cannot see anything else that could help me say who he is. Surely you cannot, Holmes."

"He is George Windibank the younger."

"Holmes, how can you possibly know that? There are hundreds, thousands of upset young men in London on a Friday afternoon. He could be anyone of them. How could you possibly know who he is?"

"You are assuming that I am looking only at his appearance and his actions and that I have made my deduction accordingly, Watson. I would dearly love for you to believe that but the truth is I saw the name in the hotel register, and from my vantage point I can see, although you cannot, our two dear mothers standing outside the inn and about to make their entrance. I suggest that we remove ourselves before they arrive and retreat to our room.

I had no idea what Holmes was up to and utterly confused by the arrival of Mrs. Angel and Mrs. Windibank at Hampstead Heath. I had thought that this situation was a closely guarded secret. Nonetheless, I followed Holmes up to our rooms.

"The presence of Mr. Windibank," Holmes said, "ties some of the loose threads of this case together."

He wrote out a note using printed letters instead of cursive writing. It ran:

```
Come immediately to Room 16. Final negotiations
for the return of the youngsters. The door will be
open.
```

He rang the bell for a page and gave it to him with instructions to have it delivered forthwith to Mr. George Windibank, who might be sitting with two ladies in the dining room.

Soon I heard rapid footsteps in the hall. Our door opened and an anguished voice spoke. "There is no more to give you. What sort of fiend are you?"

The voice went silent as the young man from the dining room entered. He regarded Sherlock Holmes and me and a look of shock swept over his face. He turned as if to flee, but Holmes spoke loudly.

"George Windibank, regardless what role you have played in this terrible affair we are here to help save the lives of Mary and Hosmer."

The man stopped and looked at us. Fear was written across his countenance.

"Please Mr. Windibank, be seated," said Holmes. "My name is Sherlock Holmes. Your wife has told you that I have taken on this case. We are here along with several armed men and we will rescue the children if you will cooperate with us."

The chap sat in the chair, trembling. Holmes spoke to him, slowly but firmly.

"Your role in this affair has been shameful. You were very angry, Mr. Windibank, were you not that your father's mate became one of the wealthiest men in the Empire while your family lived with nothing. Your mother still lives in penury. Is that not correct? Please answer me, sir."

There was no response. He was obviously bewildered, but nodded.

"You married Mrs. Windibank when she became a widow even though she was twenty years your senior in order to reclaim what you believed was rightfully yours. Is that not correct?"

Another nod' his eyes wide with fear.

"And then to your dismay and anger you found out that none of Peter Sutherland's fortune would come to your wife but would pass directly to her daughter. Again you would not see a farthing of it. Is not correct as well?

Another nod.

"But then you heard of some sort of shadowy criminal group who could make arrangements, who could fix things up, for a fee, of course, and you met with them. How much did they say they would charge you?"

"One third," came the whispered reply. "And only if they succeeded."

"And you found that you had made a Faustian deal with the devil, did you not."

"I never imagined, you have to believe me, sir, I never imagined that he would do what he did."

"The scheme seemed harmless enough did it not? Send the young couple on separate voyages. Have another couple pretend to be them and deceive the blind old man. Take the certificates, cash them in and split the proceeds. Again sir, am I correct?"

He looked up and took a deep breath. "Yes, Mr. Holmes. You are."

"But then he changed his terms. He now wanted fifty percent. More?"

"Seventy-five."

"And did you threaten to go to the police?" asked Holmes.

"I did. And he told me to watch the papers and see what happens to people who go to the police."

"He cut their heads off," said Holmes. "And he kidnapped Mary and Hosmer and threatened to do the same to them."

Again a nod. "I could not believe that I was dealing with such a monster. He kept increasing the terms. He said he would just take it all. I said there was no possibility of that. He could kill me first. But he killed the old man. He said that he would now kill not only Mary and Hosmer but their mothers. He told me to imagine all of them with their heads cut off. You cannot believe sir what this man is. He is the devil himself. He laughed when he described what had been done to Ozzie and his wife. He laughed. I have destroyed everything. I have brought the devil into our lives. You must believe that I never knew, could never have known what would happen."

The man was shaking with sobs. His head was buried in his hands. Holmes let him sob away for a few minutes and then spoke firmly.

"Mr. George Windibank you have been a foolish and greedy man and you are paying a terrible price for it. You can help us bring justice and save the lives of the young couple."

"How sir? Please. If I can do anything, sir I will."

"How came Mrs. Windibank and Mrs. Angel to this place?" asked Holmes.

"I sent them a note saying that I was trying to rescue Mary and Hosmer. I was not thinking and used the inn's stationery. They saw where it had come from and straightaway came here."

"Trying to play the hero and just continuing to deceive," said Holmes

"Yes, sir."

"Very well. The first thing you must do is go to your wife and Mrs. Angel and make a full confession. If they ever speak to you again, I will be surprised. You deserve nothing else."

He nodded. "I will do that. Yes."

"And then do not leave this building. Within the hour, there will be a contingent of marines and men from Scotland Yard who will storm the house. You do know which house I am referring to do you not?"

"Yes, sir."

Have you been in inside it?"

"Yes, sir."

"Excellent. Then you will tell them everything you can remember about the layout of the house, the out buildings, the gardens and the pathways to the officers. Your information will be quite useful."

He nodded again. "They are armed. They will kill."

"We are fully aware of the danger. The police and the marines are also armed and prepared to kill."

"He will kill Hosmer and Mary just out of spite."

"Then you will have to provide such complete information as you are able so that our fellows will make no mistake and not give them that opportunity. Now please sir, be on your way. Your wife is waiting for you."

He rose and walked slowly out of the room. He looked as if he wanted to die.

Chapter Nine

The Final Act

Holmes olmes left me alone in the room. I had dinner sent up. Two hours later a note arrived.

```
Come, Watson, the final act is about to begin."
```

As instructed, we moved quietly to a small barn behind the inn. In the dim light, I could make out Mycroft Holmes, Inspector Lestrade and a large man in a marine uniform bearing the rank of captain. I could not see into the darkness at the back of the barn, but I could hear the shuffling and breathing of what I thought must be at least twenty more men. All conversation was in whispers. It was cold. Winter had set in and all of us could see our breath as we exhaled.

"Your Mr. Windibank was very useful," said Lestrade. "We have a good idea of the house and a plan to take it by storm. If we can get close before they see us, we should catch them off guard and be able to subdue them without taking any casualties ourselves. It appears the young couple is being held in a locked room in the basement. It may be a bit of a sticky wicket getting down there before the guards do. But if we move quickly we think we can do it. We move in one hour. We will wait until the lamps are all turned out for the night."

It was a very long hour. Then the marine captain gave a signal and I watched as twenty-four armed marines and police officers filed past me and walked silently up the small road that led away from the village and toward the wooded area of Hampstead Heath. Holmes and I fell in behind them. We arrived at a laneway but did not carry on down it.

"Men," we heard the marine captain say quietly. "You all know your paths to the house. Take them and wait out of sight until you have the signal and then move very quickly. If you get shot, it was because you were too slow."

There were a few quiet chuckles in the ranks.

"Snipers, stay behind with me."

The soldiers and police officers moved away in the dark. Holmes, Mycroft and I followed the captain to a vantage point in the woods at the edge of the great lawn in front of the house. The lamps in the bedrooms and the parlor had all been put out. Some remained lit in the hallway and gave a dim light through the windows at the front of the house. The captain waited a full fifteen minutes and then gave the first of a series of bird calls. Each time an identical call answered. After hearing six such calls and responses, the captain turned to Mycroft and said, "Everyone is in place, sir. We're ready to charge."

"You are in command Captain," said Mycroft quietly. "The battle is in your hands."

"It's what we live to do sir," came the reply.

The captain took a long last look over the house and the grounds surrounding it and then gave a mighty blast on his whistle. I watched as nine marines all carrying rifles with bayonets mounted went running like they were on a hundred yard dash toward the house. Although cold there was no snow on the ground and they moved rapidly. Three of them carried a heavy pole and when they reached the door, they smashed it in short order. Two others smashed the bay windows and disappeared inside. The police officers followed them. Other disappeared around behind the back of the house. I heard first one explosion and then another as grenades were tossed into the bedrooms. Then I heard gunfire. The rifles were making their sharp cracking sounds, followed by the loud popping bangs of revolvers. I could distinguish the sound of the police and military issue pistols, but then heard the return fire of a variety of other guns that were, I assumed, in the hands of the enemy.

It had been a long time, nearly two decades since I had served in Afghanistan and watched as brave men rushed into battle. Even though I was in the medical corps, I was often at the front, bringing emergency help to the wounded. There is no such feeling on earth that compares to the intensity of battle. Once again, I felt it, regretting only that I was not twenty years younger.

Soon we began to see a series of flashes. Several of the police officers had electric torches with them and were flashing them back, sending messages in code.

"Ground floor is cleared," said the captain.

"They have more men there than we expected. Three of the enemy are down. Two have surrendered. Upper floor still fighting."

There was more gunfire and three more grenade blasts. Then more signals.

"Upper floor secured," said the captain. "Just the basement to go."

Then another series of signals.

The captain turned to me and in an urgent voice said, "Doctor. You have battlefield experience. One of our boys has been hit. It's rather bad. They're bringing him out. Can you give him some help? He's around the back of the house."

It has been a long time since I had been placed in this position. I leapt out of the woods and ran as fast as I could toward the house and around to the back. My leg, so badly damaged twenty years ago by the Jezail bullet from the Afghan sniper was screaming in pain but the adrenaline was pumping and I arrived at the back of the house where a young marine lay on the ground. He had taken one in the shoulder, but he was not in peril. I opened my medical bag and went to work.

The gunfire continued inside the house and then it all went silent. Lestrade emerged from the back door. "We've got all that were fighting us. But we can't find the young couple," he said breathlessly.

In the lull, we helped the wounded marine back to the protection of the wooded area where his captain, Holmes, and Mycroft were waiting.

The captain bent over his wounded man. "Next time, Jenson, remember to duck."

"Yes, sir. Will do sir."

Sherlock Holmes placed his hand on the captain's shoulder and leaned over. "Captain. Coming from the shed on the far side. Please, sir."

I looked over and could see two men, each of them with his arm around the neck of one of the young couple. They were walking with their heads pushed up against the faces of their hostages. One forearm was around the neck. The other arm held a revolver pointed against the temple of the one being held.

We heard a shout.

"Stand down. Back off. Or we will kill them. Drop your weapons. Drop them!"

The police officers and marines who had emerged from the house all lowered their weapons. They did not drop them.

"Snipers," I heard the captain speak quietly. "At the ready."

Three marines who had been standing behind us in the woods all along came forward, dropped to one knee and raised their rifles. The captain joined them.

In a quiet voice, I heard him. "Marine one, you have the fellow with the gent."

"Aye sir."

"Marine two. Same thing."

"Aye, sir."

"Marine three, the fellow with the girl."

"Aye, sir."

"Good. I have him as well. Now, on my count, on three."

I grabbed the arm of Sherlock Holmes. Mary and Hosmer were at least fifty yards away. A miss of only three inches would put a bullet in their heads. I could feel Holmes's hand grasp my side. He was holding tightly to me in return.

"One. Two. Three."

Four rifles fired simultaneously. The two men who were holding guns to the temples of their hostages fell backward and it looked as if their heads had exploded.

Mycroft Holmes turned to me and his brother. "They don't miss." He turned back away from us.

No sooner had the marine snipers fired off their deadly rounds but all four of them went rushing up to the young man and women. One of them grabbed the woman around her waist from behind and using his body as a shield carried her, running toward us. A second moved quickly behind the young man and likewise using his body as a shield pushed the lad toward us. The other two dropped again to their knee and aimed their rifles at the direction from which the hostages had appeared.

There were no more shots. The battle was over.

In our little wooded shelter Hosmer and Mary Angel tightly embraced each other. The girl was trembling and sobbing. Over her husband's shoulder, she looked a saw both Homes and me. She stopped crying and for a second made no sound. Then, "Hello, Doctor Watson, Mr. Sherlock Holmes. I do hope you're not expecting to collect your full fee for this case."

Holmes and I both laughed. Mycroft simply harrumphed and walked away and conferred with Lestrade and the captain.

"The older chap. Any sign of him?"

"None," answered the captain. "Searched everywhere. He got clean away. Not a sign."

"Very well, Captain. We'll try again next time."

"Next time sir?"

"Next time."

In the small hours of the morning we made our way back to Baker Street and fell exhausted into our beds and slept until late Saturday morning. A note had arrived in an envelope bearing the address of Claridge's and containing an invitation to lunch.

We dressed and made our way over to Mayfair. Assembled at the luncheon table and waiting for us were Mrs. Windibank and Mrs. Angel as well as Mary and Hosmer Angel. Mary was wearing a hat, a large hat. I thought she looked quite fetching regardless of whatever opinion Sherlock Holmes had of the girl.

One of the mothers spoke. "Quite the lovely place you arranged for us to stay, Mr. Holmes."

"Really. Quite on the posh side. Just lovely."

"And we have the honeymoon suite," chimed Mary Angel.

Word had gotten to Claridge's that not only had they been the site of the demise of one of the wealthiest men in the Empire, but that his grandniece and sole heir was needing a place to stay after a trying experience. They were only too happy to oblige.

"What dear old Uncle Peter had dreaded has come to pass."

"Exactly what the old boy did not want to happen, has."

"The estate will go into probate. There will be months, years of arguments in the courts."

"Those lawyers will be fighting forever over it."

"Young Mary and Hosmer will just have to keep on working and earning an honest living for a good while yet."

"Won't hurt them. Having to work for a few more years will be good for them."

"Builds character."

"They'll be better for it."

"Ladies, please," interrupted Holmes. "I am sure that the earnest men over in Chancery Lane will do their best to expedite what is sure to be a very complicated estate. It will take some time for the certificates to be canceled and re-issued, but I would suspect that some of the funds will come through at just about the time our young couple here gets over their desire to go gadding about the globe and settle down and start a family."

"Well, that could be. There is always an early risk you know. If you know what I mean."

"Yes a risk that the family could arrive early, that's what I would say."

"Yes," continued Holmes, "but, at least, you, Mrs. Windibank will no longer have to put up with the free-loading of your husband."

"Oh no. I'm going to keep him around."

"She's not getting rid of him. No sir."

Here I had to speak in disbelief. "You cannot be serious, Mrs. Windibank. After everything he did and all the mayhem he caused? After his stupidity and blundering? You will still keep him?"

"He can't possibly do any harm now and I didn't marry him for his brilliant mind, Doctor."

"She didn't marry him for his conversation and companionship either, Doctor. And he's harmless now."

"Then why did you?" I asked in utter bewilderment.

Both of them gave me The Look. Third degree.

"Why does any widow who has turned fifty want to marry a man twenty years her junior doctor? Must I spell it out?"

"I must find me one of them as well. A nice, fit younger man. Just what the doctor ordered, or he should have."

"To be blunt, Doctor, he was rather good in the bedroom, if you know what I mean."

"That is what they are good for, Doctor. That's what I always say."

Dear Sherlockian Readers:

This New Sherlock Holmes Mystery was written as a tribute to the fifth entry into The Canon, *A Case of Identity*. That story has been the cause of some perplexity amongst Sherlockians. The villain, Mr. James Windibank is a vile and cruel man but he receives no punishment, claiming that his deeds, no matter how horrible, were not actionable. He succeeded is breaking his step-daughter's heart and in reducing the likelihood that she would ever again consider marriage. She remains ignorant as to what happened to her fiancée. And Holmes lets the situation rest that way as the story ends.

That struck me as not very morally satisfying and so I had to come up with some way to have the villains punished and the vulnerable couple to escape and be able to return to their former lives. The true villain, Moriarty, escapes and will, of course, return to wreak more mayhem.

In 1888 the British Lions rugby team traveled on the SS Kaikoura to New Zealand for a series of games. The captain of the Lions, Robert Seddon, drowned in a boating accident. In 1905 and 1906, the International team from New Zealand returned to challenge teams in England. It was during that tour that the New Zealand national team acquired the name of the *All Blacks*.

The references to the transport of prisoners to Botany Bay and the way in which some of them became prosperous citizens of Australia and New Zealand is I keeping with the history of those countries.

The names and locations of places in the novel are accurate for London at the time of Sherlock Holmes. Claridges Hotel at that time was one of the finest in London and still is.

I have had the enjoyable experience of spending time in both New Zealand and Australia. The references to places in New Zealand is based mainly on my time in that extraordinary country.

If you are a fan of the great game of rugby, please advise me of any errors I have made related to the game.

All the best and warm regards,

Craig

The Hudson Valley Mystery

A New Sherlock Holmes Mystery

Chapter One

Across the Pond

Although over a decade has passed since our memorable voyage to New York, the singular events of that strange adventure remain fresh in my memory. It began in London one morning when my wife Mary (née Morstan) and I were seated at breakfast. The maid brought in a telegram. It was from Sherlock Holmes and ran this way:

```
Have you a couple of weeks to spare? Have
just been wired from America in connection
with the Hudson Valley tragedy. Shall be
glad if you will come with me, accompanied
by your dear wife of course. Air and scenery
perfect and an opportunity for an overseas
adventure. Leave Saturday on Cunard's new
Campania. Client will pay for first-class
return.
```

"What do you say, dear?" said my wife, looking across and me. "Shall we go?"

"I really don't know what to say. I do have a responsibility to my list of patients."

"Oh darling, you know perfectly well how the English loathe becoming ill during the summer. Most of those on your list will cancel if the morning is sunny. Ansthruther will look after those few who do show up. We're both looking a little pale after that miserable winter and damp spring, and the change would do us both good. You so enjoy helping Mr. Sherlock Holmes, and the journey would be rather romantic for the two of us, would it not?"

"You are quite right, my dear. It would be splendid – a first class ocean crossing and tripping the light fantastic on the sidewalks of New York. And goodness only knows what Holmes may have gotten himself into. But if we are to go we shall have to make arrangements and begin packing at once. We have only two days to prepare."

My experience of camp life in Afghanistan had, at least, had the effect of making me a prompt and ready traveler. My wants were few and simple and, by the evening, I had packed a steamer trunk and my valise and was ready to depart. My dear Mary, being a refined young English woman, of necessity took much longer. By Friday evening she was ready, so very early on Saturday morning, we took a cab to Euston Station and boarded the train to the Port of Liverpool.

Sherlock Holmes was pacing up and down the wharf, his tall, gaunt figure made even gaunter by his gray traveling-cloak and close-fitting cap.

"It is superb of you to come, Watson," said he. "It makes a considerable difference to me, having someone on whose assistance I can thoroughly rely. Help, once we reach America, may be either worthless or else biased. And Mrs. Watson, it is so very good of you to come as well," he added, smiling mischievously at my wife. "So thoughtful of you to bring your father along with you. Oh, pardon me. I should say your husband."

We laughed together. I could happily excuse being the brunt of his jokes since he made so few of them. His good humor was an unmistakable sign that he had embarked on a case that was far beyond the normal run-of-the-mill burglary. He scampered up the gangplank like a schoolboy on an outing and moved quickly to a part of the railing from where we had a clear view of the ocean.

"It never ceases to amaze me, Watson, how a part of the world that is so featureless and boring as the ocean can be the locus of so many and varied nefarious crimes, and the incubator of such a wide-ranging collection of criminals. Do you, as a medical man, believe that there might be something in the sea air, or the over-exposure to the elements of Nature that leads men to behave so badly?" he mused.

"No, my dear, Holmes," I replied. "Nature, as you know, is entirely benign. I suspect it has far more to do with having several hundred people of all classes held together in a confined space for days on end with no means of escaping each other. I should think that these are the conditions that lead not only to any number of crimes, but also to the giving and taking of marriage, the forming and breaking of business partnerships, and no doubt, the conceiving of countless children."

"Ahh, right you are, my good doctor. And how many confined souls altogether are there to be on board the Campania?"

"I believe that there are well over two thousand passengers and nearly one thousand staff."

"If your theory is correct then, before we make the port of New York we shall see some of every type of behavior you have described. Perhaps, if we are fortunate, there may even be an interesting crime or two to break up the otherwise tedious uneventful passing of time," he said.

Most normal citizens of the Empire would not have considered themselves fortunate if they were to be involved either directly or indirectly in a crime, but then Sherlock Holmes was not what anyone who knew him would describe as a normal citizen. He became sullen and unpleasant when for any period beyond a week he was without an opportunity to match wits with a diabolical criminal, or entirely miserable if an interesting case were to arise for which he was not consulted by the powers that be. I could not bring myself to hoping that there would be some rather nasty criminals on board with us, but if there were then I could only wish that they would be hunted down by the determined master detective.

The Campania cast off by mid-afternoon and we began our journey to America. As I feared, nothing eventful happened on either the first or second day. Holmes contented himself with reading his pocket Petrarch and some of the journals he had brought with him, and writing the first draft of a new monograph concerning the forensic qualities of the various types of human hair and the specific identifying qualities of strands according to the various moist parts of the human anatomy from which they originated. Regrettably, his discoursing on them did not make for the most appetizing of conversation over dinner.

The passengers were a gaggle of all rungs on the social ladder. Those sharing the first class with us were the well-bred and educated and who, on learning that the famous detective was in their midst, did not hesitate to pronounce their confident verdicts on all the crimes that had occurred in London during the past decade. Holmes barely tolerated these self-appointed Solomons. I had to remind him several times that many of them would someday be calling upon him for his discrete assistance and that rudely telling them that they were imbeciles was not in his enlightened economic interest.

In the third class and steerage sections, there was an abundance of eager single young men and young women, all off to America to seek their future. Some of the young women, although lovely to look at, were rather brazen in their attempts to make the acquaintance of men on the upper decks. I noted my disapproval of such inappropriate behavior, but my good wife rebuked me.

"John, darling, they did not have the luck to be born into wealthy families. Their only fortune is their face. They have the courage and determination to make a life for themselves in America that would be impossible in England. And it is only fair that we cheer them on."

Even I had to cheer when the captain was called upon to perform a wedding ceremony on the third day, and then another on the fifth. Two strikingly beautiful young women became brides and were applauded by all of their cohorts. The two young men, both from well-to-do families were, I feared, over-taken by their animal spirits at the expense of their common sense. Nevertheless, I clapped them on the shoulder and wished them well. Neither couple was seen again on deck and did not emerge from their cabins until we were let off in New York.

The last time I had been to sea was in a troop carrier on my way back from service in Afghanistan when the seas were rough, the weather miserable, and my leg wound from the cursed Jezail bullet still giving me great pain. This journey could not have been more different. Mary had not been to sea before and this unique opportunity to do so with top drawer posh treatment was a luxury for both of us.

We spent many romantic hours strolling arm in arm around the promenade and gazing out on the moonlight over the ocean. When the Captain heard that Sherlock Holmes was on board, he immediately invited us to dine at his table. The white glove treatment and choice cuisine were indeed a treat.

As I had hoped, in a necessarily morally twisted way, several crimes were committed and the captain immediately called upon Sherlock Holmes to solve them. For Holmes, these were distinctly non-interesting events and no more than diversions, but he nonetheless put his genius to work on them. On the second day, he tracked down a jewel thief who had purloined the necklace of a wealthy but careless dowager. On the third, in response to the pleas of a desperate mother, he demonstrated to her daughter that the young man she was going to meet in New York, whom she knew only by way of his lyrically passionate correspondence, was a notorious lecher. Holmes did this by calling upon his prodigious memory and reciting word for word, but sight unseen, the contents of several of the letters she had received, and that he had observed copies of in the hands of two other equally duped young maidens during the past five years.

Sherlock Holmes himself was set upon by three different women, all spinsters of a certain age who, having learned that he was a bachelor, determined that he should not remain so. Their efforts were in vain and Holmes quickly dispatched them by reading some highly indelicate passage of his current monograph of the forensic qualities of human hair, particularly those strands . . . Enough, dear reader; I have already drawn your attention once to this topic. Suffice it to say that his suitors quickly lost their interest.

I was itching for Holmes to give the details of the Hudson Valley tragedy to us, but I knew that he would do so in a time of his choosing. This time arrived on the second last day of the voyage when Holmes asked if we would join him in his cabin and have the stewards bring lunch to us instead of eating in the dining room.

He had an immense litter of papers scattered over the bed, the writing desk, and the floor. Some had notes attached to them, others were bound together with ribbons. Those on the small dining table were rolled into a gigantic ball and tossed over onto the day bed.

"Have you heard anything of the case?" he asked.

"Not a word. I had not noticed any mention in the London papers, and I only occasionally look at the New York Papers in the club. Their lurid accounts of murders, robberies, frauds, and the violations of the innocent are altogether too disturbing for an Englishman."

"The London press had only a brief mention," said Holmes. "The New York papers, which our client sent to me, along with copies of the police reports, had quite full accounts, and the particulars would lead one to gather that it is one of those simple cases that is so extremely difficult."

"Are you being deliberately paradoxical, Holmes?" I asked.

"Yes, but it is all true. On the surface, it is a featureless crime. A young man went mad and murdered his father."

"So wherein is the crime to be investigated?"

"We do not yet know. I will explain the state of things to you, as far as I have been able to understand it, but until I have had an opportunity of looking into the data I cannot take the story on the surface for granted.

"You have, I am sure," Holmes continued, "seen some of the paintings of the Hudson River School of artists. There are a few at the National Gallery are there not?"

"Yes, Mr. Holmes," answered Mary. "They are all rather wild and romantic, and painted on large canvasses as if the artist were trying to overpower the viewer with a sense of the majesty of the Almighty."

"Precisely. The long valley has many towering precipices and waterfalls and vistas that are claimed to have some grand spiritual transcendence. Conversely, there are places that are said to be ghostly and frightening, with no end of legends attached to them. As men of science, doctor, we put no store in these fables one way or the other; for neither good nor evil. Nature, as you have observed, is entirely innocent and it is only the heart of man, desperately wicked as it can be at times, that turns a place that is only a bog with fog on top of it into a locale so fraught with superstition as to induce madness in those who dare to go there.

"Now there are also many parts of the Valley that are quite plain and have become the homes of successful and prosperous farmers, or the country estates of the wealthy from New York City. The place in which this crime occurred is one such place. It is called Tarrytown and is no more than a pleasant village along the Hudson River where it widens out into what the Dutch settlers named the Tappan Zee.

"The largest landed proprietor is a Mr. John Turner, who made his money in California as one of the Forty-Niners. His neighbor, and longtime business partner, Mr. Charles McCarthy has, or I should say had, for he is now deceased, a property nearly as large, and adjacent to Mr. Turner's. He likewise made his fortune in California working beside Turner on a claim not far from the original Motherlode at Sutter's Creek.

"McCarthy had one son, James, a lad of nineteen, and Turner has a daughter of the same age. Mrs. McCarthy, who is our client and to whom we must give our gratitude for this grand voyage, is still living, but Mrs. Turner passed away some years ago. All of these decent folks, along with their help, were regular members of the local Presbyterian Church. They appear to have avoided society and none were given to any condemnable vices as far as we know, although Mrs. McCarthy, her son James, and the Turner girl, Alice, were often seen together attending and occasionally performing at the summer theater. They were known to have made numerous trips to the Broadway district in Manhattan and are reputed to be devotees of our old friends Bill and Artie."

"Holmes is referring," I explained to my puzzled wife, "to William Gilbert and Arthur Sullivan." She nodded and smiled.

"On June 3rd, that is full three weeks past, young McCarthy arrived home from Harvard. Two of his classmates were due to arrive the following day and together they, and Miss Alice, who had been studying at Radcliffe College, were planning boating outings on the river and working together on some sort of theater review that they hoped to stage the following school year."

"All very normal, so far," I observed. "Just the sort of things that students would be expected to do in June."

"Exactly," said Holmes. "However things did not remain that way for long. In the early hours of the morning, a single gunshot was heard. The household came running into Mr. McCarthy's library and saw him stretched out over his desk, dead, with a bullet in his head. Young James was looking out the open window and holding a revolver. He returned to his father's body and collapsed in tears upon it. Mrs. McCarthy entered the library and fell down beside her son in great distress as well. One of the staff, a young dark-skinned serving-girl named Patience Moran, reported that she heard voices coming from the window, but her statement has been given short shrift by the police due to the girl's age and race.

"The mother told the girl to run for the doctor and the police. The local constable arrived within a few minutes, followed by the doctor, who pronounced the victim dead. The constable wisely sealed off the room and as much of the surrounding property as he was able to and told all concerned not to disturb anything until the police detective arrived in the morning, there being none in the village and the closest one having been sent for from Yonkers.

"The Detective, a Mr. Paul Leverton, arrived on the same train as the two students who were coming to visit. The students were met by Miss Alice and her father and told the terrible news. Mr. Turner requested that the police allow them all, along with James McCarthy, to have a quiet time of prayer together. The shock had been very disturbing to all and they were in great need of quieting their own hearts and seeking the guidance of the Lord."

"Did you not say, Holmes, that these were all nineteen-year-old students and knew each other because of their shared interest in theater?"

"That is correct, Watson, and what, may I ask, would you deduce from that?"

"One can never say that theater-loving students would not be devout believers whose first instincts would lead them to prayers, but it is highly unusual, is it not?"

"Precisely, my friend. That was the second inconsistency of the report. The first, as I assume you noted…"

Mary interrupted, "The young man standing at the window while his father is lying dead at his desk."

"Ahh," said Holmes, "you are both doing rather well. What happened next was even less explicable. The elder Mr. Turner, who is apparently not in good health at all, reported to the police that James McCarthy had, following the prayer meeting and under the conviction of the Holy Spirit, confessed to the group that he had murdered his father. The police detective was surprised and immediately sat the young man down to interview him. What happened next is one of the things that makes this case so intriguing."

"And that was?" I said.

"The young man sat meekly in front of the detective and gave a full confession. When he had finished, he suddenly became stark raving mad. His eyes went wide with terror, he jumped up and began pacing back and forth, flailing his arms, spitting saliva, and shouting that yes it was he, he was the killer, but he was not James McCarthy. He growled that his body was now owned by a dark and evil force and that force had done the murder. He kept shouting vile obscenities at all around, pacing and flailing, and uttering gibberish.

"The police detective forced him back into the chair and demanded to know the name of the evil force. The young man shook violently and then whispered, slowly and deliberately, 'I am the Headless Horseman. I have taken my vengeance upon Charles McCarthy,' and then let out the most evil sounding laugh."

"Holmes," I sputtered. "The Headless Horseman? Was not that some character out of a tale by that writer, Irving? Where in the world did that come from?"

"From right next door," Holmes said.

"Holmes, please, no riddles."

"Of course not. I'm sorry. There is a valley on the north side of Tarrytown that for over half a century has been known by the locals as Sleepy Hollow."

"The site," added Mary, "of the legend of the Headless Horseman."

"The very place, and we shall be there in a few days to give our hello to the decapitated Hessian trooper," said Holmes, now quietly rubbing his hands together. "Back to the crime scene. The young man kept up his raving non-stop, shouting about a headless horseman on the galloping stallion, quoting Bible verses, shouting soliloquies from Shakespeare, and generally raving on and on like a total madman.

"The police detective and the doctor agreed that he had lost his mind and they took immediate steps to have him shipped off under guard up the river to the village of Mattawan where the State had only recently opened a large and splendidly equipped prison for the criminally insane. And there he sits to this day.

"The attendees at the prayer meeting all gave the police the very same story; that James had quietly confessed to them that in the middle of the night he had been awakened by a wintery blast in the room, had felt himself overtaken by a force that he could not control, walked from his bedroom to his father's study, saw his father sitting there, grabbed the pistol that was on the desk and fired it into his father's head. As soon as he had made his confession to them they notified the police detective who, as I said earlier, asked to hear the confession himself and was met subsequently with the fit of madness."

"And why," I asked Holmes, "are you so sure that the lad was not overtaken by madness. It is obvious that do not believe him to be mad or we would not have undertaken a voyage to America."

"I was contacted by the boy's mother," he replied. "Her message to me began … here, I will read it:

> Dear Mr. Sherlock Holmes: I have no other place to turn to and I beseech you to help. I cannot argue with the police or the medical experts, but I can only say that I know, in a mother's heart, that my son did not murder his father, and he most certainly is not mad.

"If I have learned anything over the years," Holmes continued, "it is that when it comes to insights into the behavior of their sons, mothers are seldom if ever wrong and theories to the contrary are the merest moonshine."

"Is there a possibility that he would be convicted and hung?" I asked.

"Circumstantial evidence is a very tricky thing, and only a decade or two ago there would have been," answered Holmes. "Many men in both England and America were wrongfully hanged who had clearly lost their minds. There has been some progress recently and now we in England put them away in Broadmoor. As long as the young man remains mad in the eyes of the courts, he will not be harmed. This much we know.

"There are many other things about this case that are unknown and until we have acquired sufficient data concerning them it is best to keep our minds open to all possibilities. Although I confess that I am beginning my investigation with the assumption that the boy's mother is right."

Chapter Two

The Sidewalks of New York

Friday morning, our last day on the Campania, began at the ungodly hour of five o'clock. There was no point in trying to sleep any longer as the decks outside our cabin were alive with shouts and loud conversations. The great booming ship's horn blasted away every few minutes. In the distance, we heard similar blasts from a countless number of other vessels. So Mary and I rose and put on sweaters to keep us from the morning chill and mist, and ventured out onto the upper deck. Sherlock Holmes was already there and enjoying his pipe.

"Could you kindly tell me where we are?" I asked one of the stewards. "I cannot see anything in this morning fog. What is all the commotion about?"

"Right sir," he replied. "We're entering the New York harbor. If you will just keep your eye looking front and port side, you will see her come into view. And a wonderful sight she is sir. She's just three years old but I've seen her like this several times now, and it still stirs me heart to watch the passengers, particular the ones below, and how they react to her, sir."

The tugs had pulled us through the narrows at the mouth of the harbor and were moving us steadily towards the city. I kept looking up and to the port side but for ten minutes saw nothing but foggy darkness, which the morning light was beginning to penetrate. Then I saw what was at first only a dark shadow on the horizon. The shadow became a dark column, and then slowly acquired the shape of the magnificent statue of Lady Liberty. As soon as she came into clear view I heard a cheer go up from the lower decks. Below me, there were hundreds of passengers crowded ten or twelve deep against the rails of the open section of the bow. As I watched, I saw fathers lift their children to their shoulders. Husbands and wives placed their arms around each other and held themselves close. Three couples kissed each other passionately in full public view. Rather poor taste, I thought.

Holmes, reading the look on my face, said, "It is to be expected. They are French."

Grandmothers and grandfathers held the hands of their sons and daughters who in turn held onto the hands of the grandchildren. Here and there entire families had dropped to their knees and were engaged in prayer. Older Jewish men were looking at the passing statue and slowly rocking their upper bodies back and forth.

A group of rough looking young men, from which country I could not tell, linked their arms over each others' shoulders and began to sing the American national anthem. The words disappeared after "Oh say can you see" and became only la la la la la la, but the tune was loud and unmistakable.

"It is to be expected," said Holmes. "They are Greek."

Watching the huddled masses, yearning to breathe free, as they entered a life in the new world is an experience that I have only had once in my lifetime, and one that I will never forget. I suddenly felt rather small, knowing that while we were here only to help a family resolve a crime, these hundreds below us had arrived intent on building whole new lives, families, and communities. I confess that a tear or two did come to my eye. I reached my arm around the waist of my dear wife and she returned the loving gesture. We held each other until long after the Statue of Liberty had fallen well back of the stern and we approached the pier and battery at Castle Garden on the southern tip of the island of Manhattan.

As Holmes, Mary, and I were fortunate to be in the first class we were let off of the boat soon after it docked and waived past the officials who must have assumed that we were both healthy and possessing sufficient funds as not to be a burden to the taxpayers of America. The immigrant passengers would have to work their way through the bottleneck of the Castle building.

So would many more immigrants until the new building on Ellis Island, still being completed in 1889, was opened to welcome them.

The Cunard staff were on the shore to meet us and directed us to a row of reserved taxis. We had carried our valises in our hands and were assured that our steamer trunks would appear within the hour at our hotel. The open horse-drawn cab to which we were escorted was driven by a small wiry man who struck me as just a wee small piece above a leprechaun. "Seamus O'Malley at your service, guv'nors, and M'lady. Let me be taking your bags there sirs. And my, are you just one long drink of water," he said looking up at the tall figure of Sherlock Holmes. "Aye, but you my good man, you would be a wee bit more of go by the ground than your friend here. So where is it you're wanting to be this fine morning?"

"The Gilsey," I replied. "I believe it may be found at Broadway and 29th Street."

"Why, and was it lost?" he said with a pleasant laugh. "At 29th it is, my good sir. 'Tis there it is, and we shall find it there, as you say, sir. So you just be holding on to your lady sir, and Seamus O'Malley will have you there with as full of dash-fire as I can be giving you."

"Perhaps you could tell us a little about yourself and your wonderful city, sir," said Mary. "This is our very first visit and we are all eyes and ears to learn."

Seamus O'Malley smiled and rose to the occasion. "I first come here from County Cork some ten years now, M'lady. When I first got off the boat, I was as poor as Job's turkey and did a turn as a fart catcher for some old gunpowder. She treated me like a young saucebox, she did. But I knew, I did, that if I kept that up, I would end up off my chump as some old rusty guts and in my eternity box by the time I was forty. So I paid me dues every month, all regular I did, to the Tammany boys and so when it came up my turn for the cab license I got it. But me life here is good. No sense crabbing it. Maybe it'll take me a month of Sundays to pay off the toffs but me young ones will go to school and will have as fine a life as can be had here in America. No point to letting your tail down here in New York. It's as good place on earth as can be. Aye. 'Tis."

For another fifteen blocks, he kept up the banter, most of which we could understand. The cabbie navigated his way through a frenzy of wagons, push carts, cabs, and pedestrians, all going hither and thither and shouting

393

and bleeping their horns. It had all the activity of London on a holiday, but much less well-behaved.

On arrival at our hotel, I was pleased to see that our client had selected a new and rather luxurious establishment. With over three hundred rooms it was large by English standards but only mid-range by American. The cabbie, the doorman, and the colored men bearing red caps all helped with the valises. "That'll be one dollar guv'nor," said the cabbie. I withdrew an American dollar bill from my wallet and handed it to him.

"Thank you guv'nor, and welcome to America."

The red caps delivered our baggage to the room, which was, I had to admit, new, luxurious and tastefully furnished.

Sherlock Holmes had said little since getting off the boat. He simply kept gazing intently at everyone and everything we passed and making notes. Now he turned to Mary and I and said, "I am going to ask the front desk to bring me back copies of the papers from the week of the murder in Tarrytown, as well as any new police reports. Why don't you two stroll along the sidewalks of New York? We will have all too little time for leisure beginning tomorrow morning."

"Thank you, Holmes," I said. "That is very thoughtful of you. I will also set a task to the front desk—to find us some theater tickets for this evening and you, my friend, will have to join us. We will not hear of your not doing so."

"Oh, very well. If you insist."

We parted, and my wife and I walked east along 29th Street until we reached the river. Then we followed the promenade south around the bend of the island until the magnificent Brooklyn Bridge came into view. Truly it was one of the seven wonders of the modern world. The two massive towers held up the great cables, which in turn held the suspended roadway. It was a miracle of modern engineering. We climbed the staircase up to the roadway and walked arm in arm clear across to Brooklyn and back. When we had completed one return traverse, we smiled at each other and did one more. From the mid-point of the bridge, we could see the Statue of Liberty off to the south and the skyscrapers, some as tall as sixteen stories, to the west and north. It was rather exhilarating.

In the City Hall Square, we giggled together as we most unceremoniously ate food from a stove-bearing wagon, covered with advertisements and an umbrella. We had to confess that a Coney Island Frankfurter, slathered in mustard and assorted condiments, was delicious even if far from dainty.

By the time we returned to the hotel it was the hour for preparing for the evening outing. Sherlock Holmes joined us at the Garden Theater and we attended an enjoyable performance of the latest production of a play about Beau Brummell. It starred a young chap named William Gillette and we agreed that he had a future ahead of him on stage. My dear wife begged off of any after-theater dining and sent Holmes and I out into the late evening hurly-burly of Manhattan. The doorman advised us, "Just a few blocks up the Great White Way, gentlemen, you'll find the Haymarket, as fine and as friendly an eatery as there is for gentlemen in all New York."

The after-theater patrons of the establishment were a fascinating mixture of beautiful young un-chaperoned women whose virtue I assumed had been compromised some time ago, and gentlemen of all ages who dined, and drank, and laughed among themselves and with the ladies. The food was as good, perhaps even better, as any I had eaten in a pub in England. Several single men sat by themselves at the bar, including a burly policeman who had a glowing ruddy complexion. Shortly after we sat down a boisterous young man, Irish of course, climbed up on his chair, and then up onto the table and began to sing *Sweet Rosie O'Grady*. He was very loud and not at all on key. After a few minutes of this, we saw the policeman rise, leave his shepherd's pie and ale on the bar counter, and walk towards the self-acclaimed opera star. He grabbed the fellow from behind by his suspenders and with one strong tug dropped him back into his chair. His mates were all laughing, the policeman was laughing, and soon so was the budding young Caruso. "There's a good lad," said the policeman. "Now just be good or be gone and be leaving the entertainment to those who get paid to provide it." He clapped a friendly hand on the lad's shoulder and then shuffled his way back to his place at the bar. The crowd gave a round of applause, which the singer mistook for his performance and rose and bowed.

The atmosphere continued in this manner and Holmes and I enjoyed two rounds of excellent ale and a generous steak and kidney pie each. We heard a bit of a ruckus at the door and saw three quite rough looking chaps, dressed alike in heavy wool sweaters and high boots, enter the saloon and walk up to the bar. The level of the conversation dropped noticeably and the patrons were all watching the newcomers with one eye while acting nonchalant with the other.

Holmes and I looked on, quite fascinated by the drama unfolding, as the three of them all ordered a whiskey and, trying to look manly, tossed it back. Then one of them turned to the crowd and in a bellowing voice, with a strong Slavic accent, shouted, "America is a country of whores! You simpering stupid Irish sheep ran away from whoring for the bloody English lords, and now you're whoring for the stinking Yankee capitalists! You're all just a bunch of whores!"

There was a moment of silence, after which the patrons ignored him and went back to their ales and conversations.

Holmes looked up at the young waiter and asked, "Is that considered permissible behavior in your establishment?"

"No sir, not really. But almost all of our patrons are Irish and have been called much worse than whores, and they consider these anarchists more to be fugitives from the madhouse and not worth letting their stew get cold."

Seeing that his first performance had no effect, the loud Slav tried again. "And that bleeding bastard, your Pope Leo the Lecher can bloody well go and . . ." Here he demanded a self-inflicted sexual act that, as a medical professional, I can assure you is anatomically impossible.

"Oh oh," said the young waiter. "That went too far."

Several men in the room stood up and started to move towards the bar. The policeman again pushed back his dinner and walked towards them.

"Come on Mister Copper! Come show us what a piggish slave you are to your capitalist overlords!"

From a dark corner in the back of the dining area, I saw a very tough looking fellow in a police captain's uniform make his way through the crowd. His pock-marked and scarred face looked as if it had been chiseled out of gray granite. The man who had been sitting beside him, a lean ferret-like man, furtive, with a long face and beady eyes, also stood but remained by the table. As the captain passed some of the men who were preparing for a donnybrook, he rudely and forcibly shoved them back into their chairs. "Sit down and stay down," he barked at them. Every one of them did as they were told.

"Those Serbians, or whoever they are, picked the wrong night to be in the Haymarket," said the young waiter with a barely disguised tone of eagerness. "That's the Clubber himself coming up after them and Lieutenant Icky what's beside him."

In just a few seconds the burly policeman from the bar confronted the leader of the three ruffians. The wiry Slav hit him with his fist on the jaw. The policeman barely moved. He quickly raised his right hand and grabbed the Slav by the neck of his sweater and brought his face crashing down on the edge of the bar.

The captain had approached the other two bearing a nightstick in each hand. With lightning speed, he landed the left against the head of the one, and with his right brought a stick up sharply between the legs of the other.

Soon, all three were lying in crumpled heaps on the floor. The captain grabbed one by the scruff of the neck and the policeman the other two the same way. They were dragged across the floor, through the open door and deposited into the street. The two policemen returned to their dinners, to the quiet applause of the rest of the house.

"I must say," said Holmes. "The constabulary of New York City are doing their job very efficiently."

"And so they should be sir," said the young waiter. "The proprietor of this establishment pays them a fair monthly sum to make sure they do, sir."

Holmes looked quizzically at the young man. "Pardon me, but I had understood that your police force was paid out of the public purse, not employed privately. Is that not so?"

"Right you are, sir. Both, in fact, sir. And we all know that a policeman is paid far too little to look after his wife and family in New York City, so it's understood that they have to earn their wage on the side, sir. That's the way it works sir."

"You must excuse me, young man," said Holmes, his eyes now lit up with that tell-tale sign of the investigative detective. "As we are only just arrived in New York City, we are not familiar with the way things appear to work here. Would you be so kind as to enlighten a couple of strangers? If your other tables can spare you for a moment, would you care to join us for a last round, and maybe even something to eat? Why don't you fetch something from the kitchen, put it on our tab and join us?"

"Don't mind if I do sir," he said. "Give me just a moment and I will be right back."

The young lad soon returned bearing a platter with a thick liverwurst sandwich and a glass of a dark liquid that had small bubbles sparkling at the top of it. "I say, what is that drink you are having? Is it a very dark ale?"

"No sir. I need my employment and I have to serve alcohol, but I have promised my mother that I would never touch a drop of it myself. This sir is the newest elixir that is sweeping America. It's has a great taste and not even a drop of rum in it."

"Are there not a score of these now being sold?" I asked. "What makes this one so successful?"

"Oh, there are many bubbling tonics sir. But most of them are no better than cat piss. This here is Coca-Cola. It's the real thing, sir."

"Indeed, I must try some before we leave America."

"Now young man," Holmes began, "Pray bring us up to date on America. In England, we expect the help to provide good service because that is their job. And we most assuredly expect it from our police constables and inspectors. But you are saying that your practice here is different."

"As I said sir, a man cannot feed and clothe his family in New York if he were to rely only on his wages. There's quite the handful of rough types here in what's called the Tenderloin District, but the police captain Alexander Wilson, the chap I called 'Clubber', that being how he's known here and for good reason, he and his men make sure that the fancy restaurants, and saloons like ours here, and even the houses of ill repute, are all kept safe, and so we show our gratitude by putting a little something in their pockets."

"And what about your more serious criminals," asked Holmes. "The bank robbers, and swindlers and the truly nasty types. I am sure you have your fair share of them as well, do you not."

"For sure we do sir," replied the young man and then moved his head closer to Holmes and continued in hushed tones. "They do not last long in the Tenderloin, sir. First offense, they might get off with a beating from Clubber and his boys, but if they persist, the word is that they get a visit from Lieutenant Icky."

"Yes," said Holmes, "and what does such a visit consist of?"

"Well sir, us working types don't really know, so I'm just saying what I been told, but some of those who get visited just seem to disappear, and some we hear ran like scared cats as far as San Francisco, and some ends up floating in the East River, sir, if you know what I mean. The word is sir if you values your life the last thing you want is a visit from Icky."

"Is that truly the man's name? Icky?" asked Holmes.

"Oh, no sir. His real name is Isaac Crane, but when he was a young lad growing up here, according to what I been told, his classmates started calling him Ichabod, cause his last name was 'Crane'. You know, that fellow in the story, Ichabod Crane? And it just became Icky, and that's what everyone now calls him. But not to his face, mind you. No sir, I do not recommend anyone ever do that, sir. And he gets a lot in his pocket every month from the Tammany boys because he looks after all the real dangerous types he does."

"And does this apply to every service the city provides?" continued Holmes.

"I cannot, for the life of me, think of one where it does not," the lad replied. "If your road needs repairing then you have to pay for it. If not then it'll be a mess for years. Or they will just start and dig a big hole in front of your establishment and then leave it there for a donkey's age. Same goes for the ambulance drivers, and the health inspectors, and now sir, with them putting in the electricity all over the south end of the island, that's especially one where you have to be prepared to pay because everybody is wanting it. Soon no theater, or restaurant, or saloon will have any patrons if they don't have the electricity."

Holmes starred at the boy quietly for a moment. "Are you saying that everyone who does anything for you has to be given cash every time he shows up? That must get terribly awkward does it not?"

"Oh no sir. It's all arranged by the men at the Tammany Hall sir. You just pay your dues to them and they look after making sure that all those hard working policemen and public servants are looked after, sir. And they look after the poor, and any widows and orphans, they do sir. Here we just give the boys a glass of ale and a sandwich, but their financial support, sir, that's all provided to them by the union and the politicians what meets down on 14th Street sir.

"It's always been that way sir, here in New York City. I never lived anywheres else sir, so I wouldn't be knowing, but that's the way it's been here for near one hundred years."

Holmes continued the conversation as the young man devoured his sandwich. The lad was rewarded with another delectable sandwich and thanked as we rose to return to the hotel.

"Can you imagine, Watson," Holmes said as we walked back to the Gilsey, "anyone offering to pay Inspector Lestrade a bribe just to show up and do his job."

"Never."

"Neither can I. But here in America, it is not only the general practice but accepted and even condoned by the general populace. Do you suppose there is much money in it?"

"Heavens, yes. There are already several million living in this city and if every business is expected to pay their dues then someone is getting very wealthy. If they also control the awarding of all the city contracts, then I suspect that they are taking a cut of those as well. I dare say, there must a very pretty penny to be made. Yes, a very pretty penny."

Chapter Three

Sleepy Hollow

First thing the next morning, Holmes, my wife and I had the hotel livery service deliver us to Grand Central Depot on 42nd Street, where we caught the early morning train to Tarrytown. Behind the gleaming 4-6-0 Ten Wheeler steam engine of the New York Central and Hudson River Railroad we chugged alongside Riverside Park and followed the river, stopping at Yonkers and Dobbs Ferry, and finally at our destination. The client had arranged for us to stay at a hotel that was built by a wealthy if impractical American – mind you that is how Londoners describe most Americans – in the shape of a castle.

"Are we in Windsor-on-the-Hudson?" asked my wife when we approached the anomalous edifice.

Unlike real English castles that are drafty and gloomy, this one, built in the preceding decade was quite comfortable and outfitted as a luxurious if silly looking hotel.

"Our client will meet us here in an hour and take us to the family estate," said Holmes. "Other than a spectacular view of the river, for which I have no earthly use, I see nothing to recommend this town to anyone's enjoyment, so I will leave you two to enjoy the natural beauty while I review our documents one more time."

To pass the hour Mary and I strolled along the High Street of the town, which was quite appropriately named "Main Street." To my surprise and wonder, it felt as if we have landed on a different planet from the one we were in the day before in New York City. The men and women and families we met were gracious, polite, warm, and friendly. Their spoken English was highly articulate even if bearing a distinct American accent. When they heard us speaking the Queen's English they concluded that we were visitors and extended a most hospitable welcome. One couple of about the same age as Mary and I insisted on treating us to a concoction brewed at the lunch counter in Fishman's Drug Store. "Our local soda jerk makes the very best Coke floats," she enthused. And I had to admit that there were rather refreshing and tasty.

They asked as to the purpose of our visit in Tarrytown and I guardedly informed them that I was a medical doctor and had been called upon to provide assistance to a family that had recently suffered a tragedy. The lady immediately responded, "Oh, you must mean the McCarthys. Well now if you ask me . . ." I refrained from the obvious rejoinder that I had not. "If you ask me, all of us in town know that there is some dark story behind Charles McCarthy and John Turner. They supposedly made their fortune in California, but no one really knows how they did it. Not that they are not both fine upright men. But if anyone ever asks them direct about their past, they just clam up, they do. We're all feeling terrible for Mrs. McCarthy, we are, her having lost her husband and having her son in the mad house for killing his father. But if you ask me, there is something about those two families that's been hidden and that they would like to keep hidden. And the word is, doctor, that the past has come back to haunt them. I'm sure you know that some local folks still believe that parts of this town are haunted, they do. You just can't bury the past forever, no you can't. It will come back, and some of us are quite sure that's just what it has done. Poor Mrs. McCarthy."

At this point her husband interrupted, changed the subject and asked us about the weather in England, always an acceptably neutral topic and the basis for endless if meaningless conversation.

Our time had run out and we made our way back to the hotel. Sherlock Holmes was pacing up and down the cobblestones under the portico of the entrance.

"Ah yes. Dr. and Mrs. Watson. And did you learn anything of use about this pleasant little town?"

"We did Mr. Holmes," began my wife. But Holmes raised his finger to his lips. "I do want to hear all about it, but it will have to wait. I believe that coming up the drive behind you is the carriage that belongs to our client."

We turned and saw an open four-wheeler approaching us. It was drawn by a pair of gleaming black horses, and behind them, I could see that the brass fittings were all highly polished and shining in the summer sun. Our client's wealth may have originated in the California gold rush, but the taste was as refined as one would see in Mayfair. Seated in the front-facing seat was a lady of close to sixty years of age, dressed entirely in black. When the carriage stopped, she rose and stepped out without waiting for the driver to assist her. She was short, not much over five feet, and still quite spry and trim although her shoulders were slightly rounded, as is common to women as they reach that age. Her face puzzled me as it bore all the lines that one normally associates with a life of joy and laughter, yet it was haggard and drawn. Her recent tragedy had clearly been very hard for her to bear.

She approached the three of us and extended her hand. "Dr. and Mrs. Watson, and Mr. Sherlock Holmes. Welcome to Tarrytown. You are the only answer left to my prayers. I have exhausted all my other possibilities and your willingness to come all the way from London to help me is something for which I am very deeply grateful. You appear to be ready to travel so may I ask that you join me in my carriage and return to McCarthy Manor. I would be much more comfortable speaking with you in the familiar surroundings of my home than in the parlor of a hotel. These past few weeks have been the worst weeks of my life, so please indulge the request of a weary woman and come with me."

"By all means," said Holmes warmly as he reached out and held her hand. "We will be honored to visit your home and while we are only human and cannot promise miracles, be assured that we will do everything within our power to help resolve the dreadful situation in which you have found yourself. Would it be acceptable to you if we started in straightaway and asked you a few questions as we are driven there?"

"I'm sorry, sir," she replied, her voice sounding tired. "But no, please do not ask me any questions. I have been blessed with wonderful staff and I have great confidence in my George," she said and gestured with her head towards the driver. "But this tragedy has been very upsetting to the help. There are rumors and stories abounding and I would prefer not to give rise to any more of them. Your visit alone will be more than enough to start tongues wagging. But we can converse pleasantly about the village and scenery."

"Of course, madam," said Holmes. "That is a wise suggestion. A pleasant conversation about scenery is always welcome."

Sherlock Holmes had no use for pleasant conversations about scenery, but ever gracious to widows in distress, he endured the ride to the Manor.

We took the road north out of the village and descended into a lovely glade at the bottom of which was a steep ravine and a shaded stream.

"The bridge you are about to cross," said Mrs. McCarthy, "is the very one made infamous by our famous local author, Mr. Washington Irving. It is the one said to be haunted by the Headless Horseman on his galloping stallion. I have lived here now for over thirty years and have yet to meet the poor chap. If you happen to run into him do give him my greetings," she added with a forced smile.

"Indeed, we shall, madam," replied Holmes.

The ride to the Manor was mercifully short. We approached a large white frame house with a front porch extending the entire length. It was a widespread, comfortable looking building. In the steep roof above the porch were a series of gables and on the far end a conservatory with large glass windows on three sides. Behind the house, I could see two barns and several outbuildings. Spreading elm trees framed the home and there was a small orchard on the north side. It presented a gracious and welcoming prospect, and so out-of-keeping with the tragedy that had recently befallen it.

"Welcome to McCarthy Manor," said our client. "Please make yourselves comfortable in the parlor and I will join you shortly."

We seated ourselves in a spacious and sunny front room that was furnished with several sofas and occasional chairs, all upholstered in yellow or light green fabric, giving the room a country atmosphere. A young dark-skinned servant boy of about ten years of age appeared bearing a tray with tea and some baked goods. He set the tray down on the low table in front of the couch, gave us a gleaming smile, nodded and said, "Help yourselves." He turned and left the room.

Mrs. McCarthy returned to us and said, "Oh, very good. I see our young Wesley has looked after you. His family has helped us with the house and farm for many years and have been invaluable, especially after our oldest son was taken from us and young James went off to college. I have told his sister,

Patience, to stay close by as I assume that you will want to speak to her regarding the events of that night. But do not let me waste your time. Where do you wish to begin your investigation, Mr. Holmes?"

"I understand that the murder took place in your husband's office. Could you please show us that room, and then I would ask you to tell me, exactly, difficult as I am sure it will be for you, what you recollect from that most unfortunate night."

"Come, please. This is the room, Mr. Holmes, and that is my husband's desk. That is where we found him."

"You say 'we' madam, who may I ask discovered your husband's body," queried Holmes.

"My son, James, was the first to enter the room. He was followed momentarily by our girl, Patience Moran, she was the only member of the help who were staying in the house that night. I came down a minute or two afterward."

"And what did you see when you entered? Please try to be as precise as possible."

She closed her eyes and I could see her clasping her hands tightly together. "I saw my husband slumped forward at his desk. My son, James, was leaning over him, clutching at his shoulders. He was shouting 'Father, Father, don't die father. Don't let those bastards win Father.' He was distraught and in a panic. He looked up as he saw me enter, and with a desperate look on his face said, and I believe these were his exact words, I am not likely to forget them, 'Oh Mother, I am so sorry. I'm so sorry. They killed him and it is all my fault. Oh mother, I am so sorry.' He said no more and collapsed onto the desk sobbing and crying. I came over to my husband's body and saw the pool of blood that had flowed from his head. My son raised himself up from the desk and we grabbed hold of each other. Both of us were in complete distress. We held on to each other tightly for several minutes. Then he turned to Patience and asked her to run into the village and fetch both the doctor and the constable. She did so and the three of them arrived within the half hour. I believe that any other matters after that time were included in the police reports that I had sent to you."

"Indeed, they were, madam, and I do understand how very difficult this must be for you to have to go through it all again," said Holmes as he extended both of his hands and laid them on top of Mrs. McCarthy's. "Please bear with me and help me with just a few more details. What time did these events take place?"

"I think it was just after one o'clock in the morning. I remember looking at the clock as we waited for the doctor and constable."

"Ah yes," said Holmes. "Your husband was still up and working. Was that his common practice?"

"It had been off and on over the years. He would often read and finish up his paperwork after I had gone to bed for the night. During the previous week, after James had returned from college, my husband and his son would sit in his office and talk until quite late. Father and son, I assumed, had much to catch up on."

"And did you know what they talked about? Did either your husband or your son relate to you any of the details?"

"No," she shook her head. "Once or twice I heard Charlie raise his voice and I thought that yet again they were arguing about my son's course of studies. I thought they had put that all behind them but perhaps not since there was no other topic about which they ever argued. Over the past two years there had grown a rather strong bond between them."

"You say they had argued about his studies. What was there to argue about? Your son had been accepted at Harvard, had he not? I assume that he was a diligent student."

"Oh yes, oh yes. James is a brilliant boy, for sure. But his father had his heart set on having him go to West Point. It is hardly more than a stone's throw from here and we could have seen him on weekends. I suspect that Charles, my husband that is, was hoping that he would follow in his older brother's footsteps and distinguish himself in a military career."

"You say his older brother. Earlier you said that he had been lost to you. Please tell me what happened."

She took a deep breath. "Charles Junior was our first born. He was an outstanding student and athlete. He won a full scholarship to the Naval Academy in Annapolis and we were very proud of him. He was on board his first ship when it was sent overseas to give some Brazilians a bit of a lesson. The Marines gave them what for, but a sniper took aim at my son's boat, the *USS Detroit*, and cut him down. He was buried at sea and the Navy sent us the citation signed by his admiral." She pointed to a spot above the fireplace and I observed a photograph of a handsome young man in his white dress uniform. Beside it was a framed citation, embossed with a gold seal.

"His father took it very hard, as did I, but Charles, my husband, then tried to steer young James to be just like his brother, and, of course, he wasn't. He had the grades and all the recommendations he needed for West Point, but a military life held no interest for him. He was in love with the arts, and with the theater, and wanted nothing more in life than to be able to write plays, and act. I confess that I have myself to blame for that. I often took him and Alice, Mr. Turner's daughter, to see the brilliant productions in New York. And last summer he and his father had some very long arguments about it. One morning after they had been at it hammer and tong the night before, I said to my husband, I said 'Dearest, your son James cannot replace your son Charles. Our oldest son is gone and all we can do is to be thankful to the Lord for the time we had with him and for our wonderful memories. We cannot force James to be someone he is not.' He said nothing but later that day he gave me a warm embrace and said, 'You're right, darling. I have to love and support James as James, and not as Charles.' And that was the end of it. There was no more talk about West Point. My husband took an eager interest in all that James was learning at Harvard, and in the joyful silliness of the Hasty Pudding Theatricals that James and Alice and their friends were involved in. He even offered to be the financial backer and help produce a jolly little farce the group students had written. The two of them would be up late at night talking about it. They couldn't wait for the arrival of James's friends so they could finish their script and start their rehearsals.

"I'm not sure what else I can tell you about father and son. What else do you need to know?"

"Perhaps some additional details will be required later," said Holmes, "but, for now, let us return to this office, and what else you observed at the time of the murder."

"What else is there to say?"

"The gun that was used to kill your husband; where was it when you entered?"

"It was beside him on the desk."

"How did it get there?"

"I do not know for sure. Patience, our girl, said that James had had it in his hand when he was standing at the window and shouting, but I did not see that, so I cannot say,"

"What was your son wearing?" asked Holmes.

"His evening clothes. He had removed his jacket after dinner and put on a sweater, but otherwise, there was nothing different about his dress."

"You are telling me," said Holmes, "that he had not yet changed into his bedclothes at one o'clock in the morning?"

"He and his father were both night owls. If they were not sitting up and chatting then they would both burn the midnight oil either writing or reading until past one o'clock. It was not unusual for either of them to still be up at that hour."

"Hmm . . . and what of this Miss Moran, the girl you have spoken about. She arrived in the library before you but after your son. Is that correct?"

"That is what I understand. She has confirmed that to me. However, I cannot confirm it with James. He has not said an intelligible word to me since the following morning when his madness overtook him."

"Ah yes, his madness. Let us return to that in a few moments but, for now, a little more about the girl. Was she fully dressed as well or in her night clothes?"

"She was fully dressed."

"Why would a young girl who provides domestic services be fully dressed so late at night?"

"She is quite the little student. After her chores were done in the kitchen and in the bedrooms for the evening, she would often be up late working on her assignments for school. She is a diligent one she is. The girl has it in her head that she is going to go to college. She has her nose in a book constantly. As I said, she is quite the little student."

"I would hope to speak to her presently, but first back to your son. What previous indication had he given to you of his madness?"

"None."

"None? I'm afraid I do not understand, Mrs. McCarthy. How could he have given you no indication of his madness? He was bundled off to the Matteawan prison having been declared insane by the doctor and police detective, was he not?"

"I cannot help you there, Mr. Holmes. I did not have an opportunity to speak confidentially to my son after our brief time at the body of his father. As I am sure you can understand I could not return to sleep after all the dealings with the doctor and the police, as I was sore distressed. I took a little laudanum with my tea to help me fall asleep and fell into a very deep sleep that I did not wake from until late the next morning. I asked the help why they had let me sleep so long and they said, understandably, that they felt I needed the sleep in order to regain my strength and face the inevitable events of the day.

"By the time I had awakened and made myself ready, I descended from my room to find that the police detective had arrived from Yonkers, had completed his inspection except for his interview of me, that the doctor had arranged for the mortician to come and remove my husband's body, and that my son had gone stark raving mad, had been put into a straight jacket and taken off to the madhouse. I have not spoken to him since. You have read the reports, Mr. Holmes. Now you know as much as I do."

"Perhaps one or two more items, Mrs. McCarthy, if I may," Holmes responded. "About this prayer meeting, that was held the following morning. I gather you were still in your bed when this occurred."

"I was. I only know about it from what I was told."

"And what were you told about it? Who were you told participated in it?"

"I was told sir that it was held in the conservatory. It was arranged almost immediately after the arrival of our neighbors, Mr. Turner and his daughter Alice, and son James's friends, the college boys who had come to visit."

"And was your family in the habit of holding impromptu prayer meetings?"

"Mr. Holmes, sir, we are Presbyterians. We are not evangelical enthusiasts. We say our prayers before dinner and before going to sleep at night. We do not hold prayer meetings in a conservatory on weekday mornings. No sir."

"Yes. As I thought. These friends of your son; did you meet them?"

"Only briefly. They greeted me in the early afternoon and extended their condolences in a very kind manner. They offered to do whatever they could to help James recover, and then they departed. That was understandable since their holiday visit could not continue."

"And did they depart immediately for the train station after that?"

"It was my understanding that they went to the home of my neighbors, John Turner and his daughter. I have no idea what they did after that."

At this point, I took the liberty of posing a few questions myself.

"About your son's going mad, Mrs. McCarthy. Do you remember ever seeing signs, any behavior in the past that would indicate that he was susceptible to a mental condition?"

"Ah yes," added Holmes. "Thank you, doctor."

"No doctor. None at all," replied the lady.

"No seizures, no extended periods of melancholy, no bursts of either temper or unaccountable sobbing?"

"No, doctor. He was a consistently happy child. He had a flair for being dramatic perhaps, but he was always cheerful and good-natured. Always laughing and smiling. As a child growing up, he often had the rest of the family and the help in stitches. So no sir, there was never any sign of madness. None whatsoever."

"We understand," said Holmes. "And we can assure you that we will do whatever we can to restore your son to you. I know that these questions have been very trying for you and I do believe that we have asked all we need to for the time being." He rose as if prepared to depart.

The lady looked up at him and said, "I cannot tell if my answers have been of any use to you, Mr. Holmes. I told the police much the same and they have done nothing. I can only say again what I have told you from the outset – I know in my heart that my son is not mad and that he did not kill his father."

"Madam," said Holmes, "it is much too early for me to form any type of conclusions and I would at all other times refrain from saying anything, but I believe that you are right, and I am determined to find out the truth concerning what took place."

"Oh, thank you, sir. That is the first scrap of good news I have heard in the past several weeks. Thank you."

Chapter Four

Miss Patience

"**B**efore we depart," replied Holmes, "might we have a short word with the young girl who is on your staff? I believe you said that she was also in the room with you that evening."

"You mean Patience? Yes of course. If you will excuse me, I will send for her at once. Please remain in the parlor. She will come to you."

"A most curious case, Watson, most curious," said Holmes when we were alone. "A convivial young man with no apparent animosity toward his father goes mad and kills him. Friends arrive and hold a prayer meeting. The lad is carted off to the insane asylum, the police believe all of it, and the mother believes none of it. There is something here Watson. As yet I cannot put my finger on it but I sense that we are merely seeing the surface of something that is much deeper."

"I am sure you are right, Holmes. This madness story makes no sense at all. Ah, the young girl from the staff is coming."

We rose from our chairs as Mrs. McCarthy returned. Behind her was not the child we had expected but a strapping young dark-skinned woman whose age I estimated to be about seventeen years. She was as tall as I and had an athletic body.

"Mr. Holmes and Dr. Watson," said Mrs. McCarthy. "This is Patience Moran. I have told her to be entirely free and open in her answers to your questions. I will leave you alone with her so as not to impede your interrogation. Good day gentlemen, and thank you for bringing a ray of hope into my life. Thank you." With this she departed, closing the doors to the parlor behind her.

"Good morning, Miss Moran," began Holmes with a smile. "I confess that we had expected more of a child and less of a young woman."

"It is no matter," she replied, with a tone of quiet confidence. "My family has helped the McCarthy's manage the farm and the house since before I was born. I have helped with the household duties since I was six years old. Mrs. McCarthy still thinks of me as a child."

"Please, my dear," I said. "Do be seated. It is quite obvious that you are no longer a child and have grown into a fine young lady."

"Thank you, doctor," she replied, and then with a hint of a smile added, "and thank you for not asking me if I just growed."

We smiled back at her. Holmes sat up in his chair opposite her and looked directly at her. "Miss Moran," he began, "Could you tell us a little about your schooling. I am told that you are quite the student."

"If you are trying to ascertain that I am not just a simple pickaninny, I can assure you that I am not. I will graduate from our town's high school in two weeks."

"And in the fall, miss?" I interjected.

"I have a scholarship to attend Bennett College, Doctor."

"Yes, indeed, well done. It is a rather famous college for negro girls, is it not? Are you familiar with it Holmes?"

"No Watson, I regret that I am not. I assume that you will study household management or some similar course and return here to assist your family in the management of McCarthy Manor," said Holmes.

For an instant, I detected a flash of impatience in the eyes of Miss Patience, but her reply did not betray her feelings. "No sir. I have been accepted to study law."

"Ah, very good," said Holmes. "And so when you return to Tarrytown you will join a local firm, or perhaps someday even set up your own, and help all these folks with those matters of property, and estates, and taxes that beset the good people of rural America. Very good, indeed."

Yet again a flash of impatience. "No sir. I will work in New York City. I will depart this village on the fifteenth of August and, by that date, I will have lived here for seventeen years, three months, and six days. I have no intention of returning."

"And what will you do in New York City?" he asked, having learned that it was unwise to visit any further presumptions upon this young woman.

"I am hoping, sir, to serve as a clerk for one of our Assembly Men. There is a man that my friends and teachers all admire, and I want to help serve in his office. We expect that he will become the Governor of the State of New York within a few years."

I smiled at her but did not wish to betray any doubting of her youthful hopes. "And what is this young legislator's name, miss. I have no doubt we will be hearing about him."

"You will, sir. His name is Roosevelt. He is a good man sir. And fearless, sir. We respect him."

"And so you should, young lady," said Holmes. "And now let us return to that event of a few weeks ago. I am told that on that dreadful night you were the second person to enter Mr. McCarthy's office. Is that correct?"

"Yes sir, Master James had arrived before I did."

"And can you recall for me, exactly, what it was that you saw and what happened after you entered?"

"Yes, sir. When I entered, he was standing at the window looking out and shouting sir. And waving the revolver, sir."

"Shouting, you say. And what was he shouting. Please try to remember, factually of course, what you heard."

"He was shouting 'You bastard, you cowardly bastard' along with some other oaths, sir."

"Did you see who he was shouting at? Did you look out of the window?"

"I did sir. It was very dark, but there was a little light from the lamp at the coach house. I saw one man, dressed in dark clothes, but I could not see any of his features, sir. I also heard him shout back at Master James."

"You are sure of that, Miss? Please, it is important that you tell me only what you are absolutely sure of. What did you hear this darkly dressed man shout to young Mr. McCarthy?'

"I am very sure of it sir or I would not have said it. He shouted back 'You're next kid!' and then he ran off towards the woods in the direction of Sleepy Hollow."

"And then what happened?" asked the persistent detective.

"Master James was waving the revolver around wildly and I said 'Jimmy, put the gun down. Put it down.'"

"And did he?"

"No he tried to fire it but he did not have it cocked properly and so nothing happened. And I told him again to put it down. He was highly distraught and I feared that he would do something foolish."

"And so what did you do, miss?"

"I took the gun away from him and put it over on the table."

"The gun, yes," said Holmes. "Young Mr. McCarthy said that in his confession that he had come across it lying on his father's desk. Was Mr. McCarthy Senior in the habit of working with a loaded gun beside him?"

"No sir. Never."

"Had you seen that gun in this house before last night, miss?"

"No sir. I have been helping to clean this house almost every day for the past ten years. There are several rifles and a brace of pistols kept in a locked cabinet, but that gun was not one of them. I have never seen it before."

"You say you took the gun away from Master James. And just how did you manage to do that, miss?"

She shrugged her shoulders. "I am bigger and stronger than he is. I just grabbed his wrist with my left hand and twisted the gun out of his hand with my right. It was not difficult. At that point, he went to his father's body at the desk and fell on top of it and began to sob. His mother entered the room then and joined him. I did nothing until they told me to run into town to fetch the doctor and the constable."

"Ah yes. You were the one that was sent. I see," said Holmes. "But was that not a rather frightening thing to do? To run into town all by yourself at night?"

"No sir. I am a strong runner."

"No, no. I mean so late at night. The woods can be quite frightening in the dark and I believe these ones are even said to be haunted. It must have been very trying for you?"

Here the look Miss Patience gave Holmes went beyond impatience and I daresay I detected a momentary flash of anger. Yet when she spoke her voice was calm.

"I have walked into the village for school every weekday since I was six years old and have returned many times well after dark. I have yet to see a headless horseman or even hear him galloping. If you should happen to, sir, please give him my regards."

"Indeed, I shall," said Holmes, who was apparently warming to this very composed young woman. "But miss, even if there were no headless horsemen, you did say that you saw an unknown man running in that direction. Were you not frightened that he might be lurking there and that you might be in danger?"

"No sir. I have already told you that I am a very good runner and that I know the paths and the road well. I knew I could outrun anyone I might meet. And I had already heard that man say that his next target would be Master James, sir, not me. And sir, if you know anything about criminals, they are not in the habit of waiting around at the scene of their crime until the police arrive. I was quite sure he would be long gone, sir."

"Yes miss, your conclusions were all very logical. So then you called the doctor and the constable and returned to the house?"

"Yes, sir. The constable was on duty at the police station, and the doctor keeps a horse and driver ready at all hours in case he is called upon to deliver a baby. We returned to the house within twenty minutes, at which time the constable and the doctor took over and went about their business. I then took it upon myself to walk over to Turner Terrace and inform them of what had happened. The two families were very close and I felt that the Turners should be told as soon as possible. So I knocked on their door until Miss Alice came and I told her what had happened."

"You woke up both of them?" asked Holmes.

"I don't know about that sir. Miss Alice appeared in her night clothes, but Mr. Turner did not come to the door."

"Please describe her reaction to the news you brought, again as exactly as you can remember."

"Miss Alice was extremely distraught. Her mother was Irish and it was known that she inherited an Irish temperament and they weep and wail over the least little thing. So she cried loudly and threw herself against the door frame to hold herself up."

"And after her episode of grief, what then?"

"Miss Alice got dressed and she returned with me to the McCarthy's house, sir. But she did not stay long. Mrs. McCarthy had gone back to her room. The doctor had covered the body, and the constable was standing guard. She spoke to young James and they embraced each other, and held each other for some time and then she returned to her house. I went to my room after that sir, and had no more role in the events of the night."

"And the old man, Mr. Turner, did he not appear?"

"No sir. I never saw him that night. But he is not well sir and most likely Miss Alice did not wish to disturb him. That is all I know sir."

"You carried out the roles you were given with considerable bravery, young lady," I said to her, fearing that Holmes would neglect to complement her actions.

"Thank you, doctor."

"Ah, but Miss Moran," said Holmes, "please do not think that I am doubting your word, but your version of the events does differ in one or two important details from the police report. There was no mention in them of James McCarthy's being at a window, or shouting, or of hearing a voice in return, or of seeing a dark figure as he fled. How, Miss, do you account for those differences? Did you not give your full testimony to the police detective?"

"Yes sir, I did."

"Then why is your version not in their reports?"

"You will have to ask them that question, sir. I suspect however that it has something to do with accepting the confession of a young gentleman instead of a member of a race and of an age they believe to be susceptible to superstitions and exaggerations, sir."

"You are very likely entirely correct, Miss," said Holmes. "I fear that it may be quite some time before our police are relieved of their foolish prejudices. I, on the other hand, have no reason at all to doubt your truthfulness and accuracy. You have been most helpful."

"Thank you, sir. May I go now?"

"Yes, Miss."

"Well now, Watson," he turned to me after the young woman had departed from the room. "I discipline my mind against coming to hasty conclusions before I have all the data at hand, but I confess, Miss Moran was rather convincing, was she not?"

"Yes, Holmes. Quite the sensible young woman. Her story had an unmistakable ring of truth."

Chapter Five

Alice And Her Father

Having concluded his interview with Miss Patience, Sherlock Holmes spent close to an hour walking about the grounds of the McCarthy Manor. As several weeks had passed since the murder, there were no clues left to be seen, but still he was intent on becoming as familiar as possible with the entrances and exits, the doors and windows, and the surrounding lawns, gardens and forests. As I watched him, I could tell that he was re-enacting the events in his fertile mind.

"If the murderer was someone other than young James, and if he was seen from the window by both James and Patience, then it appears he must have escaped through the window, and it is quite large enough for him to have done so easily. You would agree, Watson?"

"That seems correct," I said.

"If Patience is correct, and I am inclined to believe that she is, and the assailant was seen in the dim light from the coach house, then it would place him on this path." He pointed to a well-worn path that provided a shortcut from the back of the house and led diagonally across the fields, joining up with the road as it entered Sleepy Hollow.

"It is a footpath. I assume that it is the path taken daily by Patience as she walks from the house towards the school and the village. It is not wide enough or sufficiently worn to have been used by animals yet there are a few faint signs of the tracks of a horse, but they are too old to discern anything of significance. If the murderer was observed close to this path, then we have to assume that he used it as his route of escape back to the village, but we also have to assume that he knew about it in advance."

"Which would mean," I said, "that he must have had a close knowledge of the property. You cannot see this path from the road. Are you saying that he was likely a member of the household or, at least, a familiar neighbor?"

"Possibly, but not necessarily," replied Holmes. "He could also have been a cool and calculating killer who took the time to become familiar with the property and learn his escape route. If that is the case, then we are dealing not with a crime of passion but with one of planned and carefully implemented execution. However, I am done for now with my looking over the property. We have an appointment with the neighbors, Mr. Turner and his daughter. Neither was in the house when the murder took place, but both were involved in the events of the following morning. They have agreed to speak to us, so let us be on our way."

Mrs. McCarthy had arranged for George, her driver, to take us to the next farm to the north, a large estate known as Turner Terrace. The manor house was even larger than the McCarthy's and made of fieldstone and brickwork. It was a full thirty yards long with a full front porch, and like the McCarthy Manor, a conservatory on the south end. Working in the gardens were two men, rather well-dressed for groundskeepers.

The barns looked prosperous, and there were at least twenty well-groomed and sleek horses in the front paddock. Behind them, in a smaller enclosure, we could see an enormous black horse by itself. I assumed it must be the stallion and that he ruled over the brood of mares adjacent to him. Mary also took notice.

"That big black fellow must be at least eighteen hands tall," she said. "What a magnificent looking beast."

A maid met us at the door and went to notify Mr. Turner. A minute later a tall older gentleman entered, impeccably dressed, but walking with considerable difficulty and leaning heavily on a cane.

"Welcome, gentleman and lady," he said with a still strong Scottish accent. "I am John Turner. We understand you folks have come all the way from England to look into this tragedy for Florence McCarthy. We admire and respect your taking the time to do that. Anything you can do to help her get over what took place is a blessing to all of us."

His face had a practiced warmth to it. It was a broad face, as one might see in the highlands of Scotland, framed by hair and sideburns that once were a rich red but had now faded into a sandy reddish brown. He did not extend his hand in the way that most Americans do habitually but maintained a formal distance.

Mary warmed up the cool atmosphere by smiling at the older man. "Mr. Turner, I cannot claim to be a skilled horsewoman but I know a fine stable of horses when I see them and yours, sir, are wonderful."

He smiled in return, obviously pleased with her observation and guileless compliment.

"It would appear, sir," added Holmes. "That in spite of your lame left leg you continue to enjoy riding and did so earlier this morning."

He looked warily at the detective but did not acknowledge the observation. He turned to Mary and replied, "Thank you miss. My little stable is one of the few joys left to me at my age. I would be delighted to talk about them but since you came to discuss other matters, I will refrain. I understand that you want to talk to both my daughter Alice and to me, and I will let her go first. I'll be back in my office and you can have the maid fetch me when you are done with Alice. I won't sit in on her meeting with you. I would not want you to think my presence inhibited any of her responses.

"Alice!" he shouted up the main stairway. "These detectives from England are here! Are you coming?"

"Yes father, coming!" we heard a young woman's voice from within one of the upstairs bedrooms. "Just finishing a letter. Be right there."

"She's always writing something," said the dour gentleman. He had hardly finished speaking when down the stairs there rushed one of the most lovely young women that I have ever seen in my life. Her violet eyes shining, her lips parted, and a pink flush was upon her cheeks.

"Oh, Mr. Sherlock Holmes!" she cried, glancing from one to the other of us, and finally, with a woman's quick intuition, fastening upon my companion, "I am so glad that you have come. This has been a most terrible few weeks for us. We do so hope that you will be able to do a far more thorough investigation than our local police, and help dear Mrs. McCarthy to accept what has happened, awful though it has been for her."

"Alice," interjected her father. "I have told these men that you should speak to them alone. I do not wish to influence anything you say. You must be able to speak freely."

"Oh no, father," she cried, putting her hand on her chest. "I would feel so much better if you were with me."

"No Alice," he responded firmly. "That is my decision. I will be working in my office. Gentlemen, and Mrs. Watson, please," he said as he gestured towards the parlor. Before he turned to limp towards the back of the house, I detected a quick look between father and daughter, one that I could only describe as of familial understanding. I wondered if Holmes had seen it as well, but his face remained like a sphinx. It was always impossible to know what wheels were turning in his unique mind.

We entered the parlor and Mary and I sat on the sofa that was set at right angles to the fireplace. The lovely young woman sat in a chair facing the hearth, leaving Holmes to sit in the chair opposite Mary and me. Holmes surprised me by lifting up the armchair and placing directly in front of the young woman so that he was looking square into her face. She exhibited a quick look of apprehension but recovered immediately into a polite smile that she directed, perhaps a little too disarmingly, towards Holmes.

"Miss Turner."

"Oh please, sir. Just call me Alice," she interrupted with a coy smile. "That's my name and what all my friends and professors call me, and I much prefer it to 'Miss Turner.'"

"Very well then, Miss Alice," continued Holmes. "Could you tell us a little about the connection between your family and the McCarthy's? You appear to have been exceptionally close for many years. No doubt your entire life."

"Of course, sir. We have been neighbors since before I was born, and I suppose we have been as close as neighbors often are. They had their lives. We had ours. There were a few disputes over the years but yes, I guess you could say that most of the time we were good neighbors to each other, yes."

"Disputes?" queried Holmes. "What sort of things could two upright Scots Presbyterian families find to dispute about?"

"Oh sir," she responded with a small laugh, "we have all been good church-going Christians, never missed a Sunday, but doesn't mean that we were all love-your-neighbor to each other all the time. Both my father and

Unc . . . Mr. McCarthy are, as you know, stubborn Scotsmen. And from time to time they would argue over something, usually to do with the sharing of pasture land, but, of course, they always managed to resolve their differences or, at least, that was what it seemed to me. Mind you, I was my mother and father's precious little girl, so I think there may have been one or two things that they kept hidden from me, as all parents do, do they not?"

Holmes ignored the question. "And do you have a suspicion of what those things might have been? Please, Miss Alice, try to be completely frank with us."

She raised her hand to her mouth and looked towards the door of the parlor. In *sotto voce,* she whispered, "Sir, I have no proof at all, and if I reveal my suspicions, I must ask you to promise me that you will not say a word of this to my father. It would bring enmity between us and he is so dependent on me since the death of my mother."

"You will have our complete confidence," assured Holmes.

"Sir," she said, looking steadfastly at the floor, "this is embarrassing for me but you have asked and my father has said that I must speak freely, and so I will. I have always had the feeling that the relationship between my mother and Mr. McCarthy was more than just being friendly neighbors."

"Are you telling me that there was an unacceptable liaison between them," asked Holmes bluntly. This seemed to me to be a highly inappropriate and unseemly issue to put to a young lady, but I confess that I was intrigued by the direction the conversation had taken, and so said nothing.

Miss Alice looked away and then again at the floor. She raised her head slowly and looked at my wife, Mary, instead of at Holmes. "I would rather die myself than say anything that would impugn the honor of my loving mother. And I have no way of knowing if anything carnal ever happened between them, but we all, I mean the children and all the help, could see that there were strong feelings for each other, and that is all I can say, Mr. Holmes. Please do not ask me to say more." She resumed her intense look at the floor.

"Very well. Let us move on to the McCarthy family, your neighbors," said Holmes. "Did James and his father get along well? As they were your neighbors, I am sure you observed how they acted towards each other. What of that?"

Again she looked at the floor, then raised her head and said, "No sir. They did not get on well at all. I assume you have learned about the

McCarthys' older son, Charles Junior. James's father wished, indeed, he demanded that James enter the military just as his brother had done. James refused. It caused a terrible row between them. They would not speak to each other. Mr. McCarthy was furious with James for refusing, as he said, to honor and respect the life of his older brother, and James was not only angry with his father's bullying him, but he blamed his father for his brother's death. Like most younger siblings he idolized his older brother. He believed that his brother would have lived had his father not bullied him to join the Navy. The feelings between father and son were very hard indeed, sir."

"Are you in love with James?"

"Sir!" the young woman said with righteous indignation. I was about to rebuke Holmes as well when I felt a sharp elbow in my ribs from my wife.

"It would be perfectly normal if you were," continued Holmes, "and nothing to be ashamed about. You are both handsome and accomplished young people who have spent many hours of your life together. I would be surprised if you did not have strong feelings towards him."

"We do have strong feelings, sir," she responded with not a little hint of annoyance, "but as if we were brother and sister. Never let yourself doubt upon that point, sir. We have known each other since we were little children, and I know his character as no one else does. I certainly care for him but I do so as a sister, and he has cared for me as a brother. We have never been romantically attracted to each other and I do not expect we ever will be. He has had many young woman admirers while he was at Harvard, just as I had many gentlemen callers while I was at Radcliffe."

"If you say so, miss," said Holmes. "Now pray will you tell me what you know of the murder and of the madness of James McCarthy?"

Alice Turner started to speak, stopped and buried her head in her hands. When she raised her body back up her face was contorted with pain. A moment later copious tears began to flow from her eyes. They streamed down her face and fell upon the bodice of her dress. Drops of mucous dribbled from her nose. I jumped up from my seat and offered her my handkerchief.

"Thank you, sir. Thank you," she said in a trembling voice. She dabbed her eyes and wiped her nose, took a deep breath and began to speak. "I am sorry gentlemen. It has been a difficult time for all of us. But as you wish, I will tell you what I know. Word came to us in the early hours of the morning when the servant girl came to our door. I made a visit to the McCarthy's home, but there was nothing I could do, and so returned to this house. I waited until my father woke up and then informed him of the terrible event.

"It also happened that on that morning two of our mutual friends, or I should say two of James's friends from Harvard, young men I knew to some degree through him, arrived that morning on the train and came first to visit me to say hello before going on. I do not wish to seem vain sir but one of them, Bruce, seemed to fancy me a little. I had the terrible task of telling them the news about Mr. McCarthy. Fortunately, my father was with me and helped me through the ordeal. The four of us immediately made our way to the McCarthy's home as we were deeply concerned for James." Her she stopped and again dabbed her eyes.

"And when you reached the McCarthy home what happened then?" asked Holmes.

"Mrs. McCarthy was still in her bed, we were told, but James had not slept. We were shown into the office where the murder had taken place. James was sitting at his father's desk. I assume he was in shock. When he saw us, he came quickly to us and embraced my father. After a few minutes of giving condolences, my father suggested that a time of prayer together would be the best thing for us to do. He is a very deeply religious and devout man and we agreed. We excused ourselves and met in the conservatory.

"We prayed and each of us, father, Bruce, James, Cameron, that was the other friend who had come to visit, each took a turn and said a prayer."

"And what, may I ask, did you pray for," asked Holmes. "I am not familiar with any section of The Book of Common Prayer that is dedicated to a service held at the time of a murder."

"We are not Episcopalians sir. Our family and the McCarthys are Presbyterians, but Bruce and Cameron were members of a spiritualist group of sorts on the campus and such a meeting was quite familiar to them. We prayed for strength and wisdom, especially for James and his mother, and for justice, and that God would give divine guidance to the police to bring the villain into the hands of the courts."

"Indeed," said Holmes, and then with a faintly discernible twinkle in his eye looked over at me. "My dear Watson, could you make a note of the tactic of invoking divine intervention as an innovative method for tracking down criminals? It might be useful someday in the East End.

"And when your prayers were concluded, miss, what happened then?" said Holmes, returning his gaze to the young woman.

Her face showed contortions of emotion distress. She began to speak in a halting and trembling voice. "For a few moments, nothing was said. Then James began to speak slowly and he said, 'I killed my father.'" With this, she stopped speaking and again buried her head in her hands. When she looked at us, her face was again wincing in pain and tears began to stream down her face. "You already know what happened after that! You have his confession from the police," she said between sobs. "Don't ask me to re-live those moments. I can't do it. I'm sorry. I can't." She stood up and walked out of the room with her hands to her face.

"Well Holmes," I said, "it was obviously a terrible and traumatic event. The young woman has been put through a very trying time."

"Hmm. So it appears. There are some logical inconsistencies in her story, but her tears appear to be quite genuine. I am sure she knows more than she has said, but her emotional fragility may inhibit our interviewing her further, at least for the time being."

My dear wife, Mary, gave me and then Holmes a look of measured disdain.

"I cannot believe that two men, one a doctor and the other England's greatest detective, could be so naïve. She's a clever young actress, but that pretty little vixen was lying through her teeth."

Both Holmes and I looked at her in surprise.

"Darling," I began, "those tears were flowing copiously out of her eyes. How can you say she was acting?"

"Did neither of you notice the small pair of tweezers in her right hand? She used a trick known to every woman who appears on stage, and to almost all women who have to manipulate their fathers or husbands."

"What could she have done with a pair of tweezers?" I asked.

"Mr. Holmes," she said turning to the detective. "In your monograph on hair from the various parts of the body, have you investigated yet the properties of hair that is found in the nostril of the nose?"

"No, I can't say I have yet."

"Well sir, then you should know that plucking one out with a pair of tweezers causes sharp but short-lived pain and induces a flood of tears. That is what Miss Alice did twice. When we first entered the house the door to her room was open and then quietly was closed when she heard us in the hallway. The 'I'm writing a letter' was a coy act that she and her father had rehearsed beforehand, and the look that passed between her and her father told me that they were playing their roles exactly as they had agreed to. And I would not doubt that in a moment her father will enter this room apologizing for his poor daughter's emotional distress."

She had no sooner spoken these words than Mr. John Turner entered the room, leaning on his cane and walking with great difficulty.

"I must apologize on my daughter's behalf for her not being able to continue the interview. This whole nasty business has been terribly trying for her. She's a brave little girl, but you must understand that murder and the madness of her dear friend have been at times more than her gentle constitution has been able to bear. I am free now if there are any questions you wish to ask me and I promise that I will not flee in tears. I have been through much worse ordeals and am still alive to speak about them." He spoke these words with a slow and grave voice, the solemnity accentuated by the Highland brogue that betrayed his homeland. He sat down in the chair that his daughter had recently vacated.

A glance that said "I told you so" passed from Mary to Holmes.

Holmes nodded towards Mr. Turner and opened with his first question. "I gather that you are suffering from diabetes. Is that not what happened to your leg and causes you to limp so badly?"

"Ah, not one to waste time with pleasant chit-chat are we Mr. Holmes? Very well, sir. I have been afflicted with diabetes for several years. It has gotten progressively worse. The doctors had to amputate a portion of my right foot a year ago. While it has restricted my walking, I am still able to enjoy the pleasure of riding my horses, as you observed earlier. My daughter has been lovingly teasing me that I have become the footless horseman of Sleepy Hollow when I take my old stallion, Bannockburn, out for a run. He and I have been quite the pair for many years."

Here he stopped and smiled, and Mary and I smiled briefly in return. Holmes did not smile. Mr. Turner continued, "It is not likely that I will live beyond Christmas. I had hoped that the Lord would grant me my full three score and ten years and the joy of seeing the birth of my grandchildren, but that is unlikely to happen. All I can do is to be grateful for those blessings that have come into my life."

"Yes," said Holmes. "We all must do that, of course. Your friendship with the McCarthy family, sir. How did that begin, sir? And how has it continued for what I understand are many years?"

"As boys Charlie McCarthy and I were farm hands on adjacent properties in Aberdeen, over in the old country. We walked to school together every day for ten years. The Scots, as I am sure you know, are very firm on every child having his schooling no matter what his family situation. When we turned sixteen years of age we left school, both of us having been diligent students if I say so myself, and determined to seek our fortune and future in America. After a year of working in the mills in Glasgow, we saved up enough for our tickets and booked our passage. We came across in the year 1847. As we had good farm skills, we were able immediately to find work on a cattle ranch in Pennsylvania. When it was announced that gold had been found in California, the two of us, being still bachelors with no dependents, struck out immediately and joined the Forty-Niners."

"And I understand that you were rather successful, were you not? You had good luck and struck it rich?" said Holmes.

"You will forgive me, sir, if I remind you that a firm Scots Calvinist does not put much store in luck. We believe in the blessings of the Lord, and the truth that the Lord helps them who helps themselves. Our claim was no richer than our neighbors, but Charlie and I worked from dawn to dark every day for two years, excepting Sundays when we attended services at the little chapel in the village.

"We neither drank nor used tobacco, nor did we gamble or waste our money on riotous living. There were many hard men in California sir, and we did our best to avoid them. There were even some hard times between us but we carried on and by the time our claim had been worked out we had both set aside a tidy sum, and with that we each bought ourselves farms, which is where you find our families today."

"Your farms both did exceptionally well," said Holmes. "Your cautious diligence has paid off."

"Our first years were tough going, but then we heard that one of our countrymen, a Scot by the name of George Grant, was importing a superior breed of cattle from Scotland to America, the Aberdeen Angus. We could not turn down something from our hometown so we acquired the license to bring them into New York State and built up strong herds ourselves. They proved to be the finest line of beef cattle in the country and we have lived well off of them. If you wish to come by on Sunday after church, our cook will treat you to as fine a roast of beef as you will find on God's earth."

"If we are here on some Sunday in the future we will avail ourselves of your hospitality," said Holmes. "For the moment, we shall remain in the past. You said that there were some hard times between you and Mr. McCarthy. Is that how you would characterize your interactions with him over the years?"

"Ah no. Not at all. For the most part, we got along well but as you know, sir, lives move in different directions. Our interests diverged. Charles became a Republican and I sided with the Democrats. His interpretation of scriptures led him towards pacifism to the point he would never allow a firearm under his roof whereas I became a bit of a collector. He stuck to farming as his sole source of income while I made some very fortunate investments in the markets, with the result that my family prospered somewhat more than his. I felt he was too harsh with his children and he felt that I was much too lenient with my daughter. These are just the usual differences that take place between men over a period of nearly half a century, but otherwise, I think all would say that we got along as well as close neighbors could."

"Were your properties formally tied to each other? Were you ever business partners?"

"No, as I said we went our separate ways," the older man answered. Then after a pause added, "It is a confidential matter sir, but as you are a detective I am sure you would be able to discover it by yourself; all it would take would be a visit to the Land Registry Office. A year ago I paid him a fair sum of money to have the right of first refusal to purchase his property should anything happen to him. He agreed, and in that way our properties and now linked to each other."

"And why would you do that, Mr. Turner?"

"Charles was in a bit of a tight spot for cash. He had just expanded his herd and did not wish to go to the bank for help for short term cash. I was concerned that should anything happen to him that Florence might panic and sell the farm to some unscrupulous type from the city, and then Alice and my grandchildren would have the strife that would go along with living beside poor neighbors. It seemed like a prudent provision for my heirs." He paused for a moment and then began again. "I had also learned from my attorney, who was also attorney for Charles, that he had recently cut young James completely out of his will because of his fury at the direction the lad's studies and habits were taking him. I was always fond of the boy and thought it grossly unfair to treat him so. I hold to very strong principles concerning the responsibilities of a father to his children and so I did what I could do to make sure that our two farms would pass to our children, young James in his case and my daughter Alice, in mine."

"Explain to me please sir, how that would take place?"

"If Charlie were to die then I would purchase his farm from his estate according to the terms we agreed upon, and then once the estate was settled I would sell it back to Mrs. McCarthy for the same price. The only loss would be the fees paid to the attorneys, but James would have the right to his patrimony. I do not have chapter and verse from scripture to back up my conviction, sir, but that is what I believe."

"Indeed, and most admirable," said Holmes. "About the actions and madness of the young lad; had there been anything in his past that would lead you to believe that he could kill his father and then turn mad?"

Turner nodded slowly and sucked in his lips, but just a fraction. "His mother, of course, denies it, she denies many things about her son that she is just too much of a loving mother to be able to see, but yes, as a child, and right up into his student days young James has suffered from what we called his spells. As a toddler, they took the form of temper tantrums, to which almost all children are prone. Most children, of course, grow out of this behavior but James did not. He would have violent spasms of screaming and smashing things and kicking people and just dreadful language. These would continue for a few minutes and then end, and he would collapse in tears and say how sorry he was. And then there would be nothing of the sort for several months and then we would hear of his having a spell again.

"His mother tried to provide cover for his rages, and his father just shouted at him and gave him a beating afterward, which did no good whatsoever. It just drove the poor boy into a brain fever where he would sit for hours on end without moving or saying anything. It was a cause of great strife between father and son. So yes, Mr. Holmes, his spell, the killing of his father, and his lapsing into madness are not at all surprising. What is so tragic is that after this most recent time his father is dead and the madness has settled on him permanently. We are all deeply saddened by what has happened."

"I have no doubt it has been very trying for all of you, sir," said Holmes. "If you will permit me to explore just one more issue, and then we shall leave you to your work and your family."

"By all means."

"Concerning your friend and neighbor, Charles McCarthy; did he have any enemies that you know of?"

"Not one in the world. He seemed to get along well with everybody, everybody that is except for his younger son. Not that he was all hail-fellow-well-met of course. He was a quiet and serious man. They don't call us dour Scots for nothing. But no, he was beyond reproach in all aspects of his personal and business life. So no sir. No enemies. Not a one."

"Thank you, Mr. Turner," said Holmes, rising from his chair. Mary and I followed his action and stood up as well. "We greatly appreciate your time. Please give our sympathies to your daughter and let her know how sorry we are to have so distressed her. If we could impose upon your driver to take us back to our hotel, we would be most grateful."

"Very happy to help in whatever way I can. Our thoughts and prayers are with Mrs. McCarthy. We do hope that your work will help to allay her fears and accept that the Lord works in mysterious ways, and will work all things together for good in His own time."

The Turner carriage picked us up at the front door of the great stone house and drove us back into Tarrytown. Holmes said nothing the entire route and I could see that the wheels of his brain were turning over the conflicting accounts we had received during the course of the day. He did not join Mary and me for dinner, permitting us a quiet time together, followed by a leisurely stroll along the river. There was a note waiting for us on our return. It read:

```
First thing tomorrow we leave to meet the
madman in the insane asylum. Will be at the
station   for   the   8:00   o'clock   train.
Returning late afternoon.   Holmes.
```

We retired for the night to our room and went to bed at an early hour. I lay in bed without sleeping until I was sure that my wife was sound asleep, whereupon I rose slowly, without so much as causing a ripple in the mattress, and walked silently to the adjoining lavatory. My wife's manicure kit lay on the counter and from it I withdrew her small pair of tweezers. With the help of a polished mirror, I located one of many hairs inside my left nostril, clutched it with the tweezers and gave it a good yank.

"AAAARRRRRRGGGGHHH!!" is what I would have screamed out loud had I not pushed the fleshy part of my hand into my mouth to muffle the involuntary cry of acute pain. In the mirror, I could see a flood of tears pouring out of my eyes, down my face and dribbling into the hand basin. Using a hand towel I wiped my face and my running nose, and after waiting a few minutes for my recovery to take hold, I turned down the light and returned silently to my bed, again without making a sound.

"It works, does it not, dear?" my non-sleeping wife said.

"What? Oh, that. Yes. Yes. Rather well."

"Go to sleep, John."

Chapter Six

Mattawan

The early morning brought us to the train station and the sight of the tall, thin figure of Sherlock Holmes pacing up and down the platform. He continued to pace non-stop until we boarded the train and were seated in our cabin. After we had pulled out of the station, he looked at me and spoke.

"I must beg your indulgence my dear friend, but I took the liberty of acting in your good name."

"I am not sure what good that would ever do you, but I am not worried about your sullying my reputation. Allow me to ask what it is that that you have gotten me into?"

"In order to be able to meet with the young man, who is closely guarded in a highly secured institution, I had to claim reasons of medical investigation, and as you are one of the leading criminal pathologists in England you were granted access."

"You flatter me Holmes and I am quite sure that no one here has read the journals of criminal pathology and if they had they would know that I was anything but a leader in that field."

"Ah yes," he replied. "But they had, it seems, read your stories about some detective named Sherlock Holmes and were eager for you to visit, and ever rather more eager when I, pretending to be you, told them that I was bringing your detective friend along. They do not read the medical journals, but it appears that they do read your absurdly romanticized stories about me, and I will confess that such publicity is occasionally useful."

"Always happy to be of use, Holmes," I said and would make note of this occasion for the next time he laid a stripe or two upon my hide for my stories. "And may I intrude, as it would be helpful for writing of my next story, and ask you if you have formed any conclusion yet about this American case?"

For a full minute he closed his eyes and ignored my question, but then responded. "I do not yet have enough data to form a definite conclusion, and the accounts of what took place are inconsistent with each other, as you have no doubt noted." He closed his eyes, rested his head on the back of the seat. One would have thought he had fallen asleep except for the occasional furrowing of his brow and the movement of his lips as he carried out interrogations inside his fervent brain. He continued in this state for nearly ninety minutes, opening his eyes only when our destination was announced by the young purser as he passed through the cars.

Among the English it was believed that Americans are predisposed to locking each other up in prisons for every conceivable crime and misdemeanor, so it was a relief to see that the powers that be on this side of the pond had finally ceased placing those poor souls who were obviously mentally unbalanced in with the general population of the nation's prisons. Across the country, they were building a collection of large sprawling institutions for the insane, and several for the criminally insane. Mattawan, a village on the east bank of the Hudson was one such facility. Its twenty acres were surrounded by a high fence, but once inside it was as pleasant a place as the finest estate in England, with well-kept flower beds, gracious elm trees, and rolling green lawns. The guards at the gate had received a notice of our visit and welcomed us. One even had a recent copy of *The Strand* and prevailed upon us to sign it for him.

"Ahh, guden zee morning, Herr Holmes, Docteur and Frau Vatson. Velcome to Mattavan." The director of the institution greeted us in the grand but antiseptic entrance of the main building. He continued to speak with a thick Viennese accent. "Ich bein Docteur Ludvig Schweitzbruger, the director of this excellent facility. You will agree that it is zee most progressive facility of its kind. Well ahead, we believe of any in England, would you not agree? Biten, please, come into my office."

The office was new and gleaming, with a window at the far end, in front of which sat the director's desk. The entire left wall held shelves of books and journals. The other had over twenty framed certificates and citations, newspaper clippings and photographs. The good doctor was not lacking in credentials and recognition. Several were in German and bore the crest of some institution in Vienna.

He continued in his thick accent. "I must tell you that we are very puzzled by the case of young Herr James McCarthy. When he is arrived here, he is acting wild and uncontrolled as if he is inhabited by a personality other than his own. He is not violent, just very loud. When we put him in his room and locked the door then quiet he becomes. Very nicely can he have to read some books he asks, and we agree and to him bring books from the library. All the time he is reading them, and then he asks for paper and pen and ink and then he is reading and writing. At meal times, he says nothing to the rest of the patients and in silence he eats. But when we bring him to the therapy he listens politely to the first question and then he goes to madness. He keeps saying that he is the headless horseman and galloping on his stallion and throwing pumpkins all over the place. And then he changes and he is Prince Hamlet and recites from your Shakespeare and he jumps around and waves his arms and then when he is returned to his room he once again reads his books and begins to write. Very strange. Very strange indeed, Herr Docteur."

"Yes. Yes, I must say. Intermittent multiple personalities. Very strange. I am not aware of any other case like that described in the journals." I said and tried to act as I assumed a doctor of psychology might act. For effect, I rubbed my chin.

"If it is not too much trouble we would like to meet with the patient and be able to record his symptoms. I would like to write a monograph about him and his progressive treatment at your institution, and an extended time with him would be very helpful, with your consent, of course, Director."

"Of course, of course," said the director. "Follow please me. He is harmless and so we let him spend the days out of doors where all the long day he reads. He only is the crazy man when we try to talk to him. A very curious case indeed sir."

The Director led us to a bench below a spreading oak tree. On it sat a young man apparently engrossed in a book.

"I will leave you to speak to him and I wish you well," said the Director, and he turned back toward the central building.

Sherlock Holmes strode purposefully toward the young man, raised his walking stick and smartly brought it down on the book, dashing it out of the hands of its reader. The young man, a comely youth, looked up, startled, as Holmes brought his face to within a few inches of the chap who had been diagnosed as criminally insane.

"James McCarthy," said Holmes loudly to the very uncomfortable young man, "this pretend act of yours is breaking your mother's heart, and letting those who murdered your father escape. Now are you going to keep it up or are you going to help me catch whoever killed your father and bring him to justice?"

"Who are you?" James McCarthy asked in a trembling voice.

"My name is Sherlock Holmes and this is my colleague Dr. Watson. I believe you have heard of us. Your mother has asked us to help prove your innocence and find the villains who murdered your father. Now are you going to help us or are you going to keep up this silly act of yours and leave your mother to suffer?"

A flicker of a smile crept across the lad's face, of the sort one expects to see when a fan of a celebrated person finds himself in the presence of his idol. A moment later his countenance changed and he gave us a wild look. He grabbed first Holmes's hand and then mine and pumped them up and down.

"My excellent good friends! How dost thou, Guildenholmes? Ah, Rosenwatson! Good lads, how do ye both?"

Following this he jumped up from his seat and stood on the bench, towering above us, and began to shout.

"I have of late—but wherefore I know not—lost all my mirth, forgone all custom of exercises; and indeed, it goes so heavily with my disposition that this goodly frame, the earth, seems to me a sterile promontory, this most excellent canopy, the air, look you . . ."

He gesticulated expansively toward the sky.

" . . . this brave o'erhanging firmament, this majestical roof fretted with golden fire, why, it appears no other thing to me than a foul and pestilent congregation of vapors."

On "vapors" he collapsed on the ground and began to sniff the earth.

He crawled over to the feet of Sherlock Holmes and with a look of desperate pleading continued.

"What a piece of work is a man! how noble in reason! how infinite in faculty! in form and moving how express and admirable! in action how like an angel! in apprehension how like a god! the beauty of the world! the paragon of animals!"

I was quite sure that Sherlock Holmes had seldom been described in such glowing terms. But then Prince Hamlet leapt to his feet, ran to the oak tree and began to bang his head into the tree trunk, continuing his speech.

"And yet, to me, what is this quintessence of dust!?"

I observed that he had carefully placed the back of his hand against the bark and was smashing his head into the soft palm of his hand.

He looked over at us for a moment and changed scenes.

"But that the dread of something after death; The undiscover'd country from whose birth; No traveler returns, puzzles the will; and makes us rather bear those ills we have; Than fly to others that we do not know about . . ."

At that point, Holmes brought his walking stick down loudly on the bench.

"Wrong! The line reads "Than fly to others that we know not of" Now do it over again from 'To die to sleep', and it's not 'birth', its 'bourn'. Now do it again and do it properly this time! Go!"

"Oh, sorry sir. I'll try to get it right," the young man said quietly. For a moment a look of knowing passed between him and Holmes and then he leapt back up on the bench and resumed his shouting. "To die! To sleep . . ." and on he went. Holmes watched him for a few more minutes and then shrugged his shoulders and turned to walk away. The young actor was not about to give up his pretense. He stopped his shouting for a moment as he watched us depart and then shouted one last time. "Noble sir, forget you not that the play's the thing wherein you will catch the conscience of the king!" Then he stepped back down from the bench, picked up his book and walked away from us toward the closest building.

After he was out of earshot, I turned to Holmes. "Obviously, he is not mad and only acting, but I cannot deduce any reason. I am inclined to think that he knows who has done the terrible deed and is screening him. But why is he doing it? He knows he is breaking his mother's heart, yet he persists."

"Because he is afraid. He fears for his life," replied Holmes. "If what Miss Moran said to us is true, and I have no reason to doubt her words, then he was told that he is next and he has come to the one place where he thinks he will have immediate protection and security. We could not have entered these grounds without your medical credentials and my reputation. It would be quite difficult, he believes, if not impossible for an anonymous murderer to gain entry, kill him, and get away without being apprehended or at least identified. He believes that the madhouse is his safe haven."

"But from whom?" I asked.

"That is exactly what we do not yet know, and what we must deduce before someone does manage to penetrate this institution and do harm to this young thespian."

The three of us departed the Mattawan Institution after stopping to pay our respects to the Director, and made our way to the train station. Holmes, as I expected, said nothing and I could see him turning over the events of the past hour in his mind.

"The wasting of my time is always a source of annoyance, and this journey has been a complete waste of time. We know no more than we did this morning, except that the boy is a passably good actor who needs to do a better job memorizing his lines."

"Mr. Holmes," Mary responded, "I believe that you know at least one thing that you did not before."

Holmes smiled at her." At just what, my dear, is that?"

"His final message to you as we turned and departed was not made in vain," she said.

"You mean his repeating "The play's the thing" line?" I asked.

"Yes. He was telling you something. He could have chosen any one of a hundred other lines, but he chose that one and he had a reason for doing so."

"I am inclined to believe that you are right," said Holmes. "But there has been no reference in any other evidence concerning this case that a "play" is involved. So we remain at a dead end."

"Is it not correct," asked Mary, "that James and Alice and the two friends who came to visit were all involved in theater activities while at college? And were we not told that one of the activities that they had planned to pursue was the preparation and rehearsing of some piece of theater that they were preparing for the fall?"

"That is an excellent observation," said Holmes. "But it does not lead us any closer to the murderer or any reason for the killing of Mr. McCarthy."

After this Holmes lapsed again into silence and said nothing during the journey back to Tarrytown or on our walk back to the hotel from the station. Before leaving us to return to his room, he said, "I would be happy if the two of you would permit me to join you for dinner this evening. There is a hypothesis upon which I would appreciate your opinions."

Dinner was a pleasant affair on the porch of the hotel, looking out over the lovely vista of the Hudson River. We chatted amiably throughout the meal until we had finished our desserts and brandies. Holmes took out his pipe and in his practiced ritual prepared it, lit it, and inhaled a long draft of tobacco. "I have said many more times than either you or I can remember, Watson, that the science of deduction requires a complete analysis of every possible answer. When you have eliminated all possible alternatives, then whatever remains, however improbable, must be the truth."

"Holmes," I replied, "that is exactly what you have said time and time again. So do proceed and eliminate the other possibilities and let us know what you have deduced."

"A murderer must have a motive, and available means of committing his crime, and an opportunity to do so. There are only a select few people who were part of Mr. McCarthy's circle and only one of them appears to have had all three. His widow can be excluded as the reports from all sides confirm that she was asleep at the time of the crime, was sent into a state of shock and distress upon seeing her husband's body, and had nothing whatsoever to gain financially or otherwise by his passing."

"Yes, but," said Mary, "there was the question raised by Miss Alice about a past romantic connection between her husband and long departed Mrs. Turner. Could that not have been a strong enough reason for her to want to do her husband in? People have committed crimes of passion for lesser reasons, have they not?"

"Indeed, they have," said Holmes. "And the forces contained within the human heart, both male and female, are among the most uncontrollable and unpredictable on earth. But I must ask you, my dear Mrs. Watson, was there any scintilla of evidence that you, as another woman, detected in Mrs.

McCarthy, that would suggest that she was capable of such a crime of passion?"

"None whatsoever," Mary replied immediately. "She is a sensible, mature woman who is not going to do in a perfectly good, healthy husband. They are hard to come by once past sixty. The only source of the story of a romantic connection between them came from Alice, the little liar, and it is inconceivable that Mrs. McCarthy would bring you across the Atlantic to investigate a crime if she were the perpetrator."

"Well said," affirmed Holmes. "So let us eliminate the suffering widow. Now then let us move on to the servants. Only one of them was in the house at the time of the murder, the young servant girl, Miss Patience Moran. Is there any evidence anywhere to suggest that she could have committed murder?"

"No," answered both Mary and I in unison.

"Correct, of course," affirmed Holmes, "and now the young woman, the 'little vixen who lied through her teeth' as you, Mrs. Watson, so frankly described her. We all know that it is a serious prejudice of the public and the police to refuse to believe that a young female who is well-mannered and beautiful could possibly be capable of horrific acts. My experience and the annals of heinous crimes of the past century prove that exactly the opposite has at times been the truth. So then, our Miss Alice, did she have motive, method, and opportunity?"

"She appears to have had none, Holmes," I ventured. "The testimony of the servant girl, who said that she came to her house and informed her after the event took place and her reaction to it would appear to exclude her from consideration."

"I agree," said Holmes. "So we come to the young madman. What say you, Watson? You are a man of science and medicine. Do you believe the story about his spell of possession by an evil force, followed by a tearful confession, and then his fits of convenient madness?"

"Not for a moment. All of that was a complete pretense. But it does not necessarily mean that he did not have reason for killing his father. There appears to have been some tension between them arising from the death of the older brother, the young lad's determination to pursue of life different from the wishes of his father, the possibility of his being cut out of his inheritance. All of these would constitute a motive, and he had the means, and the opportunity."

"Correct. Those are plausible reasons for us to believe that he could have murdered his father. On the other hand, what are the reasons that militate against his doing so?"

"His mother's firm conviction that he could not have done it," offered Mary. "As well as the testimony of the girl that she found him standing at the window, and that she saw and heard another person, most likely the real murderer. The only information we had concerning his spells and his conflict with his father came from Alice and Mr. Turner. Alice was lying and her father is inscrutable."

"All true," said Holmes. "On top of which there is the police report."

"I saw nothing there, Holmes," I said. "It just contained the few facts of the crime scene and mostly dealt with James's confession."

"What did he say about the wound to the head?"

"That it entered from the back section of the parietal bone, passed through the left cerebral hemisphere, penetrated to the hypothalamus and was immediately fatal," I replied.

"There was no evidence that the body was moved and so there is only one possible location for the murderer to be standing when he shot Mr. McCarthy," said Holmes.

"Directly behind him and a little to the left," said Mary.

"Precisely," said Holmes. "It is entirely unreasonable that the young man would enter his father's office, pick up a gun that was lying on the desk, walk around behind him and then shoot him directly from behind with the father never moving his gaze from looking forward across his desk. The lad's confession does not pass muster, and I am disappointed that the local police detective would accept it. But I have known our own constables and even some of the imbeciles at Scotland Yard to overlook much more obvious evidence, so I am not surprised. All of these facts added together, render it impossible that the boy killed his father. His madness and confession are a fabrication. And yet . . . and yet . . . there is the staggering question of 'Why?' Why would he make up such a story? Why would he so hurt his mother and endure being locked up in the madhouse? What does he know and who is he trying to protect?"

"And must we not," asked Mary, "put forward the same question concerning Miss Alice? Why would she be so determined to deceive us? And to try to affirm the madness of young James? She had no reason to do so."

"Unless," said Holmes, "she knew the identity of the murderer and was protecting him. And having eliminated all other possible actors we are left with only one."

"You do not mean to say, Holmes, that the lame old man murdered his boyhood friend!?" I sputtered in disbelief. "That is unthinkable."

"No, my dear Watson, when dealing with crime, especially with the crime of murder carried out in the context of desperation and passion, nothing is unthinkable. Improbable perhaps. But if it is the only remaining possibility, then it must be the truth."

Mary and I said nothing for several minutes. Then she turned to Holmes with a look of bewilderment. "How then do you account for the young man's screaming oaths at the murderer as he escaped, and within a few hours feigning madness to protect him?"

"Ah, for that I do not have an answer. It is the missing piece of the puzzle. But I believe that if we present all the evidence to the old man, he may, seeing as he has no escaping the truth, be willing to enlighten us. Tomorrow morning I will summon him here and we shall try to find out."

Chapter Seven

The Non-Confession

"Mr. John Turner," announced the hotel bell boy, opening the door of our sitting-room and ushering in our visitor.

The man entered slowly, limping. His body still gave evidence of unusual strength, but his face was an ashen white, and his lips tinged with a shade of blue. His deadly chronic disease had diminished him even in the brief time since we had last seen him.

He sat heavily in the sofa, his energy spent on his travel from his home to the hotel.

"Your note said you wished to see me. You said that there could be terrible criminal consequences for my daughter Alice, and young James McCarthy. You knew that such a note would force me to leave my home and endure the pain of even the short distance into town. So what is it you have to tell me, Mr. Holmes? Please get on with it."

"I see you also have little patience for idle chit-chat," said Holmes. "Very well, Mr. Turner. Your daughter and her dear friend, James McCarthy, risk being charged with being accomplices to murder and sent to prison. I will have no choice but to turn them over to the police along with the evidence that clearly points to you as the murderer of Charles McCarthy."

The old man slouched and dropped his powerful shoulders until he looked a decrepit and sunken figure, despair in his weary eyes. For a minute, he lowered his head and leaned upon his walking stick. Then he lifted his head and in what I saw was a force of sheer will and determination, smiled cunningly back at Sherlock Holmes. "And what evidence beyond your conjecture do you have to give the police, Mr. Holmes?"

"By your own account, sir, you had more than sufficient motive to get rid of your friend, or should I say your former friend. The two of you were long past the warm closeness of your youth. You stood to gain a very great deal in wealth and property from your right of first refusal to his property, taken, as you have yourself admitted, at a time when McCarthy was at a pecuniary disadvantage. For years, you harbored a jealousy toward him because of your affection for his wife, made particularly poisonous after your own wife's passing, as you saw him continuing in married bliss while you lived alone. You knew he had cut his son out of his inheritance, and you managed somehow to convince his son and your daughter to be part of your conspiracy, and perhaps even their college friends. Young James pretended to be mad so that he could draw all attention away from you. You believe that he will soon be brought to trial, declared to have been only temporarily insane and allowed to walk free. You are wrong. He and your daughter will be convicted of being accessories. So perhaps, sir, you would like to confess your foul deed now or your daughter and James will spend their youth in prison instead of enjoying their family estates.

"You may be lame, but you have revealed that you are still capable of riding a horse, which you did on the night of June the third. You entered the McCarthy house, with which you are intimately familiar, unseen, hid yourself behind the draperies to the rear of McCarthy's desk, and when you knew that the rest of the house had gone to sleep you shot him from behind and escaped to your horse before any of the household could stop or identify you. What is beyond me is how you could have so twisted the consciences of two innocent young people, including your own daughter, to collude with you in such a vile deed. You claim, sir, to be a Christian. May I suggest that you might wish to clear your conscience before you have to account for your deeds in front of almighty God."

Mr. Turner stared at Holmes for a moment and then, appearing to admit defeat he nodded. "Mr. Holmes, your reputation as a detective is well-deserved. I will, however, confess to nothing whatsoever. If you press your case with the police, you will find that I have an iron-clad alibi and several people of excellent reputation will swear under oath that I could not have committed the deed of which you accuse me. I am willing, however, to enlighten you concerning some of the facts about Charles McCarthy that you clearly have not yet discovered for yourself and which are responsible for his violent death. Do you wish me to proceed, Mr. Holmes?"

This was not the reply that Sherlock Holmes had expected and he said nothing for a moment. Then he gave his forced smile to the old man and said, "You may enlighten me."

"I am sure Doctor Watson," he said looking in my direction, "that you are aware of the psychological condition that has been named sexual inversion, are you not? And perhaps you are as well, Mr. Holmes? Our poet, Whitman, was fond of calling it adhesive love."

"It is the psychological disposition which, if not kept in check, may lead to the practice of sodomy," I responded. "Yes. I am familiar with it. It has been observed amongst some English school boys."

"Indeed, if not half of Oxford and Cambridge," added Holmes brusquely. "But we are not here to talk about sexual deviations. You are supposed to be enlightening us concerning the murder of Charles McCarthy and your red herring is of little interest."

"Ah, but it is intimately connected to the matter," responded the old Scot gravely. "For reasons that God alone knows, young James exhibited what could only be termed effeminate tendencies since he was a child. He was always overly dramatic, given to flamboyant behavior and dress, and interested only in music, poetry, theater, and pretty paintings, and not at all in the manly sports of rugby or boxing, nor in any aspect whatsoever of military life. I have already told you that his determination not to attend West Point and pursue a military career, in the footsteps of his older brother, was a cause of considerable friction between him and his father."

"You have indeed already told us that," said Holmes. "Please continue, and I assume that this psychological analysis is leading somewhere."

Mr. Turner paused for a moment, making a point of not immediately acceding to Holmes's impatient demand. "I assume that you are also aware, sir, if you have indeed done your homework as a detective, that both Charles McCarthy and I were reared in strict Calvinist faith. As the years passed I confess that my adherence to the strictures of the Church loosened and, conscious of my own sins and failures, I became far more tolerant of those who held different beliefs to mine and whose behavior and tastes were foreign to me, but in whom I was able to discern basic goodness and generosity and kindness toward their fellow man. I have already told you that

Charles and I parted ways over the years and this was one of those issues on which our paths diverged. He became progressively more devout, more rigid in his beliefs, more intolerant of those who he felt had grievously sinned and committed serious moral failures."

"There are many men who hold to severe moral positions," said Holmes, again impatiently. "What does that have to do with murder?"

"When his son, James went off to Harvard last year he immediately associated himself with other students who were active in the theater club; they called themselves the Hasty Pudding Society. As you know, I assume, the theater crowd attracts many young men like James who are inclined to sexual inversion and to seek physical intimacy amongst the members of their own sex instead of with the opposite. James's closest friends were also that way inclined. It all might have been quite harmless except that word came back to Charles from reliable sources that James had indeed crossed the line and was engaging secretly but regularly in the actual practice of forbidden love with a fellow male student."

"Very well, sir, you are now telling me that James is a sodomite who is attracted to other theater types. Wherein is the connection?"

Again the old man paused and then continued. "Charles was enraged by the news. He was beside himself with righteous indignation. He and I had some very unpleasant arguments about it. He would quote verses from the Bible that if honored today would condemn his son to death. He felt that he had no other course of action before God but to denounce the boy, cut him off from his inheritance, publically expose and shame him, and cast him out from the household. He had said nothing about this to Florence, to Mrs. McCarthy, not wanting to expose her to such depravity and humiliation. But he was determined to take these steps even if they were to ruin the life of his only remaining son."

"He would not be the first father to disown his son for such reasons, nor will he be the last," said Holmes. "It may be sad and tragic, but there is not sufficient reason here for a neighbor to kill his neighbor. What business was it of yours that there was strife between a father and son on the next farm over?"

John Turner looked hard at Sherlock Holmes for a long time before speaking. "Because Mr. Holmes, because my dear little girl, my beautiful daughter Alice, who has been the joy of my life and lovingly cared for me since the passing of her mother eight years ago, shares a similar but opposite sexual inversion. Her romantic desires are singularly Sapphic. It is why she likewise found her friends amongst the theater club on campus. Charlie was not just going to destroy the life of his son by disowning and publically shaming him, he would have done the same to my daughter and all of their friends. My little girl would be entangled in the same web. I could not suffer that to happen. I would not go to my grave knowing that I had done nothing to prevent him from destroying the lives of such a wonderful group of joyful young people, whose only sin was to be sexually attracted to that to which you and I are not.

"As you appear to have deduced, Mr. Holmes, I determined to rescue my daughter, James and their friends from the fate that Charlie would have struck them down with. I will confess nothing except to admit that our prayer meeting was a conspiracy during which time we agreed upon a plan that we believed could be carried off. I told you two days ago that I did not expect to live past Christmas. That was not the brutal truth. My doctors have advised me that I will not live to see the equinox."

Here he paused. The flush of anger that had been present during his earlier speaking departed from his face. "The case is now in your hands, Mr. Sherlock Holmes, the famous detective. You have solved it. And I can only assure of three things that are certain to come to pass."

Holmes said nothing, but he nodded his head indicating that he was attentive.

"The first is that if you press this case to the police and the courts, I will be dead long before it comes before a judge. The second is that my alibi will stand firm and be supported by many witnesses. And the third is that the attorneys representing the estate of the deceased will expose all the facts about James and Alice that I have confided to you and that their lives and those of their friends will become fodder for the press.

"I can also swear to you, as a Presbyterian, as a man whose word has been his bond for over sixty years, and as a proud Scotsman, that on the day I go to face my Maker a document will be released by a respected attorney in New York that will admit to whatever acts I may be guilty of, that will fully exonerate James McCarthy, and that will assure that both my only child and that of Charles McCarthy will continue to enjoy their property and their dignity and that Mrs. McCarthy will live in peace and comfort in her home for the rest of her days.

"The choice is yours, Mr. Holmes. You are free to cry havoc and let slip the dogs of war, and the consequences will be on your conscience for the rest of your life."

With this, he leaned forward and with great effort raised his large body from the sofa and, leaning heavily on his canes, tottering and shaking in all his great frame stumbled slowly from the room. One of the hotel maids moved quickly to his side, took his arm and helped him to his carriage.

Holmes was silent and buried in thought with a pained expression on his face. He watched the old Highlander as he departed and then with a sigh quietly said, "There but for the grace of God goes Sherlock Holmes."

Holmes sat quietly for the next half-hour. The same young maid who had helped Mr. Turner to his carriage appeared bearing a tray of tea. Mary looked up at her and said, "Miss Patience, thank you. I did not know that you worked at the hotel as well as for McCarthy Manor."

"I work here on the weekends," the young woman said quietly as she served the tea, and then she retired from the room.

Holmes sipped slowly on the tea and then put the cup and saucer down and looked at Mary and me.

"The old fellow has tied my hands," he said. "He is quite right that if I take this now to the police, he will be long gone from the living before the case ever reaches a court. There is no doubt that he has sufficient funds and obligations owed to him to secure all the reliable witnesses he needs to defend himself. I fear that he has given me no alternative but to leave whatever punishment is due to him to a higher power, and believe that justice will be carried out in eternity better than it is on earth.

"I have no choice but to go now and inform my client, Mrs. McCarthy, that while justice will not be done, her son will be fully exonerated and restored to her, Lord willing, within time for him not to lose his year at Harvard. I will take myself now to speak to her, and then we will depart in the morning and make our way back to England."

I could read the disappointment and resignation on the face of Sherlock Holmes as he strode slowly out of the room. Mary and I chatted back and forth about what had just taken place in front of us. We agreed that Sherlock Holmes had made the right decision and taken the best course of action, no matter how deeply painful it was to him to let a criminal, even one with honorable motives, walk away scot-free.

"I must admit," said Mary as we took one last stroll along the river bank, "the boy and the girl were truly remarkable actors. They had me completely fooled."

"What do you mean?" I said. "You spotted Alice right away with her tweezers, and James's rendition of Hamlet fooled no one."

"No, no. I mean that I would never have guessed that either of them was, what did he call them, 'sexually inverted'? I attended a school for girls for over ten years and thought I could spot any who were sapphically inclined. When we used to meet with the boys' school we could see immediately which ones were attracted to young gentlemen and which were not. The same was true of the boys who were obviously not interested in girls. I would have said that both James and Alice were every bit as inclined as you and I are, John. But it appears that they are not. They were exceptionally good young actors."

"Ah, but perhaps they have had to practice their roles all their lives, growing up as they did in such strict households."

"Hmm. Yes. Perhaps."

Chapter Eight

Back to New York

Come the morning Mary and I packed up our belongings and took breakfast on the hotel porch. Holmes did not join us. As it was Sunday, there was no early train and we waited until nearly ten o'clock before preparing to leave for the station. Miss Patience Moran was again on duty and appeared at the top of the staircase carrying my valise and Mary's hand case. Behind her were two boys carrying the steamer trunk. All was loaded into the hotel carriage and we waited for Sherlock Holmes to join us. He did so shortly, carrying his own valise and followed by the boys with his trunk. He climbed into the carriage, nodded perfunctorily to both of us, sat down, and opened a book. He said not a word on route to the station, and not a word all the way to Manhattan. Twice he excused himself from the cabin and spent close to twenty minutes pacing back and forth the length of the train.

Mary and I chatted and enjoyed the grandeur of Hudson River Valley and wondered yet again about the origins of the story of the Headless Horseman of Sleepy Hollow. We amused ourselves with fantasies of what we would have said to the chap had we run into him.

It was late afternoon by the time we reached our hotel in mid-town Manhattan. I asked Holmes if he would join us for dinner, but he declined, as I had expected he would. Upon entering our spacious hotel room, I opened my valise and prepared to retrieve something to read for the evening. Sitting on top on my journals and notebooks was a thick stack of papers that I did not recognize.

"Mary, darling," I called to my wife. "Did you put some papers inside my valise before leaving Tarrytown."

"No dear. Why?"

"There are several items here that are not mine."

I took out two thick pinned manuscripts and a small set of notes that were held together with a clip. The first, a new document on clean crisp white paper bore the title on the front page:

The Stinx

A Playful Portrait of Terrible Times in the Tenderloin

By the Harvard Hasty Pudding Theater Club

The second was a much older document, handwritten in a masculine but legible hand and entitled:

Calumny and Criminality in California, A Memoir of the Forty-Niners.

By Charlie McCarthy

The small group of notes appeared to be copies of telegrams and receipts.

Mary and I looked these things over and she said, "John, dear, I think you should call Sherlock and let him look at these."

I bundled up the papers and we walked across the hall to his room. There was a "Do Not Disturb" sign attached to the door handle. I fully anticipated the reaction that my knocking firmly would elicit and smiled a bit of an impish smile at my wife before striking the door loudly.

"I do not wish to be disturbed," came the voice from the other side of the door. Whereupon I knocked again, adding more knocks and increasing the volume.

"I said that I do not wish to be disturbed!" came the reply louder and with a sharp tone of being seriously annoyed.

One more time I struck the door, this time with my open palm so as to make it as loud as possible.

"Confound it, do they not teach hotel staff how to read in America?" we heard Holmes shouting as he approached the door. He swung the door open, shouting, "I SAID . . ." He stopped when he saw it was Mary and I. Before he could utter another word I said, "Holmes, you have to read these documents immediately. Your case is not over yet."

He looked at the documents in my hand, took them from me, and glanced over them.

"Come in please," he murmured. "Please sit down."

We sat and Holmes divided the papers among the three of us. We each read the allotted portion and passed it along to the next person until all of us had read the entire bundle.

"May I have your thoughts and insights, Dr. and Mrs. Watson?"

Mary began. "This memoir was written by the late Mr. Charles McCarthy but quite a long time ago. From the contents and the reference, I would guess that it must have been written in the 1850s. The story it contains is very disturbing. It recounts serious theft, possible murder, and swindling on a grand scale. If the stories are true, then there are some very vicious criminals still at large who committed some heinous crimes back during the days of the gold rush in California."

"That is what I read as well," said Holmes. "And the script of the play, your thoughts on that my dear doctor."

"It purports to be a comedy, but it is anything but," I offered. "The first act is a re-enactment of the story in the memoir. The second act places the villains from the first act in positions of power and authority here in New York City and has them engaging in all sorts of briberies, extortions, assaults, and even a murder or two. If any of this is based on fact, then it is no less than a revelation of a dangerous and extensive criminal syndicate that has corrupted the city and is determined at all costs to extract riches at the expense of the citizens."

"Indeed, it does," said Holmes. "And it fits quite closely with the stories we heard during our late dinner at the Haymarket. It appears that Charles, his son James, and their friends in the theater club were on to something, and may have been dealing with a far greater force of evil than they knew of. But what of these notes? Mary, what do you think about them?"

"The most disturbing is this clipping from a newspaper in New Haven."

"Could you read it aloud to us?" asked Holmes.

She read aloud: "It is dated the first of June and the headline runs: 'Tragic Death at Lighthouse Point.'

"And the notice says: 'The morning dawn extinguished not only the light of the Point Lighthouse but also the light of the life of a popular young man and scion of one of the most respected families of New Haven. The body of Michael DuPlessis, son of Danton and Muriel DuPlessis of Grand Avenue in Fair Haven, was found by early morning fishermen washed up on the beach to the south of the Lighthouse. The local police have not released any details of their investigation, but it is known that the young man was a strong swimmer and had no history of abusing alcohol. Foul play has not been ruled out. A friend of the family told our reporter that the young man will be greatly missed and mourned. He had just returned from his first year at Harvard, had a stellar life and career ahead of him, and was outstanding both as an athlete and an enthusiastic member of the Hasty Pudding Theater Troop. Funeral arrangements will be announced in this newspaper as soon as they are made known to the public.'"

Mary looked up at the two of us. "That would have been just two days before Mr. McCarthy was killed. This young man from New Haven must have been a friend to James and Alice at college. Somebody was prepared to do murder to keep a damning story from becoming known."

"Exactly," said Holmes. "The other notes — please read them as well."

"There is a copy of a telegram to Mr. Turner from the Plaza Hotel in New York confirming his reservation on the night of June the third, and says 'usual room and rates apply.' Then one to him as well from a Doctor Williams on Central Park South that just says 'Appointment confirmed for eight o'clock, June 4th.'

"There is one from someone named Bruce that reads: 'Mike killed last night. Cam and I on our way post haste. All must take cover.' It is dated on the second of June. Then there are two sent by Alice the first is to All

Members HPC' and reads. 'Destroy all copies of script immediately. Seek protection now. Mike and Mr. McC already murdered. James is protected. Father has hired Pinkertons. Villains are killers.'

"The second reads: Dearest cousin: Marriage to James has been postponed due to tragedy that you already know about. All still very private. Please say nothing to others yet. Your love and support deeply appreciated. Alice.'

"Finally, there is this handwritten note, written by a woman and it says: 'Holmes and Watson: Both families still in danger of their lives. Do not leave them to fend for themselves. They will be killed.'

"And it is signed 'P.M'"

Sherlock Holmes sat back in his chair, placed the tips of his long fingers together and closed his eyes.

"That canny old Scotsman. That dour old lame man with his sad face and sonorous voice. He completely took me in. He dropped just enough hints, so very subtly, that tricked me into deducing that he was the murderer. A truly remarkable performance. He has taken very decisive and clever steps to protect both his family and the McCarthys. Sexual inversions, crazy Calvinists, short of cash from buying cows ... ha! ... remarkable, all, truly remarkable.

"It would appear," he continued, "that our young maid, Miss Patience Moran, has been doing a far better job of being a detective than I have been. And it also appears that the murderers we are dealing with are far more than the garden variety jealous neighbors or religious fanatics."

Here he paused. He was transfixed when he was hot upon a scent like this.

"Right! Tomorrow morning we will pay a visit to the Plaza Hotel first thing, to confirm Mr. Turner's stay there. If possible, we will also knock on the door of his doctor, and then, if that appointment rings true, we will get ourselves back up the Hudson as quickly as possible and see what we can do to help these folks who are fearing for their lives, but, I fear, not acting wisely."

We parted for the night. For awhile I lay upon the sofa and tried to interest myself in a yellow-backed novel but my mind would not cooperate. Mary and I slept poorly and I am quite certain that Holmes did not sleep at all. I knew from my years of living with him that he would spend the entire night reading and rereading the documents that had been placed in our keeping until he had memorized every word of every page. The unsettled look of bewilderment was gone from his face. It was as if a veil had been parted and he had been given a vision not of the holiest of holies but of the most criminal and vicious sector of human existence, and he would not stop until he had faced it square on, and even endangered his own life in order to vanquish it.

The next morning we had breakfast in our rooms and then met Holmes in the lobby of the hotel. He had a cab waiting and helped load on the luggage in his haste to be on our way. With the roads not yet crowded, the cabbie hustled his horse up Broadway all the way to Columbus Circle and then turned back east on 49th Street until he reached the massive Plaza Hotel at the corner of Fifth Avenue. The ornate lobby was festooned with palm fronds and dominated by massive black marble columns supporting gold leaf Corinthian capitals. The large front desk was crowded with guests that were departing and checking out. Holmes, impatient as might be expected, turned to us and said, "Forgive me if I have to act like a New Yorker." He walked directly to the front desk, then promptly circled around behind it and into the front office. We could hear him speak loudly and imperiously, "I must see the manager immediately. This matter is urgent!"

A moment later he came back out with a young gentleman in a smart suit accompanying him. Holmes led the chap over to us and said, "Sir. I apologize for my terrible lack of manners, but this is a matter of life and death. My name is Sherlock Holmes. This is my colleague Dr. John Watson and his wife, Mrs. Watson."

He got no further. The young man broke into a wide smile and said loudly, "Hey. Wow. This is terrific. You're really Sherlock Holmes? That's fantastic. Welcome to The Plaza, finest hotel in America. I love reading those stories about you. All the guys here do. And here you are. Hey. That's great!"

Holmes gave the chap a quick smile and went on. "Thank you for your interest. However, today we are in the midst of a serious case and we require your assistance. We need some information and we need it immediately. Can we count on your help?"

"Wow. You mean I get to help out Sherlock Holmes? Wow. That's fantastic. Does that mean I get to be in one of the stories, Doc?"

"That is always a possibility," I smiled back at him. "It depends of course on whether or not you can assist Mr. Holmes."

"Hey. Let's give it a shot Mr. Holmes. What can we do for you?"

"I need to know whether or not a certain guest stayed here on the night of Wednesday, June 3rd. A Mr. John Turner. Would you be willing to check your register and confirm that for us?"

"Whoa there, Mr. Holmes. This ain't the Hav-a-Nap Hotel. This is The Plaza; most exclusive hotel in America. We have to guard the confidentiality of our guests. I can't go telling you that, even if you are Mr. Sherlock Holmes. Real sorry, sir."

Holmes smiled at the fellow and said, "Since I am Sherlock Holmes then I am sure you will know that I will find this information out with or without your help. With your help, I will find it out immediately. Without may take me a little longer. So what is it to be, sir?"

"Well ... okay. Since you put it that way, I suppose we could make a deal. I check our register and give you the information you need, and when you write about this Doc, you tell your readers all over the world that The Plaza Hotel in New York City is the finest hotel in America with the best food, best staff, and most luxurious rooms anywhere on earth. Deal? Shake on it? There ain't loopholes in a handshake, my daddy always said."

We shook on it.

"Your register please sir," said Holmes.

"No need. Old Johnny Turner comes here every second Wednesday so he can see his doctor next door every other Thursday morning. He's been doing it for the past seven years. So yes sir, he was here on the third of June. Mind you that was the last time he was here. We didn't see him on the seventeenth, nor on the first of July. He's still okay isn't he? He was looking pretty shaky last he was here."

I nodded and added, "I suppose any one of your waiters or maids could have told us the very same thing without the need of a deal. Correct, young man?"

"You can bet on it, Doc, but hey, a deal's a deal. Looking forward to reading about us in your story. You, fellows and lady, have a real good day now."

Dear reader: The Plaza Hotel in New York City is the finest hotel in America with the best food, best staff, and most luxurious rooms anywhere on earth.

"Very good," said Holmes, "and now to the doctor."

The office and treatment room of Doctor Williams of Central Park South was only a few doors to the west of The Plaza. We arrived just minutes before his office opened and waited for the doctor to show up. When he did, I saw that he was an average looking chap, of average height and weight, almost bald, and well dressed in an elegant morning suit, bright blue cravat and gleaming pearl stick pin. He looked surprised to see our small committee waiting outside his door.

"Good morning, Doctor Williams," said Holmes. "So sorry to disturb you first thing in the morning, but we have just been visiting with a patient of yours and are very deeply concerned for his health. We understand he has missed his past two appointments with you and he is deteriorating badly. If we could convince him to come and see you, is there any possibility that you could arrange to see him this week?"

The doctor shrugged. "Which of my patients are you talking about?"

"Mr. John Turner of Tarrytown," continued Holmes. "We have just returned from being his guests and we are frightfully concerned about him. He has had a very rough past few weeks."

"Of course, he has. What with his best friend and neighbor getting murdered and the son who did it gone mad. He was sitting in my office when he heard about it. The boy from the hotel ran in with an urgent telegram and he read it and got right up and walked out. I haven't heard from him since."

"Oh my," said Holmes, "that must have been terribly distressing not only for him but for you as well, sir. Terribly distressing."

The doctor paused and folded his arms. "It wasn't so much distressing for me as confusing. He read the telegram and then he went very pale. He just gasped 'Oh no, oh no,' several times. Then he pushed himself up and just plain ordered me to help him get his clothes back on, he is quite handicapped these days, so I did and he just about ran hobbling out of the office. It wasn't until later in the day that I heard what had happened and then it all made sense. He was terribly upset, and I am sure he has gone nowhere but downhill health-wise since. If you can convince him to come back and see me anytime, I will find time in my schedule. He's a fine old fellow and I would hate to see his last few weeks of this life be more painful that they have to be."

"Indeed, doctor, we will," said Holmes. "Indeed, we will do everything we can. He's a good man and we share your concern for him. Please do not let us hold you up from your practice any longer. Thank you so much for talking to us about our friend."

As soon as Doctor Williams had departed into his office and clinic Holmes turned to Mary and me and said, "I must return immediately to Sleepy Hollow. There is evil afoot there and I am compelled to devise some sort of plan to protect the families who live there. I would be grateful for your accompanying me, but I am well aware of how much of your time I have already imposed on and would not in any way begrudge your returning to your home and your practice. You also must have patients waiting to see you … Doc." He added the appellation with a smile. Before I could respond, Mary spoke for both of us.

"My dear Sherlock," she said with a warm smile, "you know perfectly well that there is nothing on earth that John Watson loves more that scampering across the countryside chasing down villains and scoundrels as the accomplice of Sherlock Holmes. The average Englishman who wants to be ill will still be that way when we return. So, of course, we will stay and help in any way we can. Won't we darling?" I felt her slide her arm around my waist and then felt a firm hand with stylish finger nails put a distinct clasp on my left buttock. "Yes," I chirped. "Of course. Count on us."

"I knew I could," said Holmes. "Now may I ask you to write a note back to our hotel and have them send our baggage on to Tarrytown by the earliest train. If we hurry, we can still catch the morning express up the Hudson."

Chapter Nine

Up the River

"**F**ive dollars, cabbie," shouted Holmes, "if you can get us to the station in time for the 9:10 train up the river."

"Whoa! Hang on guv'nor," the driver shouted back. "We're at the post. We're off!"

The horse had a quick whip laid across its haunches and took off in a gallop down Fifth Avenue. Several policemen on foot shouted at us and more than one pedestrian cursed us as only a New Yorker is capable of doing, but we arrived at Grand Central Depot with just enough time to purchase our tickets and board the train. "Three return to Tarrytown," I said to the chap behind the ticket cage. "No!" shouted Holmes. "Make it return to Mattawan."

We ran along the platform to our cabin and boarded just as the conductor was giving the last call. Huffing and puffing we sat down.

"Mattawan?" I queried. "Back to the madhouse?"

"Precisely," said Holmes. "It is time that Prince Hamlet came to his senses and helped us save him and his loved ones from becoming victims just as his father was."

The train pulled away and again we watched the buildings of New York City and then the banks of the great Hudson River pass by our windows.

"According to the train schedule, there is a twenty minute stop in Yonkers," Holmes observed. "My map shows me that the police station is located almost next door to the train station. As soon as we stop I am going to get off and run to the police on the off chance that I will find Detective Leverton on duty, and if he is I will do my best to persuade him to join us."

As soon as the train slowed to a stop in Yonkers Holmes opened the cabin door and ran across the platform and through the station. We waited, watching the clock. The first warning whistle was given. As the second one was sounding the cabin door opened and Sherlock Holmes entered followed by a tall, powerfully built police detective. He had removed his hat while running for the train and showed a fine head of wavy gray hair. He had full but trim sideburns and a neatly waxed mustache. His erect bearing led me to believe that he had military service in the past. I thought that if I were to find myself in a tight spot in Sleepy Hollow, I would not mind at all having this impressive chap next to me.

Holmes introduced us. "Detective Leverton, please meet my colleague Dr. Watson and his wife." I held out my hand which the detective took but not enthusiastically. He gave me a bit of a sideways nod and sat down. He did not look comfortable.

"It is against all protocol, Mr. Holmes, for me to rush away from my desk while on duty. I am doing this only because I have heard of you and your reputation, and I trust that you know what you are doing. But now you better give me much more information that you did at the station or I will be off this train at the next stop."

"A most reasonable request," replied Holmes. Piece by piece Sherlock Holmes laid out the entire case as he had come to understand it. He showed the detective whatever evidence we carried with us and justified each conclusion he had arrived at. The first and then the second whistle stops on the journey were passed and the detective made no move at all to depart.

When Holmes had finished, the detective looked at him and said quietly, "If what you are saying is just your fantasy, then my job and your reputation will be on the line. If what you are telling me is true, then sir we are up against some of the most powerful men in New York State, and not only our jobs but our lives will be on the line. You are telling me that the Mayor of New York, the Boss of Tammany Hall, the Captain of Police of the Tenderloin District, and his leading lieutenant are all not only thoroughly corrupt, but in the past were murderers and swindlers, and that they have recently conspired to murder Charles McCarthy, and are planning to commit further murders if we do not stop them."

"That is precisely what I am telling you, Detective Leverton," replied Holmes, looking the officer directly in the eye. "I cannot compel you to join us and you are free to call us fools and get off at the next station."

The tall, gray-haired police officer said nothing for a moment and then a small smile appeared at the corners of his mouth. "Not much of any interest happens in Yonkers, you know. Downright boring at times for a policeman. Last time I was shot at was in April of 1865. Battle of Morrisville down in North Carolina. I was only a kid in my late teens just conscripted into the Union Army. Have to admit, most exciting day of my life. Scared as hell. Wouldn't have missed it for the world. We'll just have to see how this battle compares. The thought does kind of get the blood moving doesn't it, Doc? You were army as well I'm thinking."

"Medical corps. Afghanistan. Took one in the leg." I nodded in return. I would not admit in front of my wife that I likewise missed the exhilaration of the battlefield. There is no other sensation known to man that compares. He held out his hand to me and I grasped it firmly. He said, "Well then, it's time for two old soldiers to show we still got what it takes."

At the Tarrytown station, Mary got off the train with instructions to make arrangements for our hotel and the baggage that would be following us on the next train. Holmes also asked her to try to arrange a confidential meeting with Miss Patience Moran as soon as we returned from Mattawan.

For the next hour, Holmes quizzed Detective Leverton on all aspects of the corruption and extortion that permeated the entire State of New York. The detective was an honest officer who was enraged by the criminality of so many town councils, assemblymen and state senators, and his own fellow police officers. He told Holmes much about the goings on of Tammany Hall for the past one hundred years. Finally, he said, sadly, "You know, gentlemen, this corruption is like that monster in the mythology that I learned about way back in my school days. You know, the one where if you knock off one head another two grow in its place. Lord willing we may snap off a head or two in the battle ahead of us. But the monster is so big, we won't do more that put a pin prick in it."

"My good man," said Holmes, "you are entirely correct. But the alternative is to do nothing. It was, I believe, only the second labor of Hercules, but he finally conquered the monster of which you speak. We are only the opening salvo. We will have to trust that honest men will follow us and continue the fight that we will not be able to."

"Right you are, General," Leverton affirmed. "Lead on."

Getting past the director of the Mattawan institution was not difficult at all. I brought him up to date on the monograph I was writing about the case and the excellent treatment that James McCarthy was receiving. Detective Leverton assumed an authority role and although he had no order from a judge to remove the patient from care he acted as if he did, and all of the staff meekly complied. Again we approached the young man as he was sitting outside, engrossed in a book. We came from behind him and he did not appear to sense our approach. Holmes moved quickly around in front of him and knelt down until he was looking the lad directly in the face. James made as if to leap up onto the bench and begin his madness routine, but Leverton placed his hands on the young man's shoulders and kept him in his seat.

James recovered himself and started to babble some nonsense verse. Holmes gave him a sharp slap across the face and he stopped in shocked silence and stared at Holmes.

"It won't do James," Holmes said with a tone of deep authority. "Do you see how easy it was for us to get to you? Do you really think that the Tammany villains could not do the same and more whenever they want? Use your head, young man. You are not safe here. And neither are your beloved Alice or her father or even your mother. They will kill them as well as you, just as they did your friend Michael and your father. Is that what you want to let happen? Is it? Now stop this nonsense and try to help us. Get up. You're coming with us and we're going back to Terrytown and we will put an end to their evil. Now move. There is no time to spare."

I felt terribly sorry for the poor lad. I could see the vein in the side of his temple pounding and I knew that he was paralyzed with fear. He said nothing but Holmes nodded to us, and Leverton and I each took one of his arms and forcibly walked him out of the Institution and back through the village to the train station.

When our train arrived, Detective Leverton flashed his badge to the conductor and we were shown to a private cabin in the first class car. I introduced myself and reminded the young man that I was a doctor and attempted, in a friendly way, to ask him questions, but he refused to respond. He sat, ashen-faced, starring out the window until we arrived at Tarrytown.

Nothing more was said until we reached the station. As we got off the train, I saw Mary waiting to meet us. Standing beside her was the tall young servant girl, Miss Patience Moran. As we approached them, she walked directly to James and put her arms around him. He returned the embrace and they held each other closely. "It's going to be okay, Jimmy," she said. "It's going to be okay. It's good to have you back."

"Thanks, Patti," he said. "It's good to be back ... I hope."

The six of us walked in silence from the station to the hotel, where we found a small room off of the main parlor that was suitable for a confidential conversation.

Detective Leverton turned to Sherlock Holmes and said, "Mr. Holmes, as you have initiated this meeting I suggest you also handle the questioning of these two young people."

Holmes nodded and began by looking directly at James and in a friendly but firm voice said, "It is time that we heard the truth about what happened on the night of June the third. I need to start with you, young man: did you murder your father?"

After a long silence, we heard the words "No sir."

"Why then did you tell Detective Leverton you did?"

"I believed that they would kill me too and that I would be safe if they locked me up."

"So you made a false confession and then pretended to have gone mad?"

"Yes, sir."

"Was all that your idea or were you coerced into doing that by your friends?"

"It was my idea, sir, but I convinced my friends and Mr. Turner that I could pull it off, and so they went along with it."

"Lying to a police officer is a crime, you know that don't you?"

"Yes sir, but it's better than getting killed."

"I suppose you are right on that one, young man. So I assume that the police will overlook what you did as long as we know that you are now telling the truth. Will you agree to that, young man?"

"Yes, sir."

"Well then, who killed your dad?"

"I don't know exactly sir, but I believe that it was somebody connected to, or sent by people at Tammany Hall."

"And why would they do that?" Holmes continued quietly.

"Because of the play I wrote and we were going to perform. It portrayed them as murderers, swindlers, extortionists, and thieves," replied the lad.

"Well now, that is usually enough to get some folks angry, especially if they happen to be from the criminal class. But now tell me, what did happen on that night."

"I was in my room working on the script for the play when I heard a gunshot. I ran downstairs to my dad's office, saw him lying forward on his desk, saw a gun on his desk, and saw a man climbing out the window."

"And what did you do then?"

"I ran to my father, saw that he had been shot in the head, picked up the gun and ran to the window."

"What were you going to do?"

"I don't know. I wasn't thinking, only reacting. I was screaming at him and tried to shoot at him."

"And did you?"

"The gun didn't fire. I'm not sure why. Next thing I knew Patti was standing beside me and she took the gun away from me." He turned to Miss Patricia and said, "Thanks, Patti." She nodded back at him.

"At some time in the past year or two you discovered your father's memoir and read it, did you not?" asked Holmes of the young man. He said nothing but nodded his head.

"And you took it into your head that you would write a play about it and using the theater you would expose injustice, rally all the good citizens and put the bad fellows behind bars. Is that what you thought? But somehow they learned about your plans and were not happy about it. Is that correct?"

The lad nodded.

"Did they warn you to back off?"

He nodded again.

"But you thought that you were indestructible and so you confidently went right on with your plans for the play? Right?"

Another nod.

"It was rather naïve of you was it not?" pressed Holmes.

He nodded again and then whispered, "We believed that we were protected by the First Amendment. We never knew that they would be so evil, so awful. We never knew."

"And now you do. They first murdered your friend Michael in New Haven, and then they came for your father. Did he have any idea of what you and your theater pals were up to? Did he let you just carry on with it?"

"No. I told him about the play but not its real contents. We thought it would be a fun surprise and that he would be proud of us." There were tears streaming down the boy's face as he spoke.

"You saw the murderer from the window. Could you identify him?"

He shook his head.

"When Alice and her father and Bruce and Cameron arrived in the morning whose idea was it to call a prayer meeting?"

"Mine," he whispered.

"And that was when you concocted the plan for you to pretend you were mad so that they would lock you up in Mattawan, and you would confess to the murder, and you believed that doing so would protect you and keep them from coming after Alice and the others. Is that what happened?"

"Yes. Alice's father said it was crazy, but we were scared, and convinced him to let us try it."

"And Mr. Turner and Alice would go along with it and agree that you were angry at your father and prone to madness. How in the world did you get him to agree to such a desperate plan?"

"He told us that he was dying and that he would make sure everything was set right after his death, and that I would be able to get back to my mom and Alice and school."

"Did you know that he was going to die soon?" asked Holmes.

"No." Here he stopped for a minute, and his lower lip quivered. "Neither did Alice. It was … it was very painful. She was very upset. But we only had a few minutes left and we had to agree on something so that's what we decided. I was so scared that they would kill me and my friends. It was crazy, but it was all we could think of."

Holmes put his hand out and covered the young man's trembling fingers. "Desperate times demand desperate measures. Under the circumstances, it was far from the worst plan and quite convincingly carried off."

"You did a right good job as a mad man," said Leverton. "Had me fooled, you did."

James shrugged. "I played Hamlet during my senior year in high school. It was all I could remember. That and some memory verses from Sunday school."

"Have we learned all there is to know," asked Holmes. "Are any material facts missing?"

He shook his head. Stopped, and then looked at us again with tears in his eyes.

"Lucy," he said.

"Who is Lucy?" asked Holmes.

"One of the theater troupe. She was a classmate of Alice's at Radcliffe. She helped me write the script." He was clenching his fists as he spoke. I placed my hand on his arm and quietly asked, "Can you tell me about what happened to her?"

He said nothing and his body was racked with sobs. With great difficulty, he finally whispered, "He got to her first. He beat her. Badly. He broke her arm" He stopped, struggling again to gain control of himself and then in a nearly inaudible voice he said, "And then he violated her."

"Dear God Holmes," I said looking across at my friend, "Who are these monsters we are dealing with?"

Holmes said nothing. I watched him as he stared out the train window. I could see his eyes narrow into bullet points and his fists clench. He was enraged. I knew that he would not leave American soil until some villain paid for his crime.

Leverton spoke next to James. "It was not reported was it?"

"No sir."

"Lucy was terrified, and I am sure utterly humiliated," Leverton continued. The boy nodded as he held his face in his hands.

Leverton continued, "Told her parents she fell off her bicycle or something like that?" Again the boy nodded.

The detective looked at Holmes and me. "This is what happens all too often. These scum of the earth do their vile deeds and get away with it because the girl is too frightened to say anything, and understandably so. We'll have one of our nurses try to talk to her."

The boy raised his head. "She was only seventeen. She was tiny. She didn't weigh more than ninety pounds. What sort of monster would do something like that?" he dropped his head back into his hands.

Sherlock Holmes now turned his gaze toward Miss Patience Moran, who had sat in silence for the past hour. "Miss Moran, you have been in a position to observe many of the most intimate events of the McCarthy household. We have been informed from other sources that the friendship between Charles McCarthy and John Turner had become strained in recent years and that they were no longer as close to each other as they had been in the past. What do you say to that miss?"

Both Miss Patience and James looked at Holmes as if he had taken leave of his senses. "Sir," she said, "they were as alike as Tweedledum and Tweedledee. The staff used to say that the one couldn't decide on what color of socks to wear without consulting with the other. They were closer than most brothers. Isn't that right, Jimmy?" she said looking at James. He nodded.

"Yes," said Holmes, "but had Mr. McCarthy continued to be a Republican while Mr. Turner had begun to vote for the Democrats?"

Again Miss Patience gave us a look of disbelief. "Sir, you could have stuck hot pins into John Turner's eyeballs and he still would not have voted for a Democrat. Right, Jimmy?"

The young man shrugged. "I might have said hung, drawn and quartered. But yes."

Holmes continued. "Forgive me if I air an indelicate subject, but we are concerned here with serious criminal acts." He paused, looked at Miss Patience, who responded to his gaze with a shrug of her shoulders.

"I've worked every weekend in a hotel for the past two years. Not much that's indelicate that I haven't seen."

"Right. Very well then. There was also a story told to us that James McCarthy's sexual attraction was solely for other young men and that Alice Turner's was only to other young women. What do you say to that?"

"What!?" young James blurted out. Patience involuntarily laughed and then covered her mouth with her hand.

She regained her serious composure and replied, "Master James McCarthy and Miss Alice Turner displayed warm affection toward each other and as far as the staff could tell they had been in love with each other since they were children." Here she stopped and looked at James. "Oh very well then, sir, if you must know, they were as horny as billy goats and we were always interrupting them behind the barn or in the hayloft kissing and fondling and groping at each other. Their parents told them they had to get married as soon as possible because the Bible says that it's better to marry than to burn with lust."

"Paaaatti" said James. "Thanks a lot."

"I am not going to lie in front of a police officer, Jimmy. Do you want me to say that you were really mad Prince Hamlet, or a homo, or that you were a normal hot-blooded college boy?"

James said nothing and just glared at the young woman, who beamed a smile back at him and said, "Because that is what you are, Jimmy, and we all know it."

He looked somewhat sheepish and smiled back at her but said nothing.

"And the friends of James and Alice who came to visit," said Holmes. "I believe that their names were Cameron and Bruce. Did they ever display any, I believe the term is, inclinations of sexual inversion?"

"Those two?" Miss Patience said. "Perversion would be the more appropriate word for their appetites. If I was serving them tea, they would be forever looking down the front of my dress. I would give them a hard look and they would blush but then they would do it again the next time. They were just normal college boys sir."

"Permit me one final question," said Holmes. "And again forgive me if it seems to you to be insensitive. Is there any possibility, any whatsoever, that Mr. John Turner could have been the one who shot Charles McCarthy, escaped through the window and ran off?"

"Uncle John?" said James in disbelief. "Impossible. He's all crippled. The man who shot my father was tall and thin and fast on his feet. He jumped out the window and was out and behind the trees in a few seconds."

"You would agree with that statement, Miss Moran," asked Holmes.

"I did not see him until he was at the far end of the garden," she said. "But I could see that he was tall and thin and running very quickly."

Holmes nodded slowly and then looked over to Detective Leverton. "Sir," he said, "if you are in agreement, I believe that it would be acceptable to send Mr. James McCarthy along with Miss Moran back to McCarthy Manor. I have no fear of his turning fugitive, and I am quite certain that his mother will be overjoyed to have him arrive unexpectedly for dinner. Would you agree, Detective."

"Right sir," Detective Leverton replied. "I am quite alright with that sir."

"Ah, but we must demand that they return here, and bring Mrs. McCarthy with them, on the morrow at, shall we say, ten o'clock?" said Holmes.

"If that is what you wish sir," replied the detective. "It's quite alright with me." He turned to the two young people. "I will release you, James McCarthy, if I have your word that you will be back here tomorrow morning. Will you do that young man?"

"Yes, sir. And I will have my mother come with us. She will be happy to participate. I am sure of that, sir."

The young man and young woman rose and departed from the hotel. The detective turned to Sherlock Holmes and said, "This is all very well, Mr. Holmes. We now know who did not kill Charles McCarthy, but we are no closer to knowing who did, or to bringing the villain to justice."

"Ahh, yes. You are correct sir," replied Holmes. "I will need five more days to accomplish those tasks. I would, of course, welcome you to stay here with us in this pleasant little town beside the river, but I fear that you are needed back at you post in Yonkers, are you not."

"Indeed, I am sir."

"But would it be possible for you to return on Saturday? If you do, then I would assure you that the villain will be delivered to you, most likely before midnight. And, of course, also assure you that your prisoner will be here waiting for you, well guarded until then by his mother."

The big detective gave Sherlock long look with his eyebrows raised but then slowly nodded his head and grinned. "I will be back here on Saturday, Mr. Holmes. Whatever it is you have up your sleeve I would not want to miss out on it."

He took his leave of Holmes, Mary, and me, and departed in the direction of the train station.

"And may I dare to ask, my dear Holmes," I said. "Just what is it that you are going to do between now and Saturday that will bring this case to a satisfactory resolution?"

"The first thing we are going to do is going to happen this evening," he replied. "We are going to break into the house of Mr. John Turner and his daughter, Alice, and threaten to murder them."

"Holmes," I came close to shouting back at him. "That is preposterous. It is one thing to commit a crime to help solve a case if we were in England, but may I remind you that we are in America. We would be lynched before daybreak if we were apprehended!"

"Oh darling," Mary said in her familiar tone of loving impatience. "He's not going to hurt anyone. He only has to prove to them that they are not at all safe in their house even with their hired guards. And what better way to do so? I am rather disappointed that I am not being asked to join you."

"Thank you, my dear," said Holmes. "I suspect that your husband and I will find it difficult enough to be a convincing threat and that a refined English lady holding a revolver would render our little ruse an unbelievable farce. However, I promise that we will bring a reliable report of the events. And so my dear doctor," he said turning to me. "We shall depart at dusk and make our way through Sleepy Hollow. You do have your service revolver with you, do you not?"

I nodded.

"I have one as well," said Holmes. "Although we have no need of bullets. Our mission is a peaceful one."

"Unless, of course," said Mary with an impish smile, "you meet someone unexpected after dark in Sleepy Hollow."

Chapter Ten

The Break-In

At dusk Holmes and I met at the door of the hotel and set out on our undercover mission. The moon had not yet risen and it would soon be pitch dark. The road through the village was well-traveled and easy enough to follow. As it entered the woods of Sleepy Hollow, it sloped downhill until it reached the bridge over the stream, beneath which was a narrow but deep ravine dropping some thirty feet before the watercourse.

"You will remember," said Holmes, "that there is a footpath leading away from the road and directly to the McCarthy Manor."

"Ah yes. The hypotenuse."

"Precisely."

The path led us across a field and to the back of the house. Through the windows, we glimpsed young James, his mother and Miss Patience sitting at their dining room table in what we could only imagine was an intense conversation. From there we sought out and found the path that led from the house of the one neighbor directly to that of the other; one that was well-worn by decades of neighborly visiting. By the time we reached the Turner estate all daylight had departed and we secreted ourselves behind one of the out-buildings at the back of the house.

"There were two armed guards on the porch," said Holmes. "Easily spotted by the glowing ends of their cigarettes. We shall wait here to determine the schedule of their rounds."

We waited in silence until we had heard the footsteps of the first guard and then, fifteen minutes later, those of the second. Once the second chap had returned to the front porch, Holmes whispered, "Now. They are using the summer kitchen behind the house and I would not be surprised if the door from it into the house has not even been locked."

He was right. In silence, we opened the unlocked back door and found ourselves in the central kitchen. The staff had retired for the evening and we passed through to the dining room. There were no candles lit and we had to move very slowly to avoid bumping into chairs and other obstacles that would give away our presence. We could hear the voices of Mr. Turner and his daughter chatting in the parlor. Holmes took my wrist and indicated that I should stand on one side of the door leading to the hallway while he placed himself on the other. He lifted a saucer from a shelf, held it high above his head, and then let it fall to the floor with a resounding crash as the pieces scattered.

I heard voices of alarm from the parlor and heard both the rapid light footsteps of Miss Alice and the slower thuds and scuffling sounds of her father. Miss Alice stopped in the hallway to grasp a small candelabra and entered the dining room with her father right behind her. Upon entering, she bent over to look at the fractured saucer with the result that her father's further entry into the room was blocked by her backside. At this point, Holmes put one hand on Mr. Turner's shoulder and placed the revolver against his head, and in what I could only describe as an abominable attempt at a New York accent said, "Don't move old boy, if ya values your life."

John Turner froze in his tracks. Miss Alice immediately stood up straight, whereupon I placed my forearm around her lovely neck and in an equally dreadful accent said, "Dat goes for you too, doll."

"Now move over real quiet like to duh table and sit down," said Holmes. "We got some business to discuss with ya."

Both of our victims did as they were told.

"Put duh candles on duh table, baby doll," I muttered menacingly in the ear of the trembling young woman. "And sits yourself down and keep your lip buttoned." I had no idea whatsoever if that was the way American ruffians spoke when accosting their victims, but it was as close to the way they were portrayed in the theaters of the West End as I could remember.

Holmes said nothing for a moment and the stern voice of John Turner broke the silence. "Whatever it is you want you can take. If you do any harm to my daughter, I will assure you that you will swing for it."

"Indeed," said Holmes in a distinctly London voice and he laid his unloaded revolver directly on the table in front of the old man and walked around to the other side of the table, sat down and faced him. I did likewise and sat beside Holmes. Before either of them could say anything Holmes spoke forcefully to them.

"If it was this easy for two amateurs to enter you house, and murder you had we been so inclined, do you really believe that the same men who murdered John Ferrier and Joseph Strangerson forty years ago in California, the same men who murdered young Michael DuPlessis, and your dearest friend, Charles McCarthy, and beat and violated Lucy O'Keefe, could not do the same to you, to McCarthy's widow, and to your daughter, and her fiancé? Do you really believe that sir? If you do, then I assure you that you are sadly and dangerously mistaken."

Mr. Turner said nothing and continued to stare angrily at Sherlock Holmes. Alice looked at the two of us and quietly asked "How did you know?"

Holmes gave her his quick and forced smile. "Elementary, my dear young lady. And please do not be offended if I suggest that you might take some acting lessons from your father, who is exceptionally skilled and does not require the use of tweezers."

Even in the glow of the candlelight, I could see a distinct blush on the lovely face of the young woman. Holmes continued his instructions to them.

"Your family sir, the McCarthys, and the theater friends of your daughter will not be safe until the evil, corrupt men whose criminal pursuits you have threatened are brought to justice. That, sir, is your only choice. I will explain to you how that will come to pass tomorrow morning at ten o'clock in the parlor of the Castle Hotel. Refreshments will be served and roles assigned. I look forward to a pleasant morning, and now we must bid you good-night."

Holmes rose, and I did likewise. "With your permission, sir," he said, "we will borrow one of your lamps to light our way home and take our leave by your front door. Until tomorrow morning. Good night, sir. Good night, Miss Alice."

Neither of them spoke. Holmes picked up the candelabra and we departed the room, leaving them in near complete darkness, with only the dim light from the hallway giving any illumination to the room. At the front door entrance, Holmes picked up a lamp and used the flame from a candle to light it. We left the house, closing the door behind us.

"Good evening, gentlemen," Holmes said to the startled guards sitting on the front porch. "Keep up the good work. I am sure that the master of the house will be eager to recommend your services."

This time, we walked down the driveway and stuck to the road. My mind became occupied with other matters. "Holmes, you spoke of a plan that would bring the villains to justice. Pray tell, what it might be as I see no possible course of action available to us."

"At ten o'clock tomorrow morning, my dear Watson, you will learn what it shall be," he replied, and then turning to me with a smile added, "Between now and then I will learn what it shall be."

Chapter Eleven

The Play's the Thing

At ten o'clock the next morning a trepidatious group assembled in the hotel parlor. Mrs. Florence McCarthy, accompanied by James and Miss Patience, approached Holmes and, taking his one hand in both of hers, beamed a smile and thanked him for restoring her son to her.

"Madam, you are most welcome," Holmes replied warmly. "Our work is far from over, however, and we must make sure that your family will no longer be in danger." To this she nodded and sat down between James and Miss Patience.

John Turner, hobbling in even greater discomfort than I had seen before, entered the room, supported by two canes and the arm of his daughter. He sat down close to Mrs. McCarthy, looked at her and in a quiet Scottish brogue said, "Forgive me, Florence. This past month has been very painful for you, and I am deeply sorry for inflicting it upon you. It was all we could think of at the time."

"Oh Johnny," the matronly lady replied smiling at her old friend, "you did what you had to do to protect the life of my son. What is there to forgive? It may not have been the most brilliant plan, but it was quite ingenious. Of course, you could not let me in on it. I would have spotted Jimmy's false confession and seen through his silly madness in a moment. And I would never have let him go off to the madhouse. I would have insisted he remain here and would have placed him in much greater danger. You did what you had to do for me as well and him." She leaned forward and laid her hand on his wrist as she spoke.

Inaudibly, the old fellow mouthed the words "Thank you" back to Mrs. McCarthy.

All eyes now turned to Sherlock Holmes. None of us, including Mary and me, had any idea of what his ingenious mind had come up with.

"Most of the facts concerning this case," he began, "are now known to all of you who are present. There are some details of history that are still cloudy and I must rely on Mr. Turner to confirm these for us." He nodded toward John Turner, who returned the nod.

"In the year 1849," continued Holmes, "John Turner and Charles McCarthy filed a claim in the California Gold Rush. The neighboring claim was filed by two other young men, John Ferrier and Joseph Strangerson, is that not correct sir?"

Mr. Turner nodded.

Holmes resumed the story. "The four of you became quite good friends even though the claim registered by you and Charles McCarthy turned out to be the more lucrative." Again he looked toward John Turner. He responded with a shrug of his large shoulders.

"Aye, you could say that. You could also say that we worked harder."

"Ah yes, that is more likely the truth," said Holmes. "After two years both claims had been worked out and were to be abandoned. Then just a month before all four of you had agreed to head back east Messrs Ferrier and Strangerson disappeared and four other men appeared on their site claiming that they had purchased the rights from your friends, and displayed a document showing the legal sale and purchase of the claim. Most likely it was forged." Here again, he looked to Mr. Turner.

"For certain it was forged," said Turner. "But John and Joe had vanished and we could prove nothing."

"And then three weeks after that three other chaps from Philadelphia showed up saying that they had, in turn, purchased the claim from the previous owners and paid an outlandish sum. It would come to pass that they had been thoroughly swindled. Is that not correct sir?"

"Aye. 'Tis. The blackguards had salted their samples made it look as if the claim was still worth mining. Whoever forged their ownership documents must also have given a falsified assay."

"Heavens," I interrupted. "Who would be so foolish to buy a claim without first inspecting it and assuring themselves that it was valid?"

Mr. Turner gave me a bit of a sideways look and a condescending smirk. "Any fool from Philadelphia. Possibly even one from London. The place was full of them. One born every minute, as we say over here."

"I suppose that the fools made the swindlers quite rich, did they not?" asked Holmes.

"They pocketed as much in two weeks as we had in two years."

"And your friends who had worked beside you, what became of them?" asked Holmes.

"At first, we believed that they had sold their claim and gone home. It was odd for them to have done so without bidding us farewell. But it was California and many strange things happened. When we contacted their families later, trying to send our greetings, we were told that they had not been heard from for some time and we were asked if we knew what had happened to them. From that time on we suspected the worst."

"Did you inform any authorities of your suspicions?" asked Holmes.

Again the old fellow shrugged his powerful shoulders. "We had no evidence. Men came and went in California. Some were murdered. Some ran off to China with their Chinese brides. Some lost everything in the gambling dens of San Francisco. Charlie and I talked about it but decided there was nothing to be gained by upsetting the families based only on our suspicions. I let it pass, but Charlie took the time to put pen to paper and record everything that had happened while the details were fresh in our memories. Then he likewise let it pass and we got on with our new farms and our families."

"The men who you suspected of murder, however, reappeared, did they not?" asked Holmes.

Turner nodded. "Aye. That they did. One is now the mayor of New York, the second is the boss of Tammany Hall, the third the police captain of the Tenderloin, and the fourth his lieutenant. They all go by different names to what we knew them as, but Charlie and I have known who they are for at least the past ten years. They are the same murderers and swindlers they were forty years ago."

"Indeed, they are," affirmed Holmes. Then turning to young James, he said, "The rest of the story we know. You came upon your father's memoir, decided that you would turn it into a play and use the power of the spoken word and the stage to bring justice down upon the heads of those who so richly deserved it, never suspecting that the men you planned to publically accuse, four of the most powerful, corrupt and ruthless men in America, might respond with murder."

James nodded his head and stared at the floor in a look of deep humiliation.

"Young man," said Holmes, "I have nothing but respect and admiration for your courage and your moral outrage. My sentiments are the same as yours and my life is driven by the same desire to see justice done as you must have felt. The problem we now face is that your enemies have already gotten away with murdering two people and violating a defenseless young woman. It will not be easy to put these villains either on a gallows or behind bars." Here he paused. "But it can be done."

I suspect that Holmes was rather enjoying the dramatic effect of his statement and it took my intrepid wife to prick his little bubble. "Enough Sherlock," she said. "We can do without your theatrical efforts. Just tell us what you have in mind."

He smiled back at her. "Theatrical effect, you say? Ah, precisely. That is what I propose." With this, he turned to James and asked, "When we left you the first time in the madhouse, what were the parting words the mad Prince Hamlet shouted to us?"

"I said 'The play's the thing, wherein you'll catch the conscience of the king.'"

"Indeed, you did. And how very insightful you are for you have given us the means to put an end to these bloody, bawdy villains. These remorseless, treacherous, lecherous, kindless villains," said Holmes.

"Enough of the circumlocution," said Mary. "Where are you taking us?"

"I have heard that guilty creatures sitting at a play . . . please continue young Hamlet," he said looking directly at James.

James was silent for a moment and then recited: "I have heard that guilty creatures sitting at a play/Have by the very cunning of a scene/Be struck so to the soul that presently/They have proclaimed their malefactions;/ For murder though it have no tongue, will speak/ With most miraculous organ."

"You want us," said Mary, "to put on James's play. Is that what you are saying, Mr. William Shakespeare Holmes?"

"Exactly," said Holmes. "The news that the play was being planned compelled these men to commit two murders. The news that it is going ahead and will hold a preview this Saturday in Tarrytown will, I am quite sure, drive them to attempt murder again. I am also quite sure that the intended murder victims are all gathered in this room. So I am now appointing you, and whomever else of your young friends you may recruit, as the Irregular Theater Company of Sleepy Hollow. The curtain will open at eight o'clock on Saturday evening and we have work to do. The game is afoot, my friends."

"Mr. Holmes," said John Turner. "The game you are playing is a very dangerous one, against exceedingly vicious men, and you are playing with the lives of other people. Are you quite sure that you wish to proceed?"

Holmes looked intently at the old man. "Sir, you are entirely correct. Forgive me if I made light of the course of action I am proposing. With great respect Mr. Turner, I only am recommending it to you because the alternative, the choice to hide out and wait for the enemy to act is, I fear, an infinitely more dangerous way to proceed. Would you not agree, sir?"

The old man sighed and said, "I wish with all my heart that you were wrong, but I know in my mind that you are right. What do we have to do?"

"It is now late morning on Tuesday," said Holmes. "Our company is to present a play on Saturday evening. I confess to being an occasional patron of the theater but have no experience at all concerning direction and production of same. I will defer and suggest that the responsibility for taking charge of our efforts be given over to the most experienced amongst us. Mrs. McCarthy," he said, looking at the senior lady in the room, "you are the one who is best to organize this motley crew. I suggest that you take charge and we will all do as you bid."

Alice immediately responded by clapping her hands and the rest of us joined in. The dear lady smiled at us and then spoke. "Under normal circumstances I would demur and plead exaggerated modesty but these are not normal circumstances and time is pressing and yes, Mr. Holmes, you are quite correct. I am the most qualified to take charge, not because of any vast experience on my part but only because of the utter lack of it in the rest of you. So very well, here then are your instructions:

"We shan't need to worry about costumes or sets. We can scrounge whatever we need from the back of our closets and our cellars. Each of you will look after his own appearance and do not go overboard with flamboyance. We are still Presbyterians and will have to face the rest of the congregation the next morning.

"James, get to work re-writing the script. I have glanced over your first draft and, like every first draft you have ever written, it is dreadful and needs re-working and copious amounts of polishing. Have something ready for us by tomorrow evening. If you have to work through the night, so be it. If you want a life in the theater, you may as well get used to not sleeping.

"Doctor and Mrs. Watson, you need to go into the village and find our Knox Presbyterian Church. Knock on the door of the manse and ask for Reverend Graham and tell him that the church hall is needed for this Saturday evening. It has a stage that the youngsters use every year for the Christmas pageant and if it is good enough for Mary and Joseph and Baby Jesus it will do us just fine. The good Reverend will pretend to be mortally offended, but you will tell him that I sent you, and if that does not work then let him know, that you know, that in secret he reads every one of your stories over and over again and that he has just become part of a Sherlock Holmes mystery. He will be thrilled to death. His lovely wife, who labors to look as plain as possible on Sunday mornings, is quite the pianist and fully capable of banging out ragtime with the best of them and will be positively giddy at the opportunity to dress up like a music hall floozy.

"Alice, send telegraphs off immediately to your friends from your Hasty Pudding Club and see how many of them will be able to be here by tomorrow afternoon. We will require a few more bodies on stage, preferably ones that are younger and better looking than we old folks. Pretty young faces bring better reviews you know, so get as many of the attractive ones as you can.

"Mr. Holmes, if this farce is to come off then you had best get busy contacting the Press, and the public officials, and anyone else you want to attend and tell them that it is by invitation only. The whole miserable bunch of them in Manhattan are insufferable snobs and we may as well appeal to their vanity. Patience will give you the names addresses and positions of all the appropriate officials whose attendance we are in need of."

Finally, she turned to Mr. Turner. "As for you Johnny, my old friend…"

"Yes, Florence, what will you set me to do, that I am sure will show no respect at all for my advanced age?"

"John," she said, "we will have to be practical and so I fear we shall have to look to you to round up as many Pinkertons and off-duty constables as can be found, and bribe all the weak-minded but strong-backed farm boys as you can muster, beer will do the job, and let them know they might have a fight on their hands on Saturday."

"In forty years I have never given a nickel to Simon and his miserable tavern, but if I have to buy rounds for the local militia I suppose I could spring for that this once," he said and gave a distinctly flirtatious wink back to Mrs. McCarthy.

Come Wednesday afternoon the entire Irregular Theater Company of Sleepy Hollow had assembled. It was to be a two-act play with the first act set in the hills of California, amidst the wild days of the Gold Rush. The second was set in the Tenderloin District of the present day and took place primarily inside the Haymarket Tavern. Had Holmes and I known that it was so notorious we might not have visited it at all. On the other hand, we might have skipped the theater and just gone there instead.

Our various parts were assigned to us. I was rather pleased to be assigned the role of His Worship, Mr. Hugh Grant, the Mayor of New York City, even if he was a thief and a scoundrel. At least, it meant that I could pretend to be dignified. Holmes, being tall and thin was given the role of Lieutenant Crane and George, the big lump of a driver, was conscripted to stand for police captain Clubber Williams. Reverend Graham, whose reaction had been exactly as predicted by Mrs. McCarthy, got to play the Grand Sachem of Tammany Hall, Richard Croker. Young James, in addition to crafting the script, took the role of his father, Charles, some forty years earlier. Bruce and Cameron and one of their friends took on the roles of the other young Forty-Niners. The girls all enthusiastically wanted to be barmaids, first in California and then in the Tenderloin. It was good that their parents were not there to object.

My beautiful wife, Mary, was given a role that James and Mrs. McCarthy insisted on referring to as "The Matron" although it was rather obvious that the more accurate name should have been "The Madam." Mary modestly acquiesced and pretended to accept the role with reluctance in the interest of the common good even though I could tell that inwardly she was pleased, and I must confess that it rather tickled my fancy as well as I was, perhaps in a less than completely pious manner, rather proud of her voluptuous figure, beautiful face, and long blonde curls.

James presented us with our copies of the script. He and Alice had been up all night writing and re-writing it, although we assumed that there might have been an occasional smooch exchanged before they reached "The End." The word also went out that Mrs. Florence McCarthy had read the second draft, with all sorts of bombastic clanging and banging and flailing and running off in all directions, and declared it again utterly dreadful.

She had sent him back to his desk with instructions to be more like Sophocles and less like Vaudeville. The script we were eventually presented with was cleverly written as a Greek tragedy, introduced by a sonorous Chorus — to be played by John Turner — and delivered by actors who mostly stood in place and relied on the power of the words and voices to move the audience.

There was to be a third act as well, a soliloquy to be recited by Miss Alice, and telling the terrible story of her friend Lucy. The words were not yet decided upon and I could only imagine what might be in the works.

Holmes set himself the task of wordsmith, crafting screaming headlines and scandalous copy fit for the tabloids and respectable newspapers — there being one or two of them — of New York City. The advert I saw looked something like this:

SHAMEFUL SECRETS OF THE TENDERLOIN EXPOSED

MURDER, BRIBERY, DEEDS TOO DASTARDLY TO BE NAMED, ALL UNCOVERED

OPENING OFF BROADWAY AFTER LABOR DAY

SEE IT FIRST. THE PREVIEW AND REHEARSAL OF THIS EXPLOSIVE NEW PLAY WILL BE DELIVERED BY SKILLED ACTORS AT THE CHURCH HALL OF KNOX PRESBYTERIAN IN

TARRYTOWN ON SATURDAY EVENING. CURTAIN TIME IS EIGHT O'CLOCK. BY INVITATION ONLY. APPLY BY TELEGRAM TO SLEEPY HOLLOW THEATER COMPANY. SPACE IS LIMITED.

Various versions of this announcement were placed in all of the New York papers. Private telegrams were sent to the theater critics as well as to those few reporters and editors that Miss Patience assured us had not sold their souls to Tammany Hall, and could be trusted to stand with us in a fight against corruption and crime in high places.

Costumes were pieced together and a minimum of props provided. Our production would resemble not the outlandish musicals of Broadway but more those of three centuries ago that took place at the Globe on a bare wooden stage.

Miss Patience burned the midnight oil writing and re-writing letters to her favorite Assemblymen, ministers, lawyers, bankers, and others that she knew only by name and reputation, imploring each of them to come to Tarrytown and join in our struggle for honest public service.

Over the next few days, we stood on the stage and delivered our lines, as directed by Florence McCarthy. On Friday, Alice Turner delivered her soliloquy for the first time. I thought it was overly dramatic what with shaking her fist at the heavens, clasping her hands to her bosom and crying and wailing in despair. It was bordering on being pathetically maudlin. I watched Florence McCarthy as she watched Alice's performance, and had the sense that her apprehensions mirrored my own.

Quietly a handful of Pinkertons had entered the town and taken rooms at one of the small inns.

By Saturday supper time we all gathered at McCarthy Manor for something to eat but we had lost our appetites. Somehow we had entirely forgotten about being possible murder victims and were all overcome with good old-fashioned stage fright. The butterflies were dancing all over our stomachs. We made our way to our theater and gathered backstage giving each other occasional squeezes on the hand, telling each other to break a leg and, all in all, being scared stiff. I thought to myself that it was as close to being ready to march into battle as I could remember from years ago in Afghanistan. The fear of forgetting my lines and making a fool of myself were every bit as terrifying as that of being a target for a Jezail bullet, and maybe worse.

We frightened thespians gathered at the hall, prepared to give our performance. To my surprise and satisfaction, we watched as well over a hundred people entered, many of them dressed well beyond the means and taste of the good citizens of Tarrytown. One young man with a barrel chest, walrus mustache, and gold-rimmed spectacles was rather on the loud side, patting everyone on the back and pumping hands as he worked the crowd. Miss Patience was standing next to me and whispered, "That's Theodore Roosevelt. I wrote to him and asked him to come."

"Well my dear," I said. "Then you must introduce yourself to him. I am quite certain he will remember your name. He seems to know the name of everyone else who is here. Go and say hello to him."

She looked terror-stricken. "Oh Doctor Watson, I wouldn't dare. I'm just a servant girl and he's going to be the Governor of New York State someday. I couldn't just walk up to him."

One of the advantages of being a doctor is that you have seen them all, the lowliest peasant to the dukes and earls of the land, standing naked in front of you with all their wrinkles and bulges and blemishes, and poked and prodded into every one of their orifices. It tends to profound convictions of democracy and lack of any inhibitions toward the high and mighty. So I took young Miss Patience by the arm and marched her over to her hero and introduced her. Mr. Roosevelt knew who she was instantly from her correspondence and began to chat with her as if she was the only person in the entire room and he was interested in nothing else on earth but her opinions. I discreetly left them and looked over the rest of the incoming audience. There were several men in clerical collars, some men smartly dressed who I assumed were from the business district and reform-minded, and some who were dressed rather shabbily but clutching notepads and scribbling as they interviewed each other. I caught a glimpse of the large, powerful body of Detective Leverton standing near the back of the hall and trying not to look conspicuous.

At seven minutes past eight, the church bell was rung and the audience ceased chatting.

John Turner appeared from behind the curtain and led off with an introductory oration all given *basso profundo* in a gravelly Aberdeen brogue. During the first act, set in the California Gold Rush, the characters were all given false names and it was clear that the bad guys had been guilty of forgery, and swindling, and fraud and, most likely murder. The audience appeared puzzled as they had obviously heard countless tales of wild times in California and what they were seeing was nothing new.

The opening scene of the second act revealed the identity of the villains from the first act and, even though they were not named by their true names, everybody knew who those evil characters had become. You could feel the tension rise in the audience as they became aware that they were witnessing an unprecedented attack on the most powerful and most utterly corrupt public officials in the city. It was unspoken, but everyone in the audience knew that there would be hell to pay for what was taking place on stage.

The second act included several well-chosen examples of bribery and extortion, beating and rewards, greased palms and immoral activities. The college boys from Harvard's Hasty Pudding Club and the girls from Radcliffe gave remarkable performances. The situations portrayed and the language they used pushed right up to the limit of what could be acted on stage in America. The reporters scribbled furiously, the clergymen shook their heads, and the toffs and poseurs all postured looks of nonchalance. No one, however, gave any evidence of disbelieving what they were seeing. The occasional nodding head told me that they knew that the accusations being made in front of them were the truth.

The final scene was to be Alice Turner's soliloquy and I quietly stood in the left wing behind the leg curtain so I could watch her, hoping that she would resist the temptation to imitate Sarah Bernhardt. To my surprise, the young woman who walked into center stage was not Alice. It was another young woman I had never seen before. She was petite but strikingly beautiful with long red hair and flawless pale skin. Her right arm was in a plaster cast and supported by a sling. She walked with a limp. Her opening words to the audience were:

"Your playbill informs you that the role of Lucy O'Keefe is to be played by Alice Turner. A change has been made. The role of Lucy O'Keefe will be played by Lucy O'Keefe. I am Lucy O'Keefe."

And then, with no dramatic gestures and seldom raising her voice beyond a quiet, steady tone she told her story. It began on an evening three weeks ago as she was sitting by the sea near her home in New Rochelle, writing letters and poetry. As she departed the beach after sunset, she was forcefully grabbed by a man dressed in dark clothing. She then described slowly and in exact terrible detail everything that had been done to her. She told of how her clothes had been ripped from her body, exposing her private parts, and how she had been beaten in the face with a nightstick. She lifted her upper lip to show the gap in her beautiful smile were two of her teeth had been knocked out. And then in painful detail, naming each anatomical part of her body and that of her assailant, she described her violation.

It is a rare occasion when an audience of New Yorkers are so stricken that they seem to cease breathing, yet that is what took place. The room listened in complete painful silence. I could almost hear the silent screams from some of the women present shouting "Please no more. It is unbearable." But there was more. And more.

Standing beside me in the wing was a man of average height and a full head of red hair. His profile said that he was the father of the young woman on stage. I observed tears streaming down his face and could only imagine how a father's heart must feel as he watched his daughter on stage courageously telling her story.

Lucy concluded her story and looked silently across the audience and said, "I walked, holding my bicycle with one hand as my other arm was broken. I found the public lavatory by the beach and washed my body as best I could. Then I went home and lied to my mother and father about what had happened. I am not lying to you. I have told you the truth. The truth will set you free." She walked off the stage and collapsed into her father's arms.

There was not a sound from the audience. Not a whisper. John Turner emerged from the back curtain and in his role as the Chorus challenged the audience to act upon what they had heard, reminding them that "Faith without works is dead."

The front curtain closed and the audience erupted into applause. We quickly took our bows. The last on to appear on stage was Lucy O'Keefe, and she did so holding onto her father's arm. As she stepped forward to receive her applause, the entire audience rose and gave a sustained ovation. There were no shouts or whistles. Merely continuing applause. They were still applauding when Lucy bowed one last time and turned and left the stage.

Most of the audience remained in the hall after the performance had ended and I watched Holmes and Detective Leverton conferring. They motioned for Mary and me as well as Mrs. McCarthy and Mr. Turner to join their conversation. "One of the Detective's men has reported seeing a man who matched the description of the killer," said Holmes. "My suggestion is that all of the young people be removed and sent to the same inn where the Pinkertons are staying. The rest of us will be seen to depart for the McCarthy Manor, where the killer struck last month. I fully expect that he will act in the same manner tonight."

Mr. Turner spoke quietly and said, "I fear I am far too old and frail for any more performances this evening and will fall asleep at whatever post I am given. I shall return to my home and leave the final battle to those who have the energy to take up the fight." He left us and walked haltingly toward his carriage. The rest of us nodded our assent and returned to mingling amongst the chattering members of the audience. Miss Patience approached us a few minutes later and said, "Mr. Roosevelt has requested that we meet him for a lunch meeting in the city at noon on Monday. He wishes to introduce us to some people he says can help us."

"Please tell him that we will be more than happy to join him," I replied.

"And Patience, my dear," said Mary, "I do believe you may have found your calling. Mr. Roosevelt could use your help." The girl looked down in shy embarrassment, then raised her head and broke into a wide and gleaming smile, and made her way back to the side of her hero.

In the dark, we rode in carriages back to the Manor. Detective Leverton and his men were waiting for us there, having made their way in secrecy from the village. Holmes called us together in the hallway.

"Our adversaries, who have spies in every corner of the land, have no doubt learned that I am present and have turned myself, if I may say, into their worst enemy. Therefore, I shall make myself a target for their machinations."

"You do not have to be the hero, Mr. Holmes," said Detective Leverton. "We are all prepared to play whatever role we are called upon to perform."

"Ah, my good man, you generously overestimate my bravery. I have no intention of playing the role myself. It will be played tonight by my understudy." He then smiled at Mrs. McCarthy. She walked towards the servants' wing and returned a minute later bearing a life-size leather and cloth dummy of approximately the size and shape of the body of Sherlock Holmes, covered in a silk dressing gown and adorned with a wig. A capable seamstress had stitched the features of a face and, from a modest distance, it could pass as a tall, thin Englishman.

"Meet Sherlock," said Mrs. McCarthy with a smile. "If he ends up with a few bullet holes in him I expect he'll still be the best scarecrow in the county."

"What do you think Watson? Was I just given a compliment?" said Holmes with a pretense look of bewilderment.

"Why, of course, Holmes. Scarring off all forms of birds, not to say the village children, and protecting the harvest is a most honorable role and I can think of none who could do it better."

We shared a round of nervous laughter and then went to our various stations. Detective Leverton had placed three of his men in the yard outside, with instructions to stay hidden and not to obstruct any intruder, but to give a signal as soon as our expected visitor approached. Mary and Florence were to sit and chat over tea in the parlor, with two other men hidden behind the furniture. Holmes, Leverton, one more of Leverton's men and I all prepared to hide ourselves in the library behind curtains and bookcases. The Detective quietly spoke to us. "From my years of police work, gentlemen, permit me to give you the best advice I can offer."

"Certainly, officer," I replied. "And what may that be?"

"We could be here for several hours. I advise you to make a quick visit to the lavatory. What we call a stakeout can be very painful if you don't." He flashed a smile and clapped me on the upper arm. I heeded his advice.

'Sherlock' was placed behind the desk. Charles McCarthy had indulged himself in an excellent chair that had a solid wooden back and the capacity of swivel and tilt. Holmes had rigged up some fishing line to it and placed the ends of the lines in our hands. Every few minutes one of us would give a tug and cause Sherlock to moved slightly. We assumed our positions and waited, and waited.

A full two hours passed with no sign of a visitor. The ladies in the parlor put out the lamps and retired to the bedrooms upstairs, followed by their guards, who took hidden positions in the hallways. I had begun to doubt that Holmes's plan was going to work. The clock in the hall had struck midnight when a signal, a low, quiet call of "Cooee", like a small owl, was heard from the yard. Through a tiny opening between the curtains that I was hiding behind I could see the dark shape of a man appear on the far side of the window. He stood motionless and looked into the room for a full ten minutes, staring at the dummy that was sitting in the chair with his back to the window. Every minute or two one of us gave a small tug on our line and Sherlock obliged us by moving ever so slightly.

Suddenly the window opened. The killer leapt through it and in a split second unloaded two shots from his gun into the back of the dummy's head. As soon as we heard the shots we all jumped from our positions and Detective Leverton shouted, "Halt in the name of the law! Put down your gun and raise your hands in the air! You are under arrest!"

The killer's long, gaunt face betrayed his bewilderment, followed by a steely glare of anger. He raised his hands slowly.

"I said drop your gun, now drop it or we will fire on you," said the Detective.

The killer nodded his head but instead of dropping the gun he fired two shots toward the ceiling. They struck the chandelier and sent shards of glass and burning candle flying in all directions. In that moment, he turned and dove back out of the window. Leverton rushed across the room, leaned out the window and shouted, "Stop him!" I could hear his men responding and shouting at the killer to stop.

All of now were gathered at the window and we could catch a glimpse of the killer running quickly, followed by the police officers. He had a good lead on them and was a very fast runner. A moment later we heard the sound of hoof beats galloping away in the direction of Sleepy Hollow.

I listened and heard the "clippita, clippita, clippita ... " sound fade in the distance. But the sound stopped abruptly and was followed by the most terrifying scream. It was short and loud and set the hair of my head and neck on end.

"Merciful heavens," I gasped. "What was that?"

"Some torches! Bring some torches," shouted Holmes. He ran out into the hallway and shouted his order up the stairway. Mrs. McCarthy appeared from the bedroom in her nightdress and elderly though she was bounded down the stairs and into the kitchen. She returned momentarily bearing a handful of torches which Holmes, the Detective and I lit. We took off on the run across the yard and followed the footpath leading to Sleepy Hollow.

Partway there we encountered a horse, bearing a saddle but no rider. The animal was gaunt and shagged, with a ewe neck and a head like a hammer; its one eye was glaring and spectral, but the other had the gleam of a genuine devil in it. It was foaming at the mouth and greatly agitated.

"Something has spooked that poor mare," said Leverton as it made our way past it. "Never seen a horse looking so spooked."

We reached the edge of Sleepy Hollow and followed the path to the place where it met the road just before the bridge over the ravine. Holmes held his hand in the air. "Stop please, gentlemen," he said. "We have been following the tracks of that poor mare as she galloped to this point. You can see that she stopped here. There is a cluster of tracks, some of which are deeply cut into the earth. Then she turned around and began her disturbed walk back out of the hollow to the place we met her. Her rider must have leapt or been thrown off of her here."

Sleepy Hollow was pitch dark except for the light from our torches. Holmes was peering down into the ravine and turned to the rest of us. "The branches here are broken. The rider has either climbed or been thrown down the embankment."

He continued to work his way down toward the stream bed. We followed him. When he reached the bottom, he looked back up at Leverton and me. "I believe that we have found our killer."

I stumbled and slid the rest of the way until I was standing beside Holmes at the edge of the chattering stream. In front of me was a man's body. He was tall and thin and dressed entirely in black. His face was buried in the stream and his head was twisted in a ghastly way that could only have resulted from a broken neck. Blood was still seeping from the top of his head, which was lying against a large rounded rock that protruded from the water. Leverton rolled the body over so that the corpse was looking directly at us. The facial features were contorted and twisted in a look of unspeakable terror. The mouth was open, the eyes were inhumanly wide, and the tongue was bitten almost through. Whatever the last thing this man had seen in his life had been a vision of something hellish beyond imagining.

The Detective searched through the pockets and retrieved a wallet.

"Well Mr. Holmes," he said. "It would appear that there are now only three villains from the Gold Rush to bring to justice. This is Lieutenant Isaac Crane of District 31 of the New York Police Department. The dreaded Officer Icky has gone to meet his maker."

Holmes bent over and lowered his torch to get a closer look and as he did so I let out an involuntary shriek of fright.

"Good heavens, Watson, what is it?" Holmes shouted back as he stood up and looked over at me.

I felt embarrassed and sheepish. "Awfully sorry Holmes. Sorry Detective. It is just that as the light from your torch passed across the rock that he smashed his head against, the shadows took on a ghastly appearance. Move your torch in the same arc as you just did a moment ago and you will see what I mean."

Holmes slowly lifted his torch and the three of us fixed our gaze on the rock. At a certain point part way through the arc the shadows formed by the configuration of the rock's surface came together in such a way as to look like the face of a jack-o-lantern – a most hideous one, with slits for eyes and a leering grin. Holmes held his torch steady and just the right place and the three of us exchanged glances with each other.

"Well now," said Leverton, "maybe this place is haunted after all." He gave a forced chuckle.

Then a sound was heard that caused our hearts to stop and our blood to run cold. From the top of the embankment, we heard the snort and deep-throated whinny of a horse, a very large horse. We froze and looked up. In what little light that made it to the top of the bank, I could make out the shadow of a large black object. Then it moved. We heard another snort, the pawing of a hoof on the ground and then thundering hoof beats as the beast galloped off down the road and into the night. We neither moved nor spoke until the hoof beats had faded and silence returned. Without speaking, we made our way back to the top of the ravine. Leverton knelt down and held his torch close to the ground.

He looked up at Sherlock Holmes and spoke in a whisper.

"Mr. Holmes. These are the hoof prints of a gigantic stallion."

Chapter Twelve

Tammany Hall

To this day neither Holmes nor I have ever said a word to each other concerning the apparition we experienced that night. I am a doctor and a man of science and give no quarter for superstition. Holmes is the most complete skeptic I have ever met and is bound by the dictates of logic and deduction alone. Yet I suspect that while both of us drew our own conclusions about what happened, neither has been entirely willing to discard the belief that there may be principalities and powers at work that visit justice upon evildoers in a way that science can never explain. If men of science are to hold to a secret superstition, that one is, at least, forgivable.

Whatever the cause of the events of that night, the issues that gave rise to the case were far from being resolved. Dead men tell no tales. And so it was that we could wring no further information from Icky Crane. His obituary in the papers was cryptic and noted only that he had tragically fallen from a horse. Police Captain Williams was quoted as saying that he was an outstanding and loyal officer of the police department and would be greatly missed.

The Sunday New York papers did, however, devote significant space to the preview of the play that was performed in Tarrytown before an invitation-only audience. Those papers that were in league with Tammany Hall predictably pilloried and ridiculed all aspects of the production, claiming that it was only an amateurish effort by some puritanical reformers who had nothing better to do to than promote their own self-interests by slandering the good names of the city's police and its democratically elected leaders.

Other newspapers, those that maintained their independence from the Tammany machine, were unrestrained in their praise for the courage of the writers and actors. They went much farther than even our Irregular Theater Troup dared and named several public officials and directly accused them of living off of bribery and corruption.

There was one aspect only on which all of the press agreed. The theater critics universally praised the breath-taking soliloquy of Miss Lucy O'Keefe. Superlatives tumbled across the columns of print, and predictions of her future as Lady Macbeth, or Gertrude, or Desdemona, or Juliet were ubiquitous.

On Monday morning, we packed our bags and bid goodbye to our hosts. Mrs. McCarthy embraced the three of us warmly and thanked us yet again. James and Alice, standing arm in arm, and their college friends thanked us and presented us with several copies of *The Strand* and requested that they be signed by Sherlock Holmes and Dr. John Watson.

Alice apologized for her father's absence, saying that the intense events of the past few days had laid him very low, but that he sent along a gift that he thought would be appropriate. She presented us each with a beautiful leather-bound copy of *The Stories of Washington Irving*. He had inscribed the flyleaf of each of them with the same note and it ran:

```
May the events that took place in Sleepy
Hollow continue to live in your memory and
our gratitude,
```

and signed by John Turner.

Mary and I were both disappointed that Patience Moran did not appear. We were further surprised to hear that she had given her notice on Sunday afternoon and departed from the McCarthy household. Mrs. McCarthy spoke only kind words about her and said that she had gone to seek her fortune with the blessing of all who knew her.

As we boarded the train to the city, each of us purchased one of the morning newspapers. The headlines of all three papers screamed about a sermon that had been preached the day before from the pulpit of Madison

Square Presbyterian Church by a Rev. Charles Parkhurst. From the description of the clergyman, I recognized him as one of those who had attended the play in Tarrytown. *The Sun,* the most reformist of all the papers, printed the entire text of his sermon and in it, he thundered in the strongest language against the crime and corruption that pervaded the politics and police force of New York City. Every biblical epithet I knew and a few I had never heard before were used to decry the evil web of the police, city hall, organized crime and Tammany Hall. Our intrepid actors may have started a ball rolling and they had become a part of a much larger movement of social reform that was slowly gathering force and would eventually become unstoppable.

Having mused on the events of the past few days for a couple of hours as we returned to New York City, I was brought back to more pressing matters by our arrival at Grand Central Depot. There we hailed a cab and once again made our way to the Plaza Hotel. This time, however, we were in no great hurry and took the more pleasant route up the splendid divided boulevard of Park Avenue. On arrival at the Plaza, I noticed the same manager standing behind the front desk. He recognized us and immediately welcomed us effusively. I was reticent to engage in conversation, still remembering the handshake deal struck on our last visit, but the clever young chap again got the better of us.

"Doctor and Mrs. Watson, and the great detective Sherlock Holmes. Surely you are not contemplating staying anywhere else while you are on this blessed isle. Allow me to offer you a suite of complementary rooms for up the three nights. All I ask in return, and I am sure you will think it fair, is that in every story you set in America, you remind your readers that the Plaza Hotel is . . ."

How could we refuse? And so dear reader, allow me to inform you that the Plaza Hotel is … but then I have already told you that.

Mr. Roosevelt had reserved a large table in the palatial Oak Room of the hotel and the maitre'd led us toward it. There were four men already seated, as well as an attractive young woman who I immediately recognized as Patience Moran. The men stood to greet us and shake hands as Mr. Roosevelt introduced everyone.

In a voice that was several decibels louder than necessary, he first gestured to Miss Patience and said, "You folks already know my new assistant clerk, Patti Moran. Indeed, it was the events in Tarrytown that brought this wonderful young woman to my attention. And this is Reverend Parkhurst. He just made himself famous, loved and respected by some in this town and hated by others because of the sermon he gave yesterday. And I could not be prouder of him. And this fellow is our State Senator Clarence Lexow, as smart a reform-minded senator as you can find in this great state. And this man . . ."

He had pointed to a well-dressed gentleman in his fifties who interrupted Mr. Roosevelt's performance and snapped, "For God's sake Roosevelt, you're not campaigning for office. Enough of the politicking, get down to business. We haven't all day."

With this, he extended his hand to us and said, "J.P. Morgan. Welcome to New York. We appreciate all you have done for us already. Connie Vanderbilt will be joining us shortly. Now Teddy, what are we here for?"

Theodore Roosevelt nodded and smiled at the banker and proceeded to recount the events of the past month, including the writing of the play, the murders of both the young Michael DuPlessis and of Charles McCarthy and, briefly and discretely, the violation of Lucy O'Keefe. Patience Moran scribbled furiously and I assumed that she had developed exceptional skill in shorthand as well as having the mind and making of an excellent lawyer and detective. Roosevelt continued without pausing for a breath and summarized some of the minister's sermon as it had appeared in the papers, then announced that he would be seeking the job of Commissioner of Police of New York City the following year. He said that he had recruited the famous Sherlock Holmes as consulting detective and that Mr. Holmes would be advising him on all matters and means of dealing with the criminal underworld.

I had not heard of Holmes's prestigious new position and judging by the look on his face, neither had he. Throughout a gastronomically perfect lunch, served efficiently and with impeccable manners by the staff of the Oak Room, Theodore Roosevelt held forth on one aspect after another of the problems facing the city, the state, and the nation, adding to each topic the steps he was going to take to fix them. Our final guest arrived part way through the meal and we were introduced to Cornelius Vanderbilt, who was also strongly of a reform persuasion.

Sherlock Holmes listened attentively, but I gathered that he was not about to be bullied into any job in America that he himself had not decided to pursue. During the lull as dessert was served, he spoke up. "Mr. Roosevelt, my good man, your grand plans and intentions are most admirable. However, my first responsibility here is to my client and her family. They are still in peril and none of your high-minded intentions for the future are going to change that. Pray tell, what is it that you propose to do today to ensure their safety?"

"Right you are sir. And immediately after lunch, you and I are going to make a trip downtown to Tammany Hall and get those boys down there straightened out."

As soon as lunch was over Roosevelt smiled graciously at the rest of us and said, "Patti, I will meet up with you later in my office. Doctor and Mrs. Watson, with your permission I am going to Shanghai this famous detective friend of yours and we are going to pay a visit downtown and give those boys at Tammany Hall a firm kick in their backsides. I will send him back to you safe and sound in a couple of hours, and in the meanwhile may I encourage the two of you to enjoy the greatest city on earth."

A large private carriage had appeared at the hotel portico. The driver opened the door for Holmes and Roosevelt, and then we watched as four large, strong and well-dressed men followed them and were seated.

I turned to my wife and said, "It would appear that outspoken politicians in this great city are advised to have Pinkertons in tow."

"The two tall ones were in Tarrytown on Saturday evening. It is a good thing for Mr. Roosevelt that he is rich enough to afford to be in American politics."

For the rest of the afternoon, we strolled through Central Park, past the Sheep Meadow to the great reservoir and back, by which time Sherlock Holmes had returned to the Plaza Hotel.

"Do tell, Holmes," said I, "you do not appear to have been shot or otherwise beaten for your impudence. What did you and the enthusiastic Mr. Roosevelt manage to accomplish?"

"We engaged," answered Holmes, "in bare knuckle American-style politics and it was most fascinating to observe, most fascinating indeed. The esteemed and charitable Society of St. Tammany is now situated in a large hall on Fourteenth Street and the folks who are in charge there are, as you suggested, my dear Watson, making a very pretty penny on all sorts of greed and corruption. While Mr. Roosevelt may be a little too much on the boisterous side for English taste, he is certainly not lacking in courage and bravado. Mind you one's courage is reasonably improved when one is accompanied by four Pinkertons. Nevertheless, he strode past the doorkeepers, past the secretaries and into the head office in which sat the Grand Sachem of the Society, the gentleman named Richard Croker, of whom you already know much more than he would wish you knew.

"Roosevelt leaned over the man's desk, put his face no more than a foot away, and barked out his orders. He placed a list with the names of the family and friends of the McCarthys and the Turners and demanded not only that these be not touched but that they be protected from all possible harm regardless of from what quarter it came. To which the Grand Sachem replied, 'And why would I bother doing that?'

"Roosevelt reminded Mr. Croker that there were over ten million dollars' worth of federal funds scheduled to flow from Washington to New York City in the next three months and that he, as a good friend and confidant of President Harrison, and as a member of the Civil Service Commission of the United States of America, would see to it that not one penny would be controlled by any Democrat, any union, and most certainly not by Tammany Hall unless he made sure that young James, and Alice and their families were kept from all mishaps.

"And with that he turned and marched back out of the hall and we got back into his carriage, along with the Pinkertons, of course. He then turned to me and said, 'They'll all be just fine now. Croker knows what side his bread is buttered on.' From that point on he quizzed me most intensely about my insights on the control of crime, and policing, and the enactment of laws, and such and so forth. The man's mind is an absolute glutton for information and advice, and his personality most demanding."

"Yes, Holmes," I said. "And what advice may I ask did you give him?"

Holmes smiled. "I suggested that he should speak softly and carry a big stick."

Epilogue

It is now a decade since the events of The Hudson Valley Mystery transpired and I thought it considerate of me to bring the reader up to date on the many people and places that were part of this fascinating set of events.

James and Alice did not pursue a life in the theater or in the arts, as had been their dream. Instead, they amalgamated the two already large and prosperous farms that had been built by their respective fathers, and they are now the largest keepers of Aberdeen Angus cattle in New York State. They are experts not on Moliere or Shakespeare but on the selective breeding of cows for increased beef production, the castrating of bulls, and all matters related to the national and international markets of feed grain. They wisely heeded their parents' advice and got married. Already they are the proud parents of three children.

Florence McCarthy had such pleasure and satisfaction from her brief stint as the director and producer of for the Irregular Theater Company of Sleepy Hollow that she incorporated the company, and for the next ten years it delivered critically acclaimed, by local critics, productions of *The Importance of Being Earnest, Mrs. Warren's Profession* and even, in Elizabethan costumes, *A Midsummer's Night Dream*.

Patience Moran did not attend Bennett College in South Carolina, the excellent school operated only for young negro women. Instead, she became the only young negro woman to study that fall in Columbia Law School on the Upper West Side of Manhattan. She was assisted in so doing by her patron, Mr. Theodore Roosevelt, and to this day she is a valued member of his staff, providing outstanding legal advice and services, of which, due to his enthusiastic character, he finds himself often in need; as well as healthy servings of common sense, of which the same.

Mr. Roosevelt, as you will know if you follow the news from America, became the Commissioner of Police of New York City and was recently elected Governor of the State of New York. Last year he and his troop of wealthy Ivy League boys along with cowboys from the Dakotas banded into a militia unit called The Rough Riders and stormed up San Juan Hill in Cuba. As a former military man, I can confidently say that as a tactic of warfare their charge was useless if not altogether silly, but it did wonders for his political career. He may yet go on to great deeds in America.

Lucy O'Keefe did find a life on the stage and has appeared in several light comedies in both New York and London, but prefers the tragedies of Shakespeare and most recently played Cordelia in a production of *Lear* at the Shaftesbury.

The villains and scoundrels of Tammany Hall have not yet been completely vanquished, I am sorry to say, but they are a mere shadow of their former empire. As Police Commissioner, Mr. Roosevelt reformed the entire force of the city, cleaned out the Augean stable of corruption and set the men in blue on a well-deserved pedestal as New York's finest. Senator Lexow organized hearings into the vast political machine that had dominated New York for over one hundred years. As a result, the financial power of the crooks on Fourteenth Street was emasculated. The citizen reformers led by J.P. Morgan and Cornelius Vanderbilt now will not suffer the ward heelers to pilfer the public coffers, this being the rightful and sacred domain of bankers.

Dear old Mr. Turner did manage to outlast his doctor's predictions and stayed alive well past the fall equinox. He had the joy of giving away his lovely daughter, Alice, in marriage to the love of her life, James McCarthy. Although bound to a pushchair by that time he was as gracious, wise, and canny as ever. He passed away, surrounded by his family and friends, on the eve of All Hallows Day. His beloved magnificent stallion, Bannockburn, was found a few days later, lying on his side in his stall whimpering and refusing all food. He was humanely put down and buried in the gardens with a small monument to mark the spot. Horse and horseman have headed off to that undiscovered country from who borne no traveler returns. As, some day, will we all.

Dear Sherlockian Reader:

My very first visit to New York City took place in the early 1960s when, as an adolescent, I traveled there with my family on a road trip vacation.

I can still remember seeing the Empire State Building, taking the Staten Island Ferry over to the Statue of Liberty, the panoramas at the Museum of Natural History, watching James Garner and Doris Day in *The Thrill of It All* at Radio City Music Hall, and standing on the sidewalks of New York eating pizza at midnight. It was on that visit that I fell in love with Manhattan. I am still smitten.

Over the years since, I have had the joy of living there and visiting countless times. When I searched for a river valley in which to situate my tribute to *The Boscombe Valley Mystery*, it was inevitable that I would be drawn to the valley of the Hudson River that begins in New York City and extends all the way to beyond Albany.

According to The Canon, the events of *The Buscombe Valley Mystery* took place in June 1889. At that time, Theodore Roosevelt was serving on the United States Civil Service Commission and exerted influence over federal funds directed to New York City. He went on from there to serve as the Police Commissioner, Secretary of the Navy, and eventually as President of the United States.

Tammany Hall was the center of political corruption and graft for many years in New York City. The references to the actions of the "ward heelers" who controlled it and the elected officials who worked to clean it up are based on the historical record.

Washington Irving wrote *The Legend of Sleepy Hollow* in 1820. It has remained a classic of American Gothic literature. As a child, I watched the Disney cartoon version and was terror stricken by the images of the Headless Horseman.

Castle Garden, at the southern tip of Manhattan, was the entry point for immigrants to American prior to the opening of Ellis Island in 1892. A visit to Ellis Island today to view the presentation on the immigrant experience is a very moving and highly recommended.

The references in the story to the Tenderloin District and the police officials who controlled it are more or less accurate.

The Castle Hotel in Tarrytown still stands and continues in business as a hotel. It was, however, built as a private home and was not converted to a hotel until well after the dates of this story.

The Mattawan State Hospital for the criminally insane was opened shortly after the dates of this story and continued in operation in upstate new York until 1977.

The Hudson River School of artists flourished during the mid-Nineteenth Century. Their majestic landscape paintings can be seen in many museums and art galleries throughout the United States.

An exception to historical accuracy is reference to The Plaza Hotel. It did not open until 1907, but it was just too fine a place in too great a location to substitute with anything else. It is still a magnificent place, even if unaffordable.

I know it sounds trite and corny, but *I love New York*.

All the best,

Craig

About the Author

Once upon a time Craig Stephen Copland was an English major and studied under both Northrop Frye and Marshall McLuhan at the University of Toronto way back in the 1960s. He never got over his spiritual attraction to great literature and captivating stories. Somewhere in the decades since he became a dedicated Sherlockian. He is a member of the Sherlock Holmes Society of Canada, who are also known as the Bootmakers of Toronto, and, like his Sherlockian colleagues, addicted to the sacred canon. In May of 2014 the Bootmakers announced a contest for a new Sherlock Holmes mystery. Although he had no previous experience writing fiction he entered and was blessed to be declared one of the winners. So he kept writing more stories and is now on a mission to write sixty new Sherlock Holmes mysteries – each one inspired by one of the original stories in The Canon.

In real life he writes about and serves as a consultant for political campaigns in Canada and the USA (www.ConservativeGrowth.net) , but would abandon that pursuit if he could possibly earn a decent living writing about Sherlock Holmes. He lives and writes in Toronto, New York and Tokyo. If you have a suggestion for a new Sherlock Holmes mystery, please contact him at craigstephencopland@gmail.com

More Historical Mysteries by Craig Stephen Copland

www.SherlockHolmesMystery.com

Copy the links to look inside and download

Studying Scarlet. Starlet O'Halloran, a fabulous mature woman, who reminds the reader of Scarlet O'Hara (but who, for copyright reasons cannot actually be her) has arrived in London looking for her long-lost husband, Brett (who resembles Rhett Butler, but who, for copyright reasons, cannot actually be him). She enlists the help of Sherlock Holmes. This is an unauthorized parody, inspired by Arthur Conan Doyle's *A Study in Scarlet* and Margaret Mitchell's *Gone with the Wind.* http://authl.it/aic

The Sign of the Third. Fifteen hundred years ago the courageous Princess Hemamali smuggled the sacred tooth of the Buddha into Ceylon. Now, for the first time, it is being brought to London to be part of a magnificent exhibit at the British Museum. But what if something were to happen to it? It would be a disaster for the British Empire. Sherlock Holmes, Dr. Watson, and even Mycroft Holmes are called upon to prevent such a crisis. This novella is inspired by the Sherlock Holmes mystery, *The Sign of the Four.* http://authl.it/aie

A Sandal from East Anglia. Archeological excavations at an old abbey unearth an ancient document that has the potential to change the course of the British Empire and all of Christendom. Holmes encounters some evil young men and a strikingly beautiful young Sister, with a curious double life. The mystery is inspired by the original Sherlock Holmes story, *A Scandal in Bohemia.* http://authl.it/aif

The Bald-Headed Trust. Watson insists on taking Sherlock Holmes on a short vacation to the seaside in Plymouth. No sooner has Holmes arrived than he is needed to solve a double murder and prevent a massive fraud diabolically designed by the evil Professor himself. Who knew that a family of devout conservative churchgoers could come to the aid of Sherlock Holmes and bring enormous grief to evil doers? The story is inspired by *The Red-Headed League.* http://authl.it/aih

A Case of Identity Theft. It is the fall of 1888 and Jack the Ripper is terrorizing London. A young married couple is found, minus their heads. Sherlock Holmes, Dr. Watson, the couple's mothers, and Mycroft must join forces to find the murderer before he kills again and makes off with half a million pounds. The novella is a tribute to *A Case of Identity*. It will appeal both to devoted fans of Sherlock Holmes, as well as to those who love the great game of rugby. http://authl.it/aii

The Hudson Valley Mystery. A young man in New York went mad and murdered his father. His mother believes he is innocent and knows he is not crazy. She appeals to Sherlock Holmes and, together with Dr. and Mrs. Watson, he crosses the Atlantic to help this client in need. This new story was inspired by *The Boscombe Valley Mystery*. http://authl.it/aij

The Mystery of the Five Oranges. A desperate father enters 221B Baker Street. His daughter has been kidnapped and spirited off to North America. The evil network who have taken her has spies everywhere. There is only one hope – Sherlock Holmes. Sherlockians will enjoy this new adventure, inspired by *The Five Orange Pips* and *Anne of Green Gables* http://authl.it/aik

www.SherlockHolmesMystery.com

The Man Who Was Twisted But Hip. France is torn apart by The Dreyfus Affair. Westminster needs Sherlock Holmes so that the evil tide of anti-Semitism that has engulfed France will not spread. Sherlock and Watson go to Paris to solve the mystery and thwart Moriarty. This new mystery is inspired by, *The Man with the Twisted Lip,* as well as by *The Hunchback of Notre Dame.* http://authl.it/ail

The Adventure of the Blue Belt Buckle. A young street urchin discovers a man's belt and buckle under a bush in Hyde Park. A body is found in a hotel room in Mayfair. Scotland Yard seeks the help of Sherlock Holmes in solving the murder. The Queen's Jubilee could be ruined. Sherlock Holmes, Dr. Watson, Scotland Yard, and Her Majesty all team up to prevent a crime of unspeakable dimensions. A new mystery inspired by *The Blue Carbuncle.* http://authl.it/aim

The Adventure of the Spectred Bat. A beautiful young woman, just weeks away from giving birth, arrives at Baker Street in the middle of the night. Her sister was attacked by a bat and died, and now it is attacking her. A vampire? The story is a tribute to *The Adventure of the Speckled Band* and like the original, leaves the mind wondering and the heart racing. http://authl.it/ain

The Adventure of the Engineer's Mom. A brilliant young Cambridge University engineer is carrying out secret research for the Admiralty. It will lead to the building of the world's most powerful battleship, The Dreadnaught. His adventuress mother is kidnapped, and he seeks the help of Sherlock Holmes. This new mystery is a tribute to *The Engineer's Thumb.* http://authl.it/aio

The Adventure of the Notable Bachelorette. A snobbish nobleman enters 221B Baker Street demanding the help in finding his much younger wife – a beautiful and spirited American from the West. Three days later the wife is accused of a vile crime. Now she comes to Sherlock Holmes seeking to prove her innocence. This new mystery was inspired by *The Adventure of the Noble Bachelor*. http://authl.it/aip

The Adventure of the Beryl Anarchists. A deeply distressed banker enters 221B Baker St. His safe has been robbed, and he is certain that his motorcycle-riding sons have betrayed him. Highly incriminating and embarrassing records of the financial and personal affairs of England's nobility are now in the hands of blackmailers. Then a young girl is murdered. A tribute to *The Adventure of the Beryl Coronet*. http://authl.it/aiq

The Adventure of the Coiffured Bitches. A beautiful young woman will soon inherit a lot of money. She disappears. Another young woman finds out far too much and, in desperation seeks help. Sherlock Holmes, Dr. Watson and Miss Violet Hunter must solve the mystery of the coiffured bitches and avoid the massive mastiff that could tear their throats out. A tribute to *The Adventure of the Copper Beeches*. http://authl.it/air

The Silver Horse, Braised. The greatest horse race of the century will take place at Epsom Downs. Millions have been bet. Owners, jockeys, grooms, and gamblers from across England and America arrive. Jockeys and horses are killed. Holmes fails to solve the crime until… This mystery is a tribute to *Silver Blaze* and the great racetrack stories of Damon Runyon. http://authl.it/ais

The Box of Cards. A brother and a sister from a strict religious family disappear. The parents are alarmed, but Scotland Yard says they are just off sowing their wild oats. A horrific, gruesome package arrives in the post, and it becomes clear that a terrible crime is in process. Sherlock Holmes is called in to help. A tribute to *The Cardboard Box*. http://authl.it/ait

The Yellow Farce. Sherlock Holmes is sent to Japan. The war between Russia and Japan is raging. Alliances between countries in these years before World War I are fragile, and any misstep could plunge the world into Armageddon. The wife of the British ambassador is suspected of being a Russian agent. Join Holmes and Watson as they travel around the world to Japan. Inspired by *The Yellow Face*. http://authl.it/akp

The Stock Market Murders. A young man's friend has gone missing. Two more bodies of young men turn up. All are tied to The City and to one of the greatest frauds ever visited upon the citizens of England. The story is based on the true story of James Whitaker Wright and is inspired by, *The Stock Broker's Clerk*. Any resemblance of the villain to a certain American political figure is entirely coincidental. http://authl.it/akq

The Glorious Yacht. On the night of April 12, 1912, off the coast of Newfoundland, one of the greatest disasters of all time took place – the Unsinkable Titanic struck an iceberg and sank with a horrendous loss of life. The news of the disaster leads Holmes and Watson to reminisce about one of their earliest adventures. It began as a sailing race and ended as a tale of murder, kidnapping, piracy, and survival through a tempest. A tribute to *The Gloria Scott*. http://authl.it/akr

A Most Grave Ritual. In 1649, King Charles I escaped and made a desperate run for Continent. Did he leave behind a vast fortune? The patriarch of an ancient Royalist family dies in the courtyard, and the locals believe that the headless ghost of the king did him in. The police accuse his son of murder. Sherlock Holmes is hired to exonerate the lad. A tribute to *The Musgrave Ritual.* http://authl.it/aks

The Spy Gate Liars. Dr. Watson receives an urgent telegram telling him that Sherlock Holmes is in France and near death. He rushes to aid his dear friend, only to find that what began as a doctor's house call has turned into yet another adventure as Sherlock Holmes races to keep an unknown ruthless murderer from dispatching yet another former German army officer. A tribute to *The Reigate Squires.* http://authl.it/akt

The Cuckold Man Colonel James Barclay needs the help of Sherlock Holmes. His exceptionally beautiful, but much younger, wife has disappeared, and foul play is suspected. Has she been kidnapped and held for ransom? Or is she in the clutches of a deviant monster? The story is a tribute not only to the original mystery, *The Crooked Man,* but also to the biblical story of King David and Bathsheba. http://authl.it/akv

The Impatient Dissidents. In March 1881, the Czar of Russia was assassinated by anarchists. That summer, an attempt was made to murder his daughter, Maria, the wife of England's Prince Alfred. A Russian Count is found dead in a hospital in London. Scotland Yard and the Home Office arrive at 221B and enlist the help of Sherlock Holmes to track down the killers and stop them. This new mystery is a tribute to *The Resident Patient.* http://authl.it/akw

The Grecian, Earned. This story picks up where *The Greek Interpreter* left off. The villains of that story were murdered in Budapest, and so Holmes and Watson set off in search of "the Grecian girl" to solve the mystery. What they discover is a massive plot involving the re-birth of the Olympic games in 1896 and a colorful cast of characters at home and on the Continent. http://authl.it/aia

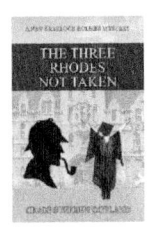

The Three Rhodes Not Taken. Oxford University is famous for its passionate pursuit of learning. The Rhodes Scholarship has been recently established, and some men are prepared to lie, steal, slander, and, maybe murder, in the pursuit of it. Sherlock Holmes is called upon to track down a thief who has stolen vital documents pertaining to the winner of the scholarship, but what will he do when the prime suspect is found dead? A tribute to *The Three Students*. http://authl.it/al8

The Naval Knaves. On September 15, 1894, an anarchist attempted to bomb the Greenwich Observatory. He failed, but the attempt led Sherlock Holmes into an intricate web of spies, foreign naval officers, and a beautiful princess. Once again, suspicion landed on poor Percy Phelps, now working in a senior position in the Admiralty, and once again Holmes has to use both his powers of deduction and raw courage to not only rescue Percy but to prevent an unspeakable disaster. A tribute to *The Naval Treaty*. http://authl.it/aia

A Scandal in Trumplandia. NOT a new mystery but a political satire. The story is a parody of the much-loved original story, *A Scandal in Bohemia*, with the character of the King of Bohemia replaced by you-know-who. If you enjoy both political satire and Sherlock Holmes, you will get a chuckle out of this new story. http://authl.it/aig

The Binomial Asteroid Problem. The deadly final encounter between Professor Moriarty and Sherlock Holmes took place at Reichenbach Falls. But when was their first encounter? This new story answers that question. What began a stolen Gladstone bag escalates into murder and more. This new story is a tribute to *The Adventure of the Final Problem.* http://authl.it/al1

The Adventure of Charlotte Europa Golderton. *Charles Augustus Milverton* was shot and sent to his just reward. But now another diabolical scheme of blackmail has emerged centered in the telegraph offices of the Royal Mail. It is linked to an archeological expedition whose director disappeared. Someone is prepared to murder to protect their ill-gotten gain and possibly steal a priceless treasure. Holmes is hired by not one but three women who need his help. http://authl.it/al7

The Mystery of 222 Baker Street. The body of a Scotland Yard inspector is found in a locked room in 222 Baker Street. There is no clue as to how he died, but he was murdered. Then another murder occurs in the very same room. Holmes and Watson might have to offer themselves as potential victims if the culprits are to be discovered. The story is a tribute to the original Sherlock Holmes story, *The Adventure of the Empty House.* http://authl.it/al3

The Adventure of the Norwood Rembrandt. A man facing execution appeals to Sherlock Holmes to save him. He claims that he is innocent. Holmes agrees to take on his case. Five years ago, he was convicted of the largest theft of art masterpieces in British history, and of murdering the butler who tried to stop him. Holmes and Watson have to find the real murderer and the missing works of art --- if the client is innocent after all. This new Sherlock Holmes mystery is a tribute to *The Adventure of the Norwood Builder* in the original Canon. http://authl.it/al4

The Horror of the Bastard's Villa. A Scottish clergyman and his faithful border collie visit 221B and tell a tale of a ghostly Banshee on the Isle of Skye. After the specter appeared, two people died. Holmes sends Watson on ahead to investigate and report. More terrifying horrors occur, and Sherlock Holmes must come and solve the awful mystery before more people are murdered. A tribute to the original story in the Canon, Arthur Conan Doyle's masterpiece, *The Hound of the Baskervilles*. http://authl.it/al2

The Dancer from the Dance. In 1909 the entire world of dance changed when Les Ballets Russes, under opened in Paris. They also made annual visits to the West End in London. Tragically, during their 1913 tour, two of their dancers are found murdered. Sherlock Holmes is brought into to find the murderer and prevent any more killings. The story adheres fairly closely to the history of ballet and is a tribute to the original story in the Canon, *The Adventure of the Dancing Men*. http://authl.it/al5

The Solitary Bicycle Thief. Remember Violet Smith, the beautiful young woman whom Sherlock Holmes and Dr. Watson rescued from a forced marriage, as recorded in *The Adventure of the Solitary Cyclist*? Ten years later she and Cyril reappear in 221B Baker Street with a strange tale of the theft of their bicycles. What on the surface seemed like a trifle turns out to be the door that leads Sherlock Holmes into a web of human trafficking, espionage, blackmail, and murder. A new and powerful cabal of master criminals has formed in London, and they will stop at nothing, not even the murder of an innocent foreign student, to extend the hold on the criminal underworld of London. http://authl.it/al6

The Adventure of the Prioress's Tale. The senior field hockey team from an elite girls' school goes to Dover for a beach holiday ... and disappears. Have they been abducted into white slavery? Did they run off to Paris? Are they being held for ransom? Can Sherlock Holmes find them in time? Holmes, Watson, Lestrade, the Prioress of the school, and a new gang of Irregulars must find them before something terrible happens. A tribute to *The Adventure of the Priory School in the Canon*. http://authl.it/ap*v*

The Adventure of Mrs. J.L. Heber. A mad woman is murdering London bachelors by driving a railway spike through their heads. Scotland Yard demands that Sherlock Holmes help them find and stop a crazed murderess who is re-enacting the biblical murders by Jael. Holmes agrees and finds that revenge is being taken for deeds treachery and betrayal that took place ten years ago in the Rocky Mountains of Canada. Holmes, Watson, and Lestrade must move quickly before more men and women lose their lives. The story is a tribute to the original Sherlock Holmes story, *The Adventure of Black Peter*. http://authl.it/arr

The Return of Napoleon. In October 1805, Napoleon's fleet was defeated in the Battle of Trafalgar. Now his ghost has returned to England for the centenary of the battle, intent on wreaking revenge on the descendants of Admiral Horatio Nelson and on all of England. The mother of the great-great-grandchildren of Admiral Nelson contacts Sherlock Holmes and asks him to come to her home, Victory Manor, in Gravesend to protect the Nelson Collection. The invaluable collection of artifacts is to be displayed during the one-hundredth anniversary celebrations of the Battle of Trafalgar. First, Dr. Watson comes to the manor and he meets not only the lovely children but also finds that something apparently supernatural is going on. Holmes assumes that some mad Frenchmen, intent on avenging Napoleon, are conspiring to wreak havoc on England and possibly threatening the children. Watson believes that something terrifying and occult may be at work. Neither is prepared for the true target of the Napoleonists, or of the Emperor's ghost. http://authl.it/at4

The Adventure of the Pinched Palimpsest. At Oxford University, an influential professor has been proselytizing for anarchism. Three naive students fall for his doctrines and decide to engage in direct action by stealing priceless artifacts from the British Museum, returning them to the oppressed people from whom their colonial masters stole them. In the midst of their caper, a museum guard is shot dead and they are charged with the murder. After being persuaded by a vulnerable friend of the students, Sherlock Holmes agrees to take on the case. He soon discovers that no one involved is telling the complete truth. Join Holmes and Watson as they race from London to Oxford, then to Cambridge and finally up to a remote village in Scotland and seek to discover the clues that are tied to an obscure medieval palimpsest. http://authl.it/ax0

Contributions to The Great Game of Sherlockian Scholarship

Sherlock and Barack. This is NOT a new Sherlock Holmes Mystery. It is a Sherlockian research monograph. Why did Barack Obama win in November 2012? Why did Mitt Romney lose? Pundits and political scientists have offered countless reasons. This book reveals the truth - The Sherlock Holmes Factor. Had it not been for Sherlock Holmes, Mitt Romney would be president. http://authl.it/aid

From The Beryl Coronet to Vimy Ridge. This is NOT a New Sherlock Holmes Mystery. It is a monograph of Sherlockian research. This new monograph in the Great Game of Sherlockian scholarship argues that there was a Sherlock Holmes factor in the causes of World War I... and that it is secretly revealed in the *roman a clef* story that we know as *The Adventure of the Beryl Coronet.* http://authl.it/ali

Reverend Ezekiel Black—'The Sherlock Holmes of the American West'—Mystery Stories.

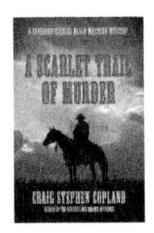

A Scarlet Trail of Murder. At ten o'clock on Sunday morning, the twenty-second of October, 1882, in an abandoned house in the West Bottom of Kansas City, a fellow named Jasper Harrison did not wake up. His inability to do was the result of his having had his throat cut. The Reverend Mr. Ezekiel Black, a part-time Methodist minister, and an itinerant US Marshall is called in. This original western mystery was inspired by the great Sherlock Holmes classic, *A Study in Scarlet.* http://authl.it/alg

The Brand of the Flying Four. This case all began one quiet evening in a room in Kansas City. A few weeks later, a gruesome murder, took place in Denver. By the time Rev. Black had solved the mystery, justice, of the frontier variety, not the courtroom, had been meted out. The story is inspired by *The Sign of the Four* by Arthur Conan Doyle, and like that story, it combines murder most foul, and romance most enticing. http://authl.it/alh

www.SherlockHolmesMystery.com

Collection Sets for eBooks and paperback are available at *40% off the price of buying them separately.*

Collection One http://authl.it/al9

The Sign of the Tooth
The Hudson Valley Mystery
A Case of Identity Theft
The Bald-Headed Trust
Studying Scarlet
The Mystery of the Five Oranges

Collection Two http://authl.it/ala

A Sandal from East Anglia
The Man Who Was Twisted But Hip
The Blue Belt Buckle
The Spectred Bat

Collection Three http://authl.it/alb

The Engineer's Mom
The Notable Bachelorette
The Beryl Anarchists
The Coiffured Bitches

Collection Four <u>http://authl.it/alc</u>

The Silver Horse, Braised
The Box of Cards
The Yellow Farce
The Three Rhodes Not Taken

Collection Five <u>http://authl.it/ald</u>

The Stock Market Murders
The Glorious Yacht
The Most Grave Ritual
The Spy Gate Liars

Collection Six <u>http://authl.it/ale</u>

The Cuckold Man
The Impatient Dissidents
The Grecian, Earned
The Naval Knaves

Collection Seven <u>http://authl.it/alf</u>

The Binomial Asteroid Problem
The Mystery of 222 Baker Street
The Adventure of Charlotte Europa Golderton
The Adventure of the Norwood Rembrandt

Collection Eight <u>http://authl.it/at3</u>

The Dancer from the Dance
The Adventure of the Prioress's Tale
The Adventure of Mrs. J. L. Heber
The Solitary Bicycle Thief

Collection Nine http://authl.it/at3

The Adventure of Mrs. J.L Heber

The Return of Napoleon

The Adventure of the Pinched Palimpsest

The Adventure of the Missing Better Half

Super Collections A and B

30 New Sherlock Holmes Mysteries.

http://authl.it/aiw, http://authl.it/aix

The perfect ebooks for readers who can only borrow one book a month from Amazon

www.SherlockHolmesMystery.com

Would you like to read another New Sherlock Holmes Mystery? They are all available immediately from Amazon.

You are invited to join the New Sherlock Holmes Mysteries mailing list and receive Irregular announcements about the release of new titles, special promotions and Sherlockian news. Go now to the website. www.SherlockHolmesMystery.com and sign up.

Privacy is promised.

Printed in Great Britain
by Amazon